FOREVER ROAD

A PERI JEAN MACE GHOST THRILLER

CATIE RHODES

PERI JEAN MACE GHOST THRILLERS

Forever Road

Peri Jean Mace: Book 1

Copyright © 2013 Catie Rhodes.

All rights reserved.

Published by: Long Roads and Dark Ends Press

Cover artwork by Book Cover Corner Content Editing by Annetta Ribken Copy Editing by Jennifer Wingard Proofreading by Julie Glover

First Printing, 2013

ISBN Ebook: 978-1-947462-02-1

ISBN Paperback: 978-1-947462-03-8

Rhodes, Catie. Forever Road/ Catie Rhodes. — 1st ed.

To all the bosses who couldn't or wouldn't pay me a living wage. If it hadn't been for you, I never would have risked pursuing my dreams.

1

An inhuman shriek sliced through the pre-dawn darkness, stabbing at the haze of sleep coating my brain. My keys slipped from my fingers and clattered to the porch's wooden floor. Cursing, I bent to retrieve them and dropped my backpack in the process. I shook my head, willing myself to wake up.

Another furious wail echoed over the pasture behind Memaw's house. Anger shooed away the last of my early morning fog. I glared at the lights blazing from the sixteen-foot travel trailer at the back of the pasture. A crash shook the trailer, and a male voice cried out in protest. A few coyotes in the pine forest howled at the disturbance. They had the right idea.

"You can't tell me what to do, you...you wall-eyed baboon." She was so loud Rae could have been standing right next to me. *Damn, that girl has a big mouth. And a nasty talent for insults.*

The muscles between my shoulder blades rolled into

hard knots. My cousin was a pimple on the ass of my existence. If she kept it up, she'd wake Memaw, our paternal grandmother. If I went out there to tell her to shut up, she'd want to fight. Both options sounded almost as fun as running from an angry alligator. Almost.

On cue, Rae let out another furious howl followed by a string of curse words.

I left my stuff on the porch, vaulted the broken chain-link fence, and jogged across the pasture. My steel-toed work boots squelched and slapped on the mud, splashing my clean blue jeans. *Of all the crappy ways to start a day.* Rae couldn't have driven me crazier if she brainstormed ways to do it.

Halfway to the trailer, a light began to glow in the pine forest behind it. It stopped me in my tracks, but only for a moment. Rae picked that moment to escalate things.

The trailer's door slammed open and banged against the aluminum siding. Chase Fischer, sans pants, stumbled out. His naked ass glowed in the waning moonlight. I groaned. *This can't end well.*

I ran the last few yards to the travel trailer, doing my best to ignore the sounds and sights coming from the woods behind it. The odor of sweat and alcohol surrounded Chase, my earliest childhood and lifelong friend. It hurt to see him associating with my trashy cousin; I couldn't even lie to myself about that.

Rae charged from the trailer, her platinum hair a wild halo backlit by the trailer's interior lights. Chase and I both took a step away from her.

"Just go." Her sandpaper smoker's voice echoed against the pines. "You're a clown and a monkey's ass."

"Come on, sugar," Chase slurred. "This dew's cold on my bare feet. You don't want me here, just let me have my pants."

He wasn't the only one uncomfortable. There was no way to un-see this crazy scene. I redirected my gaze to the tree line, hoping to lessen the shock of it. Wrong choice. The air rippled with a cacophony of whispers as ghosts of the Palmore family clamored for attention. The lights in the woods glowed brighter, and a silhouette stepped to the edge of the forest, watching us. Fear crawled up my back and sat on my shoulders, so heavy it crushed the breath out of me. *Coming so close to this part of the property was a serious error in judgment, Peri Jean.* I usually avoided the place where the Palmore family perished over a century ago.

I dragged my attention from the woods and stepped into the light spilling from the trailer's open door. Knowing Rae would attack at the first show of weakness, I shoved my trembling hands into my pockets. How she felt okay acting this way mystified me. I was no prize, but I didn't have drunken screaming matches in my grandmother's backyard at the ass-crack of dawn. It all boiled down to respect. Rae possessed none. Not for herself or anybody else.

"Your grandmother is still asleep, Raelene Georgia Mace." I stated the obvious, but I knew no other way to convince her to stop yelling. "It's not even dawn, yet."

Rae ignored me and ducked back inside the trailer. She

returned holding Chase's jeans and slung them at him with a grunt. The jeans crumpled at my feet. Stinging embarrassment prickled the back of my neck. I squeezed my eyes shut and wished myself out of the situation. When I opened my eyes, nothing had changed. I picked the jeans up and tossed them to Chase. He mumbled thanks, but I couldn't even look at him. *Why, you dumbass? Why?*

The air around the trailer cooled. That could only mean one thing. The ghosts responsible for the light show in the woods had found me. Fear stirred the coffee bubbling in my gut. I groaned at the tiny strip of pink and orange lighting the horizon's edge. Full dawn, the only thing capable of chasing these nasties away, couldn't come fast enough.

Rae stomped to the edge of the wooden deck pushed against the travel trailer, every step screeching as the metal and wood rubbed together. Her loosely belted robe hung open, displaying her enviable, though fake, breasts. She twisted her mouth into a feral snarl and said, "What you want, Looney Tunes?"

"I want you to hold it down." That only covered half of it. I wanted to run back home with my tail between my legs. With the ghosts here, I cursed myself for deciding to confront Rae.

Rae looked down her nose at me and thrust out her jaw. I halfheartedly returned her glare, too distracted by the spirits swirling around me to put my heart into it. Ghosts gravitated to me like bugs to a bug light. Too bad I couldn't zap them and make them go away. Instead, I lived a freakish horror show of feeling dead people's emotions and seeing their grisly spirits.

Rae and I squared off, each trying to intimidate the other into backing down. Chase took a few steps away from us and shimmied into his dew-wet jeans. He patted the pockets, evidently searching for his keys and cursed when he realized they weren't there.

"You know this stuff upsets Memaw." Breaking the silence first lost me a little ground, but I needed to speed things up. A ghost from the long ago fire stood not six feet from me. His tattered clothes fluttered and flapped in the early morning breeze. I smelled the reek of charbroiled flesh so acrid I bit back a gag. Every muscle in my body knotted with tension. I couldn't stop my teeth from chattering. A scream built in my chest, and I knew I wouldn't be able to hold it back much longer.

"You're not the boss of me, Peri Jean Mace." Rae propped her hands on her hips.

A million replies, all smart-assed, came to mind. I swallowed them for the sake of brevity.

"That's true." I let Rae win a small victory just so I could get away from the woods and the ghosts sooner. "Just do this for me, all right? I'll owe you one."

"You mean a favor?" Rae slouched in her robe and looked exactly like what she was—an ex-con pushing thirty and living on her grandmother's grace. *Not that I'm any younger. Or that much more successful.* Maybe I didn't have much room to judge Rae. What I said next reflected my weakening resolve.

"I'll do you a favor if you'll keep it down." *Oh, I know*

I'm going to regret this. How much remains to be seen. "Starting now."

Rae pulled out a pack of cigarettes and offered them to me. My nicotine demon, which I'd been starving for the past two weeks, begged and pleaded. I shook my head anyway.

"That's right, you quit. I gotta quit now, too." She lit her cigarette. The dim flame from her disposable lighter revealed bruises on her cheeks and underneath her eyes. I gasped, skin tightening, as I imagined how much a beating like that would hurt.

"I told her to call the cops." Chase kept a safe distance from us.

"And I said I'd take care of it...boy toy." Rae's tone brooked no argument. Chase developed a sudden interest in staring at his bare feet. I averted my eyes, too. His love life had nothing to do with me and hadn't for some time. It didn't make minding my own business any easier. My heart ached for him and the stupid choices he made.

The sun, at last, peeked over the horizon. The burned ghost man faded away with a scream in my head, although the stench of fire and roasted human flesh lingered in the air. Relief loosened my tight muscles and left me feeling giddy. *If only all ghosts faded away at daybreak.*

The growing daylight illuminated more damage on Rae's face and my throat constricted. A raised patch with a crisscross pattern decorated one cheek. Both eyes were black and puffy. Handprint bruises laced her neck, and her nose looked broken. Rae watched me look her over.

"Who did that to you?" Despite my current irritation at

Rae, fury filled me at the idea of someone beating her so cruelly. *I wonder what she did to deserve it. Oh, Peri Jean, how shitty to even think that way.*

"Go inside and fix me some orange juice." Rae jerked her head at the trailer. "I need to talk to Peri Jean."

Chase hung his head and slouched into the trailer to do his mistress's bidding. It caught my attention Rae hadn't asked for gin or vodka in her orange juice. *No telling what's going on. I bet my pinky toe I'll be in the middle of it soon enough.* I glared at her after Chase shut the door.

"What?" She smirked, and that pissed me off.

"Don't talk to him that way." Even as I spoke, the logical part of my brain pleaded with me to shut up. *Let Rae and Chase do whatever they want back here. Not my business.*

"You don't own him just because y'all are best friends." She put "best friends" in air quotes. "I bet you're all bent out of shape because you're jealous. That's right, ain't it?" Her grin reminded me of a shit-eating possum.

"When did you get like this? You were a kind person once upon a time." Rae opened her mouth to speak, but I talked over her. "He's someone's son. He has people who love him. How would you like it if people treated someone you love like shit? Wouldn't it hurt you?"

I braced myself for her fury. Instead, she shifted foot to foot, dropping those hard eyes to look at her polished toenails.

"Life ain't no cakewalk. You don't let everybody know you're the boss, they'll try to run over you." She said all this without taking her eyes off her toenails. I'd embarrassed her, and it stung me. I had no business looking down my nose at anybody, not even Rae.

"I need that favor yesterday, cousin." Rae took a hard pull on her cigarette. She squinted at me through the cloud of smoke. Calling me cousin meant she wanted something big.

"All right." A promise was a promise, and I'd keep my word. But I never doubted I'd regret this favor. Had I known how much, I'd have run right then and there. "I can't this morning. I have to clean Mrs. Rudie's house in town. Jolene wants it over and done with."

Rae muttered some words under her breath. They sounded an awful lot like, "Stingy old bitch."

I didn't ask. None of Chase's family was thrilled about his fascination with Rae. His late grandmother, Mrs. Rudie Rushing, had never minced words. No telling what kind of exchanges she and Rae had.

"So you'll keep it down if I do you this favor?" The terms had to be clear; otherwise Rae would twist things around to suit herself.

"All right." Rae tossed her cigarette butt at the deck's edge. I told myself she didn't almost hit me on purpose. "Before you go, tell me what you know about the Mace Treasure."

The change in subject caught me by surprise, although the thought of Rae digging around for a non-existent treasure didn't. "It's a load of bullshit the Chamber of Commerce uses to drum up tourist dollars."

"Awww, come on." Rae arranged her mouth into a pout. "That money's got to be somewhere. Our great-great..." she counted on her fingers, "...hell, I don't know how many greats...grandfather couldn't have just lost it."

"You sound like that stupid documentary those Hollywood people came here to make." I swept my arms wide and put on a big, phony smile. "In today's money, the Mace Treasure would have been worth at least one hundred million dollars." I dropped my arms and my smile. "But they were full of shit. And so are you if you believe in that mess."

Rae flipped me the one-fingered salute. I rolled my eyes. The formalities complete, she went inside the trailer and slammed the door behind her. The sound of her yammering at Chase shook the thin walls.

I hustled back to the house and retrieved my backpack from where I'd dropped it on the porch. A tension headache sang harmony with my worries over what I'd gotten myself into with Rae. *At least Memaw's bedroom light is still off. If this little episode didn't wake her, it's worth it.*

Now off to help Jolene clean out old Mrs. Rudie's house. A sourpuss in life, I had no reason to expect Chase's grandmother to be any different in death. The upcoming task held less appeal than taking a trip to Disneyland with my ex-husband.

2

THE SPEEDOMETER HOVERED at eighty miles per hour as I drove the short distance to Gaslight City. I thought of nothing but the scene at the trailer. Rae acted like a braying jackass, and I promised her a favor. She had me whipped. Memaw, too. I couldn't suggest we ask her to move elsewhere. The property belonged to Memaw, not me. Something had to change, but I didn't know what.

To add to the fun, now I was obligated to deliver a favor of Rae's choice. I imagined myself doing her laundry, cleaning that pigsty of a trailer, or loaning her money she'd never repay. She didn't dare ask me to hunt that stupid treasure with her. *No way. I'd eat dog food first. The canned kind.*

"Fifteen minutes late because of my idiot cousin," I mumbled as I eased into Mrs. Rudie's driveway. Jolene wouldn't care. Though I never let Chase con me into marrying him, his mother treated me like family, patronizing my odd-jobs business every chance she got.

As I climbed out of my car, a shadow moved in an upstairs window. Not every person comes back as a ghost, but it looked like Mrs. Rudie did. *That mean old cuss just won't die. I'm in for a long day.* I steeled myself for the morning's second close encounter with the spirit realm. Pretending not to see a parade of dead folks was hard work. But I knew the consequences if I didn't.

Dying had not improved Mrs. Rudie's disposition. Hell's fury had nothing on Mrs. Rudie's as Jolene and I cleaned out her house. The ghost pinched me—often—to express her displeasure. An hour after I started work, welts rose on my arms and back from her abuse. She pulled my short pixie-cut hair until it stood in tousled spikes. Jolene, the poor dear, thought the welts were caused by allergies and offered me an antihistamine.

"I apologize again for being late." I sprinkled some packing peanuts into the bottom of a box and gently set a stack of ornamental plates wrapped in newspaper on top of it. "Rae is running us ragged. Last week, during her Sunday barbecue, she started a fire back there. I managed to put it out before we had to call the VFD, but I was worried."

"Child, if you apologize to me one more time, I'll..." Jolene paused while she tried to think of an appropriate punishment and shook her head. "I don't know what I'll do. You were almost my daughter-in-law. I love you like family. You say she and Chase were outside hollering at one another? Before dawn?"

"Naw. They were inside the trailer, but I could hear them up at the house." I taped the box closed, wrote the contents in black marker, and set it aside. "And it wasn't even Chase. He never said much."

Every once in a while, I saw a flash of the specter in my peripheral vision. Mrs. Rudie's rage burrowed into my emotions, using my energy to continue her antics. The conversation with Jolene helped me pretend I saw and felt nothing. For that, I was grateful. Jolene and I never discussed my loathsome supernatural talent. Just like everybody else in town, she knew. The details of my craziness were etched permanently in the annals of Gaslight City lore. But, like most folks, Jolene's politeness quelled her curiosity about my weirdness.

"Next time my son is in the middle of some drama over there, you send his butt home." Jolene shook her head as she handed me an ornate wooden box. "Drunk or not."

"I can't make Chase do anything. If I could, things would have been different." I traced the raised carvings on the box. My mind flitted through the highlights of my long relationship with her errant son.

"It would have been yours if you had married Chase. Mama loved you." Jolene reached across me and opened the box. The recently polished silver gleamed.

"Mrs. Rudie most certainly did not love me. She tolerated me."

"Well, honey, that's all Mama really did with everyone." Jolene threw her head back and laughed, even though her eyes brimmed with tears. "Mama was one of a kind."

Whatever tolerance Mrs. Rudie had for me died with her body. Her ghost gave me another sharp pinch, this time in the sensitive area near my neck. I bit back my gasp and forced myself to admire the old bat's silver with her sweet-natured daughter.

"It's not too late." Jolene's brown eyes found mine and held them. "Chase talks about you all the time. He's hardly mentioned Rae even though he's dated her all summer. If you want to call it dating."

"I didn't end things." I packed the silver in a cardboard box labeled "dining room" in Jolene's careful schoolteacher's handwriting.

"I know that. I just wish..." Jolene broke off and shrugged. "You always want the best for your kids. You'll see."

Pushing thirty and still unwilling to be a single mother, I wasn't so sure. After growing up with neither parent on hand, I wanted to give my child the benefit of two parents who loved each other. *Maybe I want too much. White picket fences only exist in movies and children's books.* Even so, I couldn't give up hope one would show up in my life.

"Mama's china needs to go, too." Jolene opened the china cabinet and grabbed a teacup. She wrapped it in a sheet of newspaper and placed it in an empty box. Mrs. Rudie hovered around us, cooling the room better than air conditioning.

Mrs. Rudie's upset over the dismantling of her life turned the antique-filled room into a damp, unpleasant place. Jolene, if her darting eyes and shaking hands were any indication, sensed it. If asked, she'd have blamed it on nerves—too much to do on a day filled with grief.

"I appreciate you coming out so early and on a Sunday." Jolene shivered and looked around. "With Mama gone, my sisters want to split things up."

Why then did Jolene's sisters head back to Houston and Dallas the day of the funeral? The survival of my business depended on knowing when to keep my mouth shut, and so I did. The whole thing made me angry for Jolene. She had a good heart, and people took advantage of her. *She ought to tell her sisters to suck lemons.*

Mrs. Rudie hovered near. As I wrapped her prized china in newspaper, a wave of grief came from her. Confusion and sadness over the loss of her life had her stirred up. She'd move on once Jolene closed up her house for good. I knew those things because the spirits' feelings existed right alongside my own. I learned early to untangle the two sets of emotions and to keep them to myself.

Tears swam in Jolene's eyes as she arranged the china in cardboard boxes. She swiped at them and gave me a weak smile. This day couldn't be anything but hard for her. I waited for her to tell me what to do next. I knew from experience she needed to feel in control of this process.

"Look here." Jolene indicated a plain wooden box with brass accents. She grinned at me expectantly, as though I should recognize it. On the lid of the box, which sat on a cherry wood pedestal, was a monogrammed brass plaque. RM? Then, it hit me.

"This wouldn't be..." I trailed off in case I was wrong. I needed Jolene's money. I couldn't afford to offend her if this thing had belonged to somebody famous.

"Your many-greats grandfather—Reginald Mace. The founder of our little town." Jolene pulled out a drawer in the pedestal and extracted a skeleton key but stopped short of using it on the box. Staring at the wall above the antique, she wrinkled her nose. "And there's that damned ugly horseshoe. Mama always displayed both pieces together. Never understood why. Mama's gone. Let's get rid of that horseshoe."

I said nothing as she dragged a chair from the table and pushed it against the wall underneath the horseshoe. I agreed about the horseshoe's lack of attractiveness, but I wondered if Mrs. Rudie had a more practical reason for keeping the two pieces together. The bottle tree in front of Memaw's house, though pretty, was there to ward off ghosts. I had a half-formed memory of folklore having to do with iron and ghosts, but couldn't quite recall it.

"Would you climb up and get that ugly thing, shug? I'd do it myself, but I'm too fat." She patted her behind and gave me a sheepish grin. "Mama can't scold me now for getting rid of it."

Oh, if only she knew. I climbed onto the chair, bracing for Mrs. Rudie's retaliation. This reeked of bad idea, but damned if I knew a sane reason why. I pulled the horseshoe off the nail easily enough and stepped off the chair. While I hovered off balance, Mrs. Rudie struck, slamming me into the wall. Jolene's shriek scared me more than the short fall.

"I'm all right." I got to my feet and examined a scrape on my arm.

"Are you sure?" Jolene tossed the horseshoe into a garbage can and approached me, clucking over the scrape. I waved her off and made a big show of emptying the garbage can, still feeling I'd done the wrong thing. By the time I got back, she'd unlocked the box but had not opened it. She wanted to share this with me. I pasted an interested expression on my face and stood beside her.

Jolene lifted the antique box's lid.

A dark shadow rose and floated toward the ceiling. The shadow swirled and coiled in a corner; so dark it obscured the hand-carved molding. Its energy spread through the room, clammy and dreadful. The air grew heavy and close. I fought the urge to leave the room, the house, the city. *What the hell?*

Even Mrs. Rudie's formidable spirit retreated from this old nasty. I decided that iron horseshoe must have kept the ghost at bay and knew Jolene and I had screwed up. Was this dark shadow my long-dead, reputedly crazy ancestor? If so, he had some bad mojo.

Jolene and I peered inside the box. It was as plain as the outside and featured a flat surface covered with tattered green material and two inkwells with dried ink in them. The box rang with bad vibes. *Why did Mrs. Rudie hold onto it all these years? I'd have sold that thing first chance I got. Forget that iron horseshoe. I wouldn't have this in my home.* A tremor worked its way through my body, and I shivered.

"Isn't this a beautiful writing slope, shug?" Jolene's habit of calling all women shug instead of sugar made her sound less like a retired teacher and more like a southern belle. "A gentleman like Reginald Mace would have taken this on his travels."

Jolene tactfully didn't rehash the story of how Reginald Mace went from being the richest man in town to a penniless lunatic. My ancestor lost his mind after his only son, William, joined the Alaska Gold Rush. Some folks believed he squandered his fortune trying to entice the boy to come home. Others theorized Reginald hid his fortune for William to find and went too crazy to remember where he hid it. Through the latter group, the Mace Treasure legend remained alive and well years after Reginald was dead and buried.

Jolene's family likely bought the writing slope in the early nineteen hundreds when Burns County auctioned off the entire Mace estate for unpaid taxes. People who considered me mentally ill—a great number of people in Gaslight City—theorized I inherited my "mental instability" from Reginald Mace. Oh, I'd heard all the whispers. A famously crazy ancestor and a family treasure added an extra layer of unpleasantness to my childhood, repressing any interest in the treasure or researching my family tree.

I swallowed the bad feelings left over from my childhood and smiled. I couldn't lie to save my life, but sometimes politeness didn't require a lie. "It has to be close to one hundred fifty years old. I've never seen anything like it."

"Do you think we could fit it in a box? I'd hate for it to get scratched up in my SUV." Jolene removed the writing slope from its pedestal and handed it to me.

A painful current of energy burned through my arms

as soon as it made contact with my skin. The dark shadow floated down from the ceiling and swirled around me. My head swam. The air around me grew so cold, my breath puffed out in clouds of vapor. I couldn't understand how Jolene didn't see it. Maybe she didn't want to. Cycling like a whirlwind, the dark shadow floated back into the writing slope. *I bet Jolene doesn't keep this thing a week. I know I wouldn't.*

I concentrated on keeping my poker face and packaged the antique into a cardboard box and duct taped it closed, hands trembling. My skin crawled and tingled with the need to get it far away from me. A hand closed over my shoulder, and I screamed and spun around.

———

CHASE STOOD behind me with a dumb grin on his face. I searched for evidence of his night of debauchery with Rae but found none other than bloodshot eyes. He smelled of soap, deodorant, and shaving cream. His hands were steady as he took the box containing the freaky writing slope from my hands and set it on top of our growing box pile. As soon as I released my hold on the box, the tension drained away so quickly my head swam.

"I see y'all waited on me." Chase's baritone voice didn't have even the hint of a slur. It sounded just as beautiful as when we were kids, back when Chase swore he'd be a rock star. Even though his partying long ago superseded the music—and everything else—his voice still curled female toes.

Rather than answering, Jolene rushed to him and wrapped him in a grateful hug. Chase hugged her back, winking at me over her shoulder. I shook my head at him and glanced out the window to see his old truck with a flatbed trailer attached to it.

"Daddy'll be along in a few hours." Chase released Jolene and looked around the living room. "He took some folks fishing."

"Oh, it'll be late afternoon before he gets around to messing with this." Jolene planted her chubby hands on her ample hips.

"Don't matter. Me and Peri Jean can get most of this stuff loaded. I'll call him, and he can meet me at the storage place."

Jolene harrumphed but said nothing. Chase poked me in the ribs.

"You ready for a workout, Short Stuff?" Without waiting for my answer, he studied the room's furnishings, probably calculating what I could realistically carry. Chase had helped me with many heavy-lifting jobs over the years.

"Don't call me Short Stuff." I protested for form only. I knew I was a shrimp. "I think the only thing I can't pick up is the dining room table."

"Wimp." Chase made a pained face as he studied the solid oak monstrosity. "Want to start with the living room?"

Chase and I did our share of grunting and straining as we loaded the couches, chairs, end tables, and the grandfather clock onto the flatbed trailer. When we took a break, Chase lit up a cigarette and offered me one. I shook my head, and he chuckled.

"How long this time?"

"Two weeks." I made a face at him. This was only my third quit that year.

Chase laughed harder. "Is that a record?"

"No. Last year when I quit for two months was a record." I watched my old friend out of the corner of my eye. Though only a year older than me, working construction in the unforgiving Texas sun had aged his fair skin. Deep lines creased the skin around his eyes and mouth. He still looked good, but in a weathered, rugged way. Since he and Rae became an item, a tired, defeated air hung about him. It scared me. "This morning's drama. Is it really worth getting a piece of ass from her?"

"I thought we agreed a year and a half ago that we would never be more than friends again." Chase finished his cigarette and ground it out under one of his work boots. "That means my love life ain't none of your business."

"This isn't me trying to butt into your love life. This is concern over what you're doing to yourself. Your body isn't going to tolerate this kind of abuse forever." I put my hand on his back, wanting to hug him but not wanting to give him the wrong message. He was right. We could never be a couple again. But that didn't erase our bond. "I love you and worry that she's going to get you in trouble."

Chase shrugged, keeping his eyes averted. "You're the only one who gives a shit."

I snorted. "Spare me the self-pity. Nobody forces you to run around playing trailer park stud." I squeezed his arm to make him look at me. "Your son needs you to be a father to him. Do you want him to grow up thinking you don't care enough to do that?"

"Don't matter if I try or not." He shook his head when I tried to interrupt. "Last time it was my weekend with Kansas, Felicia sent him fishing with his stepfather. Haven't seen him in months."

My chief tormenter during my school years, Felicia Brent, convinced Chase to dump me and take her to the prom a million years ago when we were all teenagers. I charged into the dance and beat the snot out of Felicia in front of everybody. Chase and Felicia bonded over the drama and shared a brief marriage, which produced Chase's only child—a boy named Kansas. They divorced soon after his birth.

The trials and tribulations of adulthood changed most of us, beat the arrogance out of us. Felicia just got meaner. It didn't surprise me she used Kansas to hurt Chase, but the injustice of it infuriated me.

"Can't a judge enforce the custody ruling?"

"Judge told me to straighten out and come back." He slumped forward, digging his elbows into his knees and resting his chin on his knuckles. "Plus, last time I took them to court, Scott started harassing me. Wrote me three speeding tickets in a month. My insurance went up higher than a cat's ass."

Scott Holze, Felicia's second husband, worked as a Burns County Sheriff's Deputy. His father, the Sheriff, ran the county whatever way suited him. Scott executed his job duties the same way. My heart ached for Chase, but babying him would only encourage his mood. I scooted closer and leaned my shoulder against his.

"Listen to me. Kansas is the most positive thing you've got going for you. Do whatever it takes to get in his life." I gave him an extra squeeze for emphasis. "I'll beat Felicia up again. See how she likes that."

I'd wanted to make Chase laugh, but he slumped again, frowning.

"Maybe he's better off just knowing Scott as a father."

I looked at the sky and held out my hand, rubbing my thumb and forefinger together.

"All right," he said. "I'll play. What's that supposed to be?"

"World's littlest violin playing my hurt pumps purple piss for your pitiful ass."

Chase draped his arm over my shoulder and pulled me against him. We sat in silence for several minutes, basking in the comfort of our long friendship. Without warning, Chase tightened his grip and used his other hand to muss my hair. I flopped and wiggled and finally jerked away.

"You just wait. When you least expect it, I'll get you back." I smoothed my hair down with both hands.

"Sometimes, I don't know what I did to deserve you." He met my eyes and held them.

"Same here." I planned to convince Rae she wanted to dump Chase. Even if that meant slipping her a few bucks.

"Long as we're solving the world's problems, what was wrong with you when I got here? You looked like you'd seen a ghost." Chase had known about my link to the spirit world since we were children. Back then, I didn't know better than to tell people. That got me accused of being everything from a devil worshiper to an untreated schizophrenic over the years, but Chase never treated me any different.

"That box I had when you first came in?" I looked at Chase for confirmation he knew what I meant. After he nodded, I said, "Convince your mother to get rid of it. She doesn't want it in her house."

Chase frowned but nodded to confirm he'd do what I asked.

Jolene picked that moment to hustle outside with a pitcher of iced tea and three glasses. Chase and I turned our conversation to lighter topics. The three of us sat in the steadily increasing heat, sucking down cold, sweet tea.

"What else needs doing?" I set my tea glass back on the tray. As much as I enjoyed Jolene and Chase's company, I wanted to get home. Anticipation of negotiating a favor with Rae gnawed at me. She would ask for the moon and act cheated if I couldn't deliver. I wished time would speed up and the whole thing blow over without any high drama. About as much chance of that happening as a pile of hot garbage picking itself up.

Jolene rubbed the corner of her mouth with one finger, her face creasing into a frown as she thought. My cellphone rang. Jolene jumped, and Chase laughed.

I frowned at him as I removed the offending instrument from its dorky belt holster and checked the caller ID. Memaw. I cringed. She wouldn't call just to say howdy-do. Drama was afoot, and no doubt, Rae danced at its center.

"Yes, ma'am?" My imagination helpfully supplied every

horrible event that could have taken place. Rae burning down the travel trailer. A drug dealer or other shady type knocking on Memaw's front door.

"She's playing her music loud again." A sad lilt polluted Memaw's husky voice.

This wasn't a real catastrophe. Memaw, however, was at her wit's end. *Maybe we need to kick Rae off the property.*

"Aren't you going to your Sunday morning devotional? You love Pastor Gage's stories about his missionary work." I didn't like it when people tried to divert my anger, but this situation helped me see why they did it. Memaw's best course of action—get away from Rae. If she went out to gripe at Rae about the music, it would end up ruining her entire Sunday.

"I am, but that's—"

"Not the point," I finished for her. "I know. Let it go for now. Rae and I have an appointment to talk when I get home."

The smile faded off Chase's face as he listened. Jolene turned away, pretending not to hear. My toes curled as embarrassment heated my face.

"I'm telling her to hit the road." Memaw's voice wavered. She always put family first. She had a hard time admitting she couldn't help Rae, but by this time both of us knew the girl was too crooked to go straight. Painful, but true.

The silence stretched out between us. I knew she wanted me to tell her not to send Rae packing. I wanted the friendship Rae and I shared as kids but knew it was lost. Too many bad miles covered the road between then and now. The three of us played at an unwinnable tug-of-war.

"I bet Pastor Gage has coffee and pastries already set out." I pitched my voice low and soothing. "Why don't you go on early? I'll talk to her when I get home. Things will be fine."

"I guess I could." Weariness dragged through Memaw's voice. When she spoke again, she sounded more like her usual self. "We'll have lunch when I get home from church, so don't eat."

"Yes, ma'am." The call went dead in my ear.

"Is everything all right at your house?" Jolene peered into my eyes.

"It's nothing we can't handle." Even as fantasies of punching Rae in the face floated through my mind, I forced a smile. "Perhaps Rae will decide to move on soon."

Jolene engulfed me in one of her hugs. I hugged her back. Chase was lucky to have such a normal mother. I would never understand why he courted disaster the way he did.

Chase and I filled his flatbed trailer with Mrs. Rudie's furniture. He refused my offer to help him unload it at the storage facility. As Chase climbed into his truck and cranked it, he flashed me a smile. "Want me to help you talk to Rae?"

"As if." I waved him off and went back into the house as he drove away.

Jolene and I spent an hour loading boxes into her gargantuan SUV. Mrs. Rudie's spirit gave off sad, subdued vibes. She didn't pinch me again.

Mrs. Rudie's retreat left me with plenty of time to think about all the ways Rae got under my skin. By the time Jolene dismissed me, my anger boiled. Rae's bullshit was about to end one way or the other. I drove home, muscles rigid and jaw clenched, trying my best to figure out how to save the day. I suspected I'd go to bed with a fat lip. Turned out, I was right.

3

I HEARD the bass buzzing and thumping as soon as I turned off Farm Road 4077 into Memaw's driveway. The music couldn't have been louder at a full-out concert. My hands tightened on the steering wheel until my knuckles turned white. My brazen, silicone-stuffed turd of a cousin cared not a whit about other people's feelings. Not for the first time, I questioned Rae's end goal. Did she aim to drive Memaw and me off the property and have the whole spread for herself? Or did she have no purpose and simply delight in torturing others? If only I could figure out what she wanted, I could negotiate with her.

As my car moved under the row of towering pine trees lining Memaw's driveway, sunlight and shadow strobed over my face. The sky had already darkened from the white hue it carried in summer to the blue topaz of fall. Had Rae's drama not interfered, I'd have spent this exquisite day outside doing chores, feeling the sun on my face and the cool wind at my back. *Another day ruined, courtesy of Miss Trouble Maker. Fun, fun, fun.*

I parked my vintage Nova under the open-air carport and leaned my head on the steering wheel. *Patience.* No telling what Rae endured over the course of her childhood or in the years I lost contact with her, and how it affected her. I climbed out of my car and trekked across the pasture to the trailer.

Rae's car sat in front with all four doors open, the largest portable stereo in the world. Surprisingly, hers was the only car out there. She usually entertained a bevy of beer-drinking, thirty-year-old teenagers on Sundays. I had expected her to embarrass me before granting me an audience. At close range, the music vibrated the dirt under my work boots and ground out any sympathy for my cousin. *This sucks. It sucks to play warden. It sucks that she can't behave.* I leaned into the car and turned off the eardrum-shattering noise.

The sudden silence, though glorious at first, soon made my skin crawl. No birds chirped in the woods. No frogs hollered for rain. No crickets hummed in the grass. It was too quiet.

"Rae?" I called her name just to break that awful, dead silence. The wooden steps on the deck Chase built her a few months earlier squealed under my feet as I climbed them. The fine hairs on the back of my neck rose. Something felt wrong, but I couldn't put my finger on what. I stopped at the far edge of the wooden platform. "It's Peri Jean."

No answer. Rae never quit making some kind of noise.

She didn't seem comfortable without it. Surely, she realized her music had been cut off. That alone should have brought her raging out of her nest.

A branch popped in the woods behind the trailer. I jumped, heart racing with the urge to run. This was silly. I grew up in these woods, knew them like the back of my hand. The Palmore ghosts were gone until dark. An animal made the noise. The woods were full of animals, and they meant no harm.

Despite my pep talk, I cringed at each squeak from the unsteady wooden deck as I crossed it. Its piercing bleats shattered the stillness and jangled my nerves. Raising one shaking fist, I beat on the flimsy door. The noise boomed through the trailer and an awful silence followed.

"Rae?" My voice sounded high and childish. Scared. *I bet Rae is crouching on the other side of that door laughing at me.* My fear mixed with irritation and came out pissed off.

I knocked harder, rattling the small dwelling. "I know you're in there!" I hollered at the door, bracing for Rae to slam it open in my face. "Get out here now or I'm not doing a damned thing for you."

A squirrel chuffed curses at me for making so much racket. Other than that, my rage-infused words got no answer.

"Rae, come on." I gave the door three hard raps, bouncing it in its frame. What happened next was not on purpose. Really. When my hand came down, I bumped the doorknob. The door opened a crack. Without thinking, I swung the door all the way open, ready to give Rae the what-for.

My mind registered the red goop covering everything but quickly explained it away. Maybe she spilled some food. Red stains covered the floor, the walls, even the ceiling. A still form lay on the little foldout table. Maybe a pile of clothes.

Then, a drop of blood slid off the edge of the table, grew pregnant, and plopped onto the floor. Under the table was a pool of blood from which smaller trails of blood ran. A low hum filled my head. My stomach lurched and prepared to upend its contents. I bailed off the deck and heaved into the bushes at the tree line. Finished, I dragged a hand over my mouth. My body quaked with unspent fear.

What the hell had I just seen? *A dead person.* Sweat broke out all over my body. That thing on the table couldn't be my cousin. It didn't even look human. Had she overdosed? Or hurt herself? What if she needed help? Steeling myself, I staggered back to the trailer's open door.

My shock turned to grim realism as I took in the form on the table. I recognized the toe ring Rae always wore in the hazy light. That meant the bloody mess spread out on the table was my cousin. I forced myself to look at her face. Eyes wide, her mouth hung open in either a silent scream or a final gasp. Rae's cellphone blared its annoying ring tone.

It broke me out of the trance. Someone did this to her. I needed to call 911. I didn't want to be alone with my cousin's corpse. Through my shock, I realized I couldn't shield Memaw from this horror. *I need to get the sheriff's office out here so Memaw doesn't see Rae like this.* But I needed to get away from the sight of Rae on that table before I did anything else. I stepped back out onto the wooden deck and took out my cellphone. Rae's phone stopped ringing.

A branch cracked, this time nearer the trailer. Leaves rustled behind me. My breath caught in my throat. Somebody was with me. The killer. My throat closed. *Fight or flight*, my mind chanted idiotically. I spun around with my fists up.

The man in green came at me fast, charging up the wooden steps to join me on the deck. I threw a sloppy roundhouse. My weak punch hit him in the shoulder and bounced off. My knees went loose and liquid. They weren't going to hold me up long enough to fight off my cousin's killer.

My horrified mind took in flashes of detail. Camo hunting mask. Camo coveralls. Camo boots. Bigger than me.

I staggered and swung my fist again. The punch connected with his middle. Years of schoolyard fights paid off. He let out a pained grunt. I reared back again, leaving my torso unprotected.

He punched me in the gut and that was it. The air whooshed out my lungs. Time stopped. The slam of my pounding heart filled my head. Crows cawed in the distance. The pine trees around me blurred.

My mind kept taking little pictures. Latex gloves. He wore latex gloves. *Oh, no.* I knew why people wore those. The masked man took a step toward me. Long and lean with narrow shoulders like a woman's. Long hands and long feet. He could have been a tall woman if it hadn't been for the way he walked. *Women don't walk like that.*

My legs wouldn't work, and my empty lungs screamed for air. I flopped around uselessly until he reached me.

The masked man leaned over me and doubled up his fist. The latex glove squeaked as it rubbed against itself. Balloons. The sound reminded me of balloons. The fist hurtled toward me in slow motion.

Poor Memaw. She would find both her granddaughters dead. I didn't want her to see that. The punch connected with my face, shattering my thought process. I flew off the deck and heard the thud as my body hit the dirt. The world jumped track, and I floated into a haze of oblivion.

———

MY VISION slowly came into blurry focus. My head pounded, and I tasted blood. I whimpered. Footsteps crunched through the grass and leaves toward me. I braced myself to endure whatever the future held.

An indistinct face loomed over mine. I blinked hard. Memaw's face, red from crying, snapped into focus. I reached out to touch her, and she snatched my hand, grinding the bones together.

"Oh, thank God. You're gonna live. I was afraid they'd got you, too." Memaw's voice sounded thick and stuffy with her tears. I realized with a jolt of horror she must have seen Rae. Of course she did. I never called 911 because that man hit me. No doubt, Memaw came home from church and found us both. She pulled a cloth handkerchief out of her sleeve and dabbed at my face. "Your lip's bleeding."

"She awake?" A male voice called. Memaw nodded, and more footsteps crunched through the grass. The man who joined Memaw wore a Burns County Sheriff's uniform. He'd taken off the uniform hat, but a band where it had rested dented his light brown hair. He knelt, peering at me with intense, bottomless blue eyes. Those eyes held all the world's sorrows in them.

The guy looked familiar. Why should I know him? I didn't go for the starched uniform type, so not a one-night-stand. Then, it came to me.

"I've seen you jogging early in the mornings." My words sounded mushy, sort of unformed, as though I was talking around a mouthful of food. I reached up to touch my face and found a swollen lump where my lips used to be.

"Peri Jean, I'm Dean Turgeau." He pronounced it *two-joe*. Dean reached into his pocket, pulled out a small note-book and a pen, and smiled. The smile never touched his sad, world-weary eyes. "I'm the jogger you wave to in the mornings."

And the jogger whose butt I stared at in the rearview mirror after I passed him. He had moved into Gaslight City within the last few months. I kept meaning to find out his name, maybe make our paths cross, but I hadn't. *So this hottie is Sheriff Joey Holze's new hire. Too bad.* I kept my thoughts to myself and rolled to my knees.

"Don't move," said the hottie. *What did he say his name was? Dean. That was it.* "I've called this in, and the ambulance'll be here soon." He reached out a hand but stopped just short of touching me.

"I don't need a doctor." I tried to stand but staggered. Dean gripped my arm to steady me as the ground surged upward. His touch delivered a pleasant jolt, entirely inappropriate under the circumstances. I pulled away but couldn't quit looking at him.

"You look like you need the hospital," Dean said. Memaw nodded.

"I'm fine." I spat to clear the metallic tang of blood from my mouth.

"How'd y'all find me out here?" I pretty much guessed how things played out, but I had to talk to convince them I didn't need the hospital. The talking made my head throb worse. I reached up with both hands to hold my head together.

"I saw the trailer door hanging open and someone laid out on the ground when I got home from church," Memaw said. "I thought you and Rae got into a fight, so I came out here and saw...her. I called 911."

"I was patrolling the area," Dean said. "Got here less than five minutes after the call came in." He paused and frowned. "Your turn. What were you doing back here?"

"Rae and I had an appointment to talk after I finished work." The world around me lurched and sizzled with an unnatural crispness. *I need to sit down.*

"Where is work?"

I rattled off the address of Mrs. Rudie's former residence. "The house's owner died. Her daughter and I cleaned it out so the family can sell it."

"Was Rae alive when you found her?"

I shook my head. "I didn't touch her or try to revive her. She looked dead."

Memaw dragged me into a tight embrace. I broke off staring at Dean to hug her back. Her body trembled. I stroked her back and assured her I was all right.

"I'm confused about what happened here." Dean edged closer, his pen poised. "Your cousin was dead, but her killer was still here?"

"He wasn't in the trailer when I got here." If I didn't sit soon, I would collapse. "I found her and puked. Then, he was just there."

"Did you know him?" When I shook my head, Dean asked, "Can you describe him?"

"He wore one of those camo hunting masks." I gestured at my face. "I never saw his face."

"Your attacker was male?" Dean raised his eyebrows. "You sure?"

"He walked like a man." I thought things over. "He had bigger feet than women usually have."

"Did you see his vehicle?" Dean scribbled on the notepad, his pen scratching its surface.

"The only car here was Rae's old LTD." I pointed at the car.

"Then where did he come from? And how did he leave?" Dean said the words under his breath, maybe to himself. I answered anyway.

"There's an old path that runs through those woods. You can get out to Beulah Church Road from it or onto the Longstreet property behind us."

"Or you can cut through the Longstreet land and get to the Fischer place," Memaw said.

Dean quit writing when a sheriff's cruiser, blue and reds flashing, drove through our yard and cut across the pasture. It rolled to a stop a few feet from us. I noticed Dean clenching his jaw and grinding his teeth. The cruiser's door creaked open and Sheriff Joey Holze grunted as he hoisted his too many pounds from the driver's seat. The car rose a few inches when it no longer had to bear its burden.

Holze waddled over to stand with us, breathing hard as though he'd just run a marathon. "Just got off the phone with the Sheriff next county over. He's loaning us his crime scene van. They'll be here shortly."

"Thanks for driving out to let me know." Dean's face went still and expressionless.

"I'm gonna stay and observe." Holze hitched up his pants and stared at the trailer. "She in there?"

"Yes, sir." Dean closed his eyes and rubbed his temple. He turned back to me, seemingly ready to resume our conversation.

Holze looked me over and shook his head. "You would be in the middle of this."

Dean tilted his head as he studied me. Probably trying to figure out what kind of trouble I caused. He wouldn't have to wait long. His mean-spirited boss would fill him in first chance he got.

"What the hell does that mean, Joseph?" Memaw's stare could have brought down armies. Sheriff Joey's jowls turned purple.

"Miss Leticia, your granddaughter has a mental illness––"

"Don't you say one more word." Memaw shook her finger at Sheriff Joey. The fat man cowered. Under other circumstances, I might have bit back a laugh. My head hurt too bad to do anything but stand there swaying like a drunk at closing time.

I glanced at Dean. His handsome profile turned away from me, a few feet of distance now between us. A pang of disappointment surprised me. *This guy isn't my type anyway. Who cares what he thinks of me?*

"I'm going back to the house. I need to sit down, and I'm not doing it in that trailer." I spun on my heels and almost fell. Memaw steadied me, slightly ruining my dramatic exit.

Dean Turgeau's voice cut into my thoughts. "Don't run off. I'll come up to the house to talk to you soon as we process the crime scene."

Clammy sweat cooled my skin as I imagined Dean's questions and what I'd have to remember to answer them. Sour nausea bubbled up, and I leaned over and dry heaved. Memaw caught my arm and led me away. Two sets of eyes burned at my back.

––––––

AN HOUR LATER, Burns County Sheriff's cruisers, ambulances, and anybody who could find a reason to show up crawled all over Memaw's land. Deputy Brittany Watson—who I used to babysit—vibrated with excitement as she stood outside the crime scene holding a clipboard and checking people in and out.

Burns County, one of the smallest counties in East Texas, had a population of less than twenty thousand. Murders, when they happened, were pretty clear-cut. A wife got angry enough to shoot her two-timing husband. A drunk ran through a stop sign and plowed over a kid on his bike. Tragic, but certainly not the stuff of true crime novels. Rae's murder was different, gruesome enough to be on TV.

My jaw throbbed fit to kill, but according to Dr. Nathan Longstreet, it wasn't broken. Camo Man must have pulled his punch at the last second. If he hadn't, I'd have been in the Gaslight City ER getting my jaw wired instead of preparing iced tea in Memaw's kitchen. *It's important to be thankful for the small things.* A childhood experience left me with a terror of hospitalization so intense I'd do just about anything to avoid it. Like working in the kitchen after almost having my jaw broken. Nothing sounded better than a handful of pain relievers and sleep. But if I gave in to the impulse, I'd have to admit the extent of my injuries. Then, Memaw would make Dr. Longstreet try to convince me to spend the night at the hospital. No way in hell. So I did kitchen duty.

Somewhere between boiling water and adding the insane amount of sugar Memaw insisted on to the tea, a question occurred to me. Why didn't the camo man kill me along with Rae? The latex gloves implied a willingness to kill me. Didn't they? I thought it over as I stirred the syrupy tea. Not necessarily. They only implied a desire to mask his identity.

The camo man returned to the trailer after he killed Rae. If he wanted to kill me, he would have. Why else would he come back? Maybe he left something behind. He wore the latex gloves to make damn sure he left no prints while he retrieved...what? I just got in the way of him covering up his crime.

Cold droplets of tea sprayed my forearm, startling me out of my thoughts. My vigorous stirring had slopped it out of the pitcher. Disgusted, I wiped the sweet mess off my skin with a damp paper towel. I balanced the glass pitcher and two glasses on a tray and took it out to the back porch.

Memaw sat in a creaking wooden rocking chair, a blanket draped over her shoulders. She stared out at the crime scene with a blank expression on her face. Dr. Longstreet, who also served as Justice of the Peace, squatted next to her, murmuring something I couldn't quite hear. He quit speaking when I came close.

They both accepted tall glasses of the quintessential Southern elixir. I put down the tray and sat on the porch swing next to Dr. Longstreet. The horror of what I'd seen in the trailer wouldn't leave me. It kept circling back to haunt me. The need to cry—to let some emotion out—tightened my chest. I saved stuff like that for when I was alone, though.

"How does this work?" I spoke to keep from crying. A little explosion of pain in my jaw rewarded the effort. I put my hand to my face and probed the sore area.

"You sure you don't want to go to the hospital?" Dr. Longstreet leaned in close and looked into my eyes. When I shook my head no, he nodded. He knew I'd sooner submit to a public demonstration of my ability to see the spirit world than agree to confinement in a hospital.

"As for how this works, your guess is as good as mine." He rubbed his white mustache. "I ordered an autopsy at the investigator's request."

"Him?" I pointed at Dean Turgeau. He stood in the middle of the crime scene anthill pointing and giving orders. Every so often, he reached up to rub his temple. He was the only member of law enforcement who didn't look excited.

"Yep." Dr. Longstreet took a long sip of his tea, carefully removed a cloth hanky from his pocket, and wiped his mouth. He fixed his gaze on the pasture. The old doctor did a good job of keeping his mouth shut and would only supply information if I asked for it.

"Where's he from?" I couldn't hide my curiosity. Dean Turgeau's sweaty, defined muscles and pretty-boy face had been my daily eye candy for nearly two months. I pegged him as a transplant, but figured he was temporary—perhaps doing contract work for King Ranch Chicken or Longstreet Lumber, the county's two biggest businesses. It shocked me to learn he worked for Sheriff Joey.

"He moved here from South Louisiana. East Baton Rouge Parish. Why do you ask?" The corner of Dr. Longstreet's mouth quirked into what might have been a smile had the circumstances been appropriate.

"He was first on the scene." My words rushed out too fast. I sounded defensive. "He—"

"He and Peri Jean noticed each other." Memaw grinned, but only a shadow of her usual smile.

"We did not *notice each other*." My reply dripped with overplayed outrage. Memaw loved to joke about my love life. She called it a fiasco.

"Isn't he a little long in the tooth for you?" Dr. Longstreet raised his bushy white eyebrows.

Memaw chuckled and slapped her thigh. "Yeah, this one's probably old enough to buy beer."

"You make it sound like I date kids." I folded my arms over my chest and sniffed. "I'll have you both know they're all out of high school, well over eighteen."

Memaw and Dr. Longstreet hooted in delight and kept the barbs coming. I played straight man because we all needed the diversion. They were right about one thing, though. Dean Turgeau was too old and too straight for me.

It didn't take long for the condolence callers, or insanely curious to be more accurate, to pile in on us. Memaw and I migrated inside. Everybody wanted iced tea. I played waitress. On one of my trips to the kitchen, I saw Dean Turgeau outside our yard struggling with the latch on the gate. My libido hopped a giddy little leap.

Why this guy? He was glaringly wrong for me. The uniform only represented the tip of the iceberg. He worked for Joey Holze, who hated me ever since I could remember. He worked in law enforcement, and my best friend spent most of his time on the wrong side of the law.

The TV people say death makes survivors want to have

sex because it affirms they're still alive. Maybe that's where the sudden bolt of lust originated. A tryst with Dean Turgeau had the potential to stir up a shitstorm of epic proportions. I needed him like I needed another encounter with my camo-attired assailant. Even so, I brushed a hand over my hair—as though the action would make my hair not look like I'd just found a dead body and had my butt kicked—and stepped out onto the back porch.

4

THE SWARM of law enforcement and emergency personnel had vacated our property, and the trailer stood alone out in the pasture. Dean promised he'd come to finish the talk Sheriff Joey Fatbutt Holze interrupted, and here he was. Seeing me on the porch, he gave me that smile—which didn't touch his eyes—and rattled the gate again. I jumped off the porch, ran down the brick walk, and unwound the wire.

"Thank you." Turgeau's eyes were tight around the corners, and his full lips were white.

I held the gate open. Turgeau limped through, wincing with each step.

"You okay?" I asked. "Need some aspirin or an ice pack?"

"Naw." He limped past me and climbed the porch steps. "Leg just gets tired at the end of the day."

"What happened to it?"

Turgeau turned to face me. His blue eyes darkened to

the gray of storm clouds. "Long story. Not pertinent to this situation."

This was exactly why I stayed away from guys over twenty-five. Too complicated. Too full of old war wounds and baggage. They could turn nasty and lash out over nothing at any time.

"Feel well enough to answer questions about..." Turgeau waved a hand at the trailer sitting in the pasture and tried to smile. He couldn't quite get his face to cooperate. The anger still hovered right at the surface of his emotions.

I shrugged.

"You've had some time to think. Any idea who beat you up?" Turgeau sat on the porch swing, closed his eyes, and sighed in relief. I wanted to offer him some of the bourbon Memaw kept for medicinal purposes, but didn't want to risk his wrath again.

"Nope." There had been something familiar about the camo man, but I couldn't quite articulate it. "I did some thinking about why he didn't kill me along with Rae."

"What's your theory?" He raised his eyebrows, mischief dancing in those amazing eyes. Despite the visual effect, I prickled at his amusement.

"He came back for something linking him to the trailer and Rae. Can't you agree to that?"

"Maybe he just came back to make sure she was dead." A hint of smart-ass flickered in his grin.

"Why the hell come talk to me if you think what I have to say is silly?" I shoved my hands into my pockets and glanced through the window at the tidy kitchen, wishing I were back inside.

"It's not silly." Turgeau shrugged. "But the two of us figuring out what he came back to get is like looking for a needle in a haystack."

That made sense, and I'd been stupid. Now he knew I cared what he thought.

"Was your cousin seeing anyone?"

"Chase Fischer." I leaned against one of the wooden supports. No matter how badly I wanted to sit, I wouldn't share the porch swing with him.

"The same one who lives through the woods?" Turgeau's face was no longer pinched with pain or amused. He leaned forward, his features keen with interest.

I nodded, even though I knew this couldn't be good for Chase. "He was over there this morning, but he didn't do that to Rae. I've known Chase since—"

"Back up a second." Turgeau took the notebook and a pen out of his pocket and scribbled on the page. "The two of you talked this morning?"

"Yes. Rae was arguing with Chase. I went out there to tell 'em to shut up."

"Was Mr. Fischer..." Turgeau stared at his pad and frowned, probably too tired to think of a nice way to say it.

"Hitting her?"

Turgeau jerked a nod in response to my question and motioned me to continue.

"Not that I saw. They were arguing about whether she should report whoever beat her up."

"You're saying the beating had already happened?" Turgeau's brow creased in a frown as his pen moved across his notepad at a fast pace. I nodded, wondering if he ever got writing cramps. "Did she say who hit her?"

"No, I—"

"You didn't ask? Why not?"

"As I was about to say"—I made eye contact with Turgeau and held it—"I planned to speak with her this afternoon. I would have asked her about it then." I knew this conversation was necessary, but this man was starting to jump all over my nerves.

"What were the two of you going to talk about?"

"When I asked them to shut up, she wanted a favor in return. We were supposed to talk about what that favor entailed this afternoon."

"And you never did." He chewed on his lip. "No idea what it was?"

"Not really—wait a minute. She asked me what I knew about the Mace Treasure."

"Which is?"

"My umpteenth great-grandfather founded this town. Supposedly he went crazy and hid his fortune—"

"No, no. I know about the Mace Treasure. I watched the TV documentary. What do you know about the Mace Treasure? Or, even better, what did you tell Rae you knew?"

I sighed. "That it's bunk. My grandfather died looking for it. My uncle killed my father over it. Their best friend hung himself over it." I relished the way Turgeau's face flushed at

46

my recitation. "But there's no money. Never was. That crazy old man they think hid the money probably ground it up, smoked it, and danced naked out in those woods."

"Okay." Turgeau shook off my grisly history lesson smoothly. "Go back to this afternoon when you found your cousin. When you walked back to her trailer, you only saw her car? No sign of another vehicle?"

"No other vehicles." I explained about reaching into her car and turning off the radio. Turgeau mumbled something about fingerprints. I wanted to tell him to French kiss my butthole.

"The camo man came through the woods. Had to." I explained how I'd heard him coming but didn't pay attention. "We told you about that trail back there."

"And Mr. Fischer—the boyfriend—lives back that way. Does he ever come to see your cousin that way? Instead of driving?"

What the hell was this guy trying to say? Chase? "Well, yeah, but Chase wasn't the man who beat me up."

"You said he had on a camouflage hunting mask." Turgeau leaned back and watched me. "You don't know who beat you up. When I first saw you, you barely knew where you were."

"But I know Chase had nothing to do with this," I insisted.

Turgeau blew out a long sigh. "Okay. How?"

"Because I've known him since I was five." My certainty was hard to articulate. "He doesn't even hunt. He cried when his mother's Chihuahua got run over on the highway. Besides, he came to help his mother and I clean out his grandmother's house this morning."

Turgeau sat up straight. "When was that?"

"This morning." I said the words louder than necessary, but it sounded like I being accused of something, and it sure seemed Chase was, too. "I told you that I had to work this morning cleaning out Mrs. Rudie Rushing's house. Remember?"

Turgeau nodded and waved his hand at me to continue.

"Chase showed up between ten and eleven. He might have come earlier than that—"

I stopped speaking as Turgeau shook his head.

"I suspect she laid in there like that for a long time. Injuries like that..." He grimaced and swallowed.

The horror of this situation crashed over me. Turgeau wanted to pin the murder on Chase. And I could see him succeeding. I couldn't let that happen. He was one of the only friends I had.

———

ANGER ROSE from the well of hurt and darkness I kept buried, overriding the shock of Turgeau's accusing my best friend. "Chase did not do this terrible thing. He struggles with substance abuse, and he parties hard. That does not make him a murderer."

"Least you got part of it right. From what I hear, he's a dope head who barely pays his child support." Turgeau read in monotone from his notepad.

"Bet you got that from Sheriff Blubber Butt," I said. "His daughter-in-law is Chase's ex-wife and the mother of Chase's son, Kansas. And he's not behind on his child support—"

"He's been taken in for drunk and disorderly conduct—"

"But that was just a bar fight." My breath came in pants, and my heart kicked hard. I was fresh out of patience and ready to fight.

Turgeau held up his hand. "Calm down. Mr. Fischer will be investigated because he's a logical suspect given the nature of the crime. He will not be arrested unless we find evidence connecting him to your cousin's murder. Let's move on."

My cheeks burned. I resented Turgeau's dismissive little shutdown. And I craved a cigarette so I could blow toxic smoke in his face. He might enjoy acting like one those pretty-boy TV cops, but I had news for him. There was nothing prestigious about Gaslight City, Burns County, or anything to do with them. This was one of those places you went when nobody else wanted your sorry ass. Dean Turgeau would figure that out soon enough.

"Did you know any of Rae's friends?" Perhaps sensing my hostility, Turgeau stood. Even though he couldn't have been more than five-ten or so, he towered over me. Times like this, I hated being short.

"Just about every party animal in the county." I focused on a dirt dobber nest in the corner of the porch's ceiling and tried to let my anger go. It served no purpose other than getting me in trouble. "Look, Detective Turgeau—"

"No, ma'am. It's Deputy. Burns County Sheriff's Office is too small to have a dedicated homicide division."

"Okay, Deputy Turgeau. Rae partied a lot. I can't tell you how many different cars, trucks, and motorcycles I saw back there."

"And you didn't know any of her friends? Come on. You two were close to the same age." He gave me a knowing grin that made me want to whap him.

"You're right. We were three months apart in age." I cringed at telling him my age. No woman wants a man who looked like Dean Turgeau to know her age. Especially if it's over twenty-three. "Even so, Rae and I didn't have a lot in common. Not since we were kids, anyway."

"Why not?"

"Who gives a shit? She's dead. Talking about our problems won't bring her back." Saying those words tore a hole in my heart. Why had I been so petty? I could have talked Memaw down more than once when she got upset at Rae's antics. Instead, I went along with her, even encouraged her. "Ain't none of your business anyway."

"You have such a ladylike way of speaking." He curled his lip at me.

"I figured I'd take my cues from the gentlemanly way you've been staring at my tits for the last thirty seconds." I stood a little straighter as Deputy Dean's face darkened.

"There is a reason I am asking these questions, Ms. Mace," he said through clenched teeth. "My job is to figure out why somebody got angry enough with your cousin to do that to her. It took her a long time to die, Peri Jean. And she was likely conscious for most of it. The more I know about her, the easier it is for me to solve her murder."

Snapshots of Rae's last moments formed in my imagination. Had she made those smears on the walls when she tried to push herself to a sitting position but couldn't because it hurt too badly? Had she thought someone would come rescue her up to the very last minute? She probably hoped I'd come home and help her. But I didn't. Tears stung my throat and eyes. I sucked them down.

"After Rae's dad went to prison for murdering my father, Rae's mother moved them to San Antonio. Every time I saw her, she got a little bit wilder and nastier." Memories flooded, but I condensed them for the sake of the situation. "I didn't see her for about ten years. Next I heard, she was coming to the end of a prison sentence and wanted to know if she could move here."

"And the two of you didn't resume your childhood friendship?" Turgeau's eyes burned into me. His notepad lay forgotten on his lap, and he twirled his pen between his fingers.

"Nope. She got mean in prison—maybe before that." I picked at the paint on the wooden supports. My words spilled out, even though I knew I needed to shut up. At least we had left the subject of Chase's possible involvement in the murder. "Everything was a con with her, a way to see if she could take advantage of a situation or run over Memaw and me."

"So the two of you had some disagreements." Turgeau's voice had an understanding lilt to it. That lilt invited me to confide in him, assured me he was a good guy to talk to.

But I had enough sense to understand every word I said could paint me as a suspect.

"We did." I zipped my lips.

Turgeau stared at me, waiting to see what else I'd say. When I stayed quiet, one corner of his mouth quirked up.

"And you were with Mr. Fischer's mother all morning?" Turgeau's eyes were unreadable in the falling darkness. *Does he really suspect me? Good thing I have a rock-solid alibi.*

"Yep. I worked for Jolene Fischer from about seven until noon." I waited for Turgeau to ask why I'd worked on a Sunday morning, but he didn't. A wave of fatigue worked its way through my body. This day had to end, and soon. I needed a good long cry and a shower, and I wanted to do those things as privately as possible.

A shadow moved across Dean's face. Glancing around the yard, I saw nothing to cause it. Wordless whispers filled my head, and deep, bone-wrenching despair swelled in me. Body quivering, I stared harder at the empty yard and found the ghost near the gate. Shoulders shaking with sobs, the apparition covered her face with her hands. Still, I'd know Rae and her tangle of bleached blonde hair anywhere.

Fear, primal and irrational, bolted through me. Rae's ghost scared me because I had never before encountered my own flesh and blood in spirit form. Why now? I had a feeling I'd hate the answer.

Turgeau looked to see what had my attention. "You okay? You've had a big shock today. That doctor still here?"

I shook my head. "I'm fine. It's just starting to sink in. I won't see her again."

Turgeau pressed his lips together and put away his notepad. He shook his head. "No. Not alive."

"I'll miss her...sort of." My eyes burned with tears. I struggled to hold them in, but one ran down my cheek. Rae's ghost watched us from the gate. She stood right next to the bottle tree, which I hoped would prevent her coming closer.

Southern yard art, bottle trees are not really trees at all. They are made of a wooden pole studded with pegs to represent the branches. Each branch holds a colored bottle. The bottles are supposed to trap spirits at night, and then the morning sun burns away the trapped spirits. This bottle tree had been a gift from my surrogate father, Eddie Kennedy, when I was a little girl. Because I never saw ghosts in Memaw's house, I presumed it worked.

Turgeau squeezed my arm. "Peri Jean? You all right?"

I jumped and shivered. Turgeau leaned close and looked into my eyes.

"Where did that guy hit you? Did that doctor check you for a concussion?" Turgeau took my elbow and guided me to the porch swing and forced me to sit.

I pushed him away. "I'm all right. Just..."

"No need to explain. It's shocking. Listen, I just want to get some justice for your dead cousin. Nothing personal. It's not an attack on you or your family...or your friends." He took a card out of his uniform shirt pocket and wrote on the back before he handed it to me. "My cellphone number's on the back. Call me if you think of anything else, no matter how silly it seems."

I took the card and slid it into my back pocket.

"Sometimes...sometimes" —Dean looked out at the two-lane road in front of the house as though the right words might be there— "people surprise us. We think we know them, but we don't."

"Chase didn't—"

"He may not have." Turgeau held up his hand for me to stop. "But let me lay out an idea for you. We agree that the man who attacked you could have killed you. Both of us understand there's a reason he let you live. What if he let you live because he's Chase, and you guys have been friends since before you could talk?"

"That's not what happened—"

"Just be careful, okay?" Turgeau put his hand on my shoulder. He was trying to be nice, but he was also accusing my oldest and dearest friend of the unthinkable. I shook him off.

"Memaw needs my help inside." And I needed to get away from both Dean Turgeau and Rae's spirit. They were more than I could handle at that moment. I didn't want any part of whatever Rae wanted from me. Dean gave me too many mixed feelings. His looks appealed to me, but his complexity didn't. I didn't want his niceness or his concern. That could lead to more, and more scared me. More meant I could get hurt.

He descended the porch steps and strode down the concrete walk. As he passed through the gate—and Rae's ghost—he jerked as though something had touched him. He glanced back at me and jerked a nod. I gave him a return nod and watched him go. *Nice butt.*

I went inside but not because Memaw had any immediate need for me. She and her friends sat talking in the living room. I grabbed my cellphone and called Chase to warn him. The call went straight to voicemail. I left a terse message that the sheriff's office would be around to question him.

———

THE EVENING PASSED with even more people stopping by the house to pay their respects and condolences. Most of them probably even meant it. Many brought food, as though the gesture bought them a front row ticket to the drama. Memaw entertained them with graciousness I never could have managed.

The only visitor I had was Eddie Kennedy. My father's childhood best friend, Eddie had always been a fixture in my life. He heard the news about Rae late because he'd spent the day delivering handmade furniture to Shreveport, Louisiana. He stayed only fifteen minutes before leaving, telling me he couldn't stand the cackling from Memaw's fellow church ladies. I agreed with him but couldn't leave. I hid out in the kitchen, brewing pot after pot of coffee and longing for the moment I could go in my room and shut the door.

Voices rose in the living room, and I peeked around the wall from the kitchen. Pastor Michael Gage stood right inside the front door smiling and shaking hands. I jerked back inside the kitchen, heart slamming against my ribcage. *What a perfect end to a horrible day.*

Michael Gage had blown into town and taken over

pastor duties at Gaslight City First Baptist four years earlier. He took an immediate interest in me, which delighted Memaw. I didn't share her enthusiasm.

Memaw poked her head into the kitchen. "Come out and say hello to Pastor Gage."

I shook my head and busied myself washing coffee cups. Memaw came to stand next to me.

"He's good-looking, and he likes you," she whispered.

"He's too old for me," I whispered back. "He's fifty if he's a day."

"So? You've dated young guys, and you can date older men. He might treat you better."

"He pumps me for information about what it's like to..." I paused here. Memaw didn't like talking about my connection with paranormal. "See the things I see."

Memaw's eyes widened, and she wrinkled her nose. "Maybe he's thinks he's being polite. He won't do that today. Just come out and speak to him. He's already asked about you."

"Let me finish this round of dishes." I turned my attention back to the sink full of coffee cups and silverware.

Someone knocked on the door, and Memaw hurried back into the living room to greet them. I sagged with relief. No way I'd go out there and chat with Gage. The man creeped me out. I finished the dishes and tiptoed out to the back porch. I adopted a stooped duck walk as I skirted the house so nobody could see me through the windows. By some miracle, I made it to my window without incident and climbed inside my sanctuary.

It would irritate Memaw when she realized I had

jumped ship. She'd just have to be upset. After finding my cousin murdered and tangling with her murderer, I couldn't suffer Michael Gage's attentions without screaming.

Gage's soothing words drifted in from the living room and fell into a meaningless murmur. Good. Nobody saw or heard my escape and relocation. I opened my closet and looked for a dress fit for my cousin's funeral. As my room cooled with the onset of evening, the dampness of tears on my cheeks became noticeable. I hadn't been aware of crying.

Guilt cast the sharpest stone at my feelings—guilt that I didn't try harder to rekindle my childhood camaraderie with Rae. I told Deputy Turgeau the truth about the way time and separate paths eroded my friendship with Rae. I'd thought I didn't care, but I was wrong. I knelt on the floor near my closet, covered my face with my hands, and let the sobs come.

As the sky darkened to the color of spilled ink, the last car pulled out of the driveway. I wanted a shower in the worst way. I gathered my pajamas and robe and snuck down the hallway to the bathroom. Being in the shower gave me too much time to think. My last glimpse of Rae recurred every time I closed my eyes to rinse my face. *Someone had done that to her, made her look like that.* Turgeau's words about how it took her a long time to die ran through my head. The running water masked my sobs, and I lingered until the hot water ran out.

When I pulled back the shower curtain, humid fog hung thick in the room. I cracked the door to allow some steam to escape. Voices drifted from the living room. Memaw had company. Who the heck had come by so late?

"That Turgeau guy contacted me." Benny Longstreet's nasal voice and rapid speech were impossible to mistake. "Now they're trouncing all over my property, looking for who knows what. Probably running off my damn deer."

Benny was the much younger half-brother of Dr. Longstreet. While Nathan doctored, Benny ran the family logging business. It employed the largest number of people countywide. Benny played the role of small town big shot to the hilt with his expensive cowboy suits and his luxury trucks. Never cars. Always monstrous trucks.

Memaw made a similar complaint of the garbage now littering the pasture near the trailer. Her voice sounded shaky, and I knew she wouldn't hold out much longer. The day had worn us both down. My instinct was to go out and shoo Benny home, but I didn't quite dare. Memaw loved both Longstreet brothers like family and might not appreciate my meddling.

"I can't believe someone attacked Peri Jean," Benny said. "Does she have any idea who did it?"

"I don't guess," Memaw said. "She was pretty confused. Slipped off to her room when the house got too crowded."

"That girl's always been a loner." Benny's chair creaked as he shifted. "If I ever find out who did that to her, I'll whup his ass myself."

I bit my lip as I pictured Benny—who resembled a male Olive Oyl—flailing at some opponent.

"Brittany Watson said they're going to talk to Chase Fischer." Memaw blew out a tired sigh. "She's excited because Joey Holze picked her to assist that good-looking new Deputy. But I sure hate to see Chase dragged into this."

"Joey's hiring that Turgeau feller created some grumbling in the ranks." He skillfully sidestepped mentioning Chase. Benny's cowboy boots clopped across the hardwood floor, and the front door squeaked as he opened it.

"That so?" Memaw's old recliner squealed as she stood to see Benny out.

"Yep. Joey hired Turgeau because he had homicide experience. But I heard he had some trouble back in Louisiana. The kind that nearly got him fired." Benny would know. He had a finger in everything that went on in Burns County.

"So he decided to run away to backwoods Texas?" Memaw opened the door.

"Yep. Got shot in the leg back in Louisiana. Wife left him, and—"

Memaw closed the front door and cut off Benny's words. *Crap.* Dean Turgeau interested me, and I wanted to know more.

The heat had escaped the old bathroom while I stood there with the door cracked. Chill bumps as big as anthills stood at attention all over my body. I yanked on my pajamas and hoped for no more visitors tonight.

Condensation covered the mirror, rendering my reflection vague and blurry. Behind me stood another shadow. I gasped and spun around to see Rae's specter. My skin tightened at the sight of her. She still bore the injuries that caused her death, her white wife beater stained dark maroon with blood. Vertical slits where the knife had gone in made a random pattern across her chest. One cheek was slit open, revealing her gum and teeth. Her smoke-colored eyes stared straight ahead, the same way they had when I found her. A scream built inside me, but I cut it off. No need to alarm Memaw.

Rae's energy pulled at mine, wanting contact, wanting my help. The room's temperature dropped, and all the oxygen seemed to leave the room. My chest ached as I hyperventilated and fought to stay conscious. I put my shaking hands over my face and took deep breaths. When I dropped my hands, Rae was still there. *This can't be. The bottle tree outside the house always kept the spirits out before.*

"What do you want?" I whispered.

In the condensation covering the mirror, a line appeared. Then another, and another. The word "FAVOR" took shape like a scene in one of those straight-to-DVD horror movies. It had been a stupid question. Of course, she wanted her favor. Only now, whatever she'd originally wanted had changed. Now, she wanted me to solve her murder.

"I don't know how." I swayed on my feet. A thief in death as life, Rae had used my life force to power her little magic trick. Dizziness set in, and my lips tingled.

Rae appeared in front of me, close enough to kiss me if she'd been alive. Black spots danced before my eyes as panic took root. Rae drew so close it seemed she'd stepped into me. I shivered in the intense cold, my fingers aching with it. The bathroom lights winked out. The only sounds were my teeth chattering and my whistling gasps.

The interior of an old building came into focus. Its gray wooden walls buckled with age. It was so real, the air smelled musty and unused. This vision through a spirit wasn't my first, but that didn't make it any easier to understand.

Junk filled the room in my vision. A sheet-covered rocking chair rocked by itself. A steamer trunk sat next to the chair. Someone's handprints smeared the thick coat of dust covering the trunk. The setting was familiar, but I couldn't place it. The smell of dust tickled my nose. I sneezed and broke free of the vision and found myself laid out on the chilly bathroom floor.

The clock radio on the counter crackled to life, blaring War's "Low Rider." I scrambled to my feet and saw that the radio was set on off. I unplugged it to stop the racket. No more cowbell.

The throb of a headache worked its way up my neck and around my head and exploded behind my eyes. Something cool and wet dripped across my upper lip. Sweat? I pressed the towel to my face.

The front door closed as Memaw came back inside. She thumped down the hallway and pushed the bathroom door open. Her eyes widened at the sight of me.

"Your nose is bleeding." She grabbed the towel from me and used it to dab my face. "What happened?"

I shook my head. Memaw and I never discussed my weird little talent. It upset her if I mentioned it. Over the years, I adopted a don't-ask-don't-tell policy.

"I'll call Dr. Longstreet." Memaw turned toward the door.

"What if I promise to go see him tomorrow? I have to clean his office anyway." I washed the blood off my face and stood up straight.

Memaw frowned, but nodded. She had something else on her mind. "I'm sure you overheard my conversation with Benny." She waited a beat for me to deny or confirm. When I did neither, she continued. "He wants to buy that trailer and Rae's car."

"Aren't they part of a crime scene?" I leaned into the mirror and checked my face for any remaining blood.

"Benny says only until they finish processing it. Once they finish collecting evidence, they have to release it back to the family."

I rummaged underneath the counter and found a bottle of cleaner. I sprayed the mirror and polished it until it gleamed. Then, I started on the sink faucet. Memaw frowned but said nothing about my compulsive cleaning.

"How do you feel about selling it?" I asked. I had no interest in ever using the trailer again. I didn't want to get anywhere near it, to be honest.

"I want it out of here as soon as possible. Don't want to ever see it again." Memaw's mouth worked, and her dark eyes filled with tears. "But you did pay half for it."

"We could apply whatever we get to her funeral. Offset the expense." I scrubbed toothpaste spots off a porcelain ring holder. The cleaning, as always, soothed me. "How do we find out when the sheriff's office has released the trailer?"

"I'll do it." A sob distorted Memaw's words, and she left

the bathroom. A few seconds later, I heard her bedroom door close.

I went to bed, but sleep eluded me. Rae wanted her favor enough to cross the veil between the living and the dead to collect. No way in hell she'd just go away. Unless Dean Turgeau solved her murder, Rae would hound me until I did what she wanted.

Turgeau's interest in Chase Fischer as a suspect sent icy fear through my veins. Chase flirted with the wrong side of the law before this, but nothing serious. This could get him sent to death row. Each hour that passed without a call from him solidified the lump of dread weighing me down.

5

THE NEXT MORNING, I started to view events as Before the Murder or After the Murder. Before the murder, things had been business as usual. That meant hard work and the occasional date for me. After the murder, I didn't know what to do with myself.

In East Texas, life paused when a relative as close as Rae passed on. The family put their lives on hold until the funeral where they screamed and wailed and did whatever it took to say goodbye. Rae's body was at autopsy, though, and since we didn't know when they'd return her remains, funeral arrangements were delayed.

Meanwhile, if I didn't take jobs when they came in, people would call someone else. Next time something came up, they might decide not to call me at all.

I told Memaw all this about six times, and she told me I needed to keep busy each time. Both of us tactfully kept our mouths shut about money. Rae had no life insurance or savings to cover a funeral.

Even so, guilt consumed me as I got ready for work. A poem by W. H. Auden mentioned stopping everything when someone died. But nothing had stopped for Rae. Life just kept marching forward with little acknowledgement she'd ever existed. I fully expected Rae's ghost to show up and punish me for not properly observing her death. Or at least trying to solve her murder.

Problem was, I had no idea how to solve a murder. TV mysteries made it look simple, but TV lied. Someone other than Chase killed her. Beyond that, I had no idea where to begin. The way Rae died suggested she pissed off the wrong person. Her grating insults or her attempts to con people could have done that.

I remembered our conversation about the Mace Treasure. As I told Turgeau, plenty of people—some in my own family—had died over it. While I doubted the treasure's existence, I knew people murdered over money all the time. Money as the motive for Rae's murder didn't clear Chase as a suspect. He didn't make much money to begin with. His partying made matters worse.

I searched my memory and compiled a list of people I remembered seeing at Rae's trailer. Did I think any of them murdered her? Not really. They were just a bunch of adults who acted like teenagers. But if giving Turgeau a list of names got him off Chase's ass, it would solve one of my worries.

Memaw cracked open the bathroom door as I brushed my teeth. I jumped and threw my toothbrush across the room. It hit the wall and splattered toothpaste all over the wallpaper. Memaw winced. I grabbed a towel to wipe up the mess.

"Don't bother. I'll get it later. Come out here to the living room. We've got company." She shut the door and her footsteps receded down the hall.

I slid my feet into flip-flops and slapped down the hallway. The old wood creaked beneath my feet. The pictures on the wall slid past me, so familiar I didn't need to look at them. Just knowing they were there, seeing them in my periphery, made this place home. Some were of Memaw when she and my grandfather, George, were young. A couple of pictures showed my father and his twin brother Jesse. Closer to the hallway's end hung shots of my father and uncle with their brides, including pictures of both Rae and me as babies.

Jolene Fischer sat on the love seat picking at a cookie. Tears streaked her face.

The butterflies in my stomach danced the two-step. She was about to say something bad, and After the Murder would get even worse. I didn't know how I could take much more.

Jolene's voice shook when she spoke. "Have you seen Chase, baby?"

"No, ma'am," I said. "I've tried to call him quite a few times. No answer."

Chase's father, Darren Fischer, stepped out of the kitchen holding a steaming cup of coffee. He was tall, lanky, and fair-skinned like Chase. His skin hadn't fared any better in the sun than Chase's. Darren wore a t-shirt advertising his fishing guide service. He gave me a one-armed hug and leaned down to kiss the top of my head. "That's all right, sugar. We hoped, but…"

Memaw insisted Darren and I sit down.

"Those damned sheriffs come out to the house at the ass crack of dawn with a search warrant." Darren blew on his coffee but didn't take a drink. His soft brown eyes—so like Chase's—brimmed with tears. "They found a bloody knife wrapped in a t-shirt under his trailer."

The news slammed into me, cold and unwelcome. It shocked me enough the racket of my heart pounding drowned out all other sound. I couldn't speak.

"You don't know it's the murder weapon." Memaw sat with her legs crossed and her foot hooked around her calf. Her foot jittered.

"It's all right, Leticia." Darren hung his head. "If Chase has run off, it's because he's hiding something."

"He's not hiding anything." I stood and went to the area behind the couch, which was my usual pacing spot. As I walked back and forth, I said, "He didn't do it."

Jolene sobbed into a white, linen hanky with a purple flower embroidered into it.

"They said the knife was enough to get an arrest warrant for him." Darren spoke without inflection, never taking his eyes off the shiny hardwood at his feet.

Jolene stopped crying long enough to choke out a few words. "I can't get him to answer his cellphone, and he didn't show up for work this morning."

"Them sheriffs told Jolene that Chase would get the lethal injection for sure if he tried to flee." Darren held his coffee mug in a white-knuckled grip, and a muscle worked in his jaw. "Sheriff Holze said if we were helping him, we'd go to jail, too."

"Sheriff Joey Holze is a nitwit." I stood on my tiptoes and grabbed the pack of cigarettes I'd stashed on top of the armoire. *Oh, well. Two weeks of no smoking was better than no break at all.* My hands shook as I tore off the cellophane and popped a cancer stick into my mouth. Darren took his lighter out of his pocket and held it out to me. I lit up and inhaled with gusto.

"Peri Jean Mace!" Memaw's dark eyes were round. "I thought you quit."

"I will. Just not today." I held the pack out to Memaw who had quit with me. She shook her head and waved me away. That surprised me. Memaw had smoked all my life, and it had been my idea to quit.

"That Dean Turgeau told us Chase used the ATM to draw all the money out of his account." Darren Fischer took a sip of his coffee and grimaced.

"They said Chase's running makes him look even more guilty." Jolene put her face in her hands and sobbed. "They said if we talk to him to tell him to come in and confess. That'll be the only way to avoid the death penalty."

I paced back and forth. The knife found at Chase's was undoubtedly the murder weapon. It didn't matter if he ran or not. If Chase was caught, he'd likely be tried and convicted of Rae's murder. But he didn't do it, and I'd fight until I could fight no more to find out who did it and make them pay.

The Fischers went home, both crying. I smoked several more cigarettes and dressed for work. The nicotine high slammed into me, more intense than I remembered. One of the reasons I loved quitting for a while. I grabbed the backpack where I kept a few dollars in small bills, a receipt book, and my checkbook and went into the living room.

I found Memaw sitting in front of the silent TV, her brow wrinkled. In her lap, she folded and unfolded a paper napkin.

"I'm out of here," I said. "Got a full day. I won't be home until after dark."

"Be careful. Nothing feels right about this whole thing." She re-folded the napkin. "I have the feeling this isn't over."

I nodded because I had the same feeling. "I'll be careful. Call me if you need anything." That really meant for her call if she got worried about me. She waved me out the door.

I called Chase's cellphone seven times that day and got no answer.

———

MY MONDAYS always ended with cleaning Dr. Longstreet's offices at the hospital. We had an agreement I would clean his offices in exchange for medical care. Because the hospital employed a full-time janitorial staff, the job never took more than an hour. I suspected I came out on the winning end of our deal.

I whipped into a back parking lot at the hospital and snuck in using a side door hidden where the old part of the hospital met the new section. Gaslight City's rumor mill had the speed and tenacity of a jaguar chasing down prey. It could turn my weekly cleaning appointment into a nervous breakdown resulting in a return to the loony bin before bedtime. The fewer people I encountered, the better. I kept my head down and hurried.

"Peri Jean Mace? Girl, are you all right?"

I turned to see Mrs. Watson, grandmother of Deputy Brittany Watson, dressed in her Sunday best. Her outfit included an old-fashioned hat, which I loved. Mrs. Watson spent her days wandering the hospital and Gaslight City's nursing homes visiting people, whether they wanted her company or not.

"Yes, ma'am." I accepted her hug and held my breath against the odor of mothballs. That hat must have dated back quite a few years.

"I sure am sorry to hear about that cousin of yours. You look pale. Why don't you get Dr. Longstreet to check you into the hospital for a rest? I'll come visit you."

The rest of the conversation followed a similar vein. I escaped with an excuse about my appointment with Dr. Longstreet. That satisfied Mrs. Watson. I hurried away from her, walking as fast as my short legs would go. Intent on my destination, I almost ran into a person who stepped into my path. I looked up and groaned. I couldn't help myself.

Felicia Brent Fischer Holze stood in front of me, smirking. Chase's ex-wife wore her mousy brown hair in a highlighted bob. She had attractive, angular features, but her glittery, mean eyes and downturned mouth ruined the effect. Her athletic high school figure had degenerated to pudge after having three kids. Her unfortunate habit of wearing fashions suited to a much thinner figure accentuated the change.

"You look terrible." Her predatory smile hadn't changed in the twelve years since high school. "Too skinny. And you need a haircut."

I ground my teeth and bit back a sharp response. "Thanks for your concern. I'm on my way to the doctor's office."

She snorted. "If you see my ex, give him a message for me: I'm not bringing my son to prison to see him."

My body tensed, and I imagined my fist connecting with her face. I dropped my eyes. If I kept looking at her, I'd hit her. "Fine, Felicia. I'll tell him if I see him."

I shoved around her and fumed the rest of the way to Dr. Longstreet's office. What had Chase ever seen in that mean-spirited bitch? I wished I had dragged her into a restroom and held her head in the toilet. She deserved no better. I slipped into Dr. Longstreet's office and closed my eyes, willing away the anger. It served no purpose.

The glass separating the waiting room from the receptionist's area was dark. Good. That meant one more well-meaning person I wouldn't have to talk to.

"Peri Jean? That you?" Dr. Longstreet's voice floated from his personal office.

"It's me." I locked the door and retrieved my cleaning supplies from the closet next to the tiny restroom. I cleaned the examining rooms first. The hospital's janitorial staff, used to me doing half the work, did a slapdash job but were at least consistent. The windows and the baseboards belonged to me. I lost myself in scrubbing and buffing as the angle of the sun changed. The hospital grew quiet with the day workers gone home and the evening visitors yet to arrive.

Other than a quick wave as I passed Dr. Longstreet's office, we didn't interact. He spent the evenings catching up on paperwork and didn't want me cleaning his office anyway. He claimed I hid things.

I clicked on the lights to the reception area. The receptionist had left the surfaces clear for me to wipe down. I pulled her chair away from the long counter, and the appointment book fell off its seat and hit the floor, fanning open.

I crouched to pick up the book and flipped pages to find the correct date. The book opened to the Thursday before Rae died. Rae Mace was listed for an appointment at 3:00 p.m. In the column for reason was scrawled "pregnancy test" in Rae's childish penmanship.

The appointment book slipped from my fingers and fell to the scarred linoleum with a dull slap. My lunch sat in my stomach like a poisonous rock as I picked up the book again and reread the appointment. Pregnant? I shouldn't have been surprised, but I was.

Had the pregnancy been at the heart of her request for a favor? I raced through the possibilities, reminding myself that none of it mattered now. Chase drifted into my thoughts again. Had he known? Too bad the jerk wouldn't answer his phone so I could ask him.

Dr. Longstreet coughed in his office. Though I couldn't ask Chase about Rae's possible pregnancy, I could ask Dr.

Longstreet. I took a few steps toward his office and stopped. He might not tell me. *What about doctor-patient confidentiality? It might be against the law for him to talk about Rae's health.* Then I remembered promising Memaw I'd see him about my nosebleed.

I walked down the short hall and knocked on the door-frame of his office. Dr. Longstreet glanced up from his paperwork and set down his pen. I wiped my hands on my pants and forced myself to cross the threshold.

"I promised Memaw I'd see you about—"

"That's right." He nodded. "Leticia called me earlier today. Said not to let you leave without talking to you. So you had a headache along with a nosebleed last night?"

Dr. Longstreet approached me and tilted my head back. He shined his penlight into my eyes without waiting for an answer.

"It's not a big deal," I told him. "It's just stress."

"Headache along with a nosebleed can be a symptom of some pretty serious things. Especially when you've been hit in the head recently." Dr. Longstreet stared me down, concern evident in his bottle-green eyes.

"Last night was first time I ever had a nosebleed without getting into a fight." I squirmed, uncomfortable under the scrutiny.

"You're telling the truth, aren't you?"

I nodded.

"Have you been...seeing things? At all?" Dr. Longstreet mashed his lips together and cocked his head to one side while he studied me.

I said nothing. Talking about seeing ghosts landed me in the loony bin once upon a time. Never again.

Evidently understanding my reluctance to speak, Dr. Longstreet tried a different tactic. "Have you had headaches? Ones that won't go away?"

"No." I desperately wanted this part of my talk with the doctor to end. "But I can call you if I do."

"Do you promise? Your grandmother needs you right now, more than ever."

"I know."

A worry line appeared on Dr. Longstreet's brow, and he took a breath to speak but stopped. His eyes, usually so calm and comforting, swam with something I couldn't identify.

It was now or never if I wanted to ask about Rae. I screwed up my courage. "Was Rae pregnant?"

"I can't tell you." Dr. Longstreet dropped his gaze and studied my dusty work boots.

"She's dead. Why not?" I doubted this was a sound argument, but it was all I had.

Dr. Longstreet slowly raised his head.

"Well," I said, "was she?"

Dr. Longstreet dropped his head, but nodded an affirmative.

"Did she act upset?" I remembered Rae sounded sober Sunday morning and saying she was going to quit smoking.

"Quite the opposite." Dr. Longstreet touched his throat and grimaced as though he drank a shot of vinegar. "She knew she was pregnant. Those drugstore tests are as accurate as anything I can do here. She wanted confirmation so she could hit the father up for money. She had a lot of questions about proving paternity and what courts do in these situations."

Pure Rae. Always looking for an angle to dupe people. I closed my eyes and shook my head. "Thank you for telling me."

"You call me if the nosebleeds persist, hear me?" he said.

"Yes, sir. I will."

My mind swarmed with speculation as I walked to my car. Chase Fischer was already liable for child support on his son, and he had trouble paying that. Jolene donated a portion of it more months than not to keep Chase out of legal trouble. No, Chase's child support money wouldn't have made much difference in Rae's life.

Rae's interest in paternity proceedings and her interest in the treasure both came back to money. My cousin spent her final days alive looking for a way to get her hands on some cash. Maybe she had wanted to leave town, start over somewhere else. But nobody would have killed her over that. Her owing someone money made more sense.

I thought about Rae's partying. Had she gotten into debt with a local drug dealer? Possible. But all drug trade in Burns County traced back to Tubby Tubman. He didn't kill women over drug debt. He forced them into prostitution. They didn't last long after that.

That left one possibility. Rae had someone in mind to blame her pregnancy on. Someone she thought had money. Had he killed her for it?

———

MULLING OVER RAE'S PREGNANCY, I pointed my car toward Memaw's house and drove fast. My 1971 Nova was the only thing I had left of my father Paul, who died—more accurately, was murdered—when I was seven years old. Paul was a big mystery to me. Not much more than a blur in my memory. Now older than he ever got to be, I was haunted by Paul's memory, but not his ghost. I knew my daddy drove his Nova like a hotrod. But that was about it.

Halfway down Farm Road 4077 to Memaw's house, the speedometer read ninety miles an hour. Lined with pine trees, the two-lane blacktop stretched out in front of me for what seemed like eternity. The tension drained out of my body as I drove. Times like this, I fantasized about driving away from everything and everybody. I'd never do it because of Memaw. It would hurt her too much. But the fantasy gave me a much-needed break from reality.

A set of headlights appeared in my rearview and bore down on me in seconds. I eased off the accelerator so Mr. or Ms. I'm in a Big Hurry could pass. The approaching vehicle slowed down and tailgated me. My face stretched into a smile.

The white pickup truck belonged to Chase. Relief made me lightheaded. Chase was okay. He flashed his headlights and honked three times.

I swerved off the road and bolted out of my Nova as soon as I had it in park. Chase slid out of his truck and ambled toward me. He held out his arms as I ran at him. I slammed into him, wrapping my arms around his waist.

We hugged hard and stepped back to look at each other. Chase touched the cheek where the camo man's fist had made contact.

"That looks like a sunset." Chase squinted at the bruise. I pushed his hand away.

"It's not all that bad." It was, though. My jaw still hurt when I chewed food. But I had more important things to discuss with Chase. "What the blue hell are you doing here? The cops are after you. They'll arrest you if they catch you."

"I know." The evening wind blew Chase's shaggy, sun bleached hair back from his face. The dusk made shadows on his face, creating the momentary illusion of extreme age. His hand shook as he lit a cigarette. "Tubby told me."

Tommy Tubman would know. His main income came from selling drugs, but he bought and sold information, too. And prostituted women. And ran an illegal gambling operation.

"How much do you know?" I asked.

"I know you found Rae's body." He squeezed my arm, maybe to comfort me or maybe to tell me he was glad I wasn't dead too. "And I know some man wearing a camouflage mask beat you up. Did you catch him killing Rae?"

"No." I shook my head, my body tensing as I remembered what happened. "I found Rae's body. I barfed. Then he was just there. I think he killed her and took off but realized he forgot something and came back. I was in the way."

"Forgot what?" Chase cocked his head to one side.

I shrugged and shook my head. "How did you know not to go home?"

"I was unloading Gramma Rudie's stuff at the storage buildings. When that loud-assed parade of cop cars rolled past, I figured some bad shit had gone down. I called Felicia." Chase stared at his faded work boots and kicked at the gravel.

I shook my head. That bitch never even mentioned she'd talked to Chase. And why had he called her instead of me? No way I'd pass along her message. It would do nothing but upset and hurt Chase. For the millionth time, I wondered why he ever hooked up with her.

Even in school, Felicia loved being in the know. She cozied up to teachers, offering to do small tasks for them, which put her in the position of knowing the behind-the-scenes drama. As an adult, she found even better ways to get information. Her job at the most popular beauty salon in town and her marriage to Scott Holze, Sheriff Joey Holze's only son, gave her a direct line to everything happening in Burns Country and beyond.

"So what did Felicia say?" I used every ounce of self-control I possessed to keep my voice empty of anything for Chase to get defensive about.

"What you already know. That you found Rae murdered," he said. "Felicia still can't keep anything to herself. She told me the sheriff wanted to talk to me."

My mind put the pieces together, and it was all I could do not to roll my eyes. "So you went out to Tubby's and got stoned."

"I didn't know what else to do." Chase put his hands out palms up in silent mime for "duh."

"When did you draw your money out of the ATM?"

Chase's mouth dropped open.

"The sheriff's office got a search warrant for your house. I guess they accessed your bank accounts." I waited a beat for it to sink in. "They found a bloody knife at your trailer, and they're pretty sure it's the murder weapon."

"Oh, shit." Chase squeezed his eyes shut. "You know that buck knife I carry? I left it at Rae's Sunday morning. I was slicing limes with it. I just left it open on the table. Was that the knife they found?"

"I don't know." My chest was tight, like I needed to cry or scream. I dug in my pocket and got out my cigarettes. Despite the dire circumstances, Chase grinned when he saw them. "If it was your knife they found—with your prints all over it—you're going to have a hard time proving you didn't do it. So you better figure out who did kill Rae."

Chase looked the same way he did the day his mother's dog got run over. His mouth worked, but he said nothing and turned away from me. *The man has more of a flare for the dramatic than most women.* It had probably fueled attraction between him and Rae.

"Come on. Who did this? You spent more time with Rae than anybody else." I gripped his arm and pulled him around to face me.

The roar of glass pack mufflers interrupted me, so loud it drowned out anything else I said. I let go of Chase and turned to watch the car approach.

It was an old GTO, restored and glossed to the nines.

The white moon of the driver's face turned to stare at Chase and me standing on the roadside. The engine gave a throaty roar as it picked up speed, and the taillights disappeared into the deepening twilight.

The hair on the back of my neck stood up. Chase, wanted by the law, shouldn't be out in the open. I started to suggest we go somewhere else, but Chase began talking as soon as the muffler's roar faded.

"Rae had another boyfriend." He snorted at the expression on my face. "Come on. We were just, you know, partying together. It wasn't true love. You saw her all beat up." Chase frowned. "She wouldn't say who did it, but I got my ideas."

"Did she say what instigated the beating?"

"Instigated? Oh, no. She just kept saying everything was ruined." Chase paced back and forth.

Ruined. The drama level sounded about right. But what had Rae meant? She had needed money. She confirmed her pregnancy on Thursday. She might have tried to squeeze the baby's father for money. Maybe he beat her. Then, Sunday morning, she asked me about the treasure. For her to be interested in such a long shot, she must have been desperate.

"Do you know if she owed anybody money? Or needed money for something?"

"Rae owed somebody money?" Chase shook his head. That was answer enough.

"Well, who was the other boyfriend?" I asked. Even giving Deputy Turgeau someone other than Chase to investigate would help.

"No clue. I saw them together once, didn't know the guy. He wore a leather vest and cap. I never mentioned it to Rae because—"

"She wasn't the love of your life," I finished for him.

"Hell, Peri Jean, you don't have to say it that way." His mouth twisted. "You make it sound like I'm glad she's dead."

"I know you're not glad." I paced too, massaging my temples. "Can you tell me anything that would help find this other boyfriend?"

"He used to text message her all the time." Chase shrugged. "She'd get all secretive and brush me off when one came in."

"So his number has to be on her cellphone." Then, I remembered. "You know, her cellphone was ringing when I found her."

"If that nutsack who hit you did come back for something, it could have been the phone. 'Cuz he knew his number was on it." Chase resumed pacing.

Numb disgust spread through me. Even though I had no idea if Rae's cellphone had been found and taken into evidence, I knew in my gut Chase was right. The phone was gone. The camo man took it after he beat me up. The one easy out for Chase had dried up before I even knew about it.

"Did she have an address book or a journal? Anything that might have his name in it?" I scanned the road for more cars. We needed to wrap this up. Anybody— including Sheriff Joey Fatbutt—could drive by and spot us.

"No. But won't the cops pull her cellphone records?" Chase had a sad, hopeful look on his face.

"Rae had one of those pay-as-you-go phones you buy at the gas station. I know because I bought it for her. The sheriff's office probably can't even obtain her records." I closed my eyes and ran my hands through my hair. *Jeezum crow. These dead ends would send Chase to death row.*

"Sunday morning, after you left, Rae got a text message. Right after that, she wanted me to leave." All that was visible of Chase was the glow of his cigarette. I couldn't see the expression on his face, which would have told me a great deal more than his words.

"She didn't say what was up?"

"Nope. She just said I had to go right then." Chase dragged hard on his cigarette and crushed the butt under his work boot. Red embers flew up around his boot and went dark in an instant. "I saw who sent the text message."

My heart picked up speed. Why hadn't he told me straight away? "So who was it?"

"It was a nickname." Chase blew out a long sigh. "Low Ryder."

Another ugly nickname. Maybe someone had killed her over those. Her code name for Chase had been John Holmes.

"Wait a second. You said Low Rider? Like the song by War?" The first night Rae appeared to me popped into my memory. That night, the clock radio came on by itself and played that very song.

"No," Chase said. "All one word separated by a line and spelled with y."

I was out of ideas and told Chase so. Finding out this Low_Ryder character's identity was key, but I didn't know where to start.

"They catch me, I'll get the lethal injection." Chase interrupted my train of thought.

"You won't either. Even if I have to help you escape the country." My oldest friend was definitely not going to be convicted of a murder he didn't commit.

Chase pulled me into a hug. He stank of fear. I hugged him back, my memory replaying the highlights of our long relationship. He was both an albatross and a blessing. I considered mentioning Rae's pregnancy but decided against it. If he didn't know, he didn't need to.

"Listen to me." I pulled back from Chase. "You stay out of sight. I'll work on this. Call me if you think of anything that will help." I gripped his shoulders and shook him. "Stop ignoring my calls."

"I've got a better idea," he said.

"What?"

"Let's just get in your car and drive." He grabbed both my hands. "Start over somewhere. We could try again... you know, being together. Take that forever road."

Chase and I emerging from the ashes of our teenage romance as friends was a fluke. The fact our friendship survived our most recent attempt at romance tested fate. Chase couldn't clean his life up for me or anybody else, and I wasn't going to give my heart to a man who partied like a teenager. Hell, I could find a guy a lot younger than Chase if I wanted to settle for that.

"You don't want to spend the rest of your life hiding." I

hoped this response would divert the topic from Chase and I running away together. "And neither do I."

"You're right." Chase nodded. "We'll save running away for a last resort."

He didn't understand when I snorted laughter, and I suppose it was part of his charm. I hugged him again, and we said our goodbyes.

As I drove the rest of the way to Memaw's, I mulled over what little I knew. Low_Ryder. Rae's quest for money. Her pregnancy. The rocking chair and the trunk from my vision. None of it tied together in a way that made sense.

A few times, movement flickered in the seat beside me. I didn't turn my head to look beside me because I knew it was Rae. A cold wave of horror crept over me and stayed for the trip's duration. The idea of her never going away scared me.

6

GASLIGHT CITY DATED BACK to the early days of Texas's statehood. A great deal of effort was made to preserve the city's older structures. The Chamber of Commerce played up the historic angle, selling it and tales of the Mace Treasure to tourists.

Once a year, Gaslight City hosted an event called Heritage and History Week—better known by the residents as H & H Week. Events always ran the final week of October through the first weekend of November.

Visitors took candlelight tours of the historic homes, ghost tours, participated in mock treasure hunts, silent auctions, and perused classic car shows. At all these events, there would be many opportunities to spend money. The festivities culminated with a costume party and street dance in the downtown area on Saturday night.

People came from all over the United States to revisit their roots or imagine having roots in East Texas, where the atmosphere was just as much the Deep South as it was Old West.

As luck would have it, Rae had been murdered exactly one week before the kickoff of H & H Week. This was my busiest time of year. If things went right, I'd make more during this two-week period than I usually cleared in three months. Rae's murder made it hard to concentrate on earning money I'd need and hustling the way I usually did.

Tuesday morning, I had an early appointment to clean one of the town's many bed and breakfasts. Afterward, I canvassed the downtown area and left a flyer advertising my services with every business owner who would take one.

I purposefully planned my route so I'd end up in front of Dottie's Burgers and Rings. Dottie served the crispiest onion rings I had ever eaten. By the time I headed down the alley leading to Dottie's entrance, my stomach grumbled in anticipation. Just as I reached for the door, it opened in my face. I jumped out of the way.

"Excuse me."

Deputy Dean Turgeau stepped onto the sidewalk. We hadn't spoken since the day of Rae's murder.

"Hey." In Dottie's plate glass window, I watched my reflected face stretch into a big, stupid grin. The five days since Rae's murder hadn't changed the way Dean filled out his uniform. It never hurt to look, and when a man looked like Dean Turgeau, it might even be considered medicinal.

Whatever reaction I expected from Dean was a far cry from the one I got. As soon as he realized it was me, the expectant smile faded off his face. His lips thinned, and his eyes narrowed. He shoved his hands in his pockets and completed his transformation with a scowl.

"Ms. Mace." Turgeau's voice was downright icy. *So much for the mild attraction I'd sensed the day of Rae's murder. Now ain't that a shame.*

"Is there a problem?" My tennis shoes scraped on the sidewalk. I shuffled foot-to-foot. Damn me for letting this guy intimidate me. We hadn't even slept together.

"A problem?" He barked out a hateful laugh and cupped his chin between his thumb and forefinger, pretending to think. After a beat, he widened his eyes. "I know! You didn't tell me you and Chase Fischer were each other's booty call."

"What?" I knew what he meant, but I didn't understand why he was so upset about it. In a town the size of Gaslight City, people had histories.

"Y'all were real hot and heavy lovers in high school. And you got insanely jealous when he broke up with you. Charged into the prom, shoved his date into a wall head-first, and kicked her after she fell down. Lucky you didn't do jail time for that."

Words failed me. That whole nasty scene was twelve years in the past. Losing my first love to my chief tormenter intensified my first taste of rejection. I reacted badly.

"No snappy reply?" Turgeau's grin was more like a grimace. "I've got more for you. You bailed Chase out of jail two years ago in Shreveport, Louisiana."

"It was just a public intoxication and a fight."

"Yeah, but it proves you've still got your old boyfriend's back." Turgeau loomed over me.

"So what? Look, I can't help it if you're too obtuse to understand how Chase and I remained friends after our relationship didn't work out." I straightened my spine and stood my ground. Backing down was not an option. Chase and I had done nothing wrong by continuing our friendship after our teen romance crashed and burned. We'd been neighbors and friends long before we were lovers.

"But did your relationship really end? The two of you went on vacation together summer before last." Turgeau put his hands on his hips and cocked out his elbows like a rooster getting ready to attack.

My mouth went dry, and my left eye twitched. Chase and I kept that trip quiet. Or so we thought. Our long relationship had evolved into a romance one last time. The vacation together proved it would never work. Chase's issues with drugs and alcohol killed us. Turgeau's knowing about it beslimed an already hurtful memory.

"So here's what I see." His lips curved into a smirk. "You and your lover boy were on the skids. Your pretty, big-tittied cousin gets out of the pen and takes up residence in the back pasture. She and your lover boy get all hot and heavy. You get pissed. And everybody in this town knows what happens when you get pissed."

"Sounds like you've been overdosing on the Gaslight City rumor mill." I struggled to keep my voice even. "If that's what you think happened, why aren't you questioning me officially?" I waited a beat, widened my eyes, and snapped my fingers. "Oh, is it because you have no proof of anything?"

"Oh, there's proof out there somewhere. I just need to

find it." He narrowed his eyes. "And, when I do, your ass is going away forever."

"Want some advice? Don't believe everything those old men playing dominoes in there"—I pointed at Dottie's—"tell you. They're worse than a bunch of old women at a sewing circle. It's just talk, Deputy. Don't let rumors make a fool of you."

Turgeau's tanned skin flushed to boiling red. "You wanna talk about gossip? Let's do that. What's this I hear about you seeing ghosts?" Turgeau raised his eyebrows. His gaze drifted over me, and his nostrils flared. "Is that real or is it just another excuse to feel sorry for yourself?"

"Don't mess with me, you braying jackass." The air between us tightened. He'd gone to no man's land, and I'd do the same. "That ugly mess of trouble you had back in Louisiana can become common knowledge here."

"Don't fuck with me, you little freak." Turgeau leaned into my face. Fury ate up the miniscule amount of self-control I possessed.

"Get the hell out of my face!" My words echoed off the old brick buildings. People on the other side of Houston Street glanced at Turgeau and me standing too close together on the sidewalk yelling at each other. We each took a step backward.

"Where is Chase?" Turgeau checked his watch.

"Late for your ass-kissing session with Sheriff Holze?" I couldn't quit. My pride smarted, and I wanted revenge. "You two are a hell of a pair—stupid is and stupid does."

Turgeau picked that moment to deliver the deathblow. "We found the knife Fischer used to murder your cousin.

Her blood and his prints were all over the knife. If I can connect you to the murder, I've got a slam dunk."

Terror crawled over my skin, leaving an aftershock of goose bumps. I suspected the knife would have Chase's prints on it. Having the worst-case scenario confirmed scared the life out of me.

Dean watched me, drinking in my reaction. When he spoke, he sounded nice, like a guy who'd never call me a little freak. "Tell me where to find Chase, and I'll help you all I can."

"I don't know where he is." Though I told the truth, I'd have never given Chase up to this puffed up pile of monkey vomit. "Please listen to me. Chase didn't do this. You're looking for a guy named Low_Ryder."

"Who told you that?"

I could barely breathe, much less answer. I'd thrown my cards on the table, and Turgeau knew Chase and I had talked at some point in the last few days.

"Listen to me, Ms. Mace." Turgeau spoke so softly I barely heard him. He took a step closer, and the heat of his words warmed my face. "I know in my bones you've been in touch with Fischer. You may not have helped him kill your cousin. But if you're helping him evade the law, you're going to jail with him."

What I said next, I said way too loud. It started with an f and ended with you.

Turgeau squared his shoulders, turned and marched away from me. I watched his cute little butt retreat, but the fear beating in my chest kept me from really enjoying it. I peeked into the plate glass window of

Dottie's. A dozen sets of wide eyes watched me, waiting to see what crazy thing I did next. To hell with having a burger and rings. I turned away and walked the few blocks to my car.

As I passed the museum, I heard the doors squeal open and slap shut. I tensed. Only one person was likely to come out of the museum to talk to me, and I didn't want to talk to her.

———

"Hey, Peri Jean!" Hannah's shoes clattered on the walk behind me.

I kept walking toward my Nova. Maybe she'd give up. We had nothing to say to each other. The sooner she understood that, the sooner we could both get on with our lives. Her hand closed around my arm. Reluctantly, I turned to face her.

"Long time no see," she said, smiling ear to ear. Hannah came back to town six months ago after a very public divorce from an MLB Hall of Famer. As the wife of a famous person, a small amount of fame rubbed off on her. She appeared in an issue of *Sports Illustrated*, had a walk-on part in a TV show, and even did a stint on the Home Shopping Network. Hannah's life away from Gaslight City may have been impressive, but her return seemed less than victorious.

Twenty years ago, we were best friends. When we were both eight years old, Hannah's father died. I knew all about dead fathers and the way it made mothers distant. I tried extra hard to be a good friend to Hannah to keep her from being lonely.

When her father's ghost appeared to me, I knew what he was. But I didn't understand it was taboo to see him and interact with him. He showed me where he'd hidden Hannah's Christmas gifts. Hoping to cheer my friend, I told her where to find them. Hannah's mother, who hadn't known about the gifts, wanted to know how her daughter found them. Hannah told.

I ended up in a children's mental hospital where they tested me for schizophrenia. Memaw fought to get me released while my own mother did a great impression of a pile of shit. Hannah never spoke to me again after that day. Her mother moved them to Houston soon after. On their infrequent visits, her uncle—none other than Sheriff Joey Fatass—kept her sequestered. The times we met in public, Hannah wouldn't even make eye contact with me.

After all that, how exactly did she expect me to respond to her jaunty greeting? Her smile faded as she took in my less than thrilled countenance.

"I saw you talking with Dean Turgeau." Hannah stepped out of my personal space and shoved her hands into the pockets of her linen slacks.

"That what you call it? Talking? And what business is it of yours?"

She flushed. "Dean is one of those cops who genuinely wants to see justice served. Underneath the bluster, he's pretty tenderhearted." When I said nothing, she took another step away from me. "I'm the one who told him about the job opening at the sheriff's office."

Still I said nothing. I didn't know what to say. Dean Turgeau wanted to charge my best friend with a murder he didn't commit and see him sentenced to the death penalty. If possible, he would connect me to that crime and send me to prison, too.

"I-I wanted to invite you up to my apartment for a drink...or whatever you'd like." Hannah stood almost ten feet from me now. Her eyes darted between the museum and me. I could tell she really wanted to go back inside, leave this ugly scene behind her.

"Not today," I said. Excuses flitted through my mind, but I saw no need to give her any of them. Before she could recover and suggest an alternate plan, I turned and walked away.

The entire drive home, I bitched to the empty car about Hannah Kessler. She pushed my buttons like nobody else. My tirade cut off in mid-sentence when I pulled into Memaw's yard.

Jolene's SUV sat beside the carport. My throat tightened as my heart tried to crawl out of my chest. She might have news about Chase. With the police looking for him in connection to Rae's murder, it couldn't be anything but bad.

———

I HURRIED into the living room to find Jolene sitting on the loveseat and Memaw in her recliner. Their silence scared me worse than finding them wailing and crying would have.

"Sit down, baby." Memaw didn't look at me. The top of my head prickled. Memaw always made eye contact when she spoke to me. Whatever she had to say couldn't be good.

"What's going on?" The old brocade covered wing chair squeaked as I sat down. I gripped the arm and watched as my fingers turned white.

"Deputy Turgeau called after you left this morning. Your cousin's remains are being released Friday." Memaw grabbed the box of tissues on the end table and hugged them to her. I noticed for the first time she wore her Sunday clothes. "I talked to Hooty at the funeral home. Long as you're fine with it, we'll cremate her and have a memorial service here at the house on Friday or Saturday."

I nodded. "I'll pay half the costs."

"You most certainly will not." Memaw locked eyes with me, and we engaged in a short, silent battle. It was a sign of her grief that she surrendered first. "Hell. I'll leave everything to you when I'm dead. Pay yourself back then."

"Don't talk like that," I said.

Jolene took a crumpled tissue out of her purse and dabbed at her eyes with it. She couldn't be this upset over Rae. It had to be something with Chase. The hush in the room added to my paranoia.

"Where's Chase?"

Jolene shook her head and shrugged. Tears welled in her eyes and slid down her cheeks. The tension in my back let up, and I sat back in the chair. Chase hadn't been apprehended. One less thing to worry about.

"Well, what's wrong then?"

"Darren got into a fight today." Jolene took a hitching breath.

Chase's father was not a fighting man. All the years I'd known him, he'd been quiet and easygoing.

"Someone at Dottie's told him they'd be cheering when Chase got the death penalty for murdering Rae." Memaw spoke the words tonelessly. She had the glassy-eyed stare of someone at her wit's end. I didn't know what to do for her.

"Who said that?" I directed the question at Jolene. She glanced at Memaw, who shook her head.

"Let it drop, shug." Jolene reached over and patted my knee. "We've got to worry about burying your cousin now."

My throat tightened. This signaled the end. I'd have to tell Rae goodbye, and we had so much unfinished business. I tried to swallow past the painful lump lodged in my throat.

"Dean Turgeau said Rae bled to death and it took some time. Hours. . ." Memaw fiddled with a hole in the tissue box. "If someone had found her sooner, she might have..." Memaw's face twisted. She wept into a handful of Kleenex.

"He didn't need to tell you that." My irritation with Deputy Dean went up a few notches. He had no right to talk that way to my grandmother.

"He was angry," Jolene said to me, tears streaking down her face. "He said he would nail the ass of whoever did this."

That explained some of Turgeau's fury outside Dottie's. He had an unpleasant job. I didn't forgive him, but I understood.

I pushed myself out of the old wing chair, knelt beside Memaw's cracked old recliner, and wrapped my arms around her thin body. She seemed to be nothing more than skin and bones. When had she gotten so skinny?

Memaw and I put our heads together and cried. Rae had been a turd, but she'd been our turd. There would be no replacing her. Feeling Jolene's gaze on me, I glanced up. Her son—and my best friend—was missing. She had to be near a breakdown.

"Honey," Jolene said, "if you do hear from Chase, please get him to come home. We've already talked to Rainey Bruce, and she says she can do plenty for him."

Major ouch on the Fischer checkbook. I cleaned Rainey's office and did light filing when she needed it. Her invoices were staggering, but she was the best attorney in this part of Texas. If I wanted to confess I'd seen Chase, I needed to do it now. But I couldn't make myself. It would put Jolene and Memaw at risk of legal trouble. If anybody got in trouble, it would be me and me alone. I slumped into the loveseat, ignoring the desire to spill my guts.

The atmosphere in the room stilled, the hum of the electric lights and the ticking clock suddenly strident. A shadow flew across the room, and Rae materialized behind Jolene's chair. The ghost looked even worse than before, her eyes sunken and dark-ringed. Defensive wounds on her hands and arms gaped open. Her hands rested on the chair's back, showing her blackened nail beds. A chill enveloped the room.

"Must be a cool front coming through." Jolene shivered. She gave her arms a brisk rub and stood. "I need to go anyway, let you two get some rest."

As Jolene gathered her things, Memaw rushed into the kitchen and grabbed a foil-covered dish off the counter. She came back into the living room and pushed it at Jolene, who immediately began to argue.

"Peri Jean," Memaw said, "get the chocolate pie Elaine Watson brought."

I jumped up to obey, only half-listening to Jolene's protests and Memaw's convincing Jolene she should take some food. I grabbed a jug of store-bought sweet tea for good measure and exited the kitchen carrying both items.

Rae's ghost remained behind the chair where Jolene sat a few seconds earlier. Fear tingled at the base of my spine. I couldn't handle Rae's continued presence in the house. Aside from her appearance, she no longer belonged in this world. I had to solve her murder so she could move on. I had to save my best friend from being framed for a murder he didn't commit. My life had gone from status quo to shitstorm in less than a week.

"I'll help you carry this stuff out," I said. Memaw held open the door. Jolene led the way to her SUV. We set the food inside the cavernous vehicle.

"Thank you for always being there for my son." Jolene didn't look at me as she arranged the food in the back of her SUV.

Guilt for not giving Jolene the comfort of knowing I had seen Chase ate at me, twisting my guts.

"I'm gonna tell you something." Jolene's voice lost its

usual twang. "I saw something the Saturday morning before Rae's murder."

Jolene's nearly accent free words raised the hair on the back of my neck. Though highly educated, she enjoyed playing the part of East Texas good old girl to the hilt. She wore her Texas pride like a favorite dress.

"Darren got up Saturday morning with heartburn. I ran up to Thomas's Git and Go to buy some antacids. An older model black car sat in the parking lot. I noticed it because Darren wants to buy something like it to take around to these antique car shows.

"When I got out of the SUV, I heard two people arguing inside the car. It had tinted windows, and the sun was barely up, so I couldn't tell who was in there. I went in the store and bought what I wanted. When I came back out, Rae had gotten out of the car. She was all beat to hell and crying. She walked around the side of the building and went in the bathroom." Jolene clasped her hands in front of her and stared at them.

"What did you do?" Remembering the black car passing Chase and I as we stood talking on the roadside, I shivered. *It had to be the same one.*

"God help me, I left." Jolene's eyes brimmed with tears. "I know the Christian thing would have been to follow that girl into the bathroom and call the police for her. But I didn't. She scared me. I resented her influence in my son's life. And so I left."

"Did you tell Deputy Turgeau about this?" I asked. This could only help me prove someone other than Chase needed investigating.

"I did. He wrote it down on his notebook, but then he went right back to acting like Chase murdered Rae." Jolene bared her teeth as she remembered. The flinty-eyed woman in front of me might chew up Dean Turgeau and spit him out for messing with her son.

Jolene's seeing that black car bothered me. I flashed back on the argument I had with Dean Turgeau on the sidewalk a few hours earlier. Parked cars had lined the street. Intent on giving Deputy Dean a piece of my mind, I paid them no attention. Now that I thought about it, I remembered the black GTO had been one of the parked cars.

7

BACK AT THE HOUSE, I found Memaw warming up funeral food for our lunch. She heaped each plate with a large variety. Covered dishes crammed both the refrigerator and the counter. Most of it would likely spoil before we could finish it.

"Have you called Barbie to see if she'd like to fly out for the funeral?" Memaw asked as soon as we sat down to eat.

I kept my eyes on my plate as a tornado of emotion raged inside. I didn't understand why Memaw would ask such a thing. We rarely discussed the woman who gave birth to me. Her lack of interest in having a daughter ached like nothing else ever had.

"No." I hoped my terse answer would satisfy Memaw. I didn't want to talk about Barbie. She made me feel worthless, as though nobody could ever possibly want me. The feelings of worthlessness pissed me off. If I got angry, Memaw would too.

"Why not?"

"She won't be interested, and she'll manage to make me mad." I ate a forkful of pasta salad, barely tasting it, and chewed carefully, forcing myself to swallow.

"You need to call her. She should know what happened." Memaw said this as though it settled the matter. It did not.

"If you want her to know, you call her." The rage from Barbie's years of rejecting me tightened my voice, made it harsh and defensive.

"Don't use that tone with me, Peri Jean Mace. You're not too big to switch." Memaw thrust her jaw out and stabbed a dumpling with her fork.

"She's not interested in anything down here." I struggled to keep my voice even. Memaw's bullheadedness on this subject baffled me. She never talked bad about Barbie, but she didn't need to. Her feelings on the matter were obvious.

"Well, you need to make an effort." Memaw nearly shouted, not her usual approach. "Once I'm gone, she's the only close family you'll have."

"That's the same as having none." I gulped down my food and took my plate to the sink. Memaw huffed and puffed after me, red-faced and mad. Once Leticia Gregson Mace's temper was out of the bottle, bad stuff happened. But I was mad, too, dammit. *My mother doesn't care if I drop off the face of the earth. Memaw knows that. Why pressure me to contact Barbara?*

"Why are you so insistent on me calling her? This is

something you could do if you want it done. But I can save you the time and effort. She's going to blow you off." I said all this in a breezy tone of voice, which I knew would only stoke Memaw's anger.

"Because the call has to come from you or it won't mean anything to her."

"It won't mean anything no matter which of us calls her." I shrugged and went into the laundry room. I shut the door behind me out of habit. The machines heated up the house, and we kept the door shut to combat their effect.

"Don't you walk off from me, young lady." Memaw stomped after me and slammed the door open. The force of her anger surprised and confused me. She had always shown sympathy when I spoke to her about the way my mother's indifference hurt me. "You can't just ignore your connection to her."

Without another word, she slammed the door closed. Her footsteps pounded through the house. I finished loading the washer, started it, and returned to the kitchen to clean up our lunch. Nobody stuck by me other than Memaw, and I did everything I could to make things easy for her because I wanted to. *Could I do this? It would only cost me some pride. And isn't Memaw worth a little pride?*

Memaw's footsteps thumped down the hallway. She had changed clothes and now wore khaki pants and a t-shirt. To my surprise, she seemed calm. She set about making coffee.

"Barbie—I mean Barbara—was still a teenager when she had you." Memaw didn't look at me as she scooped grounds into a filter and filled the carafe with water. "After your daddy died, she just didn't know what to do with herself."

"So she ran off with a traveling country singer and dumped me on you to raise?"

Memaw stomped her foot. "Why do you have to be so unforgiving? We all do stupid things when we're young. People can change." She raised her eyebrows at me.

My face heated. I had my own history of idiotic choices. My short, first marriage. The reason I understood Chase's romance with drugs and alcohol. All the times I raised my fists instead of letting insults roll off my shoulders. People can learn from mistakes and change. But not Barbara. Not in my experience, anyway.

"Because," I said, "all she has ever done is hurt me. I'm the one who is crazy if I keep giving her the chance to do it."

"But you'll never know if you don't try."

I didn't argue any more. I'd call Barbara, and Memaw knew it. It was no secret between the two of us that I longed for a relationship with my mother. I wished I could change the thing about me she couldn't stand, but I could no more stop seeing dead people than an elephant can ungrow his trunk.

After we put the kitchen to rights, Memaw called a local homeless ministry. They agreed to take the surplus of food off our hands. Memaw said she'd have it to them within the hour.

"I forgot to mention Deputy Turgeau said to go ahead

and sell the trailer to Benny," Memaw said as we loaded casserole after casserole into her old sedan. "While I'm out, I'll stop by his office and see when he wants to pick it up."

"I'll go ahead and clean it out this afternoon." I didn't look forward to the upcoming chore, but I owed it to Rae. "The obvious junk can just be thrown away, right? I'll only put aside things we might want for keepsakes."

Memaw's eyes filled with tears, and her chin trembled as she nodded. She drove away without another word. I waited until she pulled out of the driveway before I wiped my own tears off my cheeks. It helped my feelings to take care of this last piece of business for Rae. But that didn't mean I looked forward to it.

All that blood had been baking in the closed up trailer for two days. My hastily eaten lunch might come back for a sequel. I didn't look forward to going in there, but I did look forward to seeing if I could find any clues to Low_Ryder's identity.

———

I WENT INSIDE to change into work clothes and gather boxes and garbage bags. Just as I pulled on my bra, someone banged on the front door.

"Just a second," I yelled. Whoever was out front only knocked harder. I fastened my bra with shaking hands, pulled on a t-shirt, and stomped through the house. I opened the front door to a leathery-skinned blonde who had plenty of gray at her roots and a lot of tattoos on her arms.

"Hi. You must be Peri Jean." She grinned, showing me a mouthful of yellow, Chiclet shaped teeth. "I'm a friend of Rae's."

"I'm Peri Jean." I desperately brainstormed humane ways to tell this woman her friend was dead. She beat me to the punch.

"I just heard about Rae and wanted to pay my respects. Sorry it took me so long to get over here. I had to work."

"That's okay. She would have understood." Sometimes the best thing to do was lie. Rae had been incapable of actually sympathizing with her fellow man's plight.

"That's sweet of you to say, no matter how untrue it is." The woman's eyes crinkled into a smile.

We shared a laugh.

"Listen, girl, Rae had something of mine when she died. What can I do about getting it back?"

"Tell me what it is and give me your phone number." The laughter had me feeling good, and I wanted to help this friend of Rae's. "I can meet you with it or you can come pick it up."

"I thought I'd just go back there and look for it." Blondie gestured toward the back pasture, her smile gone.

"I don't think so." Alarm bells went off in my head. A trembly feeling shook me, warned me to get rid of this woman fast. "She died back there, and I'd rather you didn't see the mess."

"But she had one of my belongings. I want it back." Blondie's creased, smoker's face came with a smoker's voice to match. Eau de ashtray hung around her in a cloud.

Looking at her and smelling her made me decide to quit smoking again as soon as I solved Rae's murder.

"Just tell me what it was and give me a way to reach you. I'll be happy to return it to you."

"I think I went about this the wrong way." The woman grinned, giving me another view of her awful teeth. She held out her hand to shake mine. "I'm Veronica. I know Rae from way back."

I shook her hand, holding her bloodshot gray gaze. She squeezed too hard. I squeezed right back, enjoying the way her eyes widened.

"I know you want your belongings." I worked to keep my voice non-confrontational. "I haven't had time to clean out her trailer. I don't know what all's back there."

"That's all right. I can just dig through until I find what I want." I'd seldom seen eyes hard as granite, like hers. They chilled me. Veronica was more than just a bully. Her eyes hinted at true craziness.

"No." I kept emotion out of my voice, leaving no room for negotiation or an opening to try to talk me into caving.

"If that's how you gonna be, fine." She gave me the finger and walked backward down the steps.

I laughed at her, but I had to force it. My heart beat so hard I could barely breathe. The encounter over, my adrenaline spike gave way to dizziness. I leaned against the doorjamb.

Veronica turned her back on me and stomped out to her ratty, midsize car. She gave me another hard look before she got inside. Roaring the engine, she spun the car around, throwing gravel, and raced down the driveway.

The visit shook me up enough to dig out my cellphone. My fingers hovered over the buttons, but I couldn't quite make myself dial the sheriff's office. An encounter with sourpuss Dean Turgeau might be worse than Veronica and her teeth.

While I thought it over, my cellphone's screen tiled and then went blank. "Damned worn out piece of technology belongs in the trash," I muttered. I checked our landline and found it working. By then, I decided against calling the law. What would they do anyway?

Time to get about my business. In a plastic box in the pantry, I found a padlock and hasp. I'd clean out the trailer and secure it. Make it a little harder for Veronica to break in if she decided to take matters into her own hands.

I loaded my supplies into a wheelbarrow and started the journey across the pasture. As I trudged, I thought about Veronica's visit. *Had she been the one Rae owed money? If so, what on earth for? Toothpaste?*

———

THE TRAILER'S reek assaulted me when I opened the door. I put my hand to my mouth and gagged. A clutter of magazines and paper plates littered the floor, mashed down by dozens of trampling feet. A half-eaten TV dinner on the counter crawled with flies. Blood stained the entire place.

Memaw and I bought this trailer for fishing vacations at Lake Sam Rayburn, a couple of hours south. Neither of us would want to use it again. The smell alone was enough to turn me off for life.

Once my stomach behaved, I opened the trailer's windows and got to work. Into a garbage bag went the make-up, costume jewelry, and flashy clothes. A few magazines and DVDs of romantic comedies joined them. Everything had been stepped on or had blood on it.

I opened a cabinet and backpedaled when I saw the contents. The type sold in toy stores, the Ouija board looked innocent. But I didn't care to touch it. I needed no help contacting the spirit world. *Why did Rae have this?* I grabbed the thing with a towel-covered hand, dropping it in the trash bag.

Before too long, I decided any hints to the murderer's identity were sitting in a crime lab somewhere. The remaining items in the trailer were junk. It had to be packed up, though.

The odor inside worsened as the temperature rose. My rising gorge threatened to make me quit. Maroon smears of blood covered the table where Rae's body had lain. The bench seat's cushions were ruined and the source of most of the odor.

I threw them outside and forced myself to get back to work. Underneath the cushions, I found storage bins containing a small tool kit, a water hose, a can of fix-a-flat, an extension cord, and several cheap plastic tarps.

The crime scene investigators had rifled through the whole mess, leaving it in a tangle. Blood had seeped through the cushion, trickled through a crack and left a crusty brown coating on the junk. I tore the contents from the bins and tossed it outside with the cushions.

Back inside the trailer, Eau de Dollar Store competed

with the stench of death. I rummaged in the garbage bag, making sure I hadn't broken a bottle of Rae's noxious perfume. Frigid fingers gripped my arm. I shrieked and spun around. Rae's apparition, now green-faced, stood behind me. A mournful moan filled the trailer, raising the fine hairs on my arms.

"If you left something in here," I said to the empty trailer, "you need to help me find it."

A cheap porcelain bowl Rae had been using for an ashtray jumped off the windowsill and clattered into the storage bin, breaking into a few pieces and scattering cigarette butts, marijuana roaches, and ash.

"Son of a donkey-loving bitch," I yelled and knelt to clean up the mess, all the while muttering colorful swear words I bet would have impressed even Tubby Tubman. I wiped up the ash and threw the butts and roaches into a trash bag before I noticed something wrong with the wall.

The cheap particleboard siding had come loose where the storage bin met the trailer's exterior wall. I tried to push it back into place. When it wouldn't pop into place, I lost my temper and gave it a hard slam. The siding fell to one side, revealing a thin sketchbook.

I picked it up and flipped through. It held page after page of pen and ink sketches. One drawing depicted me sitting on the back porch smoking a cigarette. It captured me thinking, with arms wrapped around my knees.

"Oh, no." I whispered. I never knew Rae could draw like this. Now that I did, her loss hit me all over again.

In another sketch, Memaw squatted in her flowerbed, her big sun hat covering most of her face. The detail of veins covering the backs of her hands showed Rae had possessed real talent. A lump formed in my throat, and a wave of sadness stung my heart. *What could she have been if life had been kinder or if she'd made better decisions?*

A sketch of Chase made me stop and smile. He squinted against the sun, shirtless and holding a beer bottle. Rae had focused on what still made him handsome —the cleft chin, his expressive eyes, and his six-pack abs.

The next sketch took my breath away. A man in a bar with liquor bottles lined up behind him. He wore one of those leather biker caps that fold over the bill, the kind Marlon Brando made famous. He held his cigarette between the index finger and thumb, which drew attention to his hand and the large, fuzzily detailed ring he wore. The man's face hid in shadow under the bill of the cap.

Was this the man who sent Rae a text message the day she died? Low_Ryder? Had to be. It sucked I found this after seeing Chase. He could have confirmed the drawing depicted Rae's other boyfriend. A shadow moved in front of me. Rae again.

"Is this him? The other boyfriend?" Silence answered my question. "Can you knock twice if it's him?"

A cabinet door opened and slammed twice. Louder and harder than necessary. Death hadn't changed Rae. I thought back to my conversation with Memaw about Barbara. If death couldn't change Rae, could time change Barbara?

I snapped the book shut and tucked it into the cardboard box. It held shamefully few keepsakes. The evidence of Rae's time on earth filled only one box and two garbage bags. Tears welled up in my eyes. Her end had been abrupt, leaving so much unfinished business and potential behind. A lump clogged my throat, and I allowed myself the luxury of a few half-hearted sobs.

The door to a narrow closet space gaped open. Inside hung a man's cotton button down shirt. I pulled it off the hanger. The smell identified it as Chase's. I held the shirt to my nose and breathed deeply, staining the cloth with my tears. *How had things gotten so messed up so fast?*

I gathered the box and garbage bags and toted them outside. The small space cleaned out, I could tell I had missed nothing. Rae's life had been packed away.

The door's hollow slam had a kind of finality to it. The factory lock would do nothing to keep Rae's friend Veronica out, but I was too stubborn not to try. My cordless drill screamed as I installed a hasp on the cheap aluminum door. I locked it with the padlock and tucked the key inside Rae's sketchbook.

Inside the house, I showered and lay down. I woke up in the late evening to find Memaw left a plastic bag of baked goodies on my night table. My stomach rumbled in anticipation, and I wished I had told Memaw that Barbara could not have been a better mother than she'd been.

———

AT ELEVEN P.M. Texas time, I forced myself to call Barbara. I never thought of her as my mother. It was always Barbara with ever-changing last names. When especially angry at her, I called her Barbie, which I knew she loathed.

From the ages of eight through fifteen, I didn't even see her. On a summer day in my fifteenth year, Barbara turned up laughing and newly married to a hunky construction worker. I thought they would invite me to live with them in their Galveston home. Memaw did, too. Barbara and the hunk stayed through supper. I sat taut with fear and excitement. Memaw looked sad. Neither of us should have worried.

At the end of supper, Barbara announced her husband had a job in Louisiana starting the following week. They were driving there to look for a short lease apartment. Barbara gave me a swift kiss on the cheek, the hunk shook my hand, and they drove off as quickly as they'd come.

Three years later, I sent Barbara a letter asking if she'd come to my high school graduation. I sent the letter in March, months before graduation because I didn't want her to say I didn't give her enough warning. Six months later, I received a card from Barbara. She apologized for missing my graduation, but she had moved. She sent me a hundred bucks, which I blew on my first tattoo.

She probably had no idea I didn't graduate. The school wouldn't let me come back after I beat up Felicia, and I needed a change of scenery. I moved to Nacogdoches County, got a GED, and applied to the junior college in neighboring Angelina County.

Calling Barbara was not high on my list of want-tos, but Memaw would have my ass if I didn't. I punched Barbara's number into my cellphone before I could stop myself. The phone rang once, twice, three times.

"Hel-looo?" Barbara's voice always sounded giddy, girlish, and giggly. A hum of conversation murmured in the background. I could practically hear the cocktail glasses clinking.

"It's Peri Jean." I waited while Barbara processed who had called her.

"Well...uh...hi, Peri Jean." Barbara tittered. "What's up?"

"Rae was murdered." I could have led up to it, but I went for shock value.

"In prison? Didn't she get sent away for forgery?" The background noise faded away, and a door clicked shut.

"Hot checks and possession with intent. She got released and moved here about eight months ago."

Barbara was quiet, probably thinking up excuses to say no to whatever I asked.

"Her funeral—actually memorial service—is Saturday." My emotions writhed as I waited for her answer even though I had a good idea what she'd say. I wished I could get tough enough for her rejections not to matter.

Barbara exhaled. She finally knew what I wanted. Now she could figure out a way to proceed. "Well, baby, Ron is having an opening next week. I'm sure I can't come all the way down there."

Ron was Barbara's rich, artist husband. He'd lasted longer than the others. I suspected they'd stayed married because Barbara was getting older and couldn't swing man-to-man anymore.

"Don't worry about it." A spiteful edge crept into my voice, but I couldn't drop it. "I told Memaw you wouldn't want to come, but she wanted me to make sure. How's your life, Barbara?"

"It's good." Her giggle had a shrill edge to it. "I'm working in a boutique. Ron's still painting...of course. Dingle—that's our Labrador—is, well, dingy."

"Good to hear. You take care, okay?"

"Sure, honey. You, too." She hung up.

No invitation to visit sometime. No asking me how I was doing. I sat on my bed and wiped the tears off my face with the heel of my hand. *Why did I let Barbara do this to me? It was stupid to get so upset. Nothing changed with her, and it never would.* I wished for the nerve to tell Barbara to go to hell, but I wouldn't. No matter how much she deserved it.

When I had myself under control, I retrieved supplies for dusting. Back in the living room, I cleared off surfaces, dusted, and applied lemon oil. Memaw wordlessly watched my activity.

Glitter dusted the bookcase. Rae had worn glittery body lotion that got all over everything. What had she been doing near the bookcase? She certainly hadn't been the literary type. I wiped away the glitter.

"What'd she say?" Memaw muted the canned laughter on the television.

"She said Ron has an opening next week and for us to take care." My eyes stung with tears.

Memaw's eyes widened until the whites were visible. A ring of white appeared around her lips, and her dainty little hands clenched into fists. She said a few choice words rarely heard from a Sunday school teacher and fled to her bedroom.

I polished the armoire we used for a coat closet until I saw my reflection in it. Hard work gave me a place to hide. I didn't have to think about disappointments and how to handle them when I worked hard. I could just work and work until I got too tired to think.

8

————

"PASTOR GAGE CALLED while you were in the shower. He wondered if you'd spiff up his house for the candlelight tour of homes next week." Memaw casually took a bite of her oatmeal as she said this. She kept her eyes focused on the window where some squirrels fought over the corn we put out for them. Only the slight twitch in her cheek gave away her delight in delivering this bit of news.

"I'll call him and decline." Michael Gage had brass. He'd taken a pretty bold step, going through Memaw to get me into his house with him. Those boyish dimples and that trim physique didn't change my lack of interest in him.

"You'll do no such thing." Memaw wouldn't look at me. "I accepted for you, even negotiated you a good price for your services."

"Next week will pay enough without me having to work for him." The idea of being alone with Michael Gage and his fascination with my link to the spirit world weirded me out. I remembered hearing his wife died tragically. What if he wanted me to try to contact her? No way. Or—and this idea nauseated me—what if he had some kinky paranormal sex fetish? *Ewww.*

"But you can do this today. I looked at your schedule and told him you had today free." Memaw's dark eyes danced. She would never insist I date Michael Gage, but she wouldn't object. She laughed about my mini-romances with guys unable to be more than Mr. Right Now, but I knew they puzzled her. Our forty-five year age difference gave us different perspectives on affairs of the heart.

"Memaw," I spoke through clenched teeth, "I don't take jobs for him because he comes onto me."

"I know." Memaw wouldn't look at me. "But you should think about giving him a chance. He's a nice man. But if that doesn't work for you, then this will: it's good money. You'll need it if you're going to buy me a computer for Christmas."

I choked on my grapefruit juice. Memaw shoved her glass of water at me as I whooped and sputtered. "How did you know?"

"Sugar, you could never play poker." Memaw gave my arm an affectionate pat. "I do wish you wouldn't buy something that expensive for me."

"But you need a computer for your tutoring."

"You treat me like something special, and I appreciate it." Memaw's dark eyes glistened with tears. "I couldn't have asked for a better granddaughter."

Unshed tears stung my own eyes. Memaw expected me to know she loved me. Despite her gruff ways, I'd never doubted it. I needed to hear her kind words after the phone call with Barbara. It helped to know I mattered to at least one person in my family.

"Pastor Gage is expecting you in about an hour." Memaw knuckled the moisture out of her eyes. "You better hustle. Skip the deodorant if you want to quell his interest."

Memaw stood and gathered the breakfast dishes while I guffawed. I wanted to work for Michael Gage almost as much as I wanted to eat road kill. If Memaw said she'd negotiated a good fee for me, I trusted her judgment. But I didn't look forward to the job.

————

MY RESOLVE firmly in place and sans deodorant, I parked my Nova in the graceful, old house's driveway and marched up the wide, brick steps. Michael Gage opened the high arched door before I could knock. He wore pressed jeans and a starched shirt buttoned at the collar. A dark, five o'clock shadow—that might have been sexy on someone else—was the only sign he was an actual man and not some sort of robot.

"Peri Jean." He managed to sound surprised to see me.

"Memaw said you'd be expecting me?"

"Yes, yes. I've got some snacks for us. Come right in." He stood aside for me to enter.

Mace House was awe inspiring, and I didn't try to hide my appreciation. My ancestor Reginald Mace had been the richest man in town when he built his dream house. As the years passed, it fell into ruin. Michael Gage bought the decrepit old wreck two years earlier and announced his plan to fully renovate it. It had been a slow, painstaking process since Gage used old photographs of Mace House to guide his efforts. Rumor had it he spent over a million dollars. It showed.

"Straight through to the kitchen." Gage led me through a wide area, open to the ceilings two stories above. Rooms stood open on either side and were visible around an interior balcony on the second floor.

"This is amazing." I stopped to turn a slow circle. The highest windows had stained glass panes. A crystal chandelier's hanging prisms sparkled, dancing rainbows on the walls. Gage smiled, but motioned me along. He walked close enough for me to smell his cologne. I tried hard to understand his interest in me but couldn't. We had nothing in common.

The kitchen, a twentieth century addition, stood at the far end of the house. It was modern, with gleaming stainless steel appliances and granite countertops. Gage had set out a tray of cheese and crackers. A bottle of wine and two glasses sat next to it. Van Morrison played softly. I bit my cheek to hide the smile tugging at my lips and choked down the laughter I wanted to bray at Gage's idea of a seduction scene.

Gage grabbed the wine bottle and tipped it over one of the glasses.

"It's nine in the morning. Besides, I don't really drink." The words came out rushed and sounded like some language in a fantasy novel. I put my palm over the wine glass to illustrate my point.

Gage glanced at me, surprise evident on his face. He recovered in seconds and nonchalantly poured his own glass of wine. It surprised me. The early hour, not the alcohol itself. Baptists traditionally abstained from drinking alcohol. In recent years, however, fewer completely abstained but most who drank did so in moderation. I wondered what Memaw would make of it but knew I'd never tell.

"I suppose Leticia told you I wanted the house deep cleaned for the Heritage and History Week candlelight tours."

"She did." I ate a cracker and some fancy tasting cheese. "I'm surprised you don't have maid service."

"I did." Gage took a sip of wine and leaned against the counter. "I had to let her go. She did a poor job."

"So you're looking for sparkling chandeliers, clean baseboards..." I trailed off, hoping he'd fill in the blanks.

"That sort of thing. Just whatever you can get done in one day. Leticia told me I was lucky to secure your services this close to the kickoff of H & H Week."

I struggled to keep my expression neutral as I listened to Gage's vague instructions. Most people had a to-do list so long I had trouble finishing it. The cynic in me suspected this dirty old man just wanted me in his house.

"This time of year is busy for me." I'd give Gage his money's worth on the cleaning, but he'd better not try any hanky-panky. He'd think he got hold of a feral cat with rabies.

"How about a tour? You can get started after that." Gage drained his wine and motioned me to come along. As I drew abreast of him, he put his arm around me. I fought the urge to slap it away and, instead, stepped out of his reach. I exited the kitchen ahead of him.

"I watched a television program about some college kids who are real life ghost busters." Gage's tone was innocent, conversational even. "Have you seen it?"

"Nope. Memaw controls the TV." I kept my tone light, but, inside, I seethed. Michael Gage never failed to bring it up. *What the hell was his problem? Did he think we'd bond over this?* If he did, he knew very little about me.

In my silence, Gage took on the role of tour guide and told me what he knew about the house and the items in it. Gage had chosen scratchy fringe and stiff-patterned upholstery for the antique furniture. Prissy angels adorned every surface. Too la-di-da for me. That is, until we got to the last room.

"I saved the best for last." Gage took my arm and led me into a room tucked away in a dark alcove on the second floor.

My *ooh* was one of real appreciation. The study almost made me forgive Gage's talent for touching me every chance he got. The low wood ceiling lent the tiny room a cozy glow. The room's size surprised me. Judging by the rest of the house's layout, I expected this room to be larger. Its size created a charm the rest of the house lacked.

A small fireplace hugged one corner. Crammed bookshelves lined the walls. Huge leather chairs invited someone to spend a lazy day sitting in them reading. Bay windows with cushioned seats looked out on the backyard, which Gage had landscaped with flagstones and controlled, manicured flowerbeds. I sat down on one the brightly colored cushions and gazed out the window.

"You like the study."

"It's the best room in the house." Sunlight glinted off the carriage house's stained glass windows. The sparkling sun glinting off all those colors mesmerized me. "Did you restore the carriage house, too?"

"I did." Gage joined me at the window and draped his arm over my shoulders. I casually reached up and pushed his arm off. I needed the tour to end soon so I could get to work. My reserve of patience ran danger-ously low.

A silhouette appeared at one of the carriage house windows. I bit back a gasp and turned from the sight. *Of course the Mace House would be haunted. What historic home isn't?* Because my family once owned the property, I had to wonder just who haunted it and why.

"Have the police come any closer to locating Chase Fischer?" Gage spoke as though my rebuff hadn't happened.

I shrugged. "I wish they'd look for the real killer. Chase didn't do that."

"I hate to say this"—Gage's facial features shifted into an apologetic grimace—"but Chase Fischer is an alcoholic and a drug addict. My mother was a heroin addict. All the signs are there. Addicts are rather unpredictable."

My skin burned as anger sprang to life. I bit back a tart retort. I was just here to do a job. Sooner I started, the sooner I could leave. Michael Gage had just ensured I'd never return his interest.

"Besides, there are no other suspects. From what I've heard, it's pretty open and shut."

"There are other people the sheriff's office needs to find and interview. One of Rae's contacts on her cellphone was someone named Low Ryder. I've heard…" I stopped just short of saying Chase's name. "Rae had another boyfriend. This Low Ryder guy."

Gage lifted an eyebrow and shook his head. "What an odd name. Low Ryder. Sounds made up. If this person is real, the authorities will find him soon enough. Tell me something. Why are you doing this? I mean, taking such an interest in Rae's murder. From what Leticia told me, you two were far from close."

"The day Rae died, I promised her a favor." This was as close to the truth as I'd get with Mr. Paranormal Fan.

"Be careful." Gage frowned. "If you snoop too much, you might find out things you were better off not knowing."

My skin tingled as a sweat broke over my body. I glanced at Gage, only to see the same genial smile and twinkling eyes I always saw. Had that been a threat? Surely not. I just needed some rest.

Gage showed me where he kept his cleaning supplies, and I got to work.

———

THE CLEANING WENT MORE QUICKLY than I expected.

Whomever Gage had hired for maid service hadn't done *that* poor a job. I again wondered if this whole thing was just a ruse to get me alone. If so, what a loser. I hoped Memaw's idea of good money and mine were close. Putting up with Gage wouldn't be worth it otherwise.

On one hand, I'd never been offered more refreshments at a job. When I asked if he kept a particular brand of furniture polish, Gage raced out to get a bottle. On the other hand, the man barely let me work.

The King of the Castle entered the study as I did my final sweep, making sure all the woodwork was dust free and the scent of lemon furniture oil hung in the air. Gage held his mail in one hand and his checkbook in the other. I rose and wiped my sweaty face on the hem of my t-shirt. That is, until I saw Gage's eyes trained on my bared belly.

"I've got a question." I strode to Gage's achievement wall and pointed to the picture of Gage in prep school. "Which one of these kids is you?"

Gage raised his eyebrows, at once surprised and pleased. He moved in next to me—too close—and pointed to a scrawny kid with a black crew cut.

"It doesn't look like you at all." It was true. I had studied the picture on and off while I cleaned in the study and didn't see a speck of resemblance between Gage and any of these kids. Just went to show how much people changed as they aged.

"How's the house coming? Everything, including the attic windows, looks fantastic."

"I'm done. If you want a quick run-through before the first candlelight tour, give me a call." I gathered my cleaning materials into the plastic crate I used to tote them around. "I've got to tell you, I saved this room for last because I like it so much."

"You're a mysterious woman, Peri Jean." His gaze oozed over me. "I find the rumors about your clairvoyance stimulating. Would you be willing to—"

The phone rang and cut him off. Gage frowned and answered. I seized the opportunity to slip away. I returned Gage's cleaning supplies and took the rest of my stuff out to my car. Gage's boldness disturbed me. He'd never before referred to my scary little talent so directly. I glanced back at the house, weighing the idea of just driving away without my pay. But running away wasn't the answer. I worked for money, not for fun. Gage would pay me my money, and I'd get away from him. I marched toward the house.

The door to the study stood half-open, exactly the way I left it. I peeked around the door to find Gage looking through his mail. Just as I started to alert him to my presence, his face twisted into a mask of rage. He crumpled the letter in his hand and threw it into the garbage can with enough force for it to bounce around. He rearranged his face in a flash when he saw me standing there. His eyes scared me.

"Would you mind emptying the trash in here before you leave?" Gage opened his leather bound checkbook and wrote without waiting for my answer. Well, la-di-da.

I grabbed the trashcan and left the room. Gage, usually so charming, had done a Jekyll and Hyde switcheroo. Curiosity about the letter's contents tugged at me, begging me to snoop. I tried to avoid giving in to my voyeuristic tendencies on the job. A reputation as a meddler would put me out of business in short order.

I retrieved an industrial sized garbage bag from the pantry and made a garbage sweep of the entire house. When I got back to the kitchen, the wastebasket from the study sat there waiting for me. The offending letter sat right on top. I knew I needed to trash it and forget it. But I wanted to know what made Michael Gage tick, what drove his weird attraction to me. I snatched the letter and stuffed it into my jeans. I took Gage's wastebasket back to his study.

Gage sat at his desk waiting for me. In my absence, he'd produced a single long stemmed rose. It sat on top of my check. It took every ounce of my self-control not to shriek laughter. I had never seen anything so cheesy.

Then, out of nowhere he said, "Now that our business is finished, will you go on a date with me?" Gage handed me the rose.

Memories of growing up the kid who got picked last for everything killed my mirth. Michael Gage did not deserve to be humiliated. His olive skin, dimples, and salt and pepper hair were far from homely. He did a good job as pastor of First Baptist Church. I just didn't feel a spark of attraction to him. His interest in my psychic ability gave me the outright willies, and I didn't want to date a man old enough to be my father.

"So what's your answer?" Gage held out my check. I took it and nearly gasped. Had Memaw quoted this price? That explained her insistence I do the job. Unless...this was even more than Memaw told him I'd charge. In that case, he was trying to buy me. I squirmed, eager to leave.

"Pastor Gage—"

"Michael. Call me Michael." Gage watched me intently. His hazel eyes were hypnotic. I tore my gaze away.

"Michael, I've had a failed marriage. One where I got a divorce." I stared at the ceiling as I tried to gather my thoughts and noticed a crack above one of the bookshelves. Foundation problems? I refocused. "I married Tim on impulse. Deep down, I knew it was a bad idea...but he wanted me, and I wanted someone to want me, so I married him anyway."

"So that's a no?"

"I think it is."

That rage I'd seen a few minutes earlier flared for a brief second. He covered it with one of his smiles. It never touched his eyes.

The back of my neck stung with nervousness and embarrassment as Gage escorted me to the front door. I'd never earned more for a day's work, but I'd never accept another job from Michael Gage. There was a reason he was single.

———

As I sat down in my Nova's well-worn seat, something scratched at my hip. The letter. In my haste to get away from Gage, I'd forgotten all about the letter. I couldn't very well sit in his driveway and read it—especially not when I could see him watching me from a window.

I drove away and cut through downtown, planning to gas up before I went home.

A pink and orange sunset streamed between the old buildings. The streets held only a few pedestrians. The huge spire of the Gaslight City First Baptist Church stood over it all, gleaming gold with the sun's last rays. I slowed almost to a crawl as I enjoyed the beauty of this magical time of day.

The museum had a closed sign on the door, but bright light streamed from the fourth floor windows. Hannah Kessler lived up there. Chase did the remodel and said she had expensive tastes. *Of course she did. Anyone who had enough money to buy a museum was used to getting what she wanted.*

An old Trans Am rumbled up the quiet street. It caught my eye because the old ones with the big gold bird on the hood were rare. The car parked in front of the museum. Dean Turgeau got out and went to the museum's door and knocked. Hannah let him in. He gave her a peck on the cheek and a hug. The two went inside laughing, their arms around each other.

Up in Hannah's apartment, the light cast Dean and Hannah's shadows in silhouette as they moved around the apartment. They laughed a lot. No wonder Hannah made a point to tell me Dean was a good guy. They were a couple.

Small towns and secrets don't mix. Hannah, of all people, knew that. I drove on, irritated she hadn't told me she and Dean were lovers. Of course, beautiful, rich

Hannah Kessler was bumping uglies with the hot new guy in town. Nothing else would be good enough for her.

"Who gives a shit?" I said aloud to the empty car. "They deserve each other." Dean was an uptight lawman. Hannah was a privileged snob. Rae's death had my whole life feeling out of whack. Soon as things calmed down, I'd find a gorgeous idiot and have a meaningless fling with him. The idea failed to make me feel better.

At the gas station, I read the letter I'd stolen from Gage by the dome light while I waited for my tank to fill.

Mikey,

I hope this is the same Michael Gage who spreads the word of God. If it is, then I'm sure you remember your good friends Jerry and Chelsea Bower from the years you spent doing missionary work in Guatemala. After thirty years of ministering to the Guatemalan people, it is time for Chelsea and me to retire. At the end of this year, we will move home to New Mexico and begin a ministry there.

I was surprised I never heard from you and Sharon after you returned to the States. People move through our lives at the will of the Lord Jesus. Sami, who is all grown up now, found this address on the internet. She'll be accompanying us to the states with plans to attend college in New Mexico.

As we packed for our move, we rediscovered some pictures of you and Sharon. Chelsea, Sami, and I had so much fun remembering the fellowship we shared. The three of us had such good times.

Chelsea and I will be in contact when we get back to the States. I hope we can renew our friendship.

Yours in the Lord,

Jerry and Chelsea Bower

And Sami Carranza. This was signed in curlicue writing with a heart over the *i*.

Michael Gage's fury over this letter made no sense to me. I didn't know the whole story, but Gage's reaction stuck with me. Pulling into Memaw's driveway, I realized why: it had scared me. His anger, about both the letter and my refusing his offer of a date, had scared me.

The living room light still shone through the curtains when I pulled into the carport. I found Memaw sitting on the couch with a bowl of ice cream. A sitcom brayed obnoxious cuteness on TV.

"How did your job for Pastor Gage go?" Memaw looked better than she had in several days. She got up and motioned me into the kitchen where she fixed me a bowl of ice cream and poured both strawberry and chocolate syrup over it. We sat at the table to eat.

"It went well. You were right about the pay. He asked me out on a date."

"Well?" Memaw's sly grin made me think she'd encouraged Gage to ask me out.

"I refused."

"How come?"

"Didn't feel right." I labored to keep my tone light. "Didn't you say he'd been married and widowed?"

"He told me his wife died in childbirth while they were out of the country on a mission. Their poor little baby died, too. Why do you ask?"

"Just curious, I guess." Maybe the old friend who contacted Gage brought back bad memories. Then something hit me. The letter's author implied he thought Gage's wife was still alive. If the guy had forgotten his wife's death, Gage had good reason to be upset. Even that explanation didn't satisfy me. The situation flipped and turned in my mind, unable to find a comfortable spot in my thoughts.

Memaw changed the subject when she noticed my contemplative mood. We talked about the festivities scheduled for H & H Week as we ate our ice cream. I rinsed the bowls while Memaw turned off the TV and went to bed.

I went to my room and paced restlessly. I wanted to discuss my life with someone. I wanted Chase. I wanted to call him and go over to his trailer and sit on his couch and talk while he listened. In return, he'd tell me his latest woes, usually something with Felicia barring him access to their son. After, we'd watch old Westerns and make fun of the actors.

Chase had to be okay. If he wasn't, I didn't know what I'd do without him. Whose life would I share in such an amiable way?

I powered up my laptop knowing I had to find something to do or I'd worry about Chase all night. As soon as the computer was ready, I ran a Google search on Michael Gage. First Baptist Church of Gaslight City's website popped up. I had never looked at the website before.

Michael Gage blogged. I couldn't believe it. He had posted before and after pictures of his renovations of Mace House. He posted a daily devotional with corresponding Bible verses to study. I noted his picture was conspicuously absent from the website. I hit my browser's back button and looked at the other search results.

Some results had to do with a radio show on which Gage appeared occasionally. There was also a link to a newspaper article about a gospel television program, which had approached Gage about appearing in a reality gospel show. Gage had declined. I clicked through two more pages of results and found a teenage Michael Gage on an older social media site and a genealogy site, which listed a Michael Gage born in the eighteen hundreds.

I gave up on Gage and ran a search on Jerry Bower in Guatemala. I found Jerry's Facebook page. Best I could tell, he used Facebook to communicate with other missionaries and his grown children in New Mexico. I wanted to send Jerry Bower a message but what could I ask him? There was no way to describe my actions other than meddling. Michael Gage hadn't done anything but act interested in me.

I closed Jerry Bower's Facebook page and ran a search on Sharon Gage. I did a quick read through of each hit, but no Sharon Gage was the correct age or seemed...right. I searched death records and had no luck there, either. Granted, I had no experience with the databases. I was about to give up when one of the hits caught my eye.

Help me find my sister. Sharon Gage... Guatemala...missionary.

I clicked on the link and a full color website came up. It featured a large picture of a light haired woman squinting into the sun. She wore a maternity shirt and looked to be in early pregnancy. The caption underneath the picture read "last known picture of Sharon Zeeman Gage." I scanned through the website, my body tightening as I read. Sharon Zeeman had married Michael Gage against her family's wishes in 2000. The couple, in lieu of a honeymoon, went straight to Guatemala to start work as missionaries.

Michael and Sharon stayed in Guatemala for about five years, during which time Sharon was estranged from her family. During the fifth year of the couple's stay in Guatemala, Sharon sent her parents a letter containing the picture featured on the website. In the letter, Sharon said she was pregnant and wanted to bury their differences for the sake of her unborn child. She and her husband planned to move back to the states in late 2005 to prepare for the birth. Nobody heard from Sharon again.

I clicked through the rest of the website and found no pictures of Sharon with Michael Gage. The Michael Gage I knew had to be around fifty years old. He'd have been forty in 2000. Sharon Zeeman Gage looked to be about my age —pushing thirty. It was possible she married a man ten years her senior.

There was an email link at the bottom of the page. I knew I had a piece of the puzzle of Sharon Gage's disappearance in Jerry Bower's letter, but I needed to think things through before I contacted Sharon's family. I could be opening a can of stink I'd regret.

9
———

THURSDAY STARTED OUT BAD. I woke to an empty house and someone banging on the front door. I stumbled through the house and answered the door yawning. Dean Turgeau stood on our front porch.

"Remember what you said about me needing proof?" Dean said. His mouth had a grim set to it, and he held his sheriff's issue uniform cowboy hat in front of him like a shield. He took one look at me and redirected his gaze to the front porch's bead board ceiling.

"Good morning to you too. About what?" I rubbed the sleep out of my face and became aware of my attire. Or lack of it. I slept in a cami and short-short set. It featured little cartoon teddy bears. Rather skimpy, and I didn't sleep in a bra.

"The other day, you said I had no proof you know the whereabouts of Fischer. And you said if I did have proof, I'd haul your ass in to question you." Dean's eyes roamed over me before he focused on the area over my left shoulder. "Well, guess what? I've got what I need to take you in for questioning. Come on."

"I'm not going to the sheriff's office." My heart did a few half-hearted somersaults before it kicked into overdrive. Sweat broke out on my scalp, itching and tingling. Was this how my Uncle Jesse felt the day they arrested him for murdering his brother, my father?

Something flickered in Dean's deep blue eyes, and his bluster disappeared. "Let's not make this harder than it has to be. Just get in the car."

"No. I want to know—"

"We got a tip from somebody who saw you with Fischer." Dean leaned on the doorjamb. "You're lucky I didn't come out here with an arrest warrant."

"Are you arresting me?" The words caught in my throat and I coughed hard, nearly gagging.

"Not yet." Dean stood very still, his body tensed. "But that's what Sheriff Holze wanted me to do. I assured him you'd come in voluntarily."

I didn't understand Dean's reluctance to arrest me. In front of Dottie's Burgers and Rings, he indicated nothing would please him more. Why the change of heart? Maybe I should do as he asked.

"I have a job in town later this morning. Let me put on some clothes and brush my teeth." Desperate for normalcy, I focused on my work schedule.

Dean mumbled something under his breath about maybe canceling the job but gave me an exasperated nod. "Go get dressed. If you run, our relationship is going to take a turn for the worse. Way worse."

In my bedroom, my hands shook as I pulled on blue jeans and a t-shirt. In the bathroom, I could barely make my trembling hands squeeze toothpaste onto my toothbrush. Finally, I got my teeth brushed and my hair combed. I went to face Dean at the front door. He looked me up and down and shook his head.

"I'll follow you to the sheriff's office." I grabbed my purse off Memaw's antique buffet and followed Dean outside to where our cars were parked.

"You're not going to try to run from me in that hunk of junk, are you?" Dean tried to smile as he stood with his door open.

My lips and cheeks tingled. A roaring started in my ears. Afraid my words would come out garbled, I just shook my head and got into my car.

———

NUMB WITH FEAR, I stared at the gold lettering on the door to the sheriff's office. Dean reached past me and held the door open as though chivalry mattered at a time like this. I took a step inside, tripped over the doorjamb, and nearly went sprawling. He caught me by the arm and righted me. Before that moment, I had wondered what it would feel like to have his hands on me. My fantasies bore little resemblance to this moment. Dean's hard, impersonal grip left me shivering.

Heads popped up and eyes widened as we walked through an open area full of desks and cubicles. The smell of burned coffee mixed with body odor assaulted my senses as a couple dozen eyes drilled into me. All the while, the endlessly ringing telephone threatened my sanity. Dean led me past a row of glassed-in offices situated around the perimeter of the room. We stopped in front of one with an open door.

The office's occupants made my skin crawl. Joey Holze and bigmouth Hannah Kessler both turned to look at me. Hannah's expression morphed into wide-eyed, open-mouthed curiosity. Joey—the galling son-of-a-bitch —grinned.

"Sheriff, do you still want to sit in on this interview?" Dean's tone held a note of sarcasm I recognized from my run-ins with him. I saw a muscle jump in his jaw. Was Burns County's newest sheriff's deputy less than enamored with his boss? *Interesting.*

Joey Holze hefted his bulk from behind his desk. He gave Hannah a one-armed hug and a kiss on the cheek. "Get on to the house, baby. Your Aunt Carly is cooking fried chicken tonight. She'd be mighty happy for you to join us."

Hannah said nothing. She just goggled at me, her mouth opening and closing in surprise. Sheriff Joey pushed past her and shut the door on her deer-in-the-headlights expression. She disappeared from my sight as Turgeau and Holze hustled me into a small room with a table and three chairs.

"Miz Mace, we got an anonymous tip that you were seen on rural farm road talking to Chase Fischer." Holze looked down at his notes. "Three days ago."

"So?" The roar in my ears had softened to a ringing. I

tried to reason this out, figure out if they could arrest me. But I couldn't think. My nervous sweat had dampened my clothes, and I could concentrate on nothing other than feeling cold. I couldn't quit shivering.

"You're not denying that you've seen Mr. Fischer? Spoken to him?" Dean Turgeau leaned across the table and frowned. I expected to see smug satisfaction in his expression but only saw curiosity and concern. That surprised me.

"I didn't say that. I just asked why it mattered if I have." I clasped my hands in front of me, hoping to hide their tremors. It didn't work.

"It matters, Peri Jean, because that means I can finally get your sorry ass out of my town." Holze bared his tobacco stained teeth in a shit-eating grin. "That loser killed your trashy cousin, and now you're aiding and abetting. For all I know, you did the killing. We all know you're capable of beating up defenseless girls at the senior prom for fooling with Chase Fischer. Even if you didn't do the killing, I can charge you as an accessory after the fact. That'll carry the same charges as whatever Chase ends up getting."

"You don't have any proof I talked to anybody." My bluffing skills sucked. I'd never admit they had me. But they did. Hadn't it always been this way? After the whole town found out about my seeing ghosts, they ostracized me and sent me to a mental hospital. My sense of injustice kindled into rage. I sat back in my chair, fuming.

"Proof? We got this anonymous witness." Holze tapped the sheaf of papers in front of him. Dean Turgeau crossed his arms over his chest and scowled.

"Well, if your source is anonymous, then you don't know who it is. If you don't know who it is, you're not going to get them to testify in court." A little ray of hope shone on my gloomy disposition. "And I bet you don't have pictures of me on the roadside with Chase Fischer, do you?"

Sheriff Joey Holze turned the color of cooked beets. His fat fists clenched. He started to sputter out a comeback, but Dean Turgeau interrupted him.

"What did you and Chase Fischer talk about? That's all we need to know. It will help us find Chase. If we don't find him soon, it'll be too late." Dean uncrossed his arms and held his hands out palms up, imploring.

"Too late for what?" The stupid questions bought me a second or two to think, and I desperately needed to think before I spoke. My life depended on what I said here in this dingy, sweat-scented room. I just knew it.

"Too late for us to help him if he really is innocent. If this turns into a manhunt, no telling what'll happen. He might end up getting hurt. Maybe dead." Turgeau let that hang in the air.

"How can you help him if you've found the murder weapon at his house?" I spat out. "Don't you want to charge him with murder? Send him to death row?"

"If he deserves to go to death row—" Sheriff Joey Holze's eyes sparkled with anger.

"Peri Jean, we are doing everything we can to investigate this case fairly." Dean didn't even look at Holze as he interrupted him. "If you'll just tell us what you and Mr. Fischer talked about, I know—"

A commotion rose outside the interview room. The three of us glanced toward the door. A strident voice neared the interview room. "You can't just go in there. I don't care if you're President of the United States—"

The door to the interview room swung open. Glenda Robbins, secretary to Holze, tried to block it with her body. "I said—"

"Move please, Mrs. Robbins." That honey rich voice belonged to Rainey Bruce, the same lawyer the Fischers had retained for Chase. Rainey was not only the youngest lawyer in town, but also the most expensive. The former Miss Texas and model towered over petite Glenda Robbins. Glenda, seeming to realize she was at a disadvantage, stepped out of Rainey's path.

"Sheriff Holze, Deputy Turgeau." Rainey greeted the men as though she hadn't just been part of an undignified ruckus. "Have you arrested my client?"

Sheriff Joey Holze wheezed and gasped. Between the gasps, he said a few words, none of which made any sense. "Been seen with Fischer...she's a bad kid anyway...always been trouble."

"Ms. Mace came here to answer some questions on her own accord." Dean stood and squared his shoulders.

"That so?" Rainey raised her eyebrows at him. With her high cheekbones and glowing mahogany skin, she resembled an ancient queen more than a small town lawyer. She had the upper hand and knew it. Before Dean formulated an answer, she turned to me. "Do you want to stay here? Answer more questions?"

"She don't have no money to pay you." Joey had rallied

and now stood next to Turgeau. His massive chest rose and fell as the excitement took its toll on him. I wished he'd have a heart attack.

"I'll front her the money." The voice came from outside the door, but I recognized it all the same. Bigmouth Hannah Kessler had come to my rescue.

Joey turned to her, his eyes widening. His mouth opened with a pop as he tried to think of words for the kind of traitor his niece had just turned into.

"I won't let you railroad her again." Hannah stared down her uncle, who had the good grace to hang his head.

"Get up." Rainey grabbed my arm and dragged me from the chair. My body went limber as relief flooded through it. I wanted to hug Rainey, but settled for letting her drag me from the sheriff's office. Behind us, Holze could be heard screaming at poor Glenda for letting Rainey into the interview room.

Once we were out on the sidewalk, Rainey hustled me to my car. Hannah followed close behind.

"Get in this car and drive away from here. Do not ever go anywhere with them alone again. Call me if they arrest you." Rainey looked down her nose at me. "And if they do arrest you, keep those fists to yourself."

I glanced down at my battle-scarred hands, my trophy from the years I'd endured schoolyard bullying. Rainey pressed a card into my hand and turned to Hannah.

"My bill will be in the mail." The former Miss Texas's smile reminded me of a lioness watching a gazelle at dinnertime. Embarrassing Holze and Turgeau had not sated her ruthless side.

Hannah gave her a stiff nod. Rainey stomped down the sidewalk and cut across the street to her office on the courthouse square, probably on her way to find someone to terrorize. She earned her reputation as the most formidable lawyer in town. Hannah turned to me, eyes wide, and her cheekbones bore hectic spots of red. I tried to imagine how Dean would feel about her taking my side. *Might make for interesting pillow talk.*

"Thank you. I won't forget this." I held my hand out for Hannah to shake. She closed her long, slender fingers around mine, and I wondered if I should let go of the negative parts of our past.

"Maybe we can go to lunch?" Hannah's smile had less confidence this time.

I shook my head. "Got work. Gonna be late if I don't get my butt in gear."

A deep flush spread out of Hannah's collar and darkened her face. She walked away from me. My face heated, the skin tightening. What a crappy way to reward someone who had just gotten me out of a serious jam. I wrapped my arms around myself as I watched Hannah retreat. All these years, I considered Hannah a jerk. But maybe I was the jerk.

I went to the job I had scheduled and worked on autopilot, insides jittering from the close call at the sheriff's office. My boss for the day noticed my distraction and showed her unhappiness by engaging me every chance she got. It didn't matter. I couldn't focus.

Razor sharp terror for Chase hacked away at my nerves. Finding Low_Ryder was the key to getting him out of this mess, and I was stuck. I still didn't understand the vision I had the day Rae died. That picture in the sketchbook had to be Low_Ryder. Had to be. Turgeau might be interested, but with no name to go with the picture, what could he do? *Continue hunting for Chase is what.* And after the scene at the sheriff's office, I didn't look forward to our next encounter.

Hannah's help confused and surprised me. She hadn't meant to hurt me when she told people how I'd found her Christmas presents. But she had. Then she ignored me for twenty years. I didn't understand what she wanted from me now, but I didn't want her to hurt me again.

I finished the work, collected my pay, and headed home, my head buzzing with problems that had no immediate fix.

———

MEMAW CALLED while I was on my way home and said Benny Longstreet wanted to pick up the travel trailer within the hour. He'd lined up a cleaning service to make it usable again, but he needed to get it to them before day's end.

Benny, a born wheeler-dealer, loved his role as the richest man in Burns County. He had either incredible business acumen or hellacious good luck. Everything he touched seemed to turn to gold. I didn't know what he was paying Memaw for the travel trailer, but I bet it wasn't much, and he'd surely double, if not triple, his money.

Though I'd agreed to sell the travel trailer to Benny, I

had a little resentment brewing. I worked my ass off for not much pay, and my half of the travel trailer wiped out my savings account the year we bought it. I sucked it up. I knew Memaw was hurting, and she needed some closure. I reminded myself we wouldn't have used it again anyway.

I dug through Memaw's file cabinet for the paperwork on the trailer and got wrapped up looking through my old report cards. My grades had been atrocious, not because the work was hard, but because being a social pariah was distracting. Something caught my eye.

I plucked an old picture from the jumble and stared at a young woman almost unrecognizable as Memaw. Those impossibly dark eyes cued me to her identity. They hadn't changed much, other than more wisdom lurking in their depths. She was possibly not even eighteen.

This was the first time I'd seen any picture of Memaw before she married my grandfather. We had a few faded, old photos of my grandfather's growing up years, but none of Memaw. She always said her family was too poor for pictures. Now I wondered.

Memaw didn't look poor. She looked like a young Elizabeth Taylor with her dark hair and bow lips. She wore a long skirt with a wide belt. Her top, while modest, did not look cheap. A jeweled barrette pulled one side of her dark curls off her face, and she wore a ring on her right hand and a bracelet on her left arm. *Why had Memaw said her family was poor?*

The noise of a rumbling diesel engine broke into my thoughts. I looked out the window to see Benny's big red Dodge dually jouncing through Memaw's pasture. I snatched the trailer's ownership papers and jogged down there to meet him. We spent the next few minutes getting the trailer hitched to his truck.

"It's a reeking mess in there," I said. "I don't envy whoever cleans it up."

"That crime scene cleanup crew is used to it. That's all they do," Benny said. He jiggled the padlock I had put on the door. "Got the key to this?"

I slapped my forehead. "It's in the house with her personal effects. I'll run down there and get it."

"Nonsense. You'll ride down there with me in Big Red." Benny patted the huge red truck's side as though it was a pet.

Benny had to help me into the monstrosity on wheels. Being short sucked. The bumpy pasture bounced us around so hard walking might have been more pleasant. When we got to the house, I expected Benny to wait in the truck, but he followed me inside. I dragged the box of Rae's effects out and removed the key from the sketchbook where I'd stowed it. Benny leaned too close to me, looking at the pictures. He wore some loud cologne I'd have never expected a man of his social standing to wear.

"Did Rae draw these?"

"Far as I know." I didn't want Benny hanging over me, so I handed the book to him and let him look by himself.

Benny leafed through the pictures, smiling, until he reached the final page. A look of horror crossed his face. I craned my neck to see what he'd found. I had to slap a hand over my mouth.

I missed this picture during my one and only perusal

of the sketchbook. On the final page, it depicted a naked man standing at the sink in the travel trailer. The man had his back turned, looking out the tiny window. He was long and lean with little stick legs and a thatch of hair over his buttocks. A giggle slipped through my fingers. Benny, unamused, grimaced and wrinkled his nose. He tossed the sketchbook back in the box.

"That garbage?"

"No. Of course not." I planned to buy a protective sleeve for the sketchbook. I wanted to show it to my future children, to share Rae's talent with them. She deserved to have something good associated with her.

Benny took a deep breath and started to speak, but instead shook his head. I waited for him to leave, but he stood looking at the cardboard box containing Rae's effects. He twirled his key ring from one finger and shifted his weight.

"Benny, I hate to run you off, but I have an appointment. You've got the keys and all the papers we had. If you need anything else..."

Benny jerked and turned his eyes to me. They darted from me to the box and back again. "Of course."

I saw him to the door and almost had to push him outside. He left the house with one last strange look over his shoulder. Icy fingers tickled at my spine.

I lied. I had nowhere to go. Benny acted so oddly after he saw the drawings in Rae's sketchbook, I just wanted him out of the house. I grabbed the sketchbook and looked at the sketch of the naked man again. Could it be Benny? Of course, I'd never seen him naked, thank God, so I had no way to know. The naked man's physique was similar enough to Benny's for me to believe they were one and the same.

Again, I considered telling Dean about the sketchbook. He really needed to see it. I wanted to tell someone about Benny Longstreet's reaction to the sketch. Dean was the logical choice. I took out my cellphone and Dean's business card but couldn't make myself call him.

I dreaded enduring his fury after the scene at the sheriff's office. Then, I thought back to his demeanor. He hadn't acted too excited. The more I thought about it, Sheriff Joey had maneuvered himself into the master of ceremonies position. And he showed the most emotion when Rainey rescued me. I remembered the way Dean acted every time Joey opened his mouth. I had the feeling Dean didn't like Joey any better than I did.

That settled it. I punched in Dean's number but stopped when I saw Memaw's headlights coming down the driveway.

She had stayed away until the shadows lengthened in the onset of full dark. I turned on the porch light and met her at the door. Lines of fatigue were etched into her face. She walked with a little drag to her step and tripped coming in the front door. I grabbed her arm and steadied her.

"Is it done?"

"It's gone." I took her tote bag and helped her out of her jacket. "I've made a stew and some onion cornbread. Why don't you go wash your hands while I dish it up?"

Memaw nodded and stumbled down the hall. She

grabbed the frame of the bathroom door to balance herself. I worried the tutoring was getting to be too much for her. Even if I wanted to, which I did, I couldn't suggest she do less of it. She said it kept her from becoming one of those old people who barely knew their own names.

I ladled the stew into bowls and cut wedges of steaming cornbread for both of us. Memaw dragged back into the kitchen wearing her housecoat and pajamas.

Rae's sketchbook lay on the table. As I cleared the dishes, Memaw leafed through the pages, tears brimming in her eyes. She wore a soft, proud smile. When she got to the last picture of the naked man with the thatch of hair over his buttocks, she burst out laughing. I noticed she covered her mouth the same way I had, as though embarrassed, but too amused not to laugh. I couldn't help smiling.

"I'll miss that girl."

I turned my back and scrubbed the pots and pans in the sink. I didn't want Memaw to see my grimace. Despite the heat coming off the hot oven, the room had a ghostly chill to it. Rae lurked somewhere near. I didn't have to miss her. She never left for me. I dreaded our next encounter, which I imagined would happen pretty soon.

———

MEMAW TOOK out her Bible and a study guide and began working through a chapter. I went to my room and called Dean Turgeau. The call went straight to voicemail. More disappointed than the situation warranted, I left my number and asked him to call me back about some information I'd like to share with him. This was the one chance he'd get from me. If he acted like an ass, we could stay enemies.

I waited fifteen minutes for Dean to return my call before I decided he wasn't going to respond to me. I yawned. The day had been a doozy. *Maybe a good night's sleep would put a new spin on things.* I put on my pajamas and got under the cover and realized my exhaustion didn't equal sleepiness. I sat up in bed and opened the book I had been reading.

The lamp beside my bed flickered on and off, and the door to my closet swung open. My heart kicked into gear as adrenaline entered my bloodstream. Footsteps rang on the hardwood and abruptly cut off to swish over the rug next to my bed. I scooted as far to the other side of the bed as I could without falling out, moaning as I scrabbled to turn on the other bedside lamp. The bed moved, and the indention of a butt appeared next to my legs.

Rae's ghost no longer wore the bloody garments in which she had died. She now wore a white dress fashioned to look like the one Marilyn Monroe wore in that famous picture of her standing over a grate, the breeze from the subway underneath making her dress fly up. Rae's version of the dress covered a lot less skin.

"I can't do this by myself. I don't know how. You have to help me," I whispered. I didn't need Memaw to hear me talking to myself. An icy breeze picked up in my room. A clump of papers blew off my dresser and littered the floor. The wind stopped swirling.

"That helped a lot." I got out of bed and stooped to pick up the papers. They fluttered out away from me. Irritated, I chased the papers around the room. Each time I got close and bent to pick them up, they moved out of my reach. Rae's amusement filled the room, malicious as when she was alive. Finally, I slammed my foot down on the papers. The wind in the room died down, and Rae faded from sight.

The papers were nothing more than a mish-mash of junk I had collected over the week. One was a mock-up of the program Memaw planned to hand out at Rae's memorial service Saturday. It featured a picture of Rae and me as children, smiling gap-toothed smiles with our arms around each other. Another was a flyer from the museum —which meant Hannah Kessler sent it—calling for volunteer tour guides well-versed in the lore surrounding the Mace Treasure. The last item was the letter I'd stolen from Michael Gage the day I cleaned Mace House.

I made a mental note not to ask for Rae's help again and sat down to reread Gage's letter. I still found the whole mystery pretty chilling, what with the missing persons entry for his wife online, or at least someone who could have been his wife.

I turned on my laptop and searched for Jerry Bower again and found a website connected with his Facebook account. I visited it and noted his email address. My common sense told me to drop the matter and mind my own business, but I couldn't quit thinking about Sharon Gage and her big smile in that picture. I didn't believe for one minute she just blew off her family after contacting them. Most likely, something bad had happened to her.

Besides that, I wanted to know more about Michael Gage. I didn't understand him. He could have had his pick of any number of women in Gaslight City. Why the fascination with me? I didn't even attend his church regularly. Most of all, I couldn't get over the fury I saw in his eyes. It contrasted sharply with the image he presented to the world.

Before I could talk myself out of it, I set up a fake email account and sent Jerry Bower the following letter:

Mr. Bower,

I am Michael Gage's secretary at First Baptist Church of Gaslight City. Pastor Gage was thrilled to get your letter. He started telling us all about his adventures in Guatemala. It sounded so exciting.

I decided to do a special program to pass out next service showing Pastor Gage's history. I wanted to include some of his Guatemala pictures if possible. You can send them to this email as a .jpg, and I'll do the rest.

Please, Mr. Bower, don't put yourself to any trouble about this request. I know you and your family are getting ready to move, and this is not the most important thing in the world.

Thank you,

Patti Harrison

I closed Jerry Bower's webpage and looked up Sharon Zeeman Gage's missing page. I stared into the smiling, freckled face of the woman in the pictures and hoped I could help her.

10

FRIDAY MORNING, I had an early appointment to help one of the bed and breakfast proprietors. She had so many bookings she rented out the carriage house where she and her husband kept an apartment and camped at her daughter's home. I helped serve breakfast to thirty guests and then worked with housekeeping to get the old house back in shape again. The mess people left in a rented room never failed to amaze me. I knew they didn't do stuff like that at home. At least, I hoped not.

My next appointment was not until much later in the day, so I went home to rest. Rae's memorial service was tomorrow. I suspected it would tire me out more than working nonstop for twelve hours.

Memaw sat at the table, a sheaf of papers before her. She scribbled comments in red, grumbling under her breath.

"Lazy kids," she said in greeting. "I'm glad you're getting me a computer for Christmas. That old piece of junk in there locks up when I try to use the comments function."

I made a mental note to go ahead and order her computer and give it to her early. It went against tradition, but she needed it now.

"The program you made for the memorial service looks great. Where did you find that old picture of Rae and me?"

"Oh, I've got a box of them. I'll never forget that day." Her smile turned wistful, and her eyes filled with tears. "The two of you and Hannah Kessler played hide and seek. You hid in an old trunk in the barn. The girls found you, but they couldn't get the trunk open. You were pounding on that trunk, screaming and hollering, so the girls came and got me. Luckily, I had the key to that stupid thing in my jewelry box."

I had forgotten all about that day. A little girl wearing an old-fashioned dress had shown me where to hide. Once I got into the trunk, she closed it. It locked by itself. My child's mind didn't recognize her as a ghost. As an adult, I'd have noticed she had no shadow. Analyzing the memory for the first time in over twenty years, I wondered if she tried to kill me.

"I remember that. You got so angry."

"Well, I told you girls not to play in that barn." She set down her pen and took off her glasses. "Want to hear a weird story? I bought the trunk at an estate sale when your grandfather and I first moved to Gaslight City. Then I decided I didn't like it and tried to sell it in my own yard sale.

"One of the ladies at the yard sale asked me where it came from. When I told her, she said the family who owned it before me had a daughter who suffocated in it. I did some research. Sure enough, a picture of my trunk was right there in the Gaslight City Gazette in an issue from the 1930s. After that, I didn't try to sell it again. I put it out at the barn and left it there. Of course, that was long before you were even thought of. Then, as luck would have it, you found it."

Yeah. Luck. A chill sank into me as I remembered that day. The little girl who convinced me to hide in there had looked funny, but I hadn't thought anything of it. Now I realized her lips had been blue. As the memory took shape in my mind, it hit me the barn and that trunk had been the setting of the vision I had the day Rae died.

My heart froze, then picked up speed. I had almost given up on deciphering the vision, but now I had it. My face tingled with excitement. I couldn't wait to get out there, but I had to play it cool with Memaw. She never wanted to discuss my ability to see ghosts, not even before it got me sent to the children's mental hospital. After she retrieved me from the mental hospital and won custody of me from Barbara, she advised me to never speak of it again to anybody.

"I haven't been out to the barn in ages," I said. "I think I might go out there and look around."

"Better take an allergy tablet," Memaw said. "It's full of dust, mold, and pollen out there. And be careful. Don't get in that trunk again."

"Give me a little credit." I did take her advice on the allergy pill.

———

Despite the sunny fall day, the barn interior resembled a black hole. Electricity had never been run to the old structure. My flashlight's glow barely made a dent in the darkness. Junk, junk, and more junk filled every available spot. The barn still smelled of horse dung and hay, even though horses never occupied the barn in my lifetime.

As I picked my way to the room's center, where I last remembered seeing the trunk, the air inside the barn cooled. Rae was with me. I shined my flashlight over the covered shapes, searching for the rocking chair in the vision. I didn't see it.

I waded deeper into the barn, opening the horse stalls and shining the light around. Nothing. I went back to the main room and picked my way around the junk. I couldn't believe I'd been wrong, but was about ready to admit defeat and go back to the house.

A hollow-eyed face appeared in the darkness, right at the edge of my flashlight's beam. I screamed and dropped my light. It rolled, splashing light over the walls.

Cursing, I picked up the flashlight. Rae—or at least her specter—stood near the middle of the room. The hair on my arms stood up, but I walked toward her anyway. Next to Rae sat the trunk. I lifted the lid. Empty.

My heart sank until I noticed the artillery box next to the trunk. I lifted it and slid the top backward. An envelope lay inside. I grinned and snatched it up. This was it, the key to the identity of Rae's murderer. I looked up and said to the empty air, "This is it. We'll get him."

For an answer, I got a swift rush of frustration and despair. It eroded my elation and left only the weight of depression. *Was she angry?* I didn't know why. I'd found the stuff she showed me in the vision. I didn't know what else she wanted me to do.

A noise above caught my attention. I looked up at the hayloft just in time to see an object hurtling toward me.

I leapt out of the way and fell into a pile of junk, scraping my arms and banging my head. The object crashed on top of the old trunk, splintering into a dozen pieces. I used my flashlight to see what had fallen. An old record player. I looked back up at the hayloft and found Rae watching me from above.

Still just as much of a bitch in death as in life. Anger replaced my fear. "You go fuck yourself, Raelene Georgia Mace."

Back in my room, I opened the envelope with trembling hands and unfolded a thin sheaf of pages with entry after entry of items and dollar figures in faded spidery script. Someone had highlighted several items in yellow: a roll top desk, some kind of chest, and a traveling slope. Augustine Dial bought the traveling slope. That interested me.

Jolene Fischer's mother, the infamous Rudie Rushing, was descended from the Dials. I had a strong suspicion the traveling slope was the same haunted writing slope I helped Jolene pack away. Why had Rae been looking for that thing? The treasure? *Oh, please. Not that again.*

I tossed the pages and the envelope down on my bed. Something rattled inside the envelope. I upturned the envelope and shook it. A business card fell out. I took one look at it and groaned. It belonged to Hannah Kessler.

Of course. Hannah Kessler had to show up in all this. I needed more time with her like I needed a meal of ground glass. I gathered up the ledger pages, planning to cram them back into the envelope, and saw a handwritten note on the back. It had lots of cross-outs and corrections. It read:

I will gladly disappear if you give me half a million dollars. Don't try and tell me you ain't good for it, cuz I know you are. Don't be resentful, neither. I got trouble on my ass, too. Otherwise, I wouldn't do you this way. We had fun together.

Well, well. Now I knew how Rae tried to cash in on her pregnancy. I suspected her blackmail scheme had backfired. That made more sense than something to do with that stupid, nonexistent treasure. If only I understood why she needed money. I had a sneaking suspicion Veronica played into it, but couldn't believe Rae owed her money. What would that disgusting crone have that Rae wanted?

Rae might have simply been looking for a big enough score to get out of Gaslight City and on the road to somewhere more glamorous. Had she been trying to escape someone, maybe Veronica? Or did it all boil down to Low_Ryder and the havoc the wrong man can wreak in the right woman's life?

As I pulled the envelope open to shove the pages back

inside, I noticed a phone number written on the inside of the envelope. It had a Tyler area code. Tyler, Texas was only an hour and some change from Gaslight City. Rae could have known someone who lived there.

I fired up my laptop. A reverse search identified it as a cellphone number. I dragged out my cellphone, restarted it —again—and called the number.

Disconnected. Another dead end. Disappointment flooded through me and re-emerged as irritation. I didn't have to be a fortuneteller to see a visit to Hannah Kessler in my future. I could think of nothing I'd rather do less than talk to her. Then I looked out the window and changed my mind.

A sheriff's cruiser rolled down the driveway and parked next to the carport. Dean Turgeau got out and stretched. I still dreaded facing him. If I had misjudged his feelings, I might have an antagonistic few minutes ahead of me.

———

DEAN KNOCKED on the front door. I waved Memaw off and answered it.

"You called my cellphone." Dean's eyes swept over me, lingering a second too long on my chest. He flushed when he met my eyes and realized I saw him.

"What's going on?" Memaw spoke from behind me.

"I don't know," Dean said. "Your granddaughter left a cryptic message on my voicemail. Said she had some information I'd be interested in."

I stepped aside and motioned Dean into the house. I

spoke to both him and Memaw at the same time. "When I cleaned out Rae's trailer, I found a sketchbook. It had a picture of two men she may have been seeing—other than Chase."

"That sketchbook?" Memaw's smile went south. "I don't want him to take it away. That's the last thing we've got left of her."

"We can make a copy of the pages Dean wants on the printer, Memaw."

"That'd be fine." Memaw went into the kitchen and sat at the table.

Dean gave me a puzzled look, and I shrugged to let him know this was odd behavior. Memaw always acted so self-assured. Lately, she'd seemed so helpless and confused. Maybe I needed to talk to Dr. Longstreet about her. It would infuriate her, but I could tell something was wrong.

I took out the box of Rae's things and let Dean look through the sketchbook. He marked the pages he wanted copied.

As I made copies, Dean moved in behind me, close enough I smelled aftershave and soap. A bolt of arousal warmed me in all the right places for all the wrong reasons. I would never steal Hannah Kessler's boyfriend away. I turned and shoved the copies at him. He glanced at them, holding the one of the biker dude close to his face and squinting at some detail.

"This it?" His tone pissed me off.

"No." I did my best to match his snotty tone. "This is not it. The rest is in my bedroom. I just found it out in the barn." I dropped my voice. "Memaw doesn't know about it."

I led the way back to my bedroom and shut the door behind us. Dean took in my room, his eyes lingering on the bed. I handed him the pages from the barn, and our fingers brushed. Both of us jerked back our hands. Dean turned his attention to the papers, raising his eyebrows as he read the blackmail note.

"If Rae's body was autopsied, you know she was pregnant."

"Who the hell told you that?" Dean's voice held an edge of anger.

"It's true, isn't it?" Dr. Longstreet didn't need to get into trouble.

Dean shrugged in response. "Tell me about the rest of this stuff."

"The pages with the highlighting are—I think—proof she was hunting the Mace Treasure."

"You said the treasure didn't exist."

"No. I don't think it does. But I also told you about people dying trying to find it."

Dean nodded. "And this phone number?"

"Disconnected."

"This is not TV. Don't you know you can get hurt playing detective?" His nostrils flared as we stared each other down.

"Somebody has to do it," I said, getting angry. "Because I know you're not following up on all the leads you have. Jolene Fischer told me about seeing Rae all beat up the Saturday before she died."

Dean rolled his eyes and snorted. "I'm sure your crystal ball keeps you apprised of my activities."

I flushed with heat, and not the good kind. I wanted to kick this ignorant dog's butt right in the gonads. Some of what I shared had to be useful. I took a deep breath, planning the insults I'd lay on him. My bedroom door opened, and Dean and I stepped away from each other.

"I brought the deputy some lemonade." Memaw's gaze darted between us. She knew she had interrupted something.

Dean smiled and thanked her for the lemonade. Memaw grinned and offered him some homemade banana nut muffins. They walked down the hall together, chatting. I followed, wishing Dean would say something rude so I'd have the chance to kick his ass into a second set of shoulders. *Crystal ball.* I'd show him.

———

DEAN SCARFED down every kind of food Memaw offered. He knew Memaw had taught school and asked her questions that got her talking more than I'd seen since Rae's death. His transformation from flaming horse's ass to charming conversationalist shocked me. He told a self-effacing story about falling into alligator infested waters while fishing in Louisiana, which had both Memaw and me laughing.

Realizing he didn't quite dare treat me rudely, I snapped up the papers I found in the barn and made copies. I might need them if I didn't figure out a way around talking to Hannah. Dean frowned as he watched me. I gave him a huge grin. I had him, and he knew it.

Finally, he announced he had to get back to work and told Memaw he enjoyed the chat. Turning to me, he held out his hand to shake. He winked at me as his fingers closed around mine. The whole thing left me too stunned for more than a mumbled goodbye. Deputy Dean confused the hell out of me.

Watching his cruiser drive off our property, I thought about his crystal ball remarks. Those stung and brought back years of schoolyard nightmares. Joey Holze must have filled Dean's head with all kinds of bull. His strong reaction surprised me. Most people branded me as a kook and moved on. Dean acted downright offended.

On the flip side, how could I forget his reluctance to arrest me? Or the genuine concern he showed the day of Rae's murder? I suspected a nice guy lurked beneath that trollish demeanor. Then there was the way he looked at me. I knew that look, and it did not fit my conclusions about Dean and Hannah being a couple. Talk about mixed signals. *Maybe it's just that time of month for Deputy Dean.*

My cellphone interrupted my thought. I snatched it, thinking for one silly moment that it might be Dean calling to apologize. But I didn't recognize the number. I accepted the call and said hello.

"Um, who is this?" The voice was high and lilting with a thick hick accent.

I took the phone away from my ear and glanced at the display again. The number had a Tyler area code. It couldn't be the number on Rae's envelope. It had been out of service.

"Who is this?"

"You called this number." The caller sounded like a sassy five-year-old. "You tell me who you are."

"This is Peri Jean Mace," I said. "I'm calling on behalf of Rae Mace."

"On behalf of? You a lawyer?" She giggled. "Just joking. I know who you are. Rae talks about you all the time. I just use that disconnect message as my voice mail to fool the bill collectors." *Bill* had two syllables. "Don't tell me Rae's standing me up tonight. I just got back into town. Got lots to tell her."

"I, um, didn't get your name." I dreaded telling this chick Rae would be standing her up for a lot of nights to come.

"I'm Dara Wyler, Peri Jean. I keep telling Rae we all need to get together."

"Dara, I hate to be the one to tell you this, but Rae died almost a week ago. We're having her memorial service tomorrow if you'd like to come."

Dara gasped. When she spoke, her voice quavered. "What happened?"

"She was murdered at her home."

Dara said nothing for so long I thought she'd hung up. I asked, "You still there?"

"I'm here," she said and sniffled.

"Listen, you wouldn't happen to know who Rae was dating would you? Any men in her life?"

"I don't think I want to get involved. Rae was into a lot of things."

"I'm not going to get you into trouble." I tried to make my voice as soothing as possible. "I just want to know what happened to my cousin."

"I can meet you at eleven tonight at The Chameleon." Dara sounded uncertain, as though she might take back her offer at any second.

"What's The Chameleon?"

Dara giggled. "It's...a dance club. Both Rae and I work there. Well, I guess Rae doesn't any more, but I do."

I glanced at the time. I had an afternoon job that ended at seven. I'd have plenty of time to change clothes and get to The Chameleon by eleven.

I asked Dara for the address, told her I'd see her at eleven, and hung up.

"Where are you going at eleven tonight?" Memaw's voice, which came from behind me, nearly scared me out of my skin.

"To see a friend of Rae's in Tyler. She didn't know Rae had passed on."

"You're going all the way over there to meet someone you don't know?"

I didn't dare tell Memaw I was meeting this someone at a strip club. What else could The Chameleon be?

"It's going to be okay." I hoped it would; otherwise, I'd have all eternity to feel guilty.

11

———

I SPENT the afternoon serving tea and cucumber sand-
wiches to the big spenders of Silver Dream Antiques. Julie
Woodson, daughter of Dottie, paid me well for my time, so
I wanted to impress her. But I struggled to keep my mind
off my plans for that evening.

I didn't make a habit of hanging out at buck-naked
dance clubs. Matter of fact, this was a first for me. As
conversations about carnival glass and art deco furniture
buzzed all around me, I wondered if Dara Wyler would
talk to me between dancing sets. Would she be clad in
some eye-averting attire?

Something else to consider: her information might
come with a price tag. Rae would have tried to dupe me for
every penny I had regardless if she knew anything useful. I
needed to keep the conversation focused on the identity of
Rae's boyfriends and anybody Rae owed money.

I raced home to get ready and found I had no clue
what to wear to a strip club. I dressed in my usual worn out

jeans and cowboy boots. To commemorate the occasion, I wore a purple silk top and actually took more than five minutes on my makeup. I spiked my short hair with gel and, not for the first time, wished I were more of a girly girl.

At the last minute, I got out Rae's sketchbook and made copies of the drawing I suspected was Low_Ryder and the drawing of the naked man. Anybody recognizing the latter drawing was a long shot, but I thought it worth a try.

Out of Gaslight City, I drove west until I hit State Highway 155. From there, I sped south, at a rate of speed I'd rather not disclose, until I hit Tyler city limits. Using directions from online, I found The Chameleon with no problem, parked in a huge parking lot, and paid too much to get in the door.

My first glimpse of The Chameleon's interior took my breath away. The roar of noise, the crush of bodies, and the underlying stench of humanity's darker side overloaded my senses. The room was a cavernous circus of flashing lights and naked flesh. On a raised dance floor at its center, a topless girl shook it for a cawing group of men waving dollar bills. *Classy.*

A scantily clad woman wearing heels so high they could have been stilts tottered toward me. "Can I get you a drink?"

"Is Dara here?"

"Sure she is." Her eyes darted to the back of the club. "There's a two drink per hour minimum if you want to stay."

"Dara and I have an appointment. Can you let her know Peri Jean is here?" I asked.

"Oh, she'll be out anytime now." Stilts's pen hovered over her order pad, prompting me.

I ordered a club soda and nearly dropped when the waitress asked for twenty dollars. She waited an extra beat for a tip. I pretended ignorance.

"You have a good time, now," she snarled and tottered away.

She probably wouldn't even bring my twenty-dollar club soda. Evidently, I'd have to look for Dara myself. I trekked into the bowels of the merrymaking establishment, fending off unwanted hands and invitations, until I reached a door marked "Employees Only."

Before I could reach out a tentative hand, the door slammed open. I backpedaled several steps. A glittery woman wearing a feather boa and not much else strode out. She seemed seven feet tall with the super high heels she'd crammed her feet into.

"Thank Gawd." Her West Texas twang was thick enough to fill a canyon. "You here with Maybelline's makeup, I hope?"

"Uh, yeah." I don't know how she thought I had makeup with me. I didn't even have a purse.

"Go on in." She snorted and held the door open. "Maybe she'll quit caterwauling and get up on stage and shake her booty."

I scooted through the open door. A dimly lit hall with doors on both sides stretched out before me. I'd have to knock on one of these doors. If I picked the wrong one, I'd be out on my butt without talking to Dara.

A door opened at the far end of the hall and several women walked out. Their style of dress was similar to the woman who'd let me in. They scrutinized me, their eyes lingering on my less than voluptuous body.

"You here to audition?" one asked. Another giggled.

A dozen lies scrambled through my head, but I told a version of the truth. "I'm looking for Dara."

"What you want? You ain't here on behalf of her sorry ex, are you?" The woman narrowed her eyes at me. Her dusky complexion shone nearly silver with the glitter she had smeared on her skin. At least I knew where Rae had picked up the habit.

"No. I have an appointment with her."

"Dara took off to Honolulu for two weeks without telling nobody. Got her ass fired for it." The girl who spoke up had cartoon heroine, big, blue eyes and pouty lips. All the other women turned and glared at her for giving me any information.

I slumped. So much for that.

"What you meeting Dara about?" The glitter-skinned girl raised her pencil thin eyebrows at me.

One of these girls might know something about Rae, but I didn't belong in their world. They'd join a convent and take a vow of silence before they helped me. Still, I had to try.

"Dara promised to help me get Rae's things out of her locker." I made this up on the spot. Maybe Rae left something here.

"Why don't Rae come get her own things?" The thickly accented words came from behind me. I turned and faced the tallest woman I'd ever seen and bit my lip to keep from smiling. She wore a Cleopatra getup, complete with the gold headdress and gold armbands.

Her question opened up two possibilities. I could tell them Rae quit and didn't want to show her face or tell the truth. I went with the truth because it left fewer reasons they could refuse me.

"She died." The hallway went still and silent.

"Whoa, whoa, wait a minute." The glitter-skinned girl held out a long fingered hand. "Rae's dead?"

"Murdered," I said.

"And who are you?" Glitter Girl asked.

"Peri Jean Mace. Her cousin."

They all nodded as though they knew my name. Dara had known who I was when we spoke on the phone. Had Rae made fun of me to these people? They seemed more interested than put off. Had she simply mentioned me in the natural course of conversation because I was part of her life? The idea hurt. In all the months Rae lived with us, I viewed her as an unwelcome intrusion. I never mentioned her name other than to complain about her. I dropped my head to stare at my feet as the overdressed girls watched me like a TV melodrama.

"Well, well, well. It all caught up with her, did it?" Glitter Girl shook her head. "Was it that crazy lady who came here to whup her ass?"

Veronica wanted to beat Rae up? So much for them

being friends. Why had Veronica been after Rae? I opened my mouth to ask, but couldn't get a word in over the din.

"No! That old horse-faced boyfriend of hers did her in." A girl who had been quiet grinned at her cleverness. Trollish laughter greeted her statement.

"I don't give a damn who did it," said Cleopatra. "Rae always mean to me. She call me Bratwurst Girl, and I am not German. I am Russian."

That explained the accent.

She looked down at me. "You don't have my makeup?"

So this was Maybelline whose missing makeup got me into this alternate universe. I shook my head.

"Shit!" Cleopatra-Maybelline slammed back into the dressing room.

I knew these women could tell me a lot. "Why was the other woman angry with Rae?"

They ignored me, whispering among themselves.

"You want the stuff out of Rae's locker?" Glitter Girl, who seemed to be the group's leader, had her hands on her hips.

"If you could help me, that would be great." I said.

"Two hundred dollars." She tipped up her chin in challenge.

"I don't have two hundred dollars." And I didn't. I had maybe another thirty.

"Well then, Peri Jean Mace," Glitter Girl tried out the name, "you are out of luck. I can't open that locker for less than, say, hundred-fifty."

"I don't have that either." This sucked. My gut said if I

had the two hundred, I could get anything out of these girls.

"Then we can't help you. This sounds like a po-lice matter, and you probably shouldn't be snooping in it at all."

The other girls murmured their agreement. They walked single file toward the pulsing music.

"Some of you have to have seen this guy." I pulled the copy of Rae's sketch from my pocket as the women pushed past me. None of them even looked at me. I tried again. "Maybe one of you knows where Dara lives?"

They kept walking. Great. All the way over here for nothing. The Nova gulped gas and cost a fortune to drive long distances. The dressing room door opened, and the Amazon who hated Rae peeped out.

"I give you tip. There's nothing in that locker. Come. I show you." She held open the door and motioned me inside.

———

THE DRESSING ROOM stank of sweat, hairspray, and desperation. The Amazon walked past a rolling clothes rack full of feathery outfits. Sure enough, a row of beat-up lockers lined one wall. I cheered my luck.

"That Keesha is scammer. She sell me movie she filmed in movie theater with her phone. Ten dollars!"

"What's your name?" I asked, realizing some of my mistake with Glitter Girl. I hadn't made it personal. The

Amazon smiled, revealing a mouth full of crooked, stained teeth. Not her best feature.

"Lloyd say my stage name is Maybelline. But my real name is Magdalene."

"Nice to meet you." We shook hands.

Magdalene swept her arm at the row of lockers. Only two had locks. I hoped Rae's was one of the locked ones. If not, this bunch would have taken whatever she had the first night she didn't show up to dance.

"If Rae had anything here is gone," she said. "But I am sure she took whatever she had with her the last night she worked."

"Why's that?" Disappointment jabbed my grinding gut. My luck sucked.

"If you want to lock up your things, you bring your own lock. And you take it all home at the end of night or Lloyd cut off lock and take what's inside." Magdalene pinched her face into a scowl and lowered her voice to imitate a man. "You leave it; you lose it."

So much for the locker idea. But now that I had Magdalene talking, she might answer the questions I'd hoped to ask Dara.

"Do you know anything about the woman Rae argued with or the boyfriend your co-workers mentioned?"

"Co-workers." Magdalene laughed. "The woman I never saw. But the man...he used to take all the girls out after closing. He had money."

I pulled the sketches out of my pocket again and unfolded them. "Do either of these look familiar to you?"

Magdalene took them. She frowned at the one I

thought to be of Low_Ryder and shook her head. She giggled at the one of the naked man and handed both back to me. "I am sorry, but no."

"Was the man who took all of you out young or old?"

"Neither. He was in middle. Homely. Big horse teeth. Rae call him BJ. But that not his name. Because she always had to call him twice before he answer."

This was good stuff.

"What about the biker guy?" Madgalene just looked puzzled, so I flashed the picture again.

"Never saw anybody like him. Sure not same as BJ. This BJ wore cowboy clothes. Like somebody on TV."

That only included about a third of Texas.

"Rae said this BJ was her ace in hole. She said she always had a plan B and C and D. And even E."

"Did she say what she hoped to achieve?"

Magdalene shrugged. "Something other than this, I guess."

"Do you know if she owed anybody money? Maybe they were trying to force her to pay?"

"Everybody here owes somebody money. Why else would you do this?"

I took a long look at Madgalene's getup. She had a point. Why would anybody subject herself to that for fun?

"What the blue blazes is going on here? Are you the girl who called earlier about an audition?" A bald-headed man with a perma-frown stomped into the dressing room. He wasn't much taller than I was and wore pressed jeans and a t-shirt the color of brains. I knew this must be the owner of the "you leave it; you lose it" edict.

"No. I came here to see Dara."

"I fired her." Baldy pointed at Magdalene. "You get back to work, or you're fired."

The poor woman click-clacked down the long hallway, wobbling a bit on her impossibly high heels. Baldy watched her go with a half-smile on his face. He turned back to me and looked me up and down. His face pinched into a disgusted scowl.

"I don't need to see you dance," he said. "You can't work here."

"But I'm here for—" I scrambled for an explanation, but Baldy grabbed the belt loop of my jeans in one hand and my arm in the other. He dragged me from the dressing room and back into the long hallway.

Only it was no longer empty. Dean Turgeau stood in it. He wore plain clothes but had his badge on his belt. As soon as he saw me, he began to laugh. His mirth stung, and I didn't fight much as Baldy shoved me out the fire exit. Relief came when the door slammed, cutting off Dean's guffaws.

What the hell was he doing there? I wondered if Sheriff Stick Up His Ass was down for a good time or on the same trail I was. Not that I cared about the first part. Oh, hell, who was I kidding? I was curious enough to get myself in trouble.

I drove home in silence. The radio would only pick up a scratchy recording of War's "Low Rider." Same song I kept hearing. Coincidence or interference from the spirit world? My mind sifted through the little I learned at The Chameleon.

The woman who threatened Rae had to be the same woman who showed up at Memaw's demanding access to the trailer. Veronica. She never did give me her last name.

I couldn't help comparing BJ to Benny Longstreet. Benny's odd response to Rae's sketchbook kept flitting around my mind. I wanted to fit him into the puzzle but had a hard time picturing him slumming with low rent strippers. Benny cultivated the image of a very religious man. He and his wife, both attendees of Michael Gage's church, involved themselves in all church activities, especially the ones involving charity work.

I didn't think all men cheated, but I thought anybody was capable of infidelity. And the churchgoers were no different than other folk. But if Benny were going to cheat on his wife, I wouldn't have picked Rae as his choice. He liked identifying himself as a rich person too much. The idea of him slumming just didn't work.

Wrapped up in my thoughts, I took no notice of the headlights hovering in my rearview mirror until the car moved in too close, flooding my car with blinding light. The road had narrowed to a two-lane highway a few miles back, and I hadn't passed another car for many miles. National forest bordered the road on both sides. I was alone with the jackass riding my bumper.

———

I CONSIDERED and rejected the idea it might be Chase. He would have flashed his lights or honked to get my attention. Besides, the vehicle behind me was a car, not a truck.

The other driver began a game of dropping back several feet and then racing forward to slam on his brakes right before he hit me. Maybe it was just a jerk who wanted to pass.

I let off the gas and slowed down, watching as the speedometer dropped to a ten-mile-per-hour crawl. The car, rather than blowing around me, simply stayed a few feet from my bumper. Fear fluttered in my belly and climbed up to my heart. My cheeks tingled with it.

I punched the gas, and my car surged forward. I leaned over the wheel as my speed picked up, glancing often into the rearview mirror. A sharp curve flew toward me. Maybe I could lose the car there. The yellow warning sign came into my vision and flashed past. I pushed hard on the accelerator. The car stayed right on my bumper.

This curve jogged right and then broke to the left. I took it, tires squealing. The other car never missed a trick and stayed right on my bumper. The sharp odor of my own sweat hit me. I couldn't win, not like this. I'd probably kill myself instead. Something had to change.

I rolled to a stop. The other car did the same. My heart slammed in my chest as I waited for something to happen. Nothing did. I put the car in park and waited, my hand trembling on the gearshift.

Just as I'd hoped, the door on the car behind me opened with a groan. I waited until I could see the silhouette of a person getting out. I popped the clutch, slammed the car into gear, and took off.

My car's engine screamed as I pushed it the last few miles to Memaw's house. Headlights appeared in my rearview mirror. I didn't dare try to fumble with my cellphone. The only thing I knew to do was get home and get inside. Once there, I could call Dean Turgeau. To hell with the humiliating scene at The Chameleon.

I barely slowed enough to make the sharp turn into Memaw's driveway. Those few seconds allowed my tormentor to catch up. It blew past, never slowing. That's when I recognized the black GTO. Dizziness numbed my lips, and I barely controlled the car enough to pull into the carport. I stood in the yard for a second, listening for the engine to turn around and come back. It simply faded into the distance.

I called Dean's cellphone and got no answer. He couldn't have done much anyway. I didn't see the license plate or know who owned the car. Needing someone to know what happened, I called Chase. He didn't answer either. I hung up without leaving a message.

12

SATURDAY CAME, and with it Rae's memorial service. Housecleaning kept Memaw and me busy most of the morning. I dodged her questions about the previous night's activities. She gave me a suspicious frown but didn't press.

Around noon, ladies from church arrived with long tables and folding chairs. After they made it clear my help was not needed, I wandered outside to be alone with my cigarettes and my thoughts.

Rae's death reminded me my life ought to mean more. In the seven years since my divorce and moving back in with Memaw, I filled my life with busywork. Now, I had a harder time ignoring the emptiness. Problem was, the right ingredient to fill the void kept escaping me.

The right ingredient didn't seem to be a man. They were entertaining enough. Once that part was over, the uncomfortable silence descended and I always found a reason to cut things off. Children sounded great, but I didn't want to do it alone. It was a vicious cycle.

I liked having my own business but didn't consider what I did especially important. It paid a little money and suited me better than working for someone else.

Seeing the spirit world and feeling the emotions of its inhabitants crippled me. I hated the imposition of the dead. No matter where I went, they climbed all over me, wanting and needing. The expectation from the living that I keep it to myself pushed at me from the other side. Both sides trapped and tortured me. It ground away at my emotions until I wanted to scream. But I couldn't because that might upset Memaw.

I lived as though in waiting for something. I made no commitments. I had nothing I couldn't walk away from. Perhaps some unsung part of me hoped I'd get a do-over. With Rae dead, I knew I wouldn't.

Gravel crunched and cut off my thoughts as a Burns County Sheriff's cruiser rolled down the driveway and parked. Dean Turgeau slid out and stretched. Brittany Watson, the youngest member of the Burns County Sheriff's Office, got out of the passenger side. She looked like a proud kid playing dress up in her uniform. I strode to Brittany, hugged her, and thanked her for coming.

Dean's intense gaze followed my actions, but he didn't speak or otherwise acknowledge me.

"Why didn't you answer my call last night? I could have had an emergency." I wasn't about to let him get away with ignoring me. "And who the hell invited you to my cousin's memorial service?"

Dean took a deep breath to speak, but Brittany broke in.

"We're here to see who shows up. Dean says sometimes the murderer comes to the funeral."

Dean shot her a death glare. The poor kid wilted. It pissed me off, and I had a bone to pick with Deputy Dean anyway.

"As for who invited me, your grandmother did." Dean took in my black dress and high heels. His eyes lingered on my legs. "I didn't answer your call last night because I was too sick of you meddling in my investigation to mess with you, and I figured you had sense enough to call 911 if you had a real emergency."

His zinger heated my anger, but I didn't have a good comeback. He was right. I should have just called 911, but the idea of Joey Holze knowing I had called for help had been too much for my pride.

"Judging from what I saw last night, I'm guessing they didn't hire you for your cousin's old job."

"I bet I found out more than you did." I wanted to add an insult but didn't.

"I doubt that," he said. "Stay out of my case. Or I'll think of some reason to arrest you."

"I've got a question for you, Deputy Turgeau."

"Why not ask your crystal ball? Isn't that what psychics do? Or do they just scam people and lie to them?" He crossed his arms. I couldn't help but notice how his biceps flexed and his pecs bunched underneath the khaki uniform shirt. Where was the man who kept me from falling down at the sheriff's office?

Brittany winced and gave me a sympathetic glance. I shrugged and shook my head to let her know it was okay. Turgeau wanted to play hot and cold. Fine. I could do it, too. We'd either have some really hot sex or get into a public fistfight. Either one was fine with me.

Dean tried to stare me down. When that didn't work, he developed a sudden interest in his highly polished shoes. "Go on and ask."

"What the hell did I ever do to you?"

"You tell the truth when it suits you. You lie when it suits you." Dean ticked off his points on his fingers. "You go around doing whatever you please without caring it could derail my investigation and jeopardize my job. And I suspect you lie about having psychic abilities to get attention."

So, he wanted to throw down, did he? "Your public relations skills suck, Deputy Dean. A bug in this red dirt out here has more detective skills than you." The man's face went slack with shock. "No wonder they ran your sour ass out of South Louisiana. Too bad we ended up with you."

Brittany gasped, and I winked at her. Turgeau's mouth moved, but no sound came out.

"Y'all take care now, and thanks for coming." I walked to the house without a backward glance. Had I turned, Dean would have seen my smile. Two could play at this game.

———

A QUIET CORNER of the living room provided a hiding place where I could observe and not be easily noticed. Turgeau wasn't the only one who had a responsibility to Rae. I wanted to find her killer too. Speaking of the devil, Rae hadn't made her appearance yet. No doubt she would, most likely at the wrong moment.

Guests trickled in, and I put Rae out of my mind. We set the inexpensive urn holding Rae's ashes and a recent, framed snapshot of her on an accent table near the door. Even with the hard lines already forming around her eyes, she'd been stunning in a platinum bombshell way. Most of our guests stopped and took a good, long look at the guest of honor. I watched them with interest. Most of them had never even spoken to Rae.

Our little living room filled quickly. The church ladies had moved Memaw's well-worn furniture to the room's edges and set out metal folding chairs with "Gaslight City First Baptist" written in black marker on their backs. Those chairs were all taken. Even more people lined the walls.

Either a lot of people wanted to pay their last respects to Rae, or they didn't want to miss a good show. When most folks had a plate of finger food and a plastic cup filled with a soft drink or iced tea, Memaw stood and rang a little bell to get their attention. She spoke in her schoolteacher voice. "Pastor Michael Gage will say a few words."

Gage took center stage near Rae's urn. Despite the casual setting, he wore a three-piece suit. It looked expensive and fell just so on his neat, wiry frame. His olive skin glowed with good health, and his salt and pepper hair was neatly clipped.

He gave me a quick glance. The fury that scared me the day I cleaned Mace House was gone. Only his usual interest remained. I inclined my head to him. I had checked the phony email account that morning. No response from Jerry Bower. *Maybe he decided to ignore me.*

Despite his lack of romantic appeal, Gage knew how to speak to a crowd. Everyone listened in rapt silence as he talked about how none of us knew when the end was coming. He claimed the only defense was to have our spiritual houses in order. I watched the guests while Gage talked, thinking about what Brittany Watson said. Was a murderer in our midst?

Darren and Jolene Fischer stood close together. Chase's absence tore at my emotions. He should have been there saying goodbye to Rae, even though he hadn't loved her. A steady stream of tears flowed down Jolene's cheeks. Darren kept his eyes straight ahead and his arm around his wife.

Across the room, Deputy Dean Turgeau watched the elder Fischers too. It didn't escape my notice Hannah Kessler stood right next to him. He frowned at me when our gazes met. I frowned right back and curled my lip in a snarl. Hannah Kessler's eyes widened, and she quickly glanced away.

Benny Longstreet's antics caught my attention more than once. As head deacon at Gaslight City First Baptist, he considered himself Pastor Gage's right-hand man. Today, Benny showed his support in the form of enthusiastic nods and constant "amens." It disrupted the quiet service. Eddie Kennedy finally asked him—not very quietly—to shut up.

"I had many a conversation with Miss Rae Mace about the way her life turned out." Gage's perfectly modulated voice caught my attention. "She said repeatedly she just didn't know what to do."

He paused dramatically and looked down at his Bible. "The answer I gave her, and the one I'll give you all today, is to turn your lives over to our Lord, Jesus Christ."

Rae never made a show of attending Sunday services. When had she had all these deep conversations with Pastor Michael Gage? Why hadn't he mentioned it when I tried to talk to him about Rae's murder? Maybe I would change my mind about that date and pump him for information. And maybe I'd win the lottery.

Memaw stood at the front of the room again. Her eyes were wet and red, but she held up well. "An old friend of Rae's will now play a song in her memory. This will mark the end of the service."

People shifted, growing impatient, but I sat up straighter. Old friend? This was the first I'd heard about anybody playing music. Hannah Kessler strode to the front of the living room carrying an acoustic guitar. *Oh, boy. This ought to be special.*

Hannah strummed her guitar a few times and looked straight at me. A flush heated my face.

"When I was a kid," she said, "I loved to play with Rae and Peri Jean. We listened to old records and sang along to them. Rae liked to sing 'Midnight Rider.' Let's see if I can do it some justice."

Hannah's guitar picking turned purposeful. She sang the song slow, her voice a mournful moan. She was good.

The finality of it all hit me with those words about the road going on forever. Rae had reached the end of her road. I bowed my head and let the tears drip off my face.

A white handkerchief found its way into my hand. I glanced up and found Dean Turgeau standing next to me. As soon as I took the hanky, he gave my shoulder a quick pat and walked away. I sobbed into the soft cloth, feeling the heat of a couple dozen stares boring down on me. I hunched my shoulders and tried to make myself as small as possible. I'd analyze Dean's giving me his hanky later.

The service ended with the last notes of "Midnight Rider." Our guests milled toward the front door chatting. Embarrassment over publicly grieving kept me rooted to my spot in the corner.

Something tugged at my hair, and I turned to find Rae next to me. *No. Not right now.* I rose to flee, saw who stood beside me, and let out a little shriek.

"Hi, sweetheart." Barbara, the woman who gave birth to me, wrapped me in a stiff, perfumed hug.

———

BARBARA RELEASED me and inched toward her husband. Their faces morphed into vapid grins, and they clasped their hands together. My mother had cut her long brown hair short, and the color was too rich not to be hiding some gray. Her lilac pantsuit looked like it came out of a magazine. She might have little padding at her bust and hips, but she still had her figure.

"I appreciate you being here, Barbara." My back bumped the wall. Nowhere to run.

"It's nothing." Barbara's gaze darted to Memaw, who had her back to us as she said goodbye to the Longstreet clan. Memaw turned, probably feeling our eyes on her. She didn't react to my mother's presence. She'd known Barbara was coming.

"Do you realize you're developing a frown line between your eyes?" For Barbara, this was an attempt to bond.

I wished for someone—anyone—else to talk to. Right then, I would have welcomed even Hannah Kessler's company. Nobody so much as glanced in our direction. Our trio was invisible to the other guests. Where had Eddie Kennedy gone?

Good thing I wasn't paying attention to Barbara. If I did, I might not have seen the armoire tipping toward my mother and stepfather. I shoved Barbara aside, ignoring her angry protest, and caught the armoire before it gained enough momentum to fall. The cold wood burned my hand. I wrangled it back into place and peeked behind it.

Sure enough, Rae stood there. Anger radiated from her in waves. It mingled with mine, giving her the power she needed to kick up a fuss. She couldn't have picked a worse time for this crap. Our tangled emotions chilled the air, and Rae's energy slammed into me, driving me backward. She'd used my energy against me.

I stumbled back and stepped on my mother's toe. She

swore. I turned to face her, an apology on my lips. What I saw there killed my apology.

Mommy dearest stared at me, her lip curled in distaste. She might not know exactly what I'd seen, but understood the gist. What she hated about me all my life had reared its head before she'd been in my presence for five minutes.

"Maybe your grandmother needs to have the house leveled." Ron the artist acted oblivious to the tension running between his wife and me.

Ron had a head of thick silver hair and a big belly. He wore an expensive looking butter colored shirt and tan trousers. His shoes looked soft enough to sleep in. On one wrist, he wore a heavy gold bracelet.

"It's cold in here too." Ron frowned and rubbed his arms now that he had my full attention. "Maybe Mrs. Mace needs to have a carpenter come in and give the place a good going over."

A little wave of humiliation rekindled my anger at the situation. Memaw and I didn't have the money to hire a carpenter and didn't need one anyway. I itched to tell rich stepdad Ron where to get off. An arm slipped around my waist. I halted my angry words.

"Thank you so much for joining us, Barbie." Memaw was a tiny woman, even shorter than me. Right then, she stood as tall as a giant.

"I go by Barb or Barbara now, Leticia." Barbara bared her teeth in imitation of a smile, a crocodile facing a lioness at the watering hole.

Rae fed off our blustery emotions, her spectral form flickering in and out of my sight. She appeared behind

Barb and Ron. Malice radiated from her translucent form. I wished her away, which did absolutely no good.

Barbara broke the staring contest with Memaw and strolled around the living room. She paused at an old picture of herself and my father from before they got married. She'd been pregnant with me, but hadn't known it yet. She traced the faces in the picture and glanced back at me. The picture popped off its shelf and plunged to the floor. The glass broke and went everywhere. Barbara shrieked and jumped back.

I tried to leave the room to get the broom and dustpan, but Memaw beat me to it. That old woman moved fast when she didn't want to be somewhere. *Why had she browbeaten Barbara into coming here? Surely, she knew it would end like this.*

"Are you seeing anyone, Peri Jean?" Barbara relaxed a little as Memaw left the room. "I saw that man give you his hanky. He's very good looking."

"He's investigating Rae's murder." I didn't comment on Dean's looks. It irked me that Barbara found him attractive too. I didn't want to share the same taste in men with her.

"Do they have any ideas on who did it?"

"They've searched Chase Fischer's mobile home." In response to Barbara's confused expression, I clarified. "Rae and Chase were seeing one another."

"It's usually the husband or a boyfriend." Ron spoke with all the authority of a true crime television addict.

"Well, you never know. The curse of the famed Mace lost fortune might have gotten her." One corner of Barbara's mouth raised in a vicious smirk.

I thought the lost Mace fortune was hogwash, too, but I stiffened at Barbara's snotty dismissal of it. "A lot of people still believe it's out there. They did a TV documentary about it."

"Your father and his brother certainly believed it. They believed it enough for Jesse to kill Paul—" Barbara shut up as Memaw hustled back into the living room carrying a broom and dustpan.

"Jesse did not kill Paul. My sons loved each other." Memaw faced Barbara. The eight inches height difference didn't matter.

Barbara stiffened and widened her eyes. Ron made a study of the old hardwood floor. Memaw and Barbara engaged in another staring contest. Memaw ended this one, turning her back on Barbara.

"It's been a long day for me, Peri Jean. I'm going to my room." Memaw's footfalls thumped down the hall, and she slammed her bedroom door hard enough to rattle the pictures hanging in the hallway.

Barb's neck had broken out in red blotches. She raised a shaking hand to smooth her perfect hair. A wave of longing hit me as I watched her. I wanted her to look at me with pride and love in her eyes. But that would never happen. She saw me as something that embarrassed her and held her back. I held my palm over my chest as though that had the power to soothe the ache there. My desire for her to leave clashed with my wish for another chance to win her love.

"Nobody's ever found the first clue to the treasure anyway."

"You don't know about the one in your family Bible?" Barbara's own frown line appeared between her eyebrows. Just like mine. "You're the only Mace who doesn't then."

Ron eased up behind my mother and slipped his arm around her waist. He spoke into her hair. "We need to get going, Barb."

"Let me show you." Barbara elbowed Ron away and marched to the bookcase where she pulled out our ancient family Bible. She peeled back the inner cover.

I yelped and reached out to stop her. Memaw would be furious if I let Barbara tear up a family heirloom. Barbara gave me a fierce hiss, and I dropped my hands. She shoved the Bible at me. The inner cover hid an ink drawing of four slim drawers with tiny pull knobs. My heart leaped with a giddy, but foreign excitement. Was this the treasure fever I heard about all my life?

"I don't get it," I said.

"Neither did your father." Bitterness puckered Barbara's cool, attractive features and aged her about fifteen years. "They searched and searched for a piece of furniture with a secret compartment in it."

"I don't remember my father having treasure fever." I tried to recall his voice, the way he smelled. Nothing came. My only memories of him were from pictures. His life was just as big a mystery to me as his death. Uncle Jesse still claimed he didn't kill his brother.

"Ask Eddie Kennedy if he's still around here." Barbara hugged herself. "Those three used to get together with Adam Kessler and talk treasure all night. I'm surprised Paul found time to knock me up. Of course, the curse of the Mace Treasure got both him and Jesse just like it did your grandfather. This supposed treasure sure is hell on your family."

"Barbie, it's time for you to go back where you came from." Memaw stood at the end of the hallway wearing her fuzzy robe, fists on her hips. Barbara shrank under Memaw's burning stare. That wild mix of emotions ran through me again. I wanted to fix everything so maybe my mother would decide she liked me. I loved Memaw for standing up for me. I wished Barbara and Ron the artist had stayed home.

Barbara and Ron left without saying another word. They just got into their rented Mustang and drove away. I saw the relieved look on Barbara's face through its window. She didn't even wave as they drove down the driveway.

Tears stung my eyes as I watched my mother leave. I wished I'd told her I loved her just to see what she said.

I went back to the bookcase to put the Bible away. A little sparkle caught my eye. I rubbed on the cover and examined my finger. Glitter covered it. I had cleaned Rae's glitter off the bookcase in my cleaning fit but apparently missed the Bible.

Rae must have known about the drawing in the Bible. That and the list I found in the barn hinted her treasure hunt entailed more than just talk. Hannah must have given her some information. Rae's possession of Hannah's business card suggested that much. But who else had information about the treasure?

One name came to mind: Eddie Kennedy.

13

I TREKKED all over looking for Eddie Kennedy. He usually separated himself from the herd and stood off to the side, watching people.

Eddie'd been my father's best friend. The two of them, along with Adam Kessler, Hannah's father, went through school together and remained friends as adults.

After my daddy's death, Eddie tried his best to be there for me. Problem was, Eddie could barely be there for himself. He suffered from bad luck with jobs, bad luck with women, and bad judgment in general. He did two things well: made things with wheels go and built exquisite items ranging from antique replica furniture to horse-drawn carriages.

I couldn't believe I had forgotten—or never knew—about Eddie and my father hunting the treasure. Had hunting the treasure caused Eddie's bad luck? An accomplished athlete in high school, a car wreck his senior year exempted him from any scholarships. That kicked off a string of choices that always ended with him getting the short end of the stick.

I loved Eddie like family. He taught me how to throw a punch and how to lift things without hurting my back. Things my daddy might have taught me had he lived to do it.

I ended my circuit of his favorite hiding places with the conclusion he'd gone home. I changed into some beat up clothes, sent him a text message, and drove to his house—a mobile home on two acres.

My text to Eddie claimed I needed him to look at my Nova, which was making a funny sound. The truth was I wanted to ask him about Barbara's revelations regarding the treasure. Now that I knew Eddie'd been interested in the Mace Treasure, Rae's interest in the treasure plus her death equaled one too many coincidences for me to stick my head in the sand. Deputy Dean had no interest in looking into this aspect of the case. I'd just have to pick up his slack.

"What's wrong with this thing, munchkin, is it's about wore out." Eddie's big butt stuck out from under my Nova's hood.

"You can't fix it?" Eddie's bulk kept me from seeing much. He backed away from my car and straightened to his full six foot six inches and glowered down at me.

"Can a dog lick his balls?"

I glanced at Eddie's one-eyed, one-eared, three-legged dog named Ugly. He gave me a big doggie grin. I shrugged.

"'Course I can fix your car." Eddie shut my hood.

"Won't be cheap. You gonna have to buy a new alternator, and soon, munchkin."

"You're kidding." I never expected such a grim diagnosis.

Eddie scowled at me. He never kidded about cars, especially not my father's old Nova. He took keeping it in running condition seriously.

"Can I ask you a question on an unrelated matter?"

"Can I tell you to kiss my fat ass if I ain't interested in answering?" Eddie washed his hands in a filthy sink and wiped them on an even filthier shop towel.

"Do you think Rae was looking for the treasure?" I held my breath. Eddie discouraged questions about my daddy and the past. I hoped this didn't qualify. Otherwise, it could irritate him enough to kick me off his property.

Without a word, Eddie turned and exited his shop. I jogged to keep up with him as he crossed his yard in a few long strides. Eddie came to an abrupt stop in front of his vintage early eighties mobile home.

"I'm having a beer. You want water or juice?" He needed a beer to answer me. That meant he knew at least some of Rae's activities during her final days.

"Water's fine." The demon of self-doubt begged me to tell him to forget it. Eddie refused to interview for the TV documentary about the Mace Treasure. His appearance on the film consisted of a brief clip of him saying that part of his life ended with his best friend's death. This little interview could turn to shit on a dime and leave me right back where I started. But it might go the other way, too, and that convinced me to go through with it.

My usual lawn chair groaned as I sat down in it. Ugly ran to me and put his head in my lap. I scratched his one ear absently. I had my theories about Eddie's silence on the treasure. Most of them tied in with his refusal to talk about my father's murder. Why had he broken his silence for Rae?

Eddie returned holding a bottled water and a six-pack of tall boys. He passed me the water and sat down in his own lawn chair, one he'd constructed out of heavy metal to withstand his bulk. Ugly immediately disregarded me and ran to his owner.

"Why you want to know this?" Eddie held a sheaf of paper in one huge mitt. The beer hissed as he cracked it open, and the smell of yeast hit me.

I started with Rae asking me about the treasure the day she died, then told him about the auction list I'd found in the barn and what Barbara showed me in the family Bible. Eddie snorted and cursed under his breath. His words sounded a lot like "stupid bitch." I pretended not to hear. Getting him started on Barbara would only keep me from learning what I wanted to know.

"What I'm about to tell you would put me in the doghouse with your grandmother on account of your granddaddy dying while looking for the treasure and on account of the trouble between your daddy and your uncle." Eddie's expression was more severe than I'd ever seen. "Only reason I'm telling you is I don't want you snooping around on your own. This is serious business."

"What's serious business? Memaw always said the treasure was just a bunch of malarkey. She thinks crazy old Reginald Mace burned his money and forgot about it."

"That might be so. But he hid some things around here, and I don't want you trying to find none of them. Now, if Leticia finds out I told you any of this, I'm gonna kick your ass."

Eddie had always treated me like a favored niece. This seriousness went against his grain. My curiosity pulled at me, stronger than quicksand. I'd promise anything to hear what Eddie had to say.

―――――

"YOUR COUSIN COME by here first week she got outta the pen." Eddie paused to light a cigarette while I mentally reeled. Rae spent the final eight months of her life looking for the treasure, and I never knew.

"She remembered her daddy and me and Paul looking for treasure." Eddie stopped speaking and regarded me with his head cocked to one side. "Don't you remember none of that?"

I shook my head.

"Well, Rae did. She musta paid better attention than you." Eddie grinned. "She said she could pay to learn what I knew."

"Did she? Pay you?"

"Naw. Told her I didn't want her money and didn't want to talk about that old shit." Eddie drained his beer and cracked open another one.

"So how did she convince you?" I could only imagine the ways Rae tried to manipulate poor Eddie.

Eddie pressed his lips together and fidgeted. "Let's just say she knew some things I thought nobody did and leave it there. That girl collected information like some people collect antiques."

"I don't understand. Did she threaten you?" I remembered the blackmail note from the barn.

"I ain't gonna tell you. Ain't safe for you to know what she knew." He scrubbed a hand over his face. "She knew too much. I think the wrong person found out."

Eddie's pained expression warned me against asking more. He'd told me all he would. Begging would only make him clam up.

"So what's that?" I pointed at the papers in his hand.

"Paul and I bought a trunk of old papers from Joey Holze's daddy—remember Big Joe? —at a garage sale. The trunk and the papers was supposedly part of the Mace estate." Eddie leaned forward and handed me the papers. Mostly copies, they consisted of scribbles, doodles, and some faded drawings.

"See them plans?" Eddie cracked open his third beer. I leafed through the papers again and decided he meant the drawings. I picked them from the pile and squinted at them.

"Reginald Mace was an architect. The man loved secret drawers, hidey-holes, all that stuff. Now what you got there is a set of plans for some kind of chest with a secret compartment in it. Paul, Jesse, and I figured it was the same secret drawers from the drawing in the family Bible."

"How did the Holzes end up having the chest that had these papers in it?"

"Hell if I know. The Mace House's furnishings got sold at county auction to pay back taxes in the year 1906. I suggested Rae see if she could find the county records. Figure out what was sold and who might have it."

"Which she must have done," I said, thinking of the list of items I found in the barn. "She had a writing slope, a chest, and a desk highlighted. Think it was any of those?"

"Probably." Eddie smiled, a little proudly I thought. "Now, I'm gonna tell you what I told her. Leave it be. Nobody will ever find anything but bad luck and sorrow wrapped up with that treasure."

"I don't want the treasure. I want to find out who killed Rae and why. The sheriff's department is looking for Chase." I didn't mention Rae's ghost haunting me. It exhausted me just to think about that part.

"Don't matter. Once you get to messing around with that treasure, it's like something knows."

"So you think the curse is real?"

Eddie didn't speak, but, instead, handed me a lone sheet of paper. It was a copy of a newspaper article from the late 1800s. The headline read:

Eccentric Philanthropist Saves Child

I scanned the article. It documented Reginald Mace saving a deaf boy from being run down by a horse-drawn carriage. I looked up at Eddie and shook my head.

"When I was serious about finding the treasure, I got ahold of some diaries talking about that incident. People stood all around watching the carriage bearing down on the boy. They was gonna let it kill him. Reginald was the only one who acted."

"Why wouldn't anybody help him?"

"Nobody wanted to help the boy because his mother, Priscilla Herrera, was thought to be a witch. Some accounts say she might'a been an Indian, some say a Cajun. All accounts agree she was a real old woman who married a real young Spaniard. A year after her marriage, she bore him a son. People thought she'd used witchcraft to attract the Spaniard and to bear a child at her age." Eddie belched. He didn't have to say excuse me. We were family.

"What does this have to do with the treasure?"

"Priscilla and Reginald struck up a friendship. One of them old diaries I read belonged to a judge from the time. He threatened to arrest Priscilla for witchcraft, and Reginald paid him to lay off. He speculated Reginald wanted Priscilla to use witchcraft to bring William back, and when she couldn't, Reginald got her to curse the treasure so nobody could have it."

Neither Eddie nor I spoke for several minutes. I didn't understand how this connected with Rae's murder. Eddie's words about Rae knowing too much echoed in my mind.

"Now you listen real careful, Peri Jean Mace." Eddie leaned close to me, so close his sour, beer breath almost choked me. "Somebody murdered your cousin, and he's still walking among us. If it was over this treasure, it ain't no wonder she come to a bad end with the curse and all. But it might not have been the treasure. You go to poking around"—he squeezed my arm for emphasis—"no telling what kind of wasp's nest you'll stir up."

I thought about Rae lying dead on the travel trailer's fold-out table. She'd sure poked the wrong wasp's nest.

———

I CAME home to a dark and empty house. A note from Memaw lay on the kitchen table.

"Baby, I went to visit Phyllis McNichols. Just needed to get out of the house."

Memaw's going anywhere after the trauma of Rae's memorial service surprised me. I figured she'd hole up in her room and spend the evening alone. That's what I intended to do.

My cellphone had locked up again, so I plugged it into the wall charger to restart it. What I saw shocked me. *Ten missed calls? Three voicemails? What the hell?*

All the calls and the voice mails were from Chase Fischer. I let out a frustrated yell. The one person I needed to talk to, and my phone acted up.

The first call came in about the time I pondered whether Ugly could lick his balls. The last call had been less than fifteen minutes ago. I bared my teeth at the phone. *Useless thing.* Soon as I could afford a new one, I'd trash it.

I accessed my voicemail. Chase's first message played.

"Hey, girl. Chase here. Listen, I got me an idea for finding this Low_Ryder guy. I need your help. Call me when you get this."

I paced the floor as the robotic female voice told me a bunch of useless stuff. My heart thundered so loud I barely heard it. Just as the tension reached an unbearable level, the second message played. Music blared over the tinny speaker. I held the phone away from my ear. Clinking and rattling noises garbled most of Chase's message. All I understood was, "Peri . . . shit. Guess you're busy . . . if you get this, meet me at . . . "

The robotic female talked again as my mind raced merrily along, showing me horrible things. Finally, the third message played. The music was gone. Chase was somewhere outside, judging by wind whistling over the speaker.

"Chase again. I can't believe I keep missing you. Remember when we used to go out to the old sawmill ruins? I need you to come out here."

Chase paused, and another voice spoke in the background. Chase said, "Hey. What you doing out here?"

The message ended.

My crappy cellphone chugged through the process of dialing Chase. The call went straight to voicemail. My scalp tickled as sweat broke out on it. The smell of my own nervousness filled my senses. Something wasn't right. I needed to find Chase. Right then.

On the way out the door, I remembered the sketchbook. If I saw Chase, he could look at the sketch and confirm he saw that man with Rae. I ran back to my room and grabbed it.

———

THE SUN SAT low in the sky when I sped down the driveway. The Nova ate up the three miles to Beulah Church Road. From there, I turned onto a red dirt road, marked only by a "No Trespassing" sign nailed to a pine tree. Nobody ever paid attention to that sign. The sawmill ruins had long been a place where kids went to party and do other stuff.

I turned onto the narrow road and slowed to a crawl. Branches scraped at my paint job, making a toe-curling squeal. My car hopscotched over deep potholes. If I bottomed out on a tall rock, Eddie would kill me. The red dirt road dead-ended after a quarter mile. I walked the rest of the way on a footpath through the woods.

By the light of my huge metal flashlight, I cut through the well-worn trail leading into the rapidly darkening woods. The ruins sat only a few hundred yards into the pines. Underneath the canopy of trees, darkness had already fallen. The astringent perfume of pine blended with the odor of rotting leaves. Shapes and shadows mingled in shades of silvery gray.

The deserted sawmill town appeared amidst the thick forest as though beamed there. At first, a few flashes of white, concrete buildings peeked out between trees. Then, without warning, the town rose in all its weird glory like a monster rising out of a still lake. Even though I knew what to expect, I stopped for a moment to stare in wonder.

The sawmill ruins consisted of three concrete shells that had once been buildings. Kids partied in the old shell that only had three sides and no roof. The other two shells had four sides and roofs.

I couldn't imagine why Chase would enter the darkness of the four-sided shells, so I went directly to the three-sided one. Light from the dying sunset filtered in and cast the whole place in a glowing orange. Empty.

"Chase?" My voice startled some roosting birds, which cried out and flew off, their batting wings the only noise in the darkening forest. The quiet closed in on me. Fear of the woods, the dark, and what else might be out here caused me to stumble as I walked around the site calling Chase's name.

Calls to Chase's cellphone went unanswered. Panic tightened my throat. Chase wouldn't just flake out of meeting me. He tended not to take life seriously enough, but this was different.

As I walked around, my pace got faster and faster until I jogged, my blood pounding in my head. The palm of my right hand ached, my fingertips numb. I opened my hand and saw I'd gripped my keys so tightly they indented my skin. I slipped my keys into my pocket and took deep breaths to calm down.

There was no use in this. I would go back to Memaw's house and wait for Chase's call. As I walked back to my car, I tripped on a branch and crashed to my knees. My hands took the impact of my fall and made a squishing noise on the leaf-covered ground. Realizing I'd landed in something wet, I jerked backward. Too late, I turned on my flashlight.

Red smudged the palms of my hands. Blood. Fear brightened and narrowed my vision. A flash of light flared behind my eyes, and a blast shook me and made my ears ring. I whipped my head around, but saw nothing and no one. Far as I tell, I was alone. I struggled to my feet and stood on my shaking legs, breathing hard. Maybe I was going crazy.

"Chase?" My voice echoed back, and I realized it was stupid to keep calling him. If the blood belonged to him, he probably couldn't answer. Around the corner of the building farthest from my car, I spotted a shape lying on the ground.

"No," I moaned. The flashlight spotlighted a hump of brown-gray fur. As I drew closer, the oblong head came into view. A dead deer. Some shithead had killed the deer, cut off the tender back strap meat, and just left the carcass to rot. Anger boiled inside me. It must have been where the blood came from. The vision of the deer's last moments would haunt me for a while. Sometimes animals left behind a powerful presence.

I turned one last slow circle and admitted to myself that Chase was gone. He'd left with whomever—probably somebody like Tubby Tubman—he'd run into out here. I trudged back toward my old Nova, mentally shaking my head at Chase. Facing murder charges, he'd gone off to party.

Something crunched underfoot, and I shined the flashlight onto the leaves, expecting another grisly surprise. Gold flashed in the flashlight's beam. I picked the object from the leaves. A matchbook.

The purple matchbook bore the words "Long Time Gone" in gold foil. A honky-tonk situated on the western edge of Burns County, Long Time Gone had a reputation as a rough place. Rumors claimed an outlaw biker gang ran contraband through it.

The second message from Chase had music playing in the background. I got out my phone. After a short struggle with the failing piece of technology, I replayed Chase's message.

I heard music, all right. Behind it, I identified the clack of pool balls and the tinkle of glass. Perhaps Chase and whomever he left with had gone back to Long Time Gone. He probably couldn't hear his cellphone because he was playing pool and getting a little drunk. I'd go find him and give him hell.

Long Time Gone wasn't a regular hangout for me, but there was a first time for everything. Using the remainder of a bottled water and some tissues, I cleaned the blood off my hands. Disgusting. My rearview mirror showed my hair sticking up. I found a trial size container of gel, squeezed a little in the palm of my hand and scrunched my short hair. If my luck was in, the mess looked stylish. I studied my outfit and grimaced. I wore a faded t-shirt with a frayed collar. My blue jeans had a rip in the knee, and my beat up cowboy boots dated back to the seventies.

Oh, well. The fashion police didn't patrol Long Time Gone. The arduous process of getting turned around and driving out of the woods earned the Nova a few deep gouges in its paint. Glad to get out of that creepy place, I almost didn't care. Almost.

14

Long Time Gone was housed in a long, low, plywood building with a wooden deck hanging off one side. It sat on a small lot cut out of the dense, longleaf pine forest covering western Burns County.

On a Saturday night, vehicles of every kind jammed the parking lot. A long line of classic muscle cars took up the parking lot's outer edge. There must have been truth to the rumors about drag racing out here.

Bikers hung out on the deck, yelling at each other, maybe due to the lasting effects of their loud pipes. They all stopped what they were doing to watch me, the newcomer, park my Nova and walk across the parking lot. When I got close, a guy wearing leather from head to toe hollered he'd buy me a drink. I pretended not to hear, and his friends jeered at him.

The heavy wooden door put up a struggle, much to the bikers' amusement. Their catcalls provided the incentive for me to muscle my way inside. The interior of Long

Time Gone hid under a haze of cigarette smoke. Politically correct no-smoking laws hadn't reached this deep into the piney woods of East Texas—thank the powers that be. I dug for my cigarettes and lit up one of the little demons. A live band played classic rock rather poorly somewhere in the smoke. Raucous shouts and thundering games of pool punctuated the music, almost keeping a beat.

"It's a five-dollar cover charge for the band." The doorman emerged from the smoke and towered over me. Tall, muscular, and intimidating, this man looked like forty miles of rough asphalt.

Between the bushy black beard obscuring his lower face and the wild tangle of his shoulder-length black hair, he fit every stereotype appropriate to the situation. I dug a crumpled five-dollar bill out of my pocket and shoved it at him.

"Lemme stamp your hand." He snatched my wrist and pressed a rubber stamp to the back of my hand. Tattoos covered his arm so completely the skin art merged into one big tattoo. It showed a naked tree, a wise owl, and the silhouettes of ravens.

I stared. I had tattoos, including a raven of my own, but nothing like this. Something so huge impressed me but also made me curious. Each of my tattoos meant something. I wondered what such an elaborate tattoo meant to this hulk of a man. The symbolism intrigued me. Under different circumstances, I might have offered to buy him a drink and let him tell me the story of it.

"Took me a year to get the sleeve. Big Billy Bob's Ink in

Arlington did 'em." He flashed a surprisingly even and white grin. "Didn't hurt a bit."

"I bet that's a lie, but it's good work." We shared a laugh. He appealed to me for all the usual reasons. For once, I didn't feel like acting on it.

"You have a good time, baby doll." He winked and dismissed me.

I skirted the perimeter of Long Time Gone. Chase was nowhere to be found in the throng of merrymakers. The doorman might have been able to tell me if Chase was there, but he'd already returned to a game of darts with a bunch of giggling, pierced girls. No way would I interrupt.

I dug in my bag until I found a snapshot of Chase and me posing in front of a tattoo parlor on Sixth Street in Austin. Armed with it, I pushed through perspiring bodies until I reached the bar. By the time I got there, sweat glued my clothes to my skin and ran down the back of my neck. The place was an oven.

The bartender might have been thirty or ninety. She had a bush of salt and pepper hair, a beaky, porous nose, and displayed wrinkled, sun-damaged cleavage over a black leather halter-top.

"What can I get you?" Her voice somehow rose above the rumble of the band.

"Cranberry juice and soda?" Alcohol robbed me of what little control I had over my second sight. I shoved another cigarette in my mouth and sat down.

"What kinda booze you want in it?"

"Nothing. Just the juice and soda." I dug in my pocket for more money.

"Same price either way." She propped her hands on her hips and cocked her head at me, squinting.

I nodded.

"Look," she said, "I know who you are. Rae sat right where you are and drew a picture of you one day."

Why did everybody who knew Rae, even just as an acquaintance, know all about me? While alive, she treated me like shit on her shoe. As a ghost, she played the same game. I didn't understand our relationship at all.

"Now, look. The management here at Long Time Gone is sorry to hear what happened to Rae. But it don't have nothing to do with us. We don't have no information for you."

My heart stuttered. What the hell did she mean? I caught a glimpse of myself in the mirror behind the bar. Deer in the headlights described me to a tee.

"Ma'am? I'm not here about Rae." I slid the picture across the bar. "I'm looking for my friend, Chase Fischer."

"I told that boy earlier—afore I kicked him out—and I'll tell you, I didn't hardly know Rae, and I don't know"— she leaned down and made an ugly face—"or *care* if some boyfriend of hers might come in here sometimes. And I don't have to talk to you anyway since you ain't the po-lice."

My mind fell over and played dead. The old hag's nastiness shocked me into confusion. Hell, I couldn't even get pissed off and punch her in the face.

"Now, I'm sorry 'bout how Rae ended up, but it don't have nothing to do with nobody here. We ain't liable." The bartender raised her arm and made a motion.

A huge hand grabbed my arm and turned me around. I was face to face with the bearded doorman again.

"You causing trouble already?" He grinned that curiously out-of-place-grin and tugged me away from the bar without waiting for an answer.

———

"WAIT A MINUTE," I struggled to get away from him, but he had no trouble holding onto me.

The doorman frog marched me to the door. The peanut gallery loved the show, shouting and cheering behind us. He pushed me out into the parking lot and stood barring my way back inside.

"I just wanted to ask some questions." Having never been thrown out of anywhere, the humiliation surprised me. The bikers on the deck hooted and hollered at the action, which made it worse.

"I can't answer your questions, ma'am." He sounded a little apologetic, but he didn't move a muscle. The top of my head barely reached his pectorals. My muscles coiled into painful knots, and the rage of impotence overflowed my emotions.

As it sometimes does with me, my anger brought on the worst of girly behaviors. A hateful lump closed my throat. Tears stung my eyes and ran in hot tracks down my cheeks. I clenched my jaw against the sobs that clawed at my throat, begging to be let out.

"Aw, shit." The doorman lost his professionalism and sagged. "Don't start crying. Please."

"My cousin was murdered." Tears blurred my words and my vision. "We just had her memorial service earlier this afternoon."

"I knew Rae and liked her." The doorman's voice softened. "I'm sorry for your loss, ma'am."

"My friend came here earlier asking about someone who might have been involved." I swiped at my eyes. "Beaky in there won't tell me anything."

"Beaky?" The doorman jerked a nod at the bar, silently asking if I meant the bartender. When I nodded, he snickered. He covered his mouth at first, but finally threw back his head and bellowed laughter at the dark sky. "You're related to Rae, all right. I think she called her Big Bird." He laughed some more and wiped tears from the corners of his eyes.

A good sense of humor, a great smile—this guy had it going on. Then why didn't I come on to him? After such a stressful week, I knew he'd make a great diversion. But I didn't feel like alley catting around. And it usually gave me such great comfort. Okay. It didn't. But it made the bad stuff, the loneliness, less intense.

The door creaked open behind us, and he cut off his laughter. Beaky stuck her head out. "Ain't she gone yet?"

He grabbed my arm and dragged me to my Nova.

"Wait a minute." I squirmed against him, but it helped almost as much as beating granite with a feather. "You knew Rae, right?"

He didn't answer, but pushed me at my old car. I turned and gave him a pleading pout.

"Get in and get going." He didn't look at me. "I can't afford to lose this job."

I sagged and ducked my head to hide my trembling chin. My detective work sucked. I'd never figure out who killed Rae. She would haunt me forever. And I deserved it. She had died a horrific death, and I failed miserably at solving her murder.

Chase couldn't depend on me to help him get free of the worst jam of his life. If he went to death row for a murder he didn't commit, I'd never forgive myself. Frustrated sobs pushed their way up my throat again, and this time I let them come. I hated myself for crying in front of this sexy, terrible man, but that didn't stop me.

"All right, all right." The bouncer stepped closer, patting my back gently with one of his huge hands.

"Look, it's just a few questions." I wiped the tears off my face with my shirtsleeve.

"You're determined...Peri Jean, right?" The doorman grinned.

"How did you know?"

"Rae talked about you every time she came in here." The doorman took his attention off me and glanced back toward Long Time Gone. "I have a break coming up. See those woods over there?" He pointed. "There's a picnic table back there. Meet me there in ten, maybe fifteen, minutes."

I MOVED the Nova to a less visible location and took the

sketchbook and a flashlight with me to the clearing in the woods. I sat at the picnic table and waited. And waited. While I waited, I thought about Rae. Everywhere I went, I learned the people she spent time with knew all about me. Judging by their attitudes, they knew good stuff.

Had Rae's life screwed her up so much she couldn't treat people well? Not even those willing to love her? The idea left a lump in my throat. I mourned, not for her death but for her life. Just as I decided to smoke one more cigarette and go home, the bouncer rushed into the clearing.

"Sorry that took so long." He flashed his killer smile again, the one that made him look like a really sweet guy who just happened to be a thug. "Fight broke out. By the time I escorted both parties to their vehicles and saw them out of the parking lot...well, you see how long it took."

"No problem." I said this as though I hadn't been ready to hit the road five minutes earlier. "You know my name, but I don't know yours."

"Wade Hill." He sat down at the picnic table and glanced at Rae's sketchbook.

"I really appreciate you doing this." I couldn't help wondering about his motivation. As long as he behaved himself, I guessed it didn't matter.

"Rae made me laugh every time she came in. I wish I had known her memorial service was today. I'd have come."

My eyes burned with unexpected tears. "So why don't we start with you telling me what happened with Chase Fischer earlier. I know he was here."

I slid the picture of Chase and me across the table. Wade took it and smiled. "Did you get a tattoo?"

I took off my jacket and showed him the raven on my arm, thinking it might interest him since he had a raven too. He leaned close and nodded his approval. Again, the light impulse to flirt with this guy, to make something happen fluttered through me. I still didn't want to enough to do it.

"Chase came in before the band started. He asked me who Rae came in here with, and I told him what little I know." Wade lit up a cigarette and blew the smoke away from me. "After, he went up to the bar and talked to...what did you call her? Beaky. She had me throw him out. I escorted him off the premises. That was it."

"So who did Rae come in here with?"

"Rae came to Long Time Gone at least once a week. This older dude would meet her." Wade chuckled. "Total middle aged dork dressed up like a bad mofo. I mean, straight out of a sixties biker movie. He had this cap...you know the one Marlon Brando wore in *The Wild One*?"

"Wait a second. You mean one of those hats where the top sort of folds over onto the bill?"

Wade nodded. Adrenaline sped into my system. Bless Chase, wherever he was. Wade had actual knowledge of Rae's Low_Ryder.

"Rae liked to sketch." I held up the sketchbook. "I think she may have drawn a picture of this guy. Will you look at it?"

"Of course." Wade reached for the sketchbook. I opened it to the correct page and passed it to him along with the flashlight. Wade nodded almost immediately. "This is him. This is the guy."

"What can you tell me about him?"

Wade's pulled the sketchbook close to his face and used the flashlight to illuminate the lower portion of the picture.

"The ring..." Wade squinted as he thought. "The pattern was a spider web with a ruby on it. I remember thinking that kind of ring could tear you up in a fistfight."

The thought raised gooseflesh on my arms. That spider ring made the pattern I saw on Rae's face the day she died. That man in the sketchbook assaulted my cousin. Wade's voice invaded my thoughts.

"One evening, this goofball and Rae were in the bar listening to the jukebox and drinking. This woman, older woman, came into the bar like a tornado. The look on their faces was priceless. You ever see that reality show about unfaithful spouses?"

I nodded.

"This was like a real-life episode." Wade stopped talking to laugh. "The older woman must have been the middle-aged dork's wife or girlfriend. Boy, was she pissed. She jumped on Rae, and those two got into it, hissing and clawing."

"Was the woman blonde with lots of tattoos?" I asked around my cigarette. "Leathery skin?"

"Definitely the rode hard and put up wet type." Wade wrinkled his nose as he remembered her. "You know her, too?"

"No, not really. She came by the house wanting me to let her dig through Rae's things. Gave me a bad feeling."

Wade sat up straight and stubbed out his half-smoked cigarette. "She what? She came to your house? You didn't let her in, did you?"

Wade's reaction stirred my curiosity. What did he know about Veronica he wasn't telling me? She scared me more than I cared to admit—at least out loud—the day she showed up at Memaw's demanding to get into Rae's trailer. I realized Wade expected me to answer.

"Not just no, hell no."

"That woman's trouble." Wade frowned. "Olivia—Beaky—the bartender who threw you out, knew the old guy and his hag real well. I'd only been here a few weeks when Rae and the woman got into a fight, so—"

"When was this fight?" I hoped to tie Veronica to Rae's beating. I wanted a reason to have it in for her.

"Oh, a month ago...maybe two."

So much for that. "Do you know the guy's name? The guy with the hat?"

"Nope. He always paid in cash too, so no credit card." Wade said. "There was one thing. He had this fine old GTO. Late sixties model probably."

My knee jerked, colliding with the table's underside. I let out a grunt of pain and reached down to massage my injury. That GTO. It had to be the same one. The one that chased me the previous night. I first saw it while talking to Chase on the roadside. How many other times had it followed me and I never noticed?

That GTO belonged to Low_Ryder, and Low_Ryder

knew Rae's bullying friend, Veronica. But I didn't have all the pieces. I didn't understand what either of them had to do with blackmail or with the treasure. For all I knew, they were the ones Rae owed money.

"Girl, you gotta go to the police with all this." Wade's brow furrowed into sexy lines that made him look fierce. I liked it. He leaned in close. "These people aren't anybody you want to fool with. I knew Rae was in over her head."

"So you wouldn't mind telling the police what you told me?"

Wade glanced back toward the bar and sighed. "Look. I need this job. If you can keep me out of it, that would help. If not, can you call me and let me go see them? Maybe Olivia won't find out that way."

I wondered how I'd get Dean Turgeau to believe me without Wade backing me up, but I agreed anyway. I programmed Wade's number into my cellphone.

"I've got to get back to work." Wade stood and seemed to mentally refocus. Gone was the nice guy who acted concerned for me and who had liked Rae. In his place stood a bruiser, a guy you didn't want to piss off. He strode out of the clearing but turned back grinning. "Call me if you ever want to go motorcycle riding."

The normal me would have left planning how many days to wait before I called him. This new me, the one I didn't understand, just thought about how I had nothing solid to tell Dean Turgeau. I wanted to call him and gloat anyway. While he focused on finding Chase, I had uncovered some clues about Rae's final months. That would wipe the smug smirk off his face.

Turning into Memaw's driveway, a black GTO blew around me and nearly deafened me with its loud pipes. My car radio came on and scanned through the stations by itself. It stopped on "Low Rider" playing on a snowy station.

Cold fear stole through me, robbing me of my breath. When I finally did exhale a shuddering sigh, it came out in a stream of vapor. I got out of the car and ran to the house.

I tried to call Chase repeatedly to find out what happened to him. Each time, my call went straight to voice mail. I prayed—the first time in years—for his safe return and wondered if I was too late.

15

My little investigation had run itself out. Dean Turgeau hadn't deigned to speak to me since Rae's memorial service. His silence pissed me off, and my Texas-sized pride prohibited me from calling him.

I tried calling Dara Wyler, Rae's stripper BFF, but she didn't bother to return my calls. She might have picked up on the fact that I wanted to wring her neck in the messages I left. Hannah Kessler was the only stone left unturned from the papers I found in the barn. I wanted to talk to Hannah almost as much as I wanted to eat dirt, especially after she rescued me from Sheriff Joey. I wanted to continue to ignore Hannah. Really, I did. But the only other thing I had to do—worry about Chase—threatened my sanity.

The best way to avoid thinking about something unpleasant was to focus on something even worse. With that in mind, I talked myself into going to see Hannah. What was the worst she could do? Start a local talk show blabbing about how weird I was? Tell her fat-assed uncle, Sheriff Joey, I had been mean to her and get him to bust me? On the drive to the museum, I kept myself busy with worst-case scenarios involving Hannah Kessler.

Despite my resolve, I sat in front of the museum in my car for another fifteen minutes. A group of blue-haired ladies exited the museum babbling excitedly. When they caught sight of me sitting in the car chain-smoking, they stopped talking and hotfooted it down Houston Street and away from me. That inspired me to get out of the car. From my vantage point, I could see into the museum. Hannah stood at a window watching me.

Now or never. I walked up the steps leading to the museum with my head down. Hannah met me at the door minus her brilliant smile. She nibbled on the corner of one perfectly painted lip and wrung her hands.

"Do you mind if I come in?" My stomach curled into the fetal position, and my heart tried to beat its way out of my chest.

"Of course." She stood aside, still unsmiling. "It's a public place."

That didn't sound too promising, but I deserved it. She'd made numerous efforts to reconnect with me. I'd rebuffed them all. To put the turd in the punchbowl, I blew her off after she rescued me from her awful uncle. I stepped inside the museum and took a deep breath. The musty smell of old building tickled my allergies. I turned away from Hannah, clapped my hand to my face, and sneezed.

Hannah stood stock still, watching me. I no longer

knew her well enough to read her expression. I plunged headlong into the speech I prepared on the drive over.

"Thank you for singing at Rae's memorial service. I should have thanked you that day. Would have been better than talking to my mother. And thanks for saving my bacon at the sheriff's office that day...again." The words felt bigger than my mouth. They were that hard to get out. *Could I be this petty?*

"You're welcome." Hannah still wouldn't meet my eyes.

"Your singing and guitar playing impressed me." The words came easier. Hannah nodded her thanks.

"I have a favor to ask."

Hannah said nothing. A clock ticked somewhere in the silent building's depths. When the wind kicked up outside, the old place groaned and creaked.

"All right." Hannah raised her chin as though going into battle.

"I found these in Rae's things." I took my copy of Rae's papers out of my bag with shaking hands. "Do you know what she was looking for? Or could tell me what you two discussed?"

Hannah took the paper and looked at it, frowning. Finally, she met my eyes. Her brow was drawn, crumpling her light eyebrows into squiggles.

I braced myself for her to shout at me to get out of her place of business, readying myself for an onslaught of caustic words.

"I've been trying to talk to you since Rae's murder." She shook the papers at me. "About this."

That knocked the wind out of me. Of all the things I

expected, this wasn't it. If only I'd known. "I apologize for my rudeness."

Hannah wrinkled her nose and bared her teeth. "Don't be so fucking formal."

She laughed at the look on my face. Unable to help myself, I laughed with her.

"I was just about to close. Come up to my apartment. Your friend, Chase—" She studied me, probably to gauge whether mentioning him upset me. "Chase designed it and did the construction himself. It's gorgeous."

Hannah turned the sign on the door to "Closed." We trooped up four flights of stairs to the former attic, now her apartment.

———

WE SAT at a mosaic-topped bar on retro bar stools with glittery red vinyl seat coverings. Hannah used an elaborate machine, which probably cost more than I made in a month, to fix us white chocolate mochas. She set my drink in front of me and pushed a plate of biscotti toward me.

"I do know how to make biscotti," she said, "but these are from Lulu's Espresso Meltdown."

"She's got good stuff in there." I took a sip of my mocha and made a sound of appreciation. Small talk isn't my specialty. Especially not with someone I considered my archenemy for twenty years. I needed information from Hannah, but I wanted to keep the door to my life closed to her.

Hiring Rainey Bruce to rescue me from Sheriff Joey

hadn't won my trust. I didn't think she had an ulterior motive exactly, but it didn't add up. After she and her mother moved to Houston, Hannah came back here every summer to visit her Uncle Joey and Aunt Carly Holze—two people who hated me with a passion. I passed within five feet of her numerous times during those visits, and she never made eye contact.

What I was and could do made people uncomfortable. I figured Hannah shared their discomfort. It hurt and made me even more of an outsider. But I accepted it. After her divorce and all those years of ignoring me, she acted as though she could just throw open her arms and I'd run into them. I didn't work that way and, therefore, didn't know what to say to her.

After a few moments silence, she sighed and sat on the barstool next to me.

"This whole thing is so crazy. I've been trying to talk to you for so long..." She took a big slug of her mocha and swallowed hard. "You coming in here out of the blue caught me off guard. Since Rae's death, I've questioned my part in it all. I'm glad you found those pages I copied for Rae. Otherwise, I don't think you'd have ever given me a chance to get it off my chest."

Anxiety sizzling in my veins, I squirmed on the barstool. So much for wanting to cut to the chase.

Hannah studied the pages I'd handed her downstairs for a moment, frowning at the practice blackmail note.

"About four months ago, Rae came to the museum asking if any records existed from the Mace estate auction back in 1906." Hannah set the pages down on the mosaic countertop and pushed them away. "I looked around and found a ledger where every item and its selling price were catalogued. I copied the pages and gave them to her and figured that would be the end of it."

During this recitation, Hannah looked everywhere in the room but at me and swallowed often. I leaned forward, impatient to hear what she had to say.

"I was wrong. Rae came back to ask me about these items she's got marked." Hannah tapped the folded pages with the back of her hand. "She had your family Bible with her and showed me a drawing inside it. Do you know the drawing I'm talking about?"

"Yes. The one of the little drawers." My heart thudded, each beat of my pulse constricting my throat. Little pinpricks of light studded my vision. I wanted answers. Getting them scared me to death.

"That's the one. Rae asked me which of these items I thought might have a secret compartment like the one in the drawing. I showed her this." Hannah's perfectly mani-cured fingernail tapped the paper. I learned forward and saw she pointed at the line where the writing slope was listed.

"Why the writing slope? Why not the cedar chest or the roll top desk?"

"Well, the roll top desk could have had it, too. Those were known to have secret compartments. But we've got the roll top desk here. I can tell you for a fact it doesn't have that little line of drawers in it. The cedar chest doesn't have it. Rae didn't realize it at first, but that's sitting in y'all's barn."

So that's how she started poking around out there. Somehow, that chest had found its way back to us. Creepy. I said, "So that left the writing slope, and Mrs. Rudie had possession of it."

"Right. And this is the part I've been trying to talk to you about, so pay attention."

What did she think I was doing? I nodded and waved my hand, urging her to keep talking.

"Rae apparently tried to talk Mrs. Rudie out of the writing slope, and she wouldn't have it. So she came back to me and asked me to appeal to Mrs. Rudie to donate it to the museum." Hannah watched my face. "At first I refused, of course. But she convinced me to go talk to Mrs. Rudie about donating it. Mrs. Rudie told me to go to hell, by the way."

Knowing Mrs. Rudie like I had, this didn't surprise me at all. This explained Rae's anger at Mrs. Rudie. The morning Rae died I thought her annoyance stemmed from Mrs. Rudie's disapproval of her relationship with Chase. *Showed what little I knew.*

"Now," Hannah said, "you're probably asking yourself how Rae convinced me to go beg that old biddy for the Mace writing slope."

I shrugged, unable to predict where Hannah was going with all this.

"She told me you were in trouble and finding the treasure was the only way to help you." Hannah's eyes searched my face. "Tell me what is going on. Please. We haven't been friends for years, and I understand why. But please let me help you."

She kept talking, but I didn't hear it. The blood rushing in my ears drowned out what Hannah said. I had to ask her to repeat herself.

"I said, 'There's no need to be embarrassed. I've been in some hairy messes myself.'" Hannah put her hand on my arm. The petty part of my brain that had convinced me to ignore her in the first place suggested I brush it off. I let the hand stay.

"I doubt you're going to believe me when I tell you that I have no idea what you're talking about."

Hannah let out a breath, and her shoulders dropped. "Really? No clue whatsoever?"

"Rae was a con artist, Hannah. She wasn't the same little girl we used to play with."

"I know, but she was so convincing." Hannah fiddled with the plate of biscotti, her expression miserable. "She sat right where you are sitting and cried. So you're not in any trouble...at all?"

"Not that I know of." Something jumped around in the back of my mind, but I couldn't catch it. I decided to change the subject. "So...I know Jolene donated the writing slope to the museum. Does it have those drawers from the drawing in the Bible?"

"Haven't checked yet. I want to." Hannah's eyes sparkled. "But see, there's a reason Jolene donated it to the museum."

I forced out a laugh even though there was nothing funny. "I know."

"Let's go see. Rae died looking for whatever's in there."

Hannah stood and took our dishes to the sink and rinsed them.

I didn't want to face the nasty spirit occupying the writing slope again, but the story Rae told Hannah bothered me. Had she really believed I was in trouble and the Mace Treasure was the only cure? Before Rae's murder, I'd have said no. Emphatically. But not now. After meeting people who knew Rae and hearing how often she mentioned me—and not to call me a bitch—it dawned on me how little I had known about Rae. *Was* I in some sort of trouble?

"Yeah, I want to see."

"Come downstairs with me. I've still got it in the receiving room." She placed the dishes in a drying rack next to the stainless steel sink and wiped her hands on a dishtowel.

I followed her from the cute little apartment with the feeling I had seen the last of anything cute for the evening.

———

"LET'S CUT TO THE CHASE," Hannah glanced back at me as we descended the endless stairs. "That thing's haunted."

I smiled at her and didn't bother with denials. Not for the first time, I wondered what normal people saw and felt when they encountered a haunted place or thing. It had to be less intense than my experience; otherwise, nobody would consider me a kook.

"Can you tell who haunts it?" She didn't turn to face

me this time. She focused on descending the steep stairs in her fashionable heels.

"I'm not that talented, but I will tell you it's like nothing I've ever encountered." Admitting this much made warning bells clang in my head as the old mistrust of Hannah clambered to the surface of my thoughts. But she was either sincere or a better actress than her appearances on TV hinted. Besides, a lifetime of pretending not to see the spirit world had tuckered me out.

"So what happens when we get in there and start messing with it?"

"Your guess is about as good as mine," I said.

Hannah led me through a maze of hallways in an unused part of the museum. She opened a door marked "Receiving Room" and motioned me inside.

The room's atmosphere held anticipation, but not the good kind. This anticipation marked the split second before blood splattered on the wall, that moment when you know everything has gone wrong, but it's too late to fix it. Every instinct I had screamed for me to run, and run fast. Once inside the room, the creepy sensation of someone watching had me looking over my shoulder.

Reginald Mace's writing slope sat on a long table. The hostile thing emanated waves of icy air no less subtle than a dog's growl. My body tightened, and I wondered if we shouldn't just leave the thing alone. Sell it online or something. Rae's claim I was in trouble stopped me from calling the whole thing off. What if she was telling the truth? I followed Hannah to stand in front of the writing slope.

The air grew so heavy and thick that each inhalation

was an effort. I glanced at Hannah to see if whatever inhabited the writing slope affected her. Chill bumps had risen on her arms, and her hand trembled as she used the key to unlock the box.

"One thing I figured out real quick after I got you into trouble is that you weren't lying about the ghost stuff." Hannah lifted the writing surface from the box and moved pieces of the writing slope around. The feeling of another presence in the room grew so strong, I expected something to appear any second. The message was clear: leave now or face the consequences. I didn't want to leave. I wanted to learn what Rae died trying to find out.

"You thought I lied about seeing your father's ghost?" I struggled to keep my voice calm. If Hannah saw nothing out of the ordinary, this thing might be bluffing.

"That's what Mom, Uncle Joey, and Aunt Carly said." Hannah shrugged. "Who do you believe when you're eight?"

She had a point. The intensity of the anger I spent the last twenty years directing at her lessened. I crept closer as Hannah straightened out a paper clip and took an inkwell out of its resting place. Her hands left condensation marks on the old wood and brass. That worried me.

"Hannah, I don't know if I'd—"

Hannah jammed the paperclip into a corner of the box. From inside the box came a click as a catch released. A million voices whispered inside my head. Though I couldn't understand the words, they broadcast anger at our intrusion. Oblivious, Hannah lifted away a panel hiding four flat drawers with tiny, black pulls. The same drawers drawn on the family Bible's inner cover appeared. A low hum resonated from the box. It sounded like something powering up. *Oh, no.* Everything leading up to this had been nothing more than a preview. I had to stop her.

"Don't touch the box anymore." I grabbed her upper arm and tried to pull her away.

"Why not? I mean it's creepy, but I think it's okay." Hannah opened the first drawer. A furious screech from inside my head knocked me off balance. I put a hand out to steady myself and tried to shake off the pain. Unaware of my agony, her face lit up with the same curiosity I remembered from childhood, and Hannah pulled the pouch from the drawer.

That's when the shit splattered. Figuratively, of course. Anger rolled through the room in waves. It drew strength from my fear, growing in intensity. A thin wisp of black swirled around, moving tentatively, seeking a home. It flowed into the pouch. Before I had time to formulate a warning to Hannah, she screamed and tossed the pouch on the floor. It landed with a heavy thud. I had just a breath of a second to wonder what could be in there. The black shadow slithered back out of it and came straight at me.

———

THE NEGATIVE ENERGY PROBED ME, its touch like electric shocks. I cried out and slapped at it, which did nothing. Gathering my will, I pushed against the energy so hard it seemed my head would explode. I didn't know what would happen if this dark thing got inside me, and I didn't want to know. I shook with the effort of trying to repel it, and a headache took root in my temples. The darkness retreated to the writing slope, cycloning around it.

"What are you doing?" Hannah came toward me, reaching for me. I could tell she knew something was wrong but not what.

"Didn't you see that?" I didn't understand how she didn't see. My second sight made it all so vivid.

She shook her head. "That pouch burned my hand. Then you seemed to be trying to fight something off."

The hum, which sounded like electricity, came back. The items on the table clattered. At the last second, I understood what was going to happen.

"Get back!" I yelled. Someone's heirloom crystal hit the concrete floor and shattered, shards rising up like a mush-room cloud. Hannah put her arms up to shield her face.

The hum increased in intensity. My ears popped the way they had the one time I flew on an airplane. We couldn't just stand here and let it decimate the entire museum. I had to get it out of here. I grabbed the writing slope, and its energy crashed into me, the force knocking me backward. My heart ached as though it might explode in my chest. I staggered toward the exit, intending to carry the horrible thing outside, dump it on the ground, and burn it. Jolts of energy traveled up my arms, shocking me, causing me to whimper. My vision went wobbly and all the color drained out of it. Each step sent a thunderbolt of pain into my back, but I forced myself to keep going.

"The safe in my office." Hannah's voice was almost lost

in the gale of whispering and pain. She grabbed my arm and towed me along. It was like pushing through hurricane force winds. We moved through the museum in slow motion, holding one another upright. When we got to the office, Hannah raced inside and opened a huge safe. I dumped the writing slope inside, and Hannah slammed the door shut.

The painfully angry force left me, leaving a confused void. I slumped to the floor in relief and sat there panting. Hannah sat down behind her desk. Her white, shocked face echoed my feelings.

"What the hell just happened?" She didn't really seem to expect an answer, so I just shook my head.

"I don't know how that made it go away, but I think it did."

"Well, of course it did," Hannah said. "The safe's iron. If an iron horseshoe'll stop a ghost, so will anything else made of iron."

"Really?" I remembered the homely iron horseshoe Jolene had me remove from Mrs. Rudie's dining room. The piece of half-remembered folklore clicked into place for me. Maybe Mrs. Rudie had known more about the writing slope, ghosts, and the Mace Treasure than anybody thought.

"Sure. Iron can sometimes keep ghosts out. So can the bottle tree I saw at your Memaw's house. They don't always work, but it's worth a try."

"How do you know this stuff?" My head gave a particularly sharp throb, and I cradled it, hoping the conversation would make me forget how much I hurt.

"Like I told you, I've had a lot of time to think about what happened between us all those years ago. I did a lot of research, went to a lot of places people thought were haunted, read a lot of books..." The color dropped out of Hannah's face and faded to a ghastly gray. "Oh fuck," she breathed.

"What's wrong?" Fear gripped me. "What?"

A drop of blood hit the carpet at my feet, and Hannah rushed toward me. She pressed a clean towel to my face. I grabbed the towel and waved away her attempts to help.

"It's okay," I said. "I had this happen the first night Rae came to me."

"I don't know if it's okay. What if that *thing* did something to you?"

"We need to clean up the blood." I ignored the other comment. Whatever damage dealing with the spirit caused was done. Worrying would only make me crazy. Cleaning would make me feel better. It always did.

Hannah searched my face for a long moment and then nodded and got out a spray bottle of some sort of industrial cleaning product. Together we dabbed at the blood, applied cleaner, and scrubbed. The stain appeared to have permanently tattooed the light colored carpet. We finally put an ice cube on the stain, hoping that would dull it. Hannah took a bottle of Kentucky bourbon out of her desk and poured herself a healthy slug of it.

"Things really went south after I poked that paper clip in the writing box," Hannah said. "It didn't do that when I was alone. I just got this horrible feeling of dread. The room was so cold I could see my breath."

"It's because of me." I hesitated before I continued but decided to go for broke. "My ex-husband and I lived in a former funeral home. My presence stirred up the spirits. It became unbearable."

"What happened?" Hannah leaned forward, elbows on her desk.

"He left one day and never came back." I sort of enjoyed the open-mouthed shock on Hannah's face. Her marriage must have ended on a nicer note than mine. I stood. Visit was over.

"Don't you want to see what was in the leather pouch?" Hannah set the little bag on the desk between us.

"You picked that thing back up after it burned you?" My old friend had brass balls. I'd have swept that thing into a dustpan and thrown it out with the garbage.

"Of course." She shrugged as if to ask what else I expected.

I didn't want to know what was inside it. The spirit had enough power to cause poltergeist-like activity. No telling what else it could do. But Rae had died while trying to find it. I couldn't refuse to look.

"Open it," I said.

Hannah grabbed the leather pouch and untied the strip of rawhide holding it together. As the rawhide fell to the desk, the dark shadow materialized. So much for iron stopping it. Or was it a different spirit connected with only the rawhide bag, like a booby trap? Did each piece of Reginald Mace's crazy treasure host one of these horrid guardians? Maybe that's why nobody ever found the treasure. And maybe that's what his deal with the witch Eddie told me about entailed.

Hannah let out a howl and dropped the pouch on the desk. "It burned me."

"Burn me once, shame on you. Burn me twice, shame on me."

She made a face and held out her hand for me to see. It was as red as if she'd slopped hot coffee on it.

I motioned her to follow me into the museum. She did so without argument, though she looked puzzled. I stopped in front of a blacksmith display. "Do you mind if we use those pincers?"

Hannah grinned.

Back in the office, I picked up one corner of the pouch with the pincers, and Hannah used an iron spike to pull open its flap. A wooden object hit the desk and bounced to the floor.

Hannah dropped to her knees. Using the iron spike, she rolled the piece of wood around, trying to get a good look at it.

"It's an angel." I squatted on the floor next to her. The angel had been carved out of wood. Its wings were spread, and it held a trumpet to its mouth. Nice figurine, but what did it have to do with treasure?

"Hand me those pincers," Hannah said. I did as she asked, and she picked up the angel and set it on her desk.

"What are you going to do with it?" I asked.

"Figure out what's important about it. What else?"

"Have fun getting burned." To show her how little I cared, I stood and looked out the window of her office.

Dean Turgeau stood over my car scribbling in a ticket book.

"That asshole!" I charged toward the museum's exit, Hannah close at my heels.

————

"WHAT'RE YOU DOING?" I stopped a few feet from Dean. His skin, tan from running outdoors, glowed in the late afternoon sun. The hair on his arms was bleached blonde from the sun. My body heated as I imagined what his skin would feel like against mine. *Focus,* I reminded myself.

"Writing you a ticket." Dean glanced behind me at Hannah who clattered up to us, already limping in her high-heeled boots. The chemistry I expected to feel between them wasn't there. *Odd.*

"I don't understand why," Hannah said. "She's not parked illegally."

"Her inspection's out." Dean closed his ticket book without tearing out the ticket. Rather than his eyes flittering over Hannah—who I had every reason to believe was his girlfriend—they rested on me. My body tightened in response. My desire for this obstinate man irritated me. I wanted to pick a fight with him to relieve some tension.

"Oh, he's right. It's an honest error, and he could cut me some slack, but he won't. He likes lording his crappy position over other people. He's a cocksmoker."

"Peri Jean!" Hannah widened her eyes and swatted at me. I moved out of her reach and engaged in a glaring contest with Dean.

"It's okay, Han," he said.

Han? Really? Who was he? Luke Skywalker?

"My feelings about Ms. Mace are less than favorable. She has bad taste in friends—present company excluded, of course."

Hannah shifted her glare to Dean. He pressed his lips together and met her gaze without flinching.

"It's not her fault," Hannah told him.

"So? She's breaking the law. She's lying to me." It might have been wishful thinking, but Dean sounded a little whiney like a kid caught doing something he shouldn't. I almost preened but realized what this conversation meant. They'd discussed me. More than once. Hannah and Dean both fit right into the Gaslight City gossip mill, the busybodies.

"Just give me the ticket," I said to Dean.

Hannah and Dean both ignored me, continuing their silent battle. Finally, Hannah spoke up.

"There wasn't any reason for you to come here and start over if all you're going to do is drag the past around with you like a badge of honor."

Dean flushed brick red. His eyes narrowed, and I figured he'd say something nasty to Hannah. Instead, he dropped his eyes. Hannah turned to me.

"And you. Tell him the truth. He only wants to solve your cousin's murder. He's a good guy and a good cop. Accept help when you need it."

My hand curled into a fist, and my face heated. *Who the hell was Hannah Kessler to lecture me?* She had all her big, fancy money to hide behind. She came back to this crummy, little town like a visiting celebrity. Did she really think she knew enough to tell me how to live? If she had anything better to do, anywhere better to go, she sure wouldn't be in Gaslight City a wash-up. My hateful words beat at me, wanting to get out and blacken the air.

"Go on," Hannah said. "Talk to each other. And go to bed with each other and get it over with. Nobody else would have either of you."

Dean gaped at Hannah, freezing in place. My head swam as the back of my neck prickled. We glanced at each other and quickly looked elsewhere.

"I'm sorry I ignored your call the other night." Dean mumbled the words at his feet, but I understood them anyway.

"I've got some stuff I need to tell you," I said. I still wanted to kick Hannah Kessler's butt, and I glared at her to let her know.

Hannah clapped her hands together. "That wasn't so bad, was it?"

Neither Dean nor I said anything. Hannah beat it back to the museum. She closed the door and locked it behind her. Wise move.

"You were right. I have been in touch with Chase." My head swam as the blood rushed through my body. "Gonna take me to jail now?"

"I didn't want to in the first place. That anonymous tip got to Sheriff Joey before it got to me." Dean still spoke to his feet.

"Then...why have you been threatening to arrest me since day one?"

"For most people, the threat of jail is a good incentive for telling the truth." Dean finally looked at me and raised his eyebrows.

"I didn't want you to arrest Chase."

"But if he didn't do this, the safest place for him might be jail. Let's say Chase didn't do it. The real killer is out there somewhere. It might be in that killer's best interest to silence Chase permanently."

For once, I didn't have a sassy comeback. Dean was right. Chase had seen Low_Ryder with Rae. He could identify him. Dean took in the expression on my face and grimaced in sympathy.

"Still not too late. I'm here. You can tell me anything."

I barely heard Dean's voice over the roaring in my ears. I remembered that final voicemail from Chase. Who had been out at the sawmill ruins with him? And why hadn't I heard from him since then?

"Have you been out to the sawmill ruins?"

"Sawmill?" Dean frowned, watching me carefully. "What does that have to do with this?"

"Can you follow me out there?" Urgency beat at me, even though I knew there was no hurry.

Dean shook his head. "Not unless you want me to call it in. I won't be off work until after dark. We could meet out there in the morning."

I drew Dean a sloppy map, which he insisted was good enough to help him find the ruins. Hands shaking, I got into my car and drove to the next job. Even though I worked until well after midnight, I didn't feel the least bit sleepy. I sat up most of the night making a list of things I needed to tell Dean the next day. I slept a few hours and woke as the sky turned gray with dawn. Replaying my part in helping Chase evade arrest, I wished for a do over and cried because those don't exist. I prayed for consequences of my ignorance not to be dire.

16

Morning dawned clear and bright with a deeper than usual blue sky. Beautiful day, horrible task ahead of me. My mind kept going over bits and pieces of the previous day.

Rae's using me to convince Hannah to do her bidding didn't shock me a bit, but it bothered me all the same. Only two possibilities existed: I was in danger or I wasn't. *Let's say Rae hadn't been lying just to get her way, and I am in danger. From what?* I'd never win a popularity contest but couldn't imagine why someone would want to harm me. I'd once mistakenly dated a man cheating on his wife, but that happened years ago. I stayed to myself too much to make any real enemies.

The other part of yesterday's events coiled into a knot I could never hope to untie. Hannah's mentioning my attraction to Dean (and his to me), like common knowledge, embarrassed the hell out of me. Now that I knew for sure they weren't a couple, I could no longer justify ignoring the pull between us. I'd have to decide to act on the attraction or let it fester. The complexity of it all made my head ache.

Unless we went out of town to do it, having a quiet fling was out of the question. Gaslight City might not have big city amenities, but our gossip grapevine surpassed the need for them. Everybody who was anybody would know Dean's and my business five minutes after it happened. Everybody else would know a half hour after that. The idea of the town gossipmongers taking a personal interest in me brought back memories of my childhood as a pariah.

Added to that, Dean had issues. He might as well carry a sign reading, "Damaged Goods." A relationship with him would take hard work. My relationship skills consisted of knowing when a relationship had reached its expiration date and extracting myself quickly and painlessly. That was it. My common sense told me to let the attraction die on the vine. Find some uncomplicated male and forget Dean. No matter how many times I told myself that, I couldn't quit remembering how he made me feel.

At the appointed hour, I met Dean at the sawmill with a thermos of coffee. He brought a box of doughnuts. We ate in silence before we ventured into the woods. The attraction—now that Hannah had pointed it out—writhed between us, begging to be recognized, acted upon.

"So why are we out here?" For once, Dean didn't sound like a tight ass.

"This is the last place Chase might have been. He

called me Saturday night and asked me to meet him out here. I came out, and he wasn't here."

"What aren't you telling me?"

"What do you mean?"

"You talk fast when you get nervous. You didn't even pause for breath when you said all that." Dean stopped and faced me. The ruins stood around us like concrete sentries, their presence both spooky and comforting. The only sounds were the wind rustling leaves and the splash of the stream feeding the old millpond.

"I got scared is all. I found a matchbook from Long Time Gone and went looking for Chase. I didn't find him."

"That didn't scare you. What did?" Dean's eyes searched mine. I saw no malice or sarcasm on his face. Despite his cutting crystal ball remarks, I decided to tell him. Hannah had been right. We needed to work together.

"There's a dead deer over there. I saw—or maybe just felt—its last moments. The hunter who killed it cut into it while it was still alive..." I stopped and shuddered.

"Show me," Dean said.

We walked without talking, footsteps crunching on the bed of dry leaves and dead grass. I skirted around the building where I'd seen the dead deer.

I braced myself for seeing a dead animal, but I wasn't prepared for what I did see. The deer that had looked so fresh only days before was half-rotted, his bones picked clean by scavengers. He'd been killed at least a month ago. The smell was unreal. How had I not noticed this?

"But there was blood here." I turned to Dean,

expecting him to make a nasty remark about my ability. "I got it on my hands. I'm not lying to you."

"My career has put me in the same room with a lot of liars. I know you aren't one of them." Dean looked as mortified as I felt about being allies for the moment.

"Show me where you fell down."

I pointed to the spot, which was still stained red with something. At this point, I wondered if it was even blood. Dean knelt down and touched the ground gingerly. The half-rotted deer, the one that had looked so fresh the night I'd been out looking for Chase, was close enough to touch.

Dean, still on his knees, peered into the patchy grass. His posture stiffened, and he drew his pen from his shirt pocket. He poked the pen into the grass and drew out a brass shell casing. In one fluid motion, he drew a plastic bag from his pocket and deposited the casing in it.

My sanity wobbled on its axis. I knew what the casing meant. Deep down, I did. I was vaguely aware of some animal making a low, mournful noise out in the woods. Then I realized the soft howl came from me and made myself stop.

Dean turned to face me. Whatever he saw made his eyes widen.

"A-a-aren't you even going to say it's not what I think it is?" My lips trembled as I spoke, and my sentence came out all warbled. The world around me got very bright.

Dean shook his head and glanced away from me. His eyes darted around before they settled on something. He gripped my arm and led me to a fallen log away from the deer, away from where he'd found the brass hull. Carefully, he helped me sit on the log.

———

"CHASE ISN'T DEAD." I needed someone to say it. Saying it didn't reassure me as much as I hoped it would, so I heaped on even more reason. "Otherwise, I'd have seen him."

Chase wouldn't go on without saying goodbye to me. Would he, though? He'd hated his life. Otherwise, he wouldn't have tried so hard to destroy himself. He didn't love partying. Dreams dashed, he was killing himself slowly. But Chase couldn't die. I needed him. I needed our shared history. I needed someone to love me who didn't have to. Dean gripped my shoulder, and I nearly jumped out of my skin.

"Talk to me, Peri Jean. Let's work together." He frowned at me. "I don't know about you, but Hannah embarrassed the hell out of me."

"Me too." We smiled at each other. Dean's smile made it all the way to his eyes. Despite my fear over Chase's whereabouts, my heart beat a little faster. "Where do you want to start?"

"Tell me the truth, everything you know about this whole, crazy thing." Dean shoved his hands in his pockets and stretched his legs out in the leaves. Our mutual attraction sat between us, huge as a white elephant. No way I'd touch that. Not until I decided for sure how bad it could blow up in my face.

"Whoever reported seeing Chase and me talking on the side of the road wasn't lying," I said. "But I think the person who saw us is the killer."

"Back up. Tell me why you think that."

"Chase said Rae had another boyfriend, a guy she listed as Low_Ryder on her cellphone. The morning Rae died, this Low_Ryder texted her, and she kicked Chase out."

Dean dug for his notepad, took it out, and scribbled in it. I leaned forward and peeked at what he wrote.

"That looks like hieroglyphics," I said.

Dean elbowed me away. "Don't lose your train of thought. Finish telling me what you know."

"I found the sketchbook and the blackmail note, which you already have. Saturday night, after I left here, I went out to Long Time Gone—"

"What the hell for? That's a rough place."

"I told you. I found a matchbook out here. One of Chase's messages had music playing in the background. I guessed he'd been there. Thought maybe he went back."

"Do you still have the matchbook?" he asked.

I dug in my jacket pocket and held the matchbook out to Dean. He produced another plastic bag and motioned me to drop it in.

"Probably no useful fingerprints on it, but we can try," he said.

"That trashy old witch who runs it kicked me out, but I talked to the bouncer. He looked at the sketchbook and said the guy with the hat—the one I showed you—used to come into Long Time Gone with Rae. He said that guy owned a vintage black GTO, extensively restored. The night I talked to Chase on the roadside, a car like that passed us. The night I went to The Chameleon, a car like that followed me home. It tried to make me wreck."

Dean turned to stare at me. "You've been chased? Why have you told me none of this?"

I took a deep breath. "Every time I've tried to talk to you, you've been an asshole. Somebody told you I can see the spirit world, and you make fun of me for it. Why would I go out of my way to talk to you?" My voice had risen unintentionally, and it echoed in the quiet forest.

Long pause.

"I deserved that," Dean said. "I've never lived anywhere this isolated, and I'm having a hard time getting my bearings. I grew up in a small town, but Baton Rouge was right up the road. We were always driving in for something." He paused and glanced at the dense forest around us. "Nothing here is what it seems. Everybody has histories, and those histories color how they interact. To an outsider like me, it seems like people make up the rules as they go along."

"We do make up the rules as we go along. That's one benefit to living in the asshole of nowhere," I said.

"If you can't beat 'em, join em?" Dean asked. I shrugged and nodded and we stared at each other. The charge of attraction between us heated until I expected to smell ozone. I waited for Dean to make the next move, and he did. Just not the one I expected. "What else can you tell me about the case?" Dean turned to a fresh page in his notebook. I almost groaned in frustration.

"There's another part to all this, one I didn't connect until the night we saw each other at The Chameleon. This woman—Veronica—came by the house and wanted to go through Rae's things. I blew her off, and she got angry. The night I went to The Chameleon, the women who work there, the dancers, mentioned a woman who showed up and tried to beat Rae up. Then, last night at Long Time Gone, the bouncer mentioned that same woman and Rae got into a fight there...over the man with the black GTO."

"You're shitting me." Dean tapped his pen on his jeans and shook his head. "I am an asshole. That explains a lot."

"Who is she?"

"Veronica Spinelli," Dean said, "is a friend of Rae's... from prison. She was released a couple of months ago. After thirty years locked up. She's a murderer, a thief, someone you don't want to mess with. Run an internet search on her. If what you read doesn't scare you, nothing will."

"I don't understand what she wanted with Rae." My mind worked to piece things together, but I didn't have enough of the puzzle.

"I'll have to see if I can find out. But you let me take care of this. Don't go off looking for her." Dean leaned forward. "She's wanted by the Smith County sheriff's office for parole violation. Veronica beat the living shit out of a woman at the halfway house where she'd been placed. The woman died from the beating."

That shocked me into silence. Veronica Spinelli could have killed Rae. From what I'd learned at Long Time

Gone, she had a motive. Rae stole her man. I couldn't believe it. All this time, I'd thought Rae's killer to be a man.

"Call me if you see her. If she approaches you, run. She can and will hurt you." Anger flashed in Dean's eyes. He stood in a quick motion and brushed off his jeans.

"I want to collect some of those leaves where we found the blood," Dean said. "It might be animal blood. If so, I can rule this out as a crime scene."

I wanted to tell him again that Chase wasn't dead because I hadn't seen his ghost, but I said nothing. I helped Dean put some bloody leaves in one of his endless supply of plastic bags. We walked back to our cars. Dean walked in silence, his brow furrowed in thought. Once we reached the cars, Dean opened the Nova's door and held it while I got inside. His mouth worked as he tried to think of a suitable goodbye for me, but something had been flitting around my mind, and I wanted to ask him about it.

"What did Hannah mean when she said it wasn't my fault?"

Dean jerked and dropped his notepad. He bent to pick it and plucked absently at his jeans leg on the way back up. His lips pressed together, and his eyes darted away from mine. "A stupid decision I made that got somebody killed. I blamed everybody but myself and even moved away to escape it. Then I met you, and I'm reminded of it every time I see you. Makes me feel stupid all over again."

I nodded. Sometimes there was nothing to say.

"You're not going to tell me it'll be all right?" Anger danced in Dean's eyes.

"Nope," I said. "Sometimes it's not all right until you tell yourself it is."

The anger faded from Dean's eyes, and a crooked smile took its place. "You're an enigma. Has anybody ever told you that?"

"My ex-husband said I was an enema. That the same thing?" It made him laugh. I started the car, and he closed the door.

———

To my complete and utter shock, the search on Veronica's name turned up pages of results. Judging by the short previews available with every result, she had been responsible for a notorious crime spree back in the early 80s.

I clicked on a link to a reasonably well-known website dedicated to profiling criminals and crimes. The bold headline read, "Romance and Murder: The Couple Who Kills Together Is Arrested Together."

Young, charismatic, creative, and deadly. Twenty-one-year-old Billy Ryder and eighteen-year-old Veronica Spinelli were all those things plus one more: ruthless.

Dallas police were unaware of this couple and their misdeeds for much of their criminal career. The young lovers preyed on their fellow criminals who wouldn't report being robbed or attacked for fear of their own crimes coming to light.

That all ended on January 29, 1982. Spinelli and Ryder knocked on the door of Natasha Whitmore's home on the pretense of buying some cocaine. Once inside Whitmore's home, the couple beat Whitmore until she agreed to give them all the drugs she had on the premises as well as all her money. Once the two had what they wanted, Veronica held a gun on Whitmore while Billy raped her.

Whitmore stayed in her home, afraid to call for help, until her children came home from school. Though Whitmore begged her children not to involve police, they knew their mom needed medical treatment. They called on a neighbor to summon law enforcement.

As soon as Whitmore talked to police, calls poured in from other victims of Veronica Spinelli and Billy Ryder. The couple targeted females likely to be home alone. They stole what they could and sexually assaulted the women. Using descriptions provided by victims, police tracked down Spinelli and Ryder at a residence in a rundown area.

After a short standoff, police took the deadly couple into custody. The home's owner, a sixty-four-year-old retiree, was found buried in the dirt floor of an outbuilding. Police recovered an estimated $25,000 worth of jewelry, drugs, guns, and cash.

And that was only the beginning.

Billy Ryder turned out to be a fake identity. The name belonged to the man whose house the couple had commandeered —the one they buried under the floor of a clapboard storage shed behind the house. Police were unable to identify Ryder using fingerprints. They suspected he had a juvenile record but were unable to find him in the system.

With time, law enforcement probably could have figured out Ryder's identity; however, Ryder escaped during his arraignment hearing. He left three people dead. The man police knew as Billy Ryder was never captured. The only known picture of him is the mug shot featured on this website.

Veronica Spinelli refused to cooperate with law enforcement. She claimed not to know Billy Ryder's real name and told police she had no idea where he might have gone. Despite the nature of her crimes, Spinelli was given a sentence of thirty years in the Texas prison system.

The website noted she was up for release this year.

I stared at the only known photo of Billy Ryder. The mug shot showed a frowning man with bottomless dark eyes and a derisive smirk. His bushy dark hair and goatee could have belonged to anybody. Even the tattoo on his neck was an unidentifiable blob.

Low_Ryder. Billy Ryder. Coincidence? I doubted it. Not when I added in Veronica Spinelli. Had those two baddies reunited to carry out some plan? Wade Hill, the bouncer from Long Time Gone, said LowRyder and Veronica had some sort of relationship with Olivia the beak-nosed bartender.

Like everybody else in Burns County, I knew the rumors about illegal activity at Long Time Gone. Most of the talk had to do with an outlaw biker gang roaming Texas and parts of New Mexico. But that didn't mean other stuff didn't go on out there. I remembered hearing about a truck driver turning up with a slit throat and an empty trailer. Maybe Veronica and Low_Ryder were back in business. They might have brought Rae in as a partner. She got involved with Low_Ryder and Veronica killed her for it.

My eyes itched and burned with fatigue. I shut off the laptop and put my face in my hands. I didn't think Billy Ryder/Low_Ryder and the horse-faced BJ were the same guy. Low_Ryder wore biker clothes while BJ wore cowboy suits. However, Veronica Spinelli had shown up both where Rae hung out with Low_Ryder and where she hung out with BJ to kick Rae's ass.

I still couldn't reason out how Billy Ryder kept from being recognized. That internet article listed all the true crime documentaries featuring Billy Ryder and Veronica Spinelli. How had he eluded arrest for so many years?

———

I HAD my proof that H & H Week had arrived on Tuesday morning. My cellphone woke me up, and I booked two appointments for local businesses later in the day. Those appointments had to be fitted in around the ones I already had. I would be stretched thin, but I had no choice if I wanted to make this year's H & H Week worth it.

For the day's first gig, I agreed to serve refreshments at a press conference for the mayor's office. The mayor's secretary demanded I wear business attire for the event. She specified pantyhose. As I shimmied into the unforgiving little bastards, Michael Gage overdressing for Rae's memorial service entered my mind.

I remembered his words about the "many conversations" he claimed to have had with my cousin. What had those two talked about? I wondered if I could get Michael Gage to tell me if I agreed to go on that date with him. It might be worth suffering his company.

In the kitchen, I poured myself a cup of coffee and waited until Memaw closed her Bible before I spoke.

"What did Michael Gage mean at Rae's memorial

service when he said he'd had many conversations with her?"

"I introduced them. Michael wrote Rae in prison at my request." Memaw packed away her Bible and took out the three-inch-thick romance novel she'd been reading.

"Why did you do that?" I cooked some toaster pastry. Breakfast of champions.

"Rae wrote asking to live with us when she got out of the pen. They were going to put her in a halfway house if she didn't have family to go to." The grim set of Memaw's mouth spoke volumes about the conflict she must have experienced. No grandmother wanted to tell her grandchild she couldn't help her, but I knew Memaw always wondered if she'd done the right thing. "I talked to Michael, and he said he would feel her out—you know, try to figure out her intentions."

"He sure didn't do a bang up job on that."

"He did the best he could." Her tone of voice indicated I had better watch it. "They seemed to connect. I could see the change in Rae after he started talking to her. You know, Michael spoke on her behalf and made sure she got her time off for good behavior."

"And they continued their relationship after she came home?"

"The powers that be at the prison agreed not to put her in a halfway house on the condition she submit to counseling by a licensed professional."

Michael Gage's counseling hadn't made Rae behave herself. I kept that observation to myself. No reason to put Memaw through any more misery. My toaster pastries popped out of the toaster, and I ate them while standing at the counter.

"What brought all these questions on?" Memaw set her romance novel aside and focused her attention on me.

"Just rehashing the whole thing in my head." I wadded up my paper towel and threw it in the garbage can. "I guess I'll do that for a long time."

I glanced at the clock. I had to leave or risk being late. The mayor's secretary wouldn't hire me again if I was even one minute late. Her influence stretched beyond our tiny City Hall, and I couldn't afford to have her blacklist me. I kissed Memaw goodbye and left.

I wanted to have another conversation with Michael Gage. No way I'd agree to be alone in his house with him again. And no way he'd agree to talk to me after I refused his offer of a date. There was but one solution, and it made me puke in my mouth a little.

On the way to my job, I called Michael Gage. He was thrilled to hear from me, and even more thrilled I had reconsidered his offer of a date. We agreed to meet that evening at Danner's Landing, Gaslight City's only nice restaurant.

I had never been less thrilled about going out with a good-looking man.

17

For my date, I chose a broomstick skirt, a peasant blouse, and my vintage cowboy boots. I accessorized with a wide leather belt and dangly earrings. As usual, my makeup and hair were understated. I'd fit in at Danner's Landing but still look like me.

Gage's eyes widened as he stood from the intimate corner table for two.

"Peri Jean." His nostrils flared as he kissed my hand. "You're beautiful. So exotic."

Gross. No doubt I looked different. People who never gave me a second glance openly stared at us. The Holzes—Sheriff Joey and Carly—studiously ignored me. I wished my nervous anticipation was for someone in whom I was actually interested. Like Dean.

Gage ordered for both of us—the house specialty—stuffed pork chops with a variety of side dishes. The complimentary bread came out, and Gage cut us each a piece. *Manners or a control thing? Interesting.* When he handed me my bread, I noticed a white, ring-shaped tan line on his left ring finger. I tried to remember if he usually wore his wedding band and couldn't. Gage saw me looking.

"My class ring from Princeton," Gage said. "It didn't match this outfit."

I laughed politely and focused on enjoying the food. Danner's Landing was expensive, and I'd only been a few times.

As we ate, Gage talked about an upcoming vote at his church on televising his sermons.

"I've told the deacons more than once it would be nothing but a distraction." He speared a new potato with more vigor than necessary. "The purpose of our church is to fellowship in the Lord. Not play at being movie stars."

I didn't know what to say to that. Not for the first or the last time that evening, it occurred to me Gage and I had nothing but humanity in common. We went from Gage's reluctance to become a local celebrity to the awful work the gardener he hired for H & H Week did. I looked for an opening to ask my questions. It never came, so I made it.

"Memaw said you'd been counseling Rae as part of her release terms."

Gage's fork stopped halfway to his mouth. "How did that topic come up?'

"Your comments at her memorial service. You said the two of you had many conversations about the direction of her life." I needed a better reason. One that might make him think a need for closure motivated me. "As you mentioned last week, Rae and I were not on the best of terms. But, now that she's gone, I feel a need to understand her better."

Gage nodded and took another bite. He frowned while he chewed.

"Rae and I both grew up in San Antonio, in the same neighborhood, in fact." Gage's eyes focused on a point beyond my left shoulder, apparently lost in memory. When he spoke again, his smile was gone. "I think I told you my mother was an addict. Rae and I had a lot to talk about."

Grief swelled in me, aching. Every time I thought I had accepted Rae's transformation from my childhood play-mate into a hard-edged criminal, some haunting thought popped into my head. I imagined the sort of topics Gage and Rae must have bonded over and realized I hadn't known Rae at all. Gage watched me, waiting for me to speak. I gathered my wits and said the first thing that came to my mind.

"You knew she'd been beaten up a few days before her death."

Gage flinched and blinked. "I was told."

"Who do you think beat her?"

"I don't know, Peri Jean. Rae had a way with words, as I'm sure you remember." Gage winked at me, his dark eyes sparkling. I realized, with surprise, he controlled the conversation. Not me. Maybe my best bet was to make him believe he wanted to gossip about my dead cousin.

"I guess we'll never really know what happened." I ate a bite of pork chop. It wasn't as good as Memaw's. "So how are the tours of Mace House going?"

Gage's eyes flashed with some emotion. Disappointment? I thought so. He wanted me to beg for the information.

"Rae was full of secrets." Gage ignored his half-eaten food and turned his full attention on me. The effect both set my teeth on edge and drew me in at the same time. Creepy feeling. "She was dating a married man, you know."

The blackmail note. That's who she had wanted to blackmail. Was Billy Ryder living right here in town, married, living a double life, and carrying on an affair with Rae? I hid my excitement as best as I could.

"Probably best not to gossip about it," I said. It was impossible to miss the pleasure in Gage's eyes. If I threatened to end the conversation, he might tell me even more. "It's over. Maybe whoever the guy was will change his ways."

"You're right. But she was so cavalier about it." He leaned forward. "Rae was only using...this man. For money. She let herself become pregnant, thinking he'd give her money to leave town."

"We had a conversation the day she died about the Mace Treasure," I said. "I suspect she wanted to find it, thinking it would solve all her financial problems. Do you know why she needed money so badly?"

"As I said at her memorial service, she was disappointed in where she'd ended up. It's likely she wanted to start over. I'm sure she thought having money would make things different. We all have our vision of what would make us happy." He had a point.

"It's normal—especially for someone like Rae—to think she can use money to erase a bad childhood and to forget the habits she learned when she was so young."

"I found a blackmail note in her things."

Gage raised his eyebrows and snorted. The information didn't surprise him a bit. "I'm sorry you had to face such an unpleasant task."

"I wonder if she gave the guy who got her pregnant the blackmail note," I asked.

"Well, it's a good guess she did. If she'd been beaten." Gage smiled, all traces of amusement gone. An arctic bead of sweat slid down my back and stopped at the waist of my skirt. I'd never claim to read minds, but I'd have sworn on a stack of Bibles Michael Gage would have beaten Rae if she'd handed him a blackmail note.

I wanted to get away from him. Right then. A dozen excuses raced through my mind. One of them had to be good enough. Someone tapped my shoulder as I tried to figure out which one. I glanced up, halfway expecting the waitress to be there to refill my tea glass. It was Hannah Kessler. My fork clattered onto my plate.

———

"Peri Jean," Hannah dragged my name out and held out her arms as though we hadn't talked in ages. Awkwardly, I stood and hugged her. She whispered, "You look miserable."

"He's a lecher," I whispered back and broke the hug.

Uninvited, Hannah sat down with us. Gage's eyes widened at the addition to our dinner party.

"I saw Peri Jean over here and just thought I'd say hi." Hannah's voice dripped sincerity, and she gave Gage the widest, shit-eating grin I'd ever seen. An air of excited anticipation hung about her.

"I don't think I've seen you in church." He held out his hand. "I'm Michael Gage."

Hannah and Gage said their howdy-dos and shook. Hannah openly stared at Gage, evidently wondering what I didn't like about him. It would have been funny had it not been so obvious and embarrassing. Seeing the beginning of the end, I ate my food quickly.

Gage, to his credit, made small talk about an upcoming revival at the church. A Christian radio station in Tyler would cover the event and encourage listeners to attend. Hannah asked questions in the right places, but Gage wasn't fooled. His suspicions grew, and so did his annoyance. His sentences became short and clipped.

The waitress stopped by for our dessert order. Hannah ordered peach cobbler with ice cream for three. By this time, Gage was so annoyed he drummed his fingers on the table and glared daggers at Hannah. When the bill came, he paid without comment and stood to leave when Hannah was in the middle of a sentence.

Hannah gave me a victory salute everybody in the restaurant saw. Gage walked ahead of Hannah and me as we exited Danner's Landing. Outside, he said nothing to either of us and left us standing underneath the green awning at the front door.

Gage's shoulders, pulled high with tension, nearly touched his earlobes. He'd never hire me for another job or ask me on another date. I felt one emotion: relief. I'd deposited his check into my bank account, and our business was finished.

Hannah burst into laughter as soon as Gage's sedan sped out of the parking lot. She howled for a few minutes, but reigned herself in when she saw I wasn't laughing with her.

"You looked unhappy." Her earnest expression was sweet and a little scary. "I just thought I could help."

"Oh, you helped all right. You got rid of him real good." I raised my eyebrows. "I didn't want to be here with him, but I've never done anything like that."

"I can tell." Hannah's bright smile could have lit up the world. "I did it all the time in high school and college."

"I can tell," I said. Hannah laughed.

"You know what?" She barely paused and obviously didn't expect me to answer. "I thought he'd incinerate when I sat down with y'all."

"He scared me. Did you see the look on his face?" I wouldn't forget Gage's tight lips and dark gaze for a while.

Hannah pulled a face that didn't look anything like Michael Gage's angry expression. We both laughed.

"Why did you do this?" I locked my eyes with Hannah, willing her to give me a straight answer. We weren't close enough for her to care whether I was unhappy.

Hannah's brow furrowed. I said nothing. The silence grew uncomfortable.

"I just want to be your friend again," she said.

"You're going to all this trouble for friendship?" I couldn't believe it.

"Not long after Mom moved us to Houston, she married my stepfather. He was rich, and that put me into a world most people just dream about." She paused, chewing her lip as she thought. "Who I married let me rub shoulders with all kinds of people—many of them famous. Most people would think these rich and famous people are the best people. But, as the years passed, I thought about you and Rae all the time, about the fun we had."

She waited for me to say something, but I didn't know what to say.

"I was surrounded by people who acted like they were my best friends, but they didn't even know me. After Carson's and my divorce was final, they dropped me, treated me like a stranger." She let out a quivering sigh. "Then, I came back here to Gaslight City, and I saw you hustling around, making a living. Not everybody is able to revisit the road not taken, but I realized I had that chance. So I took it. And here we are. I figure if I keep trying, you'll give me a chance. Not every road is forever."

Nobody had ever wanted to be a part of my life so badly. I was flattered and weirded out. A lifetime of having few friends and being the butt of the joke made me suspicious, but I'd never seen anybody look more sincere than Hannah looked right then. She was making an effort. Maybe I should, too.

"Thanks for rescuing me. I only agreed to the date because I thought he might know something about Rae's murder."

"Did he?"

"Nothing I hadn't already figured out on my own. Worth a try, I guess."

Hannah frowned. "You know, he was pissed. Do you think he'll retaliate?"

I found myself telling Hannah about the other time I'd seen Michael Gage so angry.

"Let me make sure I understand," Hannah said after I went through the story. "He got that angry over a letter from an old colleague?"

"Best I could tell." After a short internal debate, I admitted my further snooping. "Looked the guy up on line and sent him an email asking him to send some pictures of Michael Gage. I made up a story about wanting to put them in the church newsletter."

Hannah's eyes widened. "What on earth for?"

"I guess I wanted to see if it's the same Michael Gage." Hannah looked puzzled, so I explained. "I found a website for a missing woman named Sharon Zeeman Gage. Her story matched details in the Jerry Bower letter Pastor Gage got so angry about."

"So you think..." Hannah let her words trail off.

"I don't know what I think," I said. "Before I think too much, I want to find out what I can."

"Yeah. The most reasonable explanation is a case of mistaken identity."

"But if it was, why did he get so mad?" That's what kept me from dismissing the whole episode.

Hannah took a step closer to me. Her hand closed around my arm to the point of it being painful. "We'll talk about this later. Right now, listen to me. There is a woman watching us. She's coming up behind you."

"What's she look like?"

"Blonde—"

"Go to your car and call 911. She's dangerous." My heart rattled against my chest, beating so hard my vision jarred with it. My face tingled as adrenaline rushed through me.

Hannah backed away, her eyes almost comically wide.

Veronica Spinelli grabbed my upper arm and spun me around.

———

"THE OLD BITCH told me you sold the trailer." Veronica's already scary face twisted into a feral snarl. "She wouldn't let me look at what you found out there. Finally, I got her to tell me you'd come here."

"You confronted my grandmother?" My voice rose in volume as my fury took hold. After what Dean told me and what I'd seen online, I feared Veronica. But my anger at her for bullying Memaw overrode that fear.

"I want what's mine." Veronica poked me in the chest.

"Tell me what's yours. I'll be happy to give it to you." I grabbed her hand and squeezed. Veronica tightened her jaw against the pain and yanked her hand away from me.

"Don't touch me again." I said the words with my teeth clenched, hoping I looked scary. Schoolyard fights had taught me to stand my ground even when I knew I was about to get my ass whipped.

Veronica grabbed me by my blouse. I heard a seam

tear. My fists went up. Hannah came out of nowhere and hit Veronica's back at a full run. She wrapped her legs around Veronica's torso and rode her like the jockey from Hell, tearing at her hair. Veronica managed to shake Hannah off. She thumped to the ground with a pained cry.

What happened next goes to show I'd never make it in prison. I threw a punch at Veronica. The punch connected to Veronica's solar plexus just fine. Veronica even stumbled to the pavement.

She came back up with a fist-sized rock in her hand. I saw the rock hurtling at me, but I couldn't get out of the way fast enough. The rock crashed into my head with a meaty sounding thud. I hit the asphalt hard and tasted blood in my mouth. The parking lot lights got very bright. I could do nothing but listen to Veronica's footsteps running away. I floated on a cloud of misery until a flashlight's blinding beam snapped me back into awareness.

"Aw, hell. She just passed out. This ain't no emergency." Sheriff Joey Holze leaned over me, disgust plastered all over his face. He was one to act holier than thou. He'd stuffed his chubby body into a cowboy outfit, complete with hat and huge buckle making an indention in his belly.

Carly Holze—better known as Mrs. Sheriff Holze—grabbed Hannah by the arm when she tried to approach me. Hannah tried to shake off her aunt, but Carly dug her bony fingers into Hannah's bare arm.

"You okay?" I didn't want Hannah to get herself crossways with her aunt and uncle, who were her only blood relatives in Gaslight City.

"I'm all right—"

"No damn thanks to you." Carly Holze shouted over the rest of Hannah's sentence. "I always say: Once a trouble maker, always a trouble maker."

Hannah jerked away from her aunt and directed an eye roll at the starry sky. Carly, wrapped up in giving me a hateful glare, seemed oblivious to it. *Too bad.*

My head throbbed and swam. I dragged myself to my feet and staggered toward my car. I leaned against it and fumbled for my keys, my breath coming in harsh gasps. Dean Turgeau appeared in front of me decked out in his uniform. I saw two of him and rubbed the side of my face.

"Where'd you come from?"

"Someone in Danner's Landing called 911." Dean shined his flashlight in my face and took a close look at me. "You all right?"

"Veronica Spinelli did this." My words had a sluggish sound to them. "I need to get home. She visited Memaw first."

"You're not going anywhere." Dean grabbed me under my arms and steadied me against the Nova. "Except maybe to the hospital. You might have a concussion."

"Dean, listen to me." I grabbed Dean's shoulders as much to hold me upright as to get his attention. "Veronica might have hurt my grandmother."

Realization sharpened Dean's features. He turned from me and shouted for Brittany Watson. She ran to us with her shoulders back and her chin high. She wore an excited grin. I would have been amused, but my head hurt too bad.

"Go check on Mrs. Mace, Deputy Watson. Ms. Spinelli

reportedly visited her before she confronted Peri Jean here."

Brittany ran for her car and screeched out of the parking lot. Ignoring my arguments, Dean drove me to the hospital in his cop car. At Sheriff Joey Holze and Carly's insistence, the town's only ambulance drove Hannah to the ER to treat her scrapes and bruises. Who said influence didn't help?

18

At the hospital, I found myself confined in a curtained room furnished with an examining table and a stool for the doctor to sit on. The curtains provided only the illusion of privacy to anyone with normal hearing. I listened to a soap opera's worth of drama before Dr. Longstreet joined me.

"I'm fine," I told him and stood. The sooner I got out of this place, the better. The antiseptic odor and the intense glare of the overhead lights had me in a cold sweat. Too many bad memories.

"That's not what Turgeau told me. He was quite concerned about you." Dr. Longstreet approached me and shined a pen light in my eyes.

I grunted and tried to struggle away. The pinprick of light left behind an aftershock of blazing pain.

"Be still," Dr. Longstreet said. "It'll only take a moment. You might have a concussion." Eons later, he shook his head. "I don't see any signs of a concussion. You're going to look like you've been in a fistfight."

"I have been in fistfight." I got up again and pulled together my belongings. "I need to get home to Memaw. Brittany Watson went to check on her, but I never heard any more."

"Leticia's fine." Dr. Longstreet stood in front of me barring my way out. "She's staying in the hospital tonight."

"What did Veronica Spinelli do to her?" I shoved around Dr. Longstreet and pushed the curtain aside. I found myself in a sanitized maze of curtains, and I realized I had no idea where to go.

"Just wait a minute before you go off half-cocked, Peri Jean." Dr. Longstreet exited the exam room and came around me. "Your grandmother is fine. She just had a little spell, probably brought on by all the excitement."

"Then I need to see her." If Veronica Spinelli hurt my grandmother, I'd make her beg the police to arrest her sorry ass.

"Not just yet, you don't. Come on. I want to talk to you." Dr. Longstreet hustled us through a tangle of austere rooms scented with fear. I saw people wandering around who were no longer part of the living world. A little girl holding a teddy bear skipped up and down the halls. Obviously dead, her spirit form wore ghastly injuries. She emitted a loneliness so complete and poignant, it broke my heart.

I yelped when Dr. Longstreet took my arm and pulled me to his office suite. We went straight through his waiting room and past the receptionist's desk and into his office.

"Do you want a drink?" Dr. Longstreet sat down behind his desk and let out a deep sigh.

I shook my head.

"Of course. You don't drink." He produced a pint bottle of Johnny Walker from his desk and drank straight from the bottle. "Days like today have given me this head of white hair."

"What happened today?" I asked. "Car wreck?"

"How do you know?" Dr. Longstreet sat up straight and frowned at me.

I said nothing. All my life, it had been inappropriate for me to admit I could see the dead.

"You really do see them, don't you?" He knew the answer. "The ghosts, I mean."

I didn't understand this sudden change in protocol. Dr. Longstreet and I always pretended I didn't see the spirit world's occupants. We never broke character. Now he wanted me to talk about it? Or was this some kind of trick he would to use to send me back to the loony bin? I searched the recesses of my mind for all the information I could remember on involuntary commitment for mental health reasons. Clammy, slimy sweat broke out all over me.

"Yes." Dr. Longstreet's voice made me jump. "Terrible car wreck. An eighteen-wheeler hit a passenger car head on. What did you see back there? To use a tired expression, you looked like you'd seen a ghost." Dr. Longstreet took another long swig of Johnny Walker and set the bottle down on his desk.

Suddenly, I had a flash of intuition. Memaw was dead. Dr. Longstreet bought me back here so my wails wouldn't disrupt the entire hospital. He wouldn't have me back here to tell me she was fine and dandy. I called on every ounce of self-control I possessed to keep myself seated and my manner calm. I couldn't act nuts. They might not allow me to go home.

"She was less than ten, wasn't she?" I played Dr. Longstreet's game. "The little girl. She had on a pink sweat jacket and long black hair. She had her teddy bear with her, one of those expensive ones."

Dr. Longstreet jumped as though he'd been shocked. "All these years, I knew. I knew you saw things beyond the realm of what medical science can explain. As a doctor, a country doctor, I've seen things. I knew."

"Then why did we always pretend I wasn't quite right?"

"Leticia fought tooth and nail to get legal custody of you after Barbie allowed you to be committed for testing. Carly Holze spoke against Leticia both publicly and to child services. Until that happened, your grandmother believed Carly was an ally. It scared her to have misjudged someone so powerful."

"Carly Holze thought I'd somehow tainted Hannah." I saw it as an adult for the first time. "She wanted something done to me, and she had the law on her side."

Dr. Longstreet pursed his lips and frowned. "This is a small town, honey. The 'haves' have everything, including all the power. Leticia knew it. When you came home, she worried she'd lose you again."

"I don't understand why she didn't just move us away from here."

"Leticia said...she said to make you tough it out. She

said you'd have to learn to hide it or you'd never be safe."
Dr. Longstreet looked down at his desk as he spoke.

"She's dead, isn't she? Memaw, I mean."

"No." Dr. Longstreet's eyebrows shot up. He gave his
head a hard shake. "Of course she's not dead. She's resting
in a private room."

"Then why did you bring me in here?" I stood. "I need
to let her know I'm here."

"Sit down." Dr. Longstreet leveled his gaze on me. His
tone left me no choice but to comply. I sat.

"I need to tell you something. I should have already
told you, but I'm stalling." Dr. Longstreet didn't have
Benny's slick polish, but he had a certain dignity to him. I
had never seen him this way. Fear grabbed hold of me and
squeezed.

———

"LETICIA WAS RIGHT ABOUT one thing. Treating you the way
we did made you tough." Dr. Longstreet rubbed his face.
He looked twenty years older. "You never learned to trust,
though. You also grew to be very dependent on your
grandmother. So, last spring when we found out—"

"What are you saying?" It all clicked into place.
Memaw's tiredness, the way she seemed to have aged so
much in just a few months—everything started to make
some kind of terrible sense.

"I'm saying Leticia has cancer. By the time we found it,
it was already too late to..."

I forgot how to breathe. A crushing weight bore down

on me, finding every sore muscle and making it hurt worse. I couldn't handle this. Too intense. Too adult. Too permanent.

"Why wouldn't she tell me?" Some part of me wildly hoped asking enough questions would make this horrible thing not true. If I wiggled and danced enough, I might wake up in my bed, sweating out the remnants of this nightmare. But the cold truth has a certain ring. This little melodrama was real. My grandmother was dying.

"She wanted the two of you to enjoy the time you had together." Dr. Longstreet took the bottle of Johnny Walker back out of his desk. He didn't drink from it. He just set it on his desk and looked at it. "She's worried about you, worried you won't ever find someone who can love you the way she wants you to be loved."

My chest tightened as a flood of adrenaline stung my nerve endings. Cancer was a merciless executioner. It stripped away dignity and autonomy, leaving only pain and horror in its wake. Memaw took so much pride in her appearance, her intellect, and her independence. I didn't want to watch her wither into nothing, and I knew I had no choice.

"How long does she have?" Nausea rocked and rolled through me. My blouse, now soaked with sweat, clung to me. My fantasy of running away never beat at me with more urgency, but I would never leave Memaw's side as long as she needed me.

"Eighteen months, maybe two years if we're lucky. She might have to start light chemotherapy to keep herself comfortable. She'll eventually be bedridden."

The image of Memaw in a sterile hospital bed, growing thinner and weaker filled my mind. My world crumbled, a scream building in my chest. I bit it back and clenched my hands into fists, reveling in the pain of my fingernails biting into my palms. I squeezed tighter and tighter. *Maybe hurting myself would banish my fears of the future.* My apprehension built to an unbearable intensity, beating at my skin, trying to get out into the world. I took a deep breath and commanded myself to rein it in. One more breath, and I knew I could talk without screaming. I met Dr. Longstreet's eyes across the desk.

"All right. I'm ready to see her."

Dr. Longstreet didn't bother to argue. He showed me to Memaw's room. She looked frailer than ever lying on the hospital bed with her steel gray hair spread out around her head. Every vein in her face was visible. When the door clicked closed, she opened her eyes.

"You fared worse than I did." Memaw's voice was a hoarse impostor of her usual rough boom.

"Why didn't you tell me?" I hoped I didn't have to say cancer out loud.

Memaw understood I knew her secret. Maybe she'd even told Dr. Longstreet to break the news to me. She motioned at Dr. Longstreet to leave. He closed the door behind him.

"Because I knew you'd baby me. Because I knew you'd be sad. And because I don't know what you're going to do with yourself without me to push you."

I pulled the visitor's chair next to her bed and took her bony, liver-spotted hand in mine. For the first time ever, I noticed her hand and mine were about the same size. Our fingernails were the same shape. Tears stung my eyes, and my throat tightened. The tide of sorrow rushed up in my chest. I held it back, just the way Memaw always taught me. I didn't know what I was going to do either.

———

MEMAW FELL ASLEEP NOT LONG after she admitted her illness to me. I left the hospital. The parking lot gravel crunched under my heels, grinding together just like my emotions. Loneliness washed over me, devastating all other emotions, growing until I actually choked. It reminded me of getting lost in the Houston Museum of Natural Science at nine years old on Memaw's and my annual vacation.

Wandering among the endless sea of taller people whose legs all looked the same after a while made me aware of something frightening: I was too small to get myself unlost. Finally, a museum employee took mercy on me and gently helped me find Memaw. I never forgot the helpless feeling; the feeling of being too young, too inexperienced, too little to help myself. Now that feeling came back with a vengeance.

At three o'clock in the morning, I pulled up in front of Memaw's house. Lights blazed from every window. On the way inside, I muttered about the electric bill, careless Sheriff's Deputies named Brittany Watson, and all sorts of other things. It gave me something to do other than feel scared of how Memaw's last months on earth—and spending the rest of my life without her—would feel. Inside the living room, the smell of men's cologne jolted me out of my funk.

My senses on high alert, I took out my pepper spray and made a circuit of the house, which every safety video in the world warns against doing. I didn't care. Even after Veronica's beating, I thought a fight would feel good. Let out some emotion. Sure I was alone, I did another circuit through the house, this time to check for anything missing. Everything seemed to be in its place.

I smelled the odor of men's cologne only in the living room. It triggered a foggy memory, one I couldn't quite latch onto. That bothered me enough to make another circuit through the house, this time locking all the doors and windows. Even the ones in Memaw's room.

Declaring sleep impossible, I started a pot of coffee. Memaw's cancer roosted at the forefront of my brain, and I sat down at the kitchen table in her chair. I ran my fingers over the worn cover of her Bible as sorrow thrummed in my chest. My eyes stung. When I reached up to rub them, my face was already wet with tears. Deep down, where it really counted, I didn't believe I could survive losing her.

Self-pitying sobs built in my throat. I tried to hold them back as if denying the release of crying would make a bit of difference. In the end, I gave in to the sobs. I moaned. I wailed. I beat my fists on the table. None of it changed anything.

———

I MUST HAVE FALLEN ASLEEP. The next thing I knew, daylight flooded the kitchen, and the smell of burned coffee hung in the air. I got up to turn off the coffee pot and rinse the rancid brew out of the carafe.

As I filled the coffee pot with vinegar to remove the stains, I remembered the picture I found of Memaw the day Benny came by to pick up the trailer.

I always thought Memaw an orphan. I tried to remember why. Perhaps because I never met anybody from her side of the family. I had some distant Mace cousins scattered over the US, but I never met anybody directly related to Memaw.

That picture of Memaw hadn't looked like an orphan. It looked like a well-off young lady. If it hadn't been for Memaw's cancer, I probably wouldn't have given that picture a second thought. But, now that I knew, I realized how little I knew about Memaw. I didn't want her to take all these stories—stories of my heritage—to the grave with her.

I called the hospital and had them connect me to Memaw's room. Between complaining about the horrible breakfast and the sadistic nursing staff, Memaw managed to tell me she didn't want me to pick her up. She didn't know when she'd be released, and Pastor Gage had offered to give her a ride home.

I worked outside town that day for one of my regular customers, an elderly shut-in who had me cook a month's worth of meals to freeze and do light housekeeping. The job took most of my day. Memaw and I had a short conversation via cellphone after she got home from the hospital.

She warned me not to baby her. *As if I'd have the temerity to try.*

On the way home, I received an emergency call from Amanda King, owner of Amanda's Hair Flair. She said she needed my help *pronto* and begged me to come right away. H & H Week and all the madness it brought had come to town.

Amanda's Hair Flair operated out of a portable building a mile from downtown. Cars overflowed the little dirt parking lot and sat on the highway's shoulder. When I opened the door, the chaotic scene inside almost made me chicken out. A customer sat under every dryer. The waiting area was standing room only.

Felicia Holze smirked when she saw me but motioned me inside. If anything, marrying Sheriff Joey Holze's only son made her even more of a hater.

"I've got one stylist home sick, and both me and Felicia are booked up." Amanda took some money, made it disappear into the cash register, and thanked her client before speaking to me again. "I need somebody to wash towels and clean up this place. If the Texas State Board of Cosmetology came in here to inspect us right now, my ass would be grass."

"Just go on back and start the towels." Felicia snipped some more hair and returned her attention to me. She said, "Please" like she ought not have to.

Sometimes I wondered if Felicia's nastiness was a symptom of mental illness. She seemed unable to help herself. During high school, she and her minions very effectively passed a rumor I was a closet Satanist. After studying world religions in college, I knew Felicia and her buds didn't have the first clue of the meaning of Satanism. But their rumors had the desired effect. My pariah status went up to Def-Con One. She married Chase and acted as though that somehow gave her status over me, despite their marriage ending a decade ago. I believed wholeheartedly I could still whup her ass and longed to test my theory.

I wandered around the salon speaking to people I knew and collecting damp towels. At Amanda's chair, I ran into Benny Longstreet. Amanda's scissors flew over his head as she trimmed his short, dark hair. He smiled at me.

"How are things with your new acquisition?" I asked Benny.

"Cleaned, and I already have a buyer." He jammed his hand into his pocket. "I found an item you missed when you cleaned out Rae's things."

"Oh?" I shifted the wad of damp towels to my hip.

Amanda stepped away as Benny stood so he could dig in his pocket. He dropped a silver ring into my palm. It was a band perforated in the shape of a spider web with a spider in the middle. A single red ruby adorned the spider's abdomen. The back of the ring was solid.

Understanding hit me hard, and I nearly dropped the ring. This had to be the one Wade Hill told me about, the one that made those awful marks on Rae's face. But this one wouldn't fit a man. Its smaller size would have fit a woman. Was this what Veronica Spinelli wanted out of Rae's things? And what about the one Low_Ryder wore in the sketch? Every time I got a new piece of the puzzle, it made the ones I already had make even less sense.

Benny or the people he hired must have torn that travel trailer apart to find it. I thought I had done a thorough job on the trailer.

Amanda leaned in close to see the ring. "Oh, I remember this. A jewelry salesman came in one day while we were bleaching Rae's hair. Rae bought two, a little one for her and a bigger one in a man's size."

At least I knew Rae had bought both rings. I slipped the ring into my pocket and thanked Benny. My cellphone interrupted his response. The caller ID indicated it was Dara. After she stood me up and ignored my phone calls, my bullshit meter hovered in the red.

"It's Peri Jean." I didn't make an effort to sound nice.

"Girl," she said, her hick accent in full play, "I am so sorry. I heard you came to The Chameleon, but Lloyd had done told me to get out or he'd call the cops."

"I tried to call you, and you didn't answer. I had to drive all the way back to Gaslight City." I turned away from Benny and Amanda and walked into the back room to dump the towels. I grabbed the broom and came back out, still holding the phone to my ear.

"I know," Dara said, "but my roommate kicked me out. I had to find somewhere else to live, like, right then."

I knew Dara's type. The drama never ended. *No wonder she and Rae had been so close.*

"I still wanna meet you. I got a picture of Rae with this boyfriend of hers."

"You have a picture of Rae and BJ together?" I said the

words louder than I'd intended, and both Amanda and Benny looked my way.

"I sure do, and I found this envelope she must have left at my old apartment. It's addressed to you. Let me give you my new address." Dara rattled off numbers and a street. I leaned the broom against a wall and begged a sheet of paper and a pen from Amanda. I scribbled the directions to Dara's digs there at Amanda's workstation. Dara named the time, and I wrote that on the top of the page and circled it.

"Now, listen," I said, "if you stand me up, don't bother calling back."

"No, no, no. Tomorrow morning at ten sharp. I'll be there."

I hung up and raced through my duties at Amanda's. Anticipation at having another piece of the puzzle kept my mind only half on my tasks. Felicia loved that.

19

ON THE WAY out of Amanda's parking lot, I called Dean. He answered his cellphone but sounded distracted. I told him about the ring, and he asked me to meet him at the corner of Houston and Crockett Streets.

I drove over there in the deepening twilight, not knowing what to expect. Dean's and my relationship—if you could call it that—had two speeds, full-blown hate and the barest of tolerance.

Once I reached Gaslight City's small downtown area, people celebrating H & H Week filled every available parking space. I drove around the block three times before I caught someone pulling out and whipped into their spot. Horns blasted and a few entitlement minded tourists shouted at me.

A small crowd gathered at the corner of Houston and Crockett Streets. The solid wall of bodies obscured my view. I elbowed my way into the crowd and found myself standing shoulder to shoulder with Dean Turgeau. On the ground lay Mrs. Watson, bellowing like a hyena being castrated. Dean looked sick. A few tourists videoed the spectacle on their fancy cellphones.

"She won't get up," whispered Dean. "I called for the ambulance, but they're on another call and can't come right now."

"Mrs. Watson?" I spoke in a loud, clear voice. Mrs. Watson couldn't hear so well anymore. "I just saw Mr. Benoit go into Lulu's Espresso Meltdown. He asked me about you."

Mrs. Watson sat up. "Is he still in there?"

"I don't know. You'll have to go see for yourself."

Mrs. Watson stood, brushed the dust off her clothes, adjusted her wig, and headed in the direction of Lulu's. I could tell the locals from the non-locals by which ones had their mouths hanging open and which ones didn't.

Dean rallied. "Show's over, folks. Go spend some money."

The crowd left, albeit reluctantly. Several headed in the direction of Lulu's Espresso Meltdown.

"What's wrong with her?" Dean asked.

"She's lonely and feels like nobody needs her. She does stuff like this all the time."

"You said you had something for me? A piece of evidence?"

I pulled the spider ring out of my pocket. I had wrapped it in a piece of plastic wrap I found at Amanda's. Dean grinned when he saw my attempt at preserving evidence.

"I think this is a match to the ring the guy in the sketch is wearing. It might match the wounds on Rae's face."

Dean nodded and motioned me to follow him to his cruiser. There, he placed the plastic-wrapped ring into an evidence bag. While he put the bag away, I told him where and how I'd come by the ring. Things went great until I mentioned Dara's phone call and our appointment to talk.

"I'm the one who should talk to her." Dean stuck out his jaw.

"But she's willing to talk to me. I bet she'll tell me more than she'd ever tell you."

Dean closed his eyes and exhaled through his teeth. "Tell you what. For the sake of us not having another pointless argument, let's pretend you didn't tell me about Dara. But, after you meet her, tell me what she says."

"You've got a deal."

"This town is crazy. It's like another universe."

I laughed.

"I feel like I'm learning how to do this job all over again." Dean started to get inside his cruiser but stopped and turned back to me. "Want to eat an early supper with me? I've got to make it fast. We are all on overtime because of H & H Week."

I accepted. Dean insisted on buying Frito pies from Dottie's. We agreed to meet at Longstreet Park in fifteen minutes.

———

LONGSTREET PARK, a few blocks from the Mace House on

Alamo Street, had some new playground equipment and a few picnic tables. A statue of the Longstreet who started the family's lumber empire stood in the middle of the park, covered in bird droppings. I walked around the park and fidgeted as I waited for Dean, feeling more anticipation than the night I lost my virginity.

Dean's cruiser rolled into the parking lot and eased in next to my car. He got out holding a brown Dottie's bag. He led the way to a concrete picnic table. I helped him unpack containers of chili and two bags of Fritos. I poured my chips in my chili and stirred. Dean handed me a bottle of water.

"This investigation is getting crazy." Dean wolfed down fast bites of his Frito pie. "Every time I think I've got it figured out, something new shows up. Things might be looking up for Chase, but they're looking down for me."

"You sound like you wish you could just prove Chase did it and be done with it." My Frito pie sat untouched. Dean's comfort with tearing Chase's life asunder bothered me. I knew he had a job to do, but couldn't he show some empathy?

"It would certainly make my life easier." Dean watched me through narrowed eyes, his good mood fading away.

"So it doesn't matter who really killed Rae or how many lives your investigation ruins." I put "investigation" in air quotes just to be catty. "All that matters is that your life is easy."

Dean watched me in silence, that closed-up wariness clouding his eyes. He clasped his hands in front of him. The darkening sky deepened the lines on his face, and it reminded me of the last time I saw Chase. Sadness throbbed within me. I missed him so much. How could I be loyal to Chase while sitting here with Dean? His investigation threw my best friend's life into a tailspin, and I didn't know if I'd ever see him again. I needed to blame someone, so I blamed Dean.

"I gotta go," I mumbled and started for my car.

Leaves crunched behind me. I pretended I didn't hear. Dean grabbed my arm and spun me around.

"Don't you touch me." I doubled up my fist. If I blew things up, left in a rage, I could condemn Dean. It didn't matter that I knew Chase destroyed his own life. When his dreams failed, he refused to get up and try again the way grownups do. He just gave up.

"You can go to jail for assaulting a law officer." Dean, to his credit, did take his hand off me. I searched his eyes for anger so I could feed off it. Instead of anger, I saw confusion and hurt.

"Last time we did that, you ended up looking like a jackass." My words, including the nasty tone of voice, replayed in my mind. Stupid, stupid. I closed my eyes and counted to ten. When I opened them, Dean still stood in front of me, biting his lip. I prepared to eat humble pie.

"Dean, I'm sorry." I exhaled as I said the words, trying to organize all the things I'd done wrong in my mind. "Chase and I go back a long way. I don't think I'll ever be able to believe he killed Rae."

"I can't talk to you about the case's details," Dean said. "But I can say it is more complicated than I ever imagined.

And I didn't expect to meet somebody like you. That part keeps throwing me for a loop."

I didn't know what to say to that. Part of me wanted to hate Dean. The other part of me burned with attraction to him, curiosity about him. His kindness, even though buried under a mountain of surliness, showed through. Most of all, I wanted to know if his lips tasted as good as they looked, if his skin burned against mine, and if I could make his heart beat faster.

"Will you come back and sit with me?" Dean tried to smile, but couldn't quite pull it off. "Your chili's gonna get cold."

I cut off my dirty fantasies and trudged back to the picnic table, determined to act like a grownup. I managed to choke down the rest of my cold chili.

"What I said before—the thing about you and Chase murdering Rae, the stuff about the crystal ball—was uncalled for." He took a bite of his cold chili and grimaced. "I want to explain."

"There's no need." I hated stuff like this. It complicated things, opened wounds, scared me. I sipped my water and desperately hoped I didn't spew used Frito pie all over the table. Dean held out his hands, palms up. I nodded that I'd listen.

"Before I came here, I worked for East Baton Rouge Parish Sheriff's Homicide Division. I told you a little about how I came here. About making a mistake and getting somebody killed."

"You don't have to do this." If he told me, things between us could never go back to simple. Some women want this kind of openness. Not me. The idea of laying all my guts on the table instilled a breathless horror in me.

"Please listen to me." Dean's voice rose. "I'm so sick of people being afraid to let me tell them what happened, how I fucked up, how I'm a failure."

"Fine. Tell me that stuff." I took out my cigarettes and lit one up. Between the nicotine and my spinning head, maybe I'd pass out and miss his confession.

———

"About a year ago, I was working a murder case. A bad one. People kept turning up dead, but my partner and I couldn't figure out how it all connected.

"In the middle of it all, my marriage to my childhood sweetheart was imploding. She had been cheating on me, so I cheated on her. I stayed out at bars all night and came to work too hungover and exhausted to think. My partner picked up the slack.

"Eva Cassidy. That was my partner. She was a little, tiny woman—kind of like you—and so brave. She figured out who the killer was but found him while she was checking out another lead. He shot her in the chest three times. About five minutes before that happened, she left a message on my cellphone asking me to come back her up." Dean looked into my eyes. "The rip of it all was the very psychic who offered us help in the beginning turned out to be the murderer."

"And every time you see me, you think about this guy." *And how he killed Eva while you weren't doing what you were supposed to be doing.* I kept the second part to myself. Not one of us is without fault.

Dean nodded, his normally bright blue eyes dark and full of storm clouds.

"I am so sorry. Working for Sheriff Fatass and listening to him bitch about me has to make it that much worse," I said. "Is...this incident what happened to your leg?"

Dean pressed his lips together. His face turned such a complete red it extended to the tips of his ears.

"Yes, that's what happened to my leg." He spat out the words. "There's some physical therapy and other treatments I could take that might make it hurt less, but I haven't bothered."

"Why not?" As always, I thought in terms of money. "Doesn't the county offer good insurance?"

"My carelessness got my partner killed and me hurt." Dean curled his lip into a sneer. "She'll never walk in the sun again. Never see her children again. I deserve to remember her every day of my life."

"You can't feel that way. It wasn't your fault—"

"It was!" Dean slammed his fist down on the concrete picnic table and flinched from the impact. "Eva worked the case by herself because I couldn't get my shit together. She wouldn't have been out there by herself if I had been doing my job."

"And that's why you want to see Rae's murder solved?" I needed to understand this part of Dean so we could quit running in circles. "So you can know you got the bad guys?"

"Nothing that noble. Turns out, I'm still a selfish shithead." Dean's nose and cheeks were red. Tears swam in his eyes. "I got into some big trouble over my part in Eva's shooting. I wasn't asked to resign the East Baton Rouge Parish's Sheriff's Department, but it was made known I needed to. So there I was, in my late thirties and jobless. Cop work is the only job I've ever known. If I can't solve Rae's murder and make Sheriff Joey look good, he'll find a reason to get rid of me."

I walked around the table and gave him a hug. He tensed at first, pulling away from me, but leaned into me after a moment.

"What was that for?"

"You looked like you needed it." I sat back down on my side of the table.

"Joey just hired me because I knew Hannah from way back. I used to work security detail for sporting events and met her and Carson. We had a chance meeting after her divorce. She told me she was moving back home, back to Gaslight City, and her uncle, the sheriff, had a position open. She told him about me, and my homicide experience caught his interest.

"I came here, applied for the job, and he hired me on the spot. Sheriff Holze doesn't like involving the state police in his homicide investigations. He figured with my experience he'd never have to again. I figured the most I'd see is the very occasional rage murder or drug deal gone bad—"

"For what it's worth," I broke in, "that usually is all we have."

"I know." Dean smiled. "I checked. Then Rae's murder

came up almost right off the bat. Chase doing it would have tied it all up in a neat bow. I'd only have to see you checking me out in the mornings when I'm jogging, and you being," he swallowed hard, "what you are would never touch me."

I turned my face away from Dean, wanting to put my hands over my ears. I didn't. Instead, I heard myself talking about things I needed to keep quiet. It horrified me, but for some reason I couldn't stop. "It drives me crazy. All my life, people disliked me for this thing I couldn't help. Your boss is a perfect example. Nobody ever asked me if I wanted to be this way. People either think I'm something unholy or mentally ill."

Dean reached across the table and put his hand over mine, twining his warm, strong fingers into mine.

"Not me. See, I'm a pretty good cop. After Sheriff Joey gave me the lowdown about you, I asked around." He gestured at the silent houses around us. "Nobody thinks you're a fake. Some call you crazy, which means they've seen you do something that makes them damn uncomfortable. But it also means you're not a fake."

"It sucked not being able to write me off as a lying charlatan?" I bit my lip to hold back my smile. Dean dealt in absolutes, in facts. No facts existed to help him put me in a neat little category.

"Oh, it sucks. It sucked worse when I started caring whether you running around like you're on a detective show would get you in hot water."

Dean's lapel mic crackled. He answered, speaking mostly in numbers. When he stopped speaking, his face was closed. I knew he was finished pouring his heart out to me. We gathered our garbage and walked to our cars.

"Give me the address of Dara's apartment. At least I'll know where you went if you go missing." Dean shoved his notebook at me, and I copied the address.

He leaned forward and brushed my cheek with a kiss. My cheek tingled where he kissed it, and his clean scent lingered. Warmth spread over me as my heart fluttered. I closed the distance between us and kissed him. Really kissed him. He tasted as good as he looked. His arms slid around my waist and pulled me onto my tiptoes. His radio crackled again. We both groaned and pulled apart.

"Call me," he said and got into his cruiser.

———

THE AROMA of warm sugar greeted me at the door. After seeing Memaw lying in the hospital bed, it stunned me to see her working hard in the kitchen. She stood with her back to me scooping perfect tablespoons of cookie batter out of a huge mixing bowl and dropping them onto a cookie sheet. A row of pies lined the kitchen counter.

"That looks good," I said. "It smells even better."

"The church is having a bake sale. I promised to provide a few things." Memaw's idea of "a few things" went above and beyond the norm.

"Why don't you sit down? I'll finish all that."

"This is precisely why I didn't want you to know I'm dying of cancer. I knew you would act exactly like you're acting right now." Memaw turned to face me, her arms crossed over her chest and a dour look on her face.

So she wanted to talk about the thousand-pound gorilla in the room. It surprised me considering we'd spent my whole life pretending I didn't see ghosts.

"If you make yourself sick, we won't have as much time together." I laid my grievance on the table. Why not?

"I'm already sick. What is time together if I can't enjoy it?"

Both the picture I found of young Memaw and the conversation I'd had with Dr. Longstreet tormented me. So much lay between us, unmentioned. In the face of losing her forever, I wanted to know who I was.

"Good point. I'll add to it. What good is time together if all we do is keep secrets from each other?" I risked driving a wedge between us, but time was short. If I didn't do this now, I might never work up the nerve again.

"Oh hell. I just didn't want to see you upset." She widened her eyes. "Just like you are right now."

"I'm not just talking about the cancer. I'm talking about the way we dance around what I am. Dr. Longstreet told me you insisted on it. I want to know why that is."

Memaw did a double take but didn't try to pretend she didn't understand. "Honey, try to understand. I survived this kind of thing long before the day you told everybody how you knew where Hannah's daddy hid her Christmas presents."

"What do you mean?" In my naiveté, I thought she wanted to talk about my grandfather's premature death and my father's murder. Boy, was I wrong.

Memaw took a pan of cookies from the oven and set them aside. She motioned me to follow her to the table. We both sat down. Forget butterflies in my stomach. Dinosaurs could have been stomping around in there. I wondered if Pandora felt this way right before she realized she'd fucked up.

"This conversation is long overdue, and it's all my fault." Memaw hung her head, blinking rapidly. "I hope you can hear what I have to say without hating me. For a long time, you were too young to hear it. After you got old enough, things seemed so hard for you. I just...I don't know."

On TV, cheesy soap opera music always started when somebody made a statement like that. I hunched in my seat, as though that might protect me from the bad stuff. Hearing Memaw's secrets would change the way I saw things, maybe for the worse. Living in a house built of secrets had its comforts. My insistence on the truth might come back to haunt me. But it was too late to hit the undo button. Besides life doesn't have one.

"My mother could do what you do—see ghosts." Memaw let out a deep breath she must have been holding. When she spoke again, she did it in short, disconnected bursts. "So could my brother, Cecil. My twin sister, Ruth, not so much. She was like Daddy, though. So it didn't matter."

Cold, hurtful shock drowned out any coherent thought. Tears welled in my eyes. A lifetime of being the outsider flashed through my memories. Seeing ghosts was a family trait like our dark eyes and high cheekbones.

Surely, it would have helped me to know. Was this why we never went around Memaw's family? So I'd never learn how to be what I am?

"Why didn't you tell me? It would have helped me feel normal to know them." My chin trembled, and I turned away so Memaw couldn't see the tears flooding my eyes. The loss of not knowing these people tore at me.

"Maybe it would have." Memaw's eyes filled with tears, too. "But, then, they'd have made you like them."

"They are like me."

"No, ma'am. They are most certainly not like you." Memaw's words came out strong and forceful. "You're kind, honest, and compassionate. My family is...nothing you want to know or to know you."

"So you think what I am is bad?" I twisted my fingers together on the tabletop. No surprise there. The shunning, the sideways glances, the whispering. All proof I was *defective*.

"I'm going about this wrong. The same way I've done since that awful day when you were eight." Memaw crossed her arms over herself and looked at the ceiling. A tear slid down her cheek. Let's start from some kind of beginning."

———

"MY MOTHER COULD DO what you do. See the ghosts. Feel their emotions. She came from a family of—I guess you'd call them psychics. They called it Knowing. They called seeing the ghosts Seeing. Those words you could say in public without drawing too much attention.

"Daddy came from a family of traveling con artists. There is no other way to put it. None of them ever did an honest day's work. They always had an angle, a scam." For the first time, she looked at me straight on, a gleam in her eye. "Rae got it honest, darlin'.

"Daddy and Momma were the perfect pair. They'd go into a town and convince a new widow they knew where her late husband hid a fortune. Momma knew how to manipulate her gifts. She could pick up just enough about the deceased to make it believable. Or Momma might somehow know the deceased's family had murdered them. Then the blackmail would start. And everybody wants Uncle Elmer to send them a message from beyond the grave."

I laughed at that in spite of myself.

Memaw shook her head, and the sad look in her eyes hurt my heart. "It might sound funny, but it was a hard way to grow up. We never stayed in one place for long. People inevitably figured out they were being scammed, and they'd run us out of town. I hated it. I ran away at seventeen, and I've never seen them since."

"I guess I understand why you never told me." But I still wished I had known. A lifetime of feeling like a freak had a tendency to suck the joy out of life.

"If the incident with Hannah Kessler—the one that ended with you in a mental hospital— had never happened, I might have told you." Memaw raised her eyebrows. "If for no other reason, I'd have told you about my family to warn you about them. But after that, I was scared. You see, people—especially people facing something that can't possibly be real but obviously is—can be dangerous. I learned that when I was young too." Her chest hitched with a silent sob, but she got a hold of herself to continue.

"My parents had a change of life baby, a little boy they named Raymond. He was born when I was about fifteen. Cute as a button, he was. I might have spoiled him a little." Memaw spoke in a quiet voice, the tiniest of smiles curving her lips. "We were living in a town outside Dallas. The jig, as my daddy used to say, was about up. We went to bed early, planning to slip out before sunrise the next morning. Some locals set the house on fire. Everybody got out except for Raymond. The police didn't do much after some important people whispered in their ears. So, you see, I know what people can do to other people."

"But that was back in the 1950s, right? That wouldn't have happened in the 1990s." I understood the horror of Memaw's loss. But she was an educated woman. She knew things like that didn't—couldn't—happen anymore. Nothing stayed off the grid.

"Things might seem like they change, but they don't. There's a lot you have forgotten...or never realized." Memaw watched me with her eyes narrowed and her brows drawn.

"Can't you tell me? It's all over now. I'm a grown woman." My voice shook with the rest of my body. I couldn't stop shivering.

"Remember this: It'll never be over. One thing I realized back then is I have enemies in this town. And it's people I don't have a damn clue what I did to piss them off."

"But they sent me away for seeing ghosts." My voice warbled with unshed tears. "And you knew nothing was wrong with me. How could you let that happen?"

Memaw and I stood at the same time and stared at each other across the table. She held her hands out to me. "No, baby, it wasn't that way at all."

"What way was it then?" Memories of a stark white room and bright lights tore open all the scars I'd sealed and buried. Panic lodged in my throat. Voices from more than twenty years ago, voices I had done everything I knew to forget, said things like, "Schizophrenic...should be institutionalized for life...severe break with reality."

Memaw lips moved, but I couldn't hear her words. Those old voices from the mental hospital and the roar of my own paranoia were too loud. Without meaning to, I shouted, "What?"

Memaw grabbed my hands and squeezed hard.

My veneer of control snapped back into place. I put my face in my hands and muttered, "I'm sorry for yelling at you."

"No. I'm the one who's sorry." Her face had turned gray, her lips nearly white. "Your being taken to the mental hospital for testing happened before I knew what was going on."

Memaw stared at me for a long moment before I understood what she wanted. She wanted confirmation I believed her, that I didn't consider her my enemy. I nodded, and so did she. We sat back down, facing each other across the scarred old table.

"When the whole mess broke, the school called Barbie because she was your mother and—supposedly—in charge of you." Memaw's mouth twisted with bitterness she'd evidently held onto these twenty years. "According to Jolene Fischer, Barbie signed the papers for the psychological testing without a word of argument. She didn't even call to tell me what was going on...and I guess she didn't have any obligation to. Jolene called the high school and pulled me out of class to let me know."

My mouth had gone dry as dirt. I reached for a glass of tea Memaw had left on the table. Hand shaking, I almost knocked the glass over. Quick as a flash, Memaw reached out to steady the glass. I put my hands in my lap and didn't reach for it again.

"I knew Barbie would be working, so I went down to Mickey's Five-and-Dime—remember that place?—and confronted her." Memaw frowned and said her next words through clenched teeth. "She said without your daddy alive, she didn't know what to do with you."

Memaw looked at the table, her lips trembling. Her fingers twitched as she lived through it again.

"Well, what happened?" Some sick part of me needed to know what Memaw's response to my ne'er-do-well mother had been.

"I slapped her right across the face, is what happened." Memaw's mouth curled into a little smile. "They kicked me out of Mickey's for life, and I told them they could kiss me where the sun don't shine."

Laughter—the laughter of relief something unpleasant was over with no lasting injury—quivered and bubbled to the surface. A second later, our laughter filled the kitchen.

"Then I made Barbie get in the car with me, and we drove down to that hospital and signed you out." Memaw raised her eyebrows at me, still smiling. "I think it insulted her tender sensibilities."

"I thought I remembered hearing you hollering." Hazy memories of a nurse, her face pinched in worry, found me and I shook them away.

"Oh, I did holler." Memaw snorted. "On the way there, we'd stopped to get Wilton Bruce—Hooty's daddy, the judge—and he threatened them with every legal this 'n that he could think of. I'm not sure how they heard him over my shouting, but I think he made more difference than I did."

That Memaw came to my rescue wholeheartedly helped my feelings somewhat, but her secrecy about the paranormal sixth sense running in her family, my family, bothered me. My gut told me to let it go.

"Tell you what," Memaw said. "There's a new rule in this house. We won't act like you seeing through the veil is a secret. It isn't, and I'm sorry I didn't tell you the truth sooner. And if there's ever something I do that you can't understand, just ask me. When you bury things, time just buries them deeper."

We hugged and cut into a pie intended for the bake sale. Sugar and lard didn't cure everything, but it helped.

20

FOR THE SECOND time in less than a week, I made the trek to Tyler in my old gas-guzzler. This time, it cost even more because I had to pass off a lucrative appointment to one of my competitors.

I checked my rearview mirror often for the black GTO. Last Friday night taught me not to let it catch me unaware. Especially not on these lonely country roads.

By the time I reached Tyler, I was a nervous wreck. I drove past Dara's apartment the first time and had to double back. She lived in an apartment complex of five beat-up two story buildings with walk-up entrances. Since I was fifteen minutes early, I sat in the car considering what I was about to do.

A lot of things could happen once I got inside Dara's apartment. She could be playing both sides of the fence and have Rae's boyfriend up there waiting for me. If he was the same man I encountered the morning of Rae's murder, he'd hurt me again. Maybe kill me. Or Dara herself could do me harm.

I wished I traveled with some sort of weapon. I rarely thought of myself as a weak, vulnerable woman, but I was. I dug through my glove box until I found a few rolls of quarters I used when I took things to the Laundromat for clients. They'd do in a pinch. My punch would pack a lot more of a wallop with a roll clenched in my fist. I slipped the rolls into my jacket pocket and climbed out of the car.

For once, my luck was in. Had it been one of those modern cities of endless apartment buildings, I'd have never found building three, where unit 312 was sure to be.

Dara must have heard my feet ringing on the metal stairs leading to her apartment and opened the door. She beamed. "You right on time, ain't cha, girl?"

Dara turned out to be a brunette version of Rae, voluptuous with a tiny, flat waist and long, tanned legs. Her wild, brown hair stuck out every which way without being curly. She motioned me inside.

I smelled nag champa, which usually meant dope unless Dara had a spiritual side. Sure enough, I spotted a half-smoked doobie in a heavy glass ashtray on the coffee table. Apprehension spiked into my muscles, tightening them painfully. Dara might be a harmless pothead. On the other hand, the joint could be the only sign I'd get before things went to hell in a big hurry. I glanced around the apartment, praying I'd notice any warning signs I needed to run for my life.

"How come you moved?" I pretended I hadn't seen the roach. Dara might take any interest I showed as a desire to smoke with her, and I wanted that almost as much as I wanted a raging case of acne.

"My old apartment got broken into." Dara displayed the half-lidded stare and slow, careful speech of the profoundly stoned. "My roommate said it was my fault since my room was the only one messed up. People are always doing that, going back on their word, getting mad for no reason—"

"You told me on the phone you have a picture of Rae and her boyfriend and a package Rae addressed to me?" I would have to keep reminding Dara of my visit's purpose. Being with Dara reminded me of my short first marriage. It also reminded me of Chase. As much as I missed him, I didn't miss this. I couldn't wait to get back out to my car and sanity.

"I totally forgot." Dara pointed her finger at me and giggled. "Lemme go get it."

She meandered into the only other room, which I guessed was a bedroom. Several long minutes later, right as I was about to go looking for her, Dara walked slow as a turtle out of the bedroom.

"Man, I forgot where I put the stupid thing." Dara handed me a brown padded envelope addressed to me in Rae's handwriting. After I took it from her, she handed me the picture, her face set in a mask of studious concentration.

The picture had been taken in a nightclub and was dark. To make matters worse, a flickering television provided the only light in Dara's apartment. I walked into the galley kitchen and flipped on the light. A group shot, the picture showed several of the girls I met at The Chameleon. Dara, who was absent, must have been the photographer.

Right there, wearing her biggest cheese-eating grin, was Rae. Benny Longstreet sat next to her with his arm around her shoulders. A thrill worked its way through me. I'd suspected Benny had known Rae in the biblical sense, but seeing the proof of it took my breath away.

Someone knocked. Dara stared as though she had no idea what to do. Maybe she didn't.

"I'll get it." I went to admit our guest, planning to make an excuse to leave.

Dara's slack expression showed no recognition.

I pulled open the door. The person on the other side wore camouflage head to toe, but I recognized him. Benny. Before I could react, Benny reared back a fist and slugged me in the stomach. My breath whooshed out of me, and my knees loosened. Sucker punched again. Those damn coin rolls hadn't done me a bit of good.

As I struggled to pull in a breath, he yanked the picture out of my hand and shoved me to the floor. I curled into the fetal position, fully expecting him to kick me. His footsteps thundered down the metal steps as he ran away.

Dara, belatedly, screamed for help. She sounded slow and confused. A door across the way opened. A guy with no shirt and stringy, long hair boiled out of his apartment and ran after Benny, but he only went a few steps before he returned.

"You all right, lady?" He leaned over me. "Want me to call the po-po?"

I rolled onto my knees, still whooping for breath. I couldn't speak, but I shook my head. The metal stairs clanged as someone ran up them. I braced myself for Benny's return and moaned in relief when I saw Dean. He ran to me and knelt beside me.

"You all right?" he asked. I nodded.

The shirtless guy peered into Dara's apartment. "Dude...is that, like, a roach in your ashtray? You probably don't want to, like, call the po-po if you've got a roach in the ashtray."

I didn't bother to tell him that Dean was the po-po. Behind us, Dara wailed in a shrill monotone, oblivious to everything.

"Can you please stop?" Dean glared at her.

Dara continued to wail, never acknowledging two extra people were in her apartment.

"Shut up," Dean hollered.

Dara jumped. I sucked in a breath of air.

Dean pulled me to my feet. "I saw him come up here, but I hung back to see what happened. I am so sorry. Let me get you out of here."

"Get the package addressed to me off the counter in the kitchen." I pointed at it, and Dean hurried into the kitchen and grabbed it.

Dara watched us like a show on TV, her mouth half open. I thanked her for her hospitality and left her standing there with the no-shirt guy. *Maybe they'd make a love connection.*

Dean made no effort to hide his guilt. He apologized to

me numerous times on the way to car, babbling about jurisdiction and gut feelings.

"I had the morning off and decided to go out to the lake. Stopped in a convenience store for gas. Benny was in there with a bunch of road munchies. He told the cashier he was headed to Tyler on business. I just knew."

"Don't." I shook my head, still fighting to breathe. "I'm all right. Or at least, I will be. Let's see what's in this package."

I tore open the package and found nothing but a DVD. Disappointment flooded me. We'd have to wait until we got home to see what was on it.

"Don't touch it," Dean said. He used a piece of paper and a pen to get the DVD out of its case. "I've got a DVD player in the car."

"What on earth for?"

"I've got two nephews. Last time I took them out, they left it. I've been meaning to give it back, but..." He shrugged.

———

DEAN DUG around in his ratty old Trans Am and came up with a portable DVD player.

We crowded together and turned on the DVD. At first, the frame showed nothing but an empty motel room. Within seconds, a woman's giggle became audible. Rae and Benny, buck naked, walked into the room. The two must have come from the bathroom. Their bodies glistened with water.

They went straight to the bed kissing. Rae glanced at the computer several times, probably wondering if it was recording her little show. When they finally got down to business, Benny's back was to the camera. The little thatch of hair above his buttocks was perfectly visible.

I wandered away to let Turgeau watch the DVD by himself. Dean viewed the distasteful show with one hand over his mouth and one eyebrow raised. After a few minutes, he motioned me to join him.

The DVD screen showed nothing but white text on a blue background. It read:

Benny,

I am pregnant. Whether or not the baby is yours, this DVD will raise enough doubt to cost you your seat on the Gaslight City Council, your post as deacon of Gaslight City First Baptist Church, your wife and your kids, and half of your money.

I will gladly disappear if you'll give me half a million dollars. Don't try to tell me you're not good for it, because I know you are. Don't be resentful. I've got trouble riding my ass too. Otherwise, I wouldn't do you this way. We had fun together.

Rae

"She improved that letter, didn't she?" Turgeau's eyes flitted over me, and everything below my navel tightened. Heat zinged between us. *We have to do something about our attraction and soon.*

"Rae must have owed Veronica Spinelli money," I said. "I can't figure out why, though. I bet a silver dollar Veronica is in cahoots with her old partner in crime, Billy

Ryder. Maybe he helped her squeeze Rae for money. Either way, from all accounts, she threatened Rae."

"I'll give you the why," Turgeau said. "Yesterday evening, I received intelligence from Gatesville Prison from one Tonya Russell, who knew both Rae and Veronica. Ms. Russell said Rae promised Veronica money for protection in prison. Apparently Rae got Pastor Michael Gage to speak at both hers and Veronica's parole hearings, which went a long way to getting them released. I guess that wasn't enough."

"Remind me to never go to prison," I said.

We got quiet. It was human nature to bounce back, to forget we were talking about a woman who'd never feel sunlight again, have children, or learn she was above this trashy behavior.

"So what are you going to do now?" I asked Turgeau.

"Well, this might surprise you, since you think you're the only one who can properly investigate Rae's murder, but Mr. Bennett Longstreet was already under investigation. This DVD gives me enough to get a search warrant. Don't know how long it'll take me to pick him up. If you see him, run."

Dean and I ate lunch together. The heat from our kiss and the earlier contact made sitting in such close proximity a dizzying experience. Had I not had a job that afternoon and needed the money, I'd have suggested getting a cheap room at a no-tell motel.

Instead, I screwed up my courage and said, "What are you doing tonight?"

"Arresting Benny. Shift ends at eleven. Wanna come over?" His lips parted as he waited for my answer.

"I thought you weren't supposed to get involved with people in an ongoing investigation." I kept my tone light and teasing, but I sincerely didn't want to get him in trouble with his boss. Sheriff Joey would be pissed when he figured out Dean and I were seeing each other.

"After all the rules I've seen broken down at that sheriff's office, I'm not too worried about it."

"Tonight," I said.

———

I DROVE BACK to Gaslight City and spent the rest of the day working. A dizzying pirouette of desire mixed with a barrage of worst-case scenarios plagued my every task. I worked late because I couldn't stand having nothing to do until it was time to go to Dean's. Somehow, I made it to his house in one piece.

Dean lived in a rundown mid-twentieth century Tudor a few blocks from the Mace House. I pulled into the driveway and left the car running. My conflicted emotions had my thoughts writhing in a feverish mess.

I wanted to be with Dean, but the thought freaked me out a little. My romances—if they could even be called that —were destined for a short shelf life by my own design. I didn't want to navigate the complexities of a grownup relationship. So I picked men who couldn't go the distance for one reason or another. For a long time, I thought they filled the void, kept me from being lonely and horny. But I wanted more from Dean.

The first step to more lay in my very near future. No matter if it ended in happily ever after or heartbreak, I knew being with Dean would tattoo my life. I sat there in front of his house seriously contemplating backing out of the driveway and going somewhere else. A curtain in the front window twitched. *Now or never.*

I walked up the cracked sidewalk and rang the doorbell. Dean met me at the door wearing a white t-shirt and faded blue jeans. His eyes, always full of intensity and intelligence, danced with nervousness. It almost convinced me to turn tail and run. If it hadn't been for the way the t-shirt clung to his muscled chest, I probably would have.

"Hi...come on in." He held the door open, and I walked inside.

The house sat empty for several years before Dean purchased it. He hadn't done much to the house yet. Freed by the near constant humidity, the wallpaper hung in strips. The ancient, stained linoleum flooring buckled with cracks.

"Wow." I turned a slow circle and peeked into a den where Dean seemed to have set himself up. It boasted a big screen TV, a TV tray, and a fake leather bachelor couch. "You know, the wallpaper will come right off with dish soap and water. All you have to do is make a solution and spray it on the walls. I could—"

"Did you come here to give me an estimate for your services?" Dean lips twitched and almost curved into a smile.

I shook my head. I wanted to say something seductive, but I couldn't come up with words that didn't sound like dialogue from a cheesy porn movie. I moved closer to Dean, until my breasts brushed his chest. He inhaled deeply and circled his arms around my waist. I stood on my tiptoes and kissed him, inhaling the fresh scent of soap and shaving cream. Dean kissed me back hard, pulling me up and against him. My pulse fluttered as my nerve endings grew more sensitive.

I twined my arms around Dean's neck and tilted my head, allowing him to explore my mouth with his tongue. He cupped my butt and lifted me. I wrapped my legs around his waist, and he carried me into his bedroom. We didn't need words or foreplay. We'd been doing that from the moment we met.

Dean dropped me on his bed, knelt over me, and parted my lips with his tongue. The fire inside me built to an ache. We kissed and groped until I pushed Dean away and got off the bed. While Dean watched in silence, I unbuttoned my jeans and pushed them and my special occasion black lace panties to my ankles. I wiggled out of my shirt and bra and dropped them on the floor, panting from the throb of anticipation.

Dean shimmied out of his jeans and t-shirt. His body was a canvas of hard planes of sculpted muscle. Impressive. I crawled back onto the bed, and we knelt face to face. Dean pulled me against him and eased me backward onto the mattress, pulling my legs up around his waist.

I had one last second to doubt my decision, and then nothing mattered but our bodies rising and falling together. My eventual cries of ecstasy broke the stillness of the house. Dean was as good as he looked. Afterward, we lay half-dozing in each other's arms.

When Dean's breathing deepened into the pattern of sleep, I knew I needed to go. I sat on the edge of the bed and gathered my clothes off the floor. Dean opened one eye.

"Where you going?" He rose on one elbow, the sheet puddled around his waist.

"Home. I need to make sure Memaw's okay."

"That tough old woman doesn't need you coddling her. Bet she's already asleep anyway. Spend the night with me."

This was too much, too fast. We'd had a big, frustrating buildup to the sex, which had been some of the best I'd ever had. We both needed time to think things over. Subconsciously, I wanted to prepare for Dean to disappoint me. He stroked my back while I thought.

"At least stay a few more minutes." Dean reached across me and took my clothes out of my hands. He pulled me on top of him, and I lowered myself onto his hardness. His hands cupped my breasts as I rocked on top of him. This time, our movements were less frenzied, and we stared into each other's eyes as the tightness inside me built and we exploded together.

The next time I woke up from a contented doze, I could feel the lateness of the hour. Dean talked softly on his cellphone. He said goodbye and jerked on his clothes.

"That was Sheriff Holze." He rolled his eyes as he said the name.

"What did that turd want?" The notion of Joey Holze

calling while I was naked spurred me to get dressed. I got up and gathered my clothes.

"Did you know dispatch calls him at home every time something interesting comes in?" He gritted his teeth and shook his head. "Anyway, a black GTO was found burning at Beulah Church Road and 4077. Witnesses report two bodies in the car." Dean came up behind me, put his arms around me. He kissed my shoulders and neck. "He wants me to go out there, try to head off the State Highway Patrol folks."

"What on earth for?" I leaned into him, and he stiffened, drawing in a sharp breath. He slid his arms around my waist. My voice came out high and breathy. "Why not let them have the case?"

"Like I told you before, Holze wants to keep Burns County business in house. State boys can call in the Texas Rangers to investigate. Holze wants those badasses poking around his county about as much as he wants to go on a diet." Dean pulled away from me and went to his dresser where he picked up a shoulder holster rig and pulled it on with jerky movements.

"I don't see how you stand working for him." I watched Dean carefully. What he said in the next few seconds would determine whether we'd have a repeat performance.

"If only I had known before I hired on." Dean blew out a sigh. "I was in such a hurry to get out of Louisiana that I jumped."

"Think you're gonna quit?" I had to ask. If he was on

his way out of Burns County, I could handle it. But I needed to know so I could pretend it didn't matter.

He turned to me, and we watched each other for a long moment. Seeming to decide something, he leaned against his dresser, curling his fingers over the edges. Only the whiteness of his fingers gave away his trepidation. I stopped dressing and gave him my full attention.

"Next year's the sheriff's election." He said no more. There was no need. He planned to stay. I released a relieved breath I hadn't even been aware of holding.

"There's been a Holze in the sheriff's seat since the 1940s," I said. "They own that office. You've got a fight ahead of you."

"This'll be like a chess game. You know who has the power in this county. Didn't you dream of espionage and high stakes as a kid? Here's your chance to live your fantasies." Dean slipped a denim jacket over his shoulder holster.

I lived my fantasies a few minutes ago, I thought. The mistrustful part of me told me to be careful, because Dean might use me. I shut it down, determined to let this play out naturally.

"I'm game," I said. "You ready to go see the GTO?"

Dean crossed the room, his steps slow and careful. When he reached me, he pulled me to him and leaned his forehead against mine.

"I can't show up with you. Stay here." He kissed my nose. "Wait on me to get back."

"I'll go on home. I've got to get an early start anyway."

"You are determined not to spend tonight with me.

Why?" He traced my jawline with one finger, and I shivered.

I sat on the bed and pushed my feet into my cowboy boots. He watched me, waiting for my answer. I gave it in the form of a shrug. He nodded and held out his hand to me.

We walked outside with our hands linked. Dean leaned me up against the car and kissed me. Feeling eyes on us, I broke the kiss and glanced around. A shadowy figure stood in the window of the neighboring house.

"This'll be all over town by nine this morning," I said.

Dean shrugged, kissed me again, and got in his Trans Am. He turned the key, but nothing happened. He tried several more times as I looked on. Finally, I leaned down to the window.

"Need a ride?"

Dean slumped. I skipped to my car, elated I'd get to see the action.

———

DEAN ASKED me not to drive him right up to the burning GTO. I parked a short distance away and stayed in the car.

The fire had been extinguished, but smoke still rose from the wreck. The glossy black paint was bubbled and ruined. The stench of roasting flesh hung in the air. State troopers and Burns County sheriff's deputies milled around the car, shining their flashlights on the interior. Sure enough, I saw two people sitting in the car. Given the conditions, it had to be two dead someones.

I hoped the bodies were Veronica Spinelli and Billy Ryder. Veronica had driven Rae to blackmail Benny, which had motivated Benny to...I shivered at the thought. I watched as Dean showed his badge to a state trooper and the two shook hands.

Sheriff Holze pulled up in his personal car. He got out and duck walked toward the knot of law enforcement officers, red and blue lights flashing over his chubby body. He walked up to Dean and pointed at my car. Dean jogged over to me, and I rolled down the window.

"You better go home, Nancy Drew." He smiled. "There's a good possibility the Texas Rangers will take over the case as soon as the Veronica Spinelli and Billy Ryder angle comes out. Holze is furious and seeing you pissed him off even more."

"What'd you tell him?" I knew I shouldn't ask. If Dean had lied about our relationship, his answer would hurt me. But it would hurt him if he didn't lie.

"I told him I was off duty, and none of his business." Dean narrowed his eyes as he watched Holze talking to the state troopers.

"Are the bodies in the car Veronica Spinelli and Billy Ryder?" I asked.

Dean shrugged and glanced back at the crime scene. I followed his gaze and gasped at what I saw. A familiar woman stepped from the car. I thought her alive until I noticed the cooked flesh on her arms and legs. As though sensing my presence, she turned to stare at me. I cranked the car.

"Dean, I don't think it's Veronica." I tugged at the sleeve of his jacket.

"How do you—"

"Just listen," I said. "Find out where that woman who bartends at Long Time Gone is. I think Wade said her name was Olivia. He didn't give me a last name. I think that might be her in the car."

Dean glanced back at the car. "You can't..."

"You said you know I'm not a fake, right?" I put the car in gear.

Some emotion I didn't recognize flashed over Dean's face. He straightened his posture, and it was gone. "I'll check into it. Be careful driving home."

I gave him a half-hearted wave and turned the car around in the road. Tears burned my eyes, my throat tightened. I hated the way I was. This would have worked—for about a month—if Dean hadn't known the truth about me. But I made him uncomfortable. I gave Dean a wistful once-over as I drove away. He caught my eye and smiled and mimed for me to call him.

I wanted to, but I wondered if I should just let it go. Consider this an enjoyable booty call and move on. I drove the short distance to Memaw's and pulled into the carport. The house was dark, matching my mood.

I crept through the house, too aware of the pleasant soreness good sex left behind. I undressed in the darkness of my bedroom. My clothes smelled like Dean, and I threw them across the room. I didn't want to think about him right then. If I did, I'd remember the way he looked when I told him about Olivia.

21

Thursday morning, I raced around in a frenzy. I had a job to get to, but my cellphone wouldn't quit ringing. Everybody who made money off H & H Week had some last minute work they wanted done.

Three short raps sounded on the front door. I muttered a curse and raced out of the bathroom only to see Memaw headed for the door. She waved me off. Rather than go back to the bathroom, I waited to see who it was. Seeing Olivia's ghost last night meant Veronica Spinelli was still out there.

Memaw spoke pleasantly to the person at the door and sent them on their way before I had a chance to come closer. She turned holding a vase of roses. Amusement danced in her eyes, and that made me happier than the flowers. She carried the flowers into the kitchen and set them on the middle of the table. I plucked the card from the plastic holder and opened it.

Spend the night with me next time. – D.

The happy glow of euphoria spread though me.

"That's the first smile I've seen from you all morning." Memaw took her oatmeal out of the microwave and stirred it. "Is it from whoever you were with last night? He actually has money for something like this?"

I nodded and had to restrain myself from skipping back to the bathroom to finish getting ready. The flowers didn't mean Dean could handle my seeing ghosts, but they did mean he would try. That alone made my heart freeze. In a good way.

———

THE THURSDAY before the Saturday H & H street dance was always crazy. Every room in every bed and breakfast and hotel had been rented. A couple thousand extra people filled Gaslight City to bursting. Traffic moved slower than ever. I had to park several blocks away from my first job.

I had been wrong about the whole town knowing about Dean and me by nine that morning. It was nine-thirty before the first person asked me when Dean and I became a couple. I worked three different jobs that day and fielded no fewer than twenty questions about Dean.

What part of Louisiana did he come from? I didn't know. Was that last name French? I didn't know that either. Where did he go to school? Beats me. Well, what did I know about him? That he looked as good out of his clothes as in them. That one went over like a fart in church.

By day's end, I buzzed with the excitement of a new relationship. It didn't matter if I actually had one or not. I walked to my car, parked on the outer edges of BFE, a silly grin on my face. I didn't hear Dean calling my name until the second or third time. I turned with a smile on my face, but it went south when I saw the look on Dean's face.

"Wanted you to know Benny was arraigned about an hour ago." Dean swept his arm out as though throwing something away. "Bail was set, and he met it. He's back out on the streets."

"Money helps." It did. Sooner Dean learned that about Gaslight City, the better.

"That arrogant shithead." Dean balled his hands into fists. "He actually sneered at me on the way out of the courtroom."

"Thanks for the flowers. They were gorgeous." Just remembering them made me smile.

Dean shook off the irritation, changing courses so fast it made me dizzy. "Does that mean you'll come over tonight?"

I didn't answer but gave him a kiss that let him know my intent. We parted ways, and I resumed the walk to my car. My route took me past the museum. With dark falling, lights spilled from inside the museum. I glanced inside.

Hannah Kessler, looking as flustered as I'd ever seen her, stood in front of a huge group of people. She couldn't take them all on a tour at once. She wouldn't be audible over that many people rustling and coughing, and it would take forever to guide them through the displays.

Because Dean had made me feel good, and because I owed Hannah one, I went inside. The look of relief on Hannah's face almost made me laugh. I winked at her.

"Howdy, folks. I'm Peri Jean Mace. I bet at least one of you has heard of the Mace Treasure. Let me see a show of hands."

About half the group raised their hands.

"Well, my ancestor was Reginald Mace—the guy who hid the treasure and founded this town."

An excited murmur rose from the group. Hannah flashed me a grateful smile.

"Sorry I'm late," I said to Hannah. "How do you want to split up this group? I'll start my group on one end of the museum, and you start your group on the other."

Two hours later, Hannah locked the museum door and turned the sign to "Closed." Talking loud had made my throat scratchy, and my feet ached from walking.

"I never realized I knew so much about the Mace Treasure."

"You were great," Hannah said. "I think the ones who didn't get in your group wished they had."

We stood there looking at each other. I owed Hannah more than she did me. In a weird sort of way, I had come to depend on Hannah over the last couple of weeks. She was there every time I needed someone. *Isn't that the definition of friend?*

"I've got a few free hours tomorrow. Last-minute cancellation. Want me to come by and help?"

"This place has been a madhouse. Of course, I want you to come by and help. I'll even pay you for your time."

"I won't accept your money," I said. "This is the kind of thing friends do for each other."

"You're right." Hannah smiled her movie star smile. "It is."

I put my hand over my mouth to cover a yawn. Not only had I gone to bed late the night before, I had gone to bed upset. What sleep I got wasn't restful.

"I can help you clean up before I go home." The offer was halfhearted.

"No, you're tired. Is what I hear about you and Dean true?"

I smiled and shrugged. "Is that all people are talking about today?"

"The locals anyway. It's like Benny was never arrested." Hannah said. "Before you go can I show you something?"

I yawned again. "What's it got to do with?"

"Remember that wooden angel we found in the writing slope?"

My drowsiness left me, and an uneasy chill took its place. I swallowed hard and nodded.

————

WE TURNED off the lights in the front part of the museum and went to Hannah's office. I could have been walking to my execution. Since my last encounter with the writing slope, my spirit sensitivity had gotten *louder*. Things I used to ignore crawled all over me. I worried the repeated exposure to this dark spirit would break the puny shields I'd managed to erect over the years. But I worried even more about sticking my head in the sand. My best interests depended on me finding out what Rae meant about me being in danger.

Hannah removed a shoebox from her desk. Using a pair of iron tongs, she lifted the wooden angel from the box. Clammy sweat dampened my forehead, and the hair raised on the back of my neck. I'd never forget the dark spirit's havoc or the way that hideous little thing burned Hannah.

"Are you some sort of sadist?" I asked as Hannah leaned over the angel.

"Something you don't know about me," she said. "I like puzzles. When I was a teenager, my stepfather bought me a puzzle box for every occasion. I got pretty good at figuring them out."

Hannah picked up a long, wicked looking ice pick and the biggest pair of tweezers I'd ever seen. With the tweezers, she held the angel's trumpet and gave it a twist.

"Don't break it." The thing had to be worth something. Even if it wasn't, I hated to see it destroyed.

"I won't." Hannah's response was toneless. She was too invested in the task at hand to pay me much mind. She gave the trumpet another twist. It popped away from the angel's pursed lips. I bit back a gasp. Hannah poked the ice pick into the angel's mouth. That one made me yelp. The angel popped open.

"Reginald Mace liked using springs to put tension on stuff like this." Using the ice pick, she turned the angel where I could see it. When I just sat there, she said, "Come on. Look what's inside. This is what Rae wanted to find."

Nestled in the angel's belly lay a skeleton key with a

symbol not unlike the mother, maiden, crone symbol I'd seen in Celtic mythology. Hannah plucked the key from the angel with the tweezers and set it on the desk.

"Do I dare touch it?" She smiled, enjoying this. She extended her index finger and touched the key. She let out a shriek of pain, jerked her finger away, and popped it into her mouth. "You think I'd learn," she said. "But I wonder if it burns you. You are, after all, a Mace, a descendant of William—for whom the treasure was intended."

"Forget it," I said. "I'm not touching that hexed thing."

"Come on," she said. "Don't be chicken."

"Don't call me chicken." Fatigue provided fertile soil for my indignation.

"Buck buck buck." Hannah flapped her arms.

I narrowed my eyes at her and reached out a tentative finger. I let it hover over the key, unable to take the last step. Finally, Hannah reached across the desk and pushed my finger down on the key. I yelped, and we both jumped. But it didn't burn me.

"Just as I thought," she said.

"You could have burned me." I took out my cigarettes and lit up. The look of horror on Hannah's face was satisfying. I smoked with relish.

"Rae desperately wanted to find this," she said. "I wonder what it opens."

"She didn't find it soon enough to matter."

"Do you think Benny killed her?" Hannah stood, took one of her expensive lead crystal glasses out of her antique hutch, and filled it half full of amber colored liquor, a brand I'd never heard of. She held the bottle out to me, but I shook my head.

"I have a hard time imagining Benny killing anybody. He used to take me riding on his family's tractor when I was a little girl and he was a young man. He was always so nice and gentle."

Hannah sipped her liquor, watching me remember with a thoughtful look on her face.

"But he did beat me up outside the trailer and sucker punched me in the gut yesterday in Tyler. There's no denying that."

"My cousin told me they recovered a sex tape of him and Rae." Hannah's cousin was none other than Sheriff Joey's son, Scott. A sheriff's deputy, Scott was no doubt being groomed to run when Joey decided to retire. At his retirement, Joey would publicly recommend Scott for his position, and most citizens of Burns County would vote for Scott Holze without question. Dean's plan to run for Sheriff would throw a monkey wrench into the order of things.

"Your cousin isn't lying," I said, wondering if it was legal for me to tell Hannah even this much, but I'd bent the law in worse ways.

"I'm no cop, but something feels off about it all to me too." Hannah belted back her drink and poured more. "If he killed her, he did it because she blackmailed him."

I shrugged. "The day I ran into Benny at Rae's trailer, he wore latex gloves. He could have used that knife to kill her without leaving his own prints. It's possible he could have hidden it at Chase's trailer. I guess."

"But do you think he did?"

"It doesn't feel right. Benny is sneaky. If he were going to do away with Rae, I'd think he'd get her out of town to do it. Just have her disappear."

"If we're right, and Benny didn't do it," Hannah said, "the real killer is still out there. Maybe looking for this key."

My gut twisted. I had an even scarier idea.

"If Benny is the killer, he could be looking for this key. He made bail today."

"Benny's rich. What would he want with a treasure?" Hannah finished her drink and set the glass aside.

"Rich people never mind getting richer," I said. "Benny included."

"That still leaves one thing unanswered." The liquor had affected Hannah, slowing her speech and allowing her East Texas accent to creep into a few words. "Where do you fit into all of it? Rae seemed so sincere about trying to keep you from harm."

That made no sense to me either. Learning Rae talked me up to all her acquaintances had me wanting to think better of her. But running a con on Hannah fit right into her personality. Memaw said she got the con bug honest.

"I still think she could have been lying, manipulating you. You didn't see all the stuff I saw during the eight months she lived with us. The Rae we knew as kids died long before her body stopped living."

"But if she was telling the truth...somebody is out there, looking to get you alone."

It was true. Rae claimed I was in danger long before her

murder. Benny's aggression toward me started only after I threatened the secrecy of his affair with Rae. That led me to believe he had no reason left to harm me. Veronica Spinelli, a sociopath, would harm me just for the satisfaction. Her relationship with Rae pre-dated both Rae's release from prison and her move to Gaslight City. But Veronica never mentioned the treasure to me. She only wanted some item Rae possessed when she died. None of this made sense. I opened my mouth to tell Hannah that, but a thick fog hanging in the hallway outside her office distracted me.

"What is that?" I asked instead.

"Is something on fire?" Hannah sniffed the air as she half stood behind her desk.

The lamp next to Hannah's desk blew out with a dramatic spurt of sparks. Hannah and I both screamed. The office door slammed, cutting off any ambient light from the hallway. The shock of silence and darkness made the footsteps in the hallway sound thunderous.

The door cracked open, its hinges whining. Light from the hallway flooded into the office, hurting my eyes. A silhouette appeared in the doorway. I found I didn't need light to recognize Rae. Her emotions were as familiar to me as her voice would have been. My mouth painfully dry, I dragged my tongue over my lips. I tried to extract myself from the chair, got tangled in my bag, and ended up sprawled on the floor.

"What are you doing here?" I managed to croak.

Rae glided across the office, coming straight at me. I heard Hannah scrabbling on the other side of the desk, whimpering and crying. Rae stopped about a foot from me. The cold wafting off her cooled my sweat-soaked clothes until I shivered. She leaned forward and pushed the key from the angel off the desk. It fell on my chest. The chilly metal burned my skin.

As though propelled by an unseen force, Rae flew backward out of the room. The door slammed behind her. The room was quiet except for the sound of Hannah crying.

"Did you see that?" What a stupid question to ask. Of course she saw it. Otherwise she wouldn't be crying. I remembered the way my ex-husband's sensitivity to the spirit world increased when he was drunk or high in my presence.

Hannah didn't answer. She just kept crying. Shoving the skeleton key in my pocket, I crawled to my feet. I rounded the desk, knelt next to Hannah, and patted her on the back.

"I thought you knew what I saw." Shame dug into my conscience for reasons I couldn't quite describe.

"I didn't know it was like that." Hannah rose and turned on another lamp. Her face red and blotchy from crying and her makeup a streaked mess, she looked humbled and childlike.

"This is the first time I've seen you not look like a famous person," I said.

Hannah's brow furrowed in puzzlement before she realized what I meant.

"Go to hell, Peri Jean." She said it with a smile tugging

at her lips. "Your hair is sticking straight up. You look like an extra from an old music video."

Together, we put the office to rights. Obviously, Rae wanted me to have the key. Hannah insisted I keep it on me at all times. Just in case having the key would have saved Rae from the fate she met. Somehow, I doubted that. I left as soon as Hannah settled in at her apartment.

I went to Dean's and stayed half the night. But I couldn't stay all night. The idea left me feeling too vulnerable.

———

THE NEXT DAY was the most hellish Friday I ever had during H & H Week. In addition to helping Hannah at the museum, I cleaned two bed and breakfasts, filled in at Dottie's Burgers and Rings for the lunch rush, and helped Eddie Kennedy set up a booth where he'd offer carriage rides to tourists. My pockets jammed with checks and cash, I rushed to hit the bank before they closed for the weekend to deposit today's earnings. Memaw's Christmas computer cost me more than I intended because I ordered her a laptop instead of the desktop I originally chose. In light of her health situation, she needed something portable. I couldn't come any closer to thinking about Memaw having cancer without totally losing my grip.

Cars jammed the bank's one drive-through window. Apparently, all the local merchants had the same idea I did. The tourists took advantage of the only bank-run ATM in town. I swung into a parking place and hotfooted it inside. The lines were almost to the door. I picked one and settled in for a long wait.

I must have nearly fallen asleep on my feet because, when someone tapped my shoulder, I jumped and let out a little scream. Jill Frankens, the accounts manager, stood before me.

"Come on in my office," she said. "I'll help you in there."

I gratefully followed Jill to an office off the open lobby. *She must be desperate to go home at a decent hour to break protocol like this. I don't blame her.*

Once in her office, Jill motioned me to a chair in front of her desk and went to sit on the other side. A ring flashed on her hand. On closer inspection, I recognized it as her high school ring.

Jill graduated a couple of years ahead of me in school. A non-entity at Gaslight City High, she was smart, studious, and bound for somewhere else. She went away to college and made a career in Dallas until her parents began having health problems, and then she gave it all up to move back to Gaslight City.

"Just give me your deposit slip, and I'll enter it in for you after hours." She wrote out a receipt for my deposit.

"I've been trying to get in touch with you." Jill folded her hands on her desk and leaned forward. At thirty-two, she'd risen as far as she could at the First National Bank.

"Oh?" I hadn't seen any missed calls on my blasted dying cellphone.

"You had a check bounce on your account." Jill, who had always been nice to me, kept any insinuation out of her voice and a sympathetic expression on her face. A flush colored her high cheekbones.

"One I wrote?"

"No. The one Michael Gage wrote you. His bank is in New York, so it took a while to come back."

I slumped and swallowed a volley of curses Jill didn't deserve to hear. Believe me, a string of them ran through my head.

"Thank you for telling me." I struggled to keep my voice even. His check was a big one, and I'd already spent the money. The hot check meant a lot of the work I'd done during H & H Week was just going to pay back what should have been in my account.

"Here's the check." She set the offending slip of paper on her desk. I slipped it into my bag with a shaking hand. Jill pressed her lips together.

"Thanks, Jill."

"Don't worry about it," she said. "It's Pastor Gage, so I'll waive any fees when he makes it good."

It was a nice thing to do. But I couldn't help thinking, *IF he makes it good.*

———

FUMING about Gage and his bad check, I sped down Farm Road 4077 to Memaw's house. I could already taste the skillet steaks and gravy Memaw planned to cook that evening. As I rolled down the driveway, my headlights flashed over Dean's Trans Am sitting next to the carport.

What the hell? We hadn't agreed on him invading my

living space this early in the game. I parked under the carport and adjusted the rearview mirror to check for food between my teeth and smudges of dirt on my face.

Once confident I looked presentable, I bolted out of my car, stomped toward the house, bubbling with annoyance. I didn't like Dean just showing up like this. It made me nervous. I could deal with him losing interest after a few spirited rolls in the hay. After all, they all ended that way. But I never let guys come to my house. They didn't get to see where I lived and what I treasured.

Dean had taken the decision out of my hands. It burned my ass. Before I opened the door, I took a few deep breaths and counted to ten. As usual, it slowed my anger enough to let in a few rational thoughts. Call it a lesson hard learned.

Dean had shown me nothing but kindness after our initial hostilities, and—as a bonus—he was hotter than East Texas asphalt in August. If I walked in blazing mad, it determined the course of this relationship. Did I really want to throw it away over Dean doing something most people considered normal? I took another deep breath and opened the door.

I expected to smell food cooking, to hear Dean and Memaw making small talk. What I saw shocked me. Dean and Memaw sat in complete silence on the couch. The good smells I had expected to be pouring from the kitchen were absent.

Memaw's face was pale, and a full ashtray sat in front of her. Despite her cancer, she'd been smoking again.

Dean sat next to Memaw, his elbows on his knees. I recognized the look in his eyes—pity.

Fear clogged my throat, and I swallowed convulsively. My mind raced through the possibilities and hit on the one thing I'd suspected but couldn't quite prepare myself to face.

"Why don't you sit with us, honey?" Memaw scooted away from Dean to form a space between them on the couch.

"No." I backed up until I hit the front door. The wild urge to reach behind me, grab the doorknob, open the door, and run beat at me. "No."

Movement flashed in my peripheral vision, and Rae's specter floated into the room but stopped at the dark mouth of the hallway. Even she wore a compassionate expression.

"Noooo..." This time I screamed the word.

Dean shot up off the couch and came to me. He gripped my shoulders. In my state of increased awareness, I made note of the chill bumps on his arms. Rae was feeding on our emotions and recycling them to cool the room, making her presence known to Dean and Memaw. I put my hands on Dean's chest to push him away, but he pulled me to him, crushing me against him.

"The Fischers provided Chase's dental records," Dean said, still holding me tight and stroking my hair. "They wanted to know one way or the other."

"Stop it." I flailed against Dean, forcing him to squeeze me even tighter.

"It was him, Peri Jean." Dean shook against me, either

from experiencing my grief with me or from the frigid room. "Chase is dead. The ME found a bullet hole in his skull. He was already dead when someone put him in the GTO and set it on fire."

I screamed at the ceiling. *My best friend is dead.*

My knees buckled, but Dean continued holding me upright. Memaw's arm snaked around my waist, firm as iron. I jumped and turned to face her. I hadn't even heard her coming. I leaned my head on her shoulder as I had when I was a little girl.

"Let's get her on the couch, Dean." Memaw stepped away as Dean scooped me into his arms and carried me to the couch where he gently set me down. I heard myself sobbing, but I didn't feel the deep pain that usually accompanied crying. It was as though I watched the whole scene from somewhere else.

"Rae, please leave," Memaw said. "You are freezing us out."

The shock of Memaw addressing a ghost jerked me back into myself. My chest ached with my loss. I'd never get to tell Chase how much I appreciated his friendship, how important he was to me, or how much I loved him— but just not that way. He would never get better, overcome his addictions, or decide to join a band and relive his teenage dreams. Chase's son, Kansas, would never know what a great, loyal man his father was. He'd only hear Felicia's awful stories about what a terrible husband he'd been.

I curled into a ball on the couch, gasping and sobbing. My tears burned my skin as they tracked over my face.

They made plopping sounds, reminding me of rain as they wet the couch's old upholstery.

I had lulled myself into believing Chase wasn't dead because he hadn't come to see me in ghost form. That he'd gone on without telling me goodbye spiked into me like a poison dart. The pain of it all rushed over me, suffocating me. Dean's and Memaw's hands caressed me and they murmured comforting words, but I couldn't respond. My sobs turned to half-screams, which turned to whimpers when my throat grew raw. I drifted into sleep when my body grew too exhausted to continue mourning.

I woke in the middle of the night in my bed. Someone's arm weighed me down. I trailed my fingers over the arm, touching the soft hair and hard muscles distinguishing it as male. The part of my mind that had not quite woken thought Chase had come back. The rational part of my brain knew it was Dean. I turned on the bedside lamp to find him fully clothed on top of the covers next to me. He woke smoothly and squinted at me.

"I'm sorry I pitched such a fit." Speaking hurt my raw throat, and my voice came out all scratchy and husky.

"Apologize for wrecking my car or forgetting my birthday." Dean kissed my cheek and curled his arm around me to pull me closer. "Never apologize for crying when you've lost someone you love."

I snuggled into Dean even though I wanted to get up and find my cigarettes. I decided I'd quit smoking again after Chase's funeral. Dependency on the nasty little cancer sticks stunted my whole life.

"I need to ask questions about..." I couldn't quite say Chase's name.

Dean sat up and leaned against the headboard. "Okay."

"You said he didn't die when the car burned. He'd been shot?"

"The angle of the wound indicated he died instantly. I doubt he suffered." Dean pulled his arm off me and fiddled with his watch, but his eyes never left mine.

"The other body...was it Olivia?"

"We don't know," Dean said. "But probably. She's missing. We're waiting for dental records."

"Olivia had something going on with Billy Ryder and Veronica. You should have seen the way she acted when I went in there looking for Chase. She probably called Billy or Veronica and let them know where to find him." My eyes itched and burned from all the crying. I rubbed at them and winced at the discomfort.

"Sugar, you're not the only one who can investigate this case." Dean yawned. "Your boyfriend, that Neanderthal bouncer at Long Time Gone, told me the very same stuff."

"It's Billy Ryder. I just know it." And oh, how my heart burned. From anger, and grief. And guilt. If only I had trusted Dean sooner, Chase might be alive. In jail, but alive.

"Veronica's old partner in crime?"

"I just have a feeling," I said. Dean shrugged.

"It's not our case anymore, so I'll tell you I gave the Texas Rangers the sketch Rae drew. They've circulated it to law enforcement in the tri-state area."

"What about Benny?" I asked. "He's in this up to his tits."

"Dunno. One thing's for sure," Dean said. "He didn't set that car on fire. He was in jail when it happened."

I got up and dug through my dresser until I found the carton of Marlboro reds I'd hidden in there. I took out a pack, popped it against my palm a couple of times, and unwrapped the cellophane. Dean watched me light my cigarette.

"I'm quitting after Chase's funeral," I said to his unasked question.

He raised his eyebrows and grinned. Despite the grief piercing my heart, I smiled back. Cigarette clamped between my teeth, I climbed back in bed with Dean. To his credit, he didn't react to the proximity of my toxic smoke. I made another silent vow to quit.

"Billy Ryder is tying up loose ends."

"It's a good thing you realize that without me telling you," Dean said. "No more snooping around. Both him and Veronica are stone cold killers. Not sure how Benny fits in with those two losers, but he's proven he's violent."

"But I promised Rae I'd solve her murder." I stubbed out my cigarette in the ashtray I kept by my bed and clicked off the bedside lamp. I snuggled under the covers and against Dean. I had a full day of work starting in just a few short hours. Michael Gage's bounced check made me unable to cancel the jobs. Mourning would have to wait until Sunday morning.

"If you are killed solving Rae's murder," Dean said around another yawn, "what good is it going to do you?"

He began snoring lightly without hearing my response. I listened to him breathe as I stared into the dark. Dean didn't understand. Rae's murder had been one thing. I could accept that she'd gotten in over her head and just wanted her murderer brought to justice. Chase's murder flat out pissed me off. I would get Billy Ryder, and I'd knock his dick in the dirt. No matter what.

22

———

SATURDAY, and the end of H & H Week, finally arrived. I rushed from my paying job to help Hannah close down the museum before the street party. Not that I was in the mood for a street party, but even I was not tough enough to stay home alone in the wake of Chase's death. Besides, Memaw and Hannah threatened to drag me to the street party if I refused to come.

To my utter horror, Hannah bought us elaborate Victorian era costumes for the street party. She nixed my idea to go as a female gunslinger. Instead, I wore a huge skirt, a bustier, and petticoats. After she tied me into a corset, I understood why Victorian women needed fainting couches.

I hated everything about the outfit except its purple top hat and wire glasses with purple lenses. Very steampunk. The dress had no pockets, so I attached the skeleton key from the writing slope to a purple velvet ribbon and tied it around my neck. Memaw met us at the museum's front door. When I saw her gunslinger costume, I glared at Hannah.

"You wouldn't want to be Twinkies with your grandmother, would you?" Hannah trilled the words in a way that made me want to kick her in the butt. I might have tried if I hadn't been afraid I'd trip over my ridiculous getup and fall down.

We descended the museum's brick steps and joined the melee. As I did every year, I stopped to take in the scene before me. A regiment of soldiers marched past wearing both blue and gray period uniforms, antique replica rifles slung over their shoulders. The high school marching band, outfitted with kilts and drums, filed behind the soldiers. A man riding a penny-farthing bicycle weaved along behind them.

Gaslight City's namesake, the gas powered streetlights, burned brighter than usual because many merchants lowered the lights inside their businesses to resemble candlelight. For all the things I hated about Gaslight City —the caste system, the gossip, and the lack of anonymity —I loved this one night of the year enough to make up for it all.

Memaw kissed my cheek and wandered off with a marauding band of old ladies. Hannah left to dance with a handsome executive from Longstreet Lumber. Dean and I danced until his boss told him to get to work.

Alone again. The odd man out. Chase's loss throbbed within me. My throat ached from the crying I'd done anytime I could carve out a few minutes alone. I allowed myself to imagine how we'd have spent the evening.

Chase would have laughed at my dress. He'd have danced with me. I sampled food from the different booths and people-watched, reveling in my loneliness. Chase would have walked around to all the booths with me, sharing the food.

After a few drinks—and whatever else he could get his hands on—Chase would have tried to take me to bed. Subtract Dean from the picture, and I might have gone. Old flames never really died out.

Eddie Kennedy's Victorian style horse-drawn carriage appeared from time to time as he took people for romantic rides through Gaslight City's historic district. We exchanged a wave. He signaled to me to keep my chin up. *Did I look that sad?*

A puffy, middle-aged man wearing a suit that cost more than my car stepped into my path. "Peri Jean Mace? I need to speak with you. Please?"

"Aren't you? Speaking to me, I mean."

"I'm Winston Everett, Mr. Bennett Longstreet's lawyer. Mr. Longstreet wants to see you."

What the hell? As if. "I've nothing to say to Mr. Longstreet. He attacked me twice, and he's accused of murdering my cousin."

"Mr. Longstreet has offered a monetary gift for speaking with him." Winston Everett's florid cheeks stretched into a phony smile.

"The answer's still no." I put my hands on my hips and

quickly dropped them when I realized how I must look in my waist-cinching dress and top hat.

"Now, Ms. Mace—"

"Want me to call my boyfriend?" I raised my eyebrows at him. "That's him right over there with the uniform and the gun."

Winston Everett's mouth dropped open, and he walked away from me without another word. Jerk.

Bad temper boiled through me as I stalked toward the shaved ice stand. Sweat poured off me. My ridiculous getup didn't let in any breeze. Between that and my foul mood, I needed something cool. A hand closed on my arm, and I whirled around to find Wade Hill grinning in front of me. He'd left his biker attire at home and donned the topcoat and tails of a Victorian gentleman. His black hair hung in a braided queue tied with a satiny black ribbon.

Despite my feelings for Dean, a charge of lust warmed me. Had I met Wade first, would I have fallen for Dean? I would never two-time Dean, and I wanted to let things play out without a cheap cop-out on my end...but if my relationship with Dean turned bad, Wade Hill better watch out.

The band launched into a wailing, accordion-filled rendition of "Jolie Blon." The lead singer wailed the sad song in Cajun French, of which I spoke not one word but loved hearing. Wade held out his hand to me.

"May I?" he asked.

I took his hand, and we swooped around the other dancing couples. We probably looked like Mutt and Jeff, with Wade being so tall, but I didn't care. It took my mind off missing Chase.

"Jolie Blon" segued into "Luckenbach, Texas." The two songs together fit East Texas, which was a mish-mash of culture. By the time the band began a new song—Stevie Ray Vaughan's "Tin Roof Alley"—I caught Dean watching Wade and me with an unhappy expression on his face. I kissed Wade's cheek and told I'd see him around. He bowed theatrically and kissed my hand.

I wandered through the crowd alone, missing Chase more than ever. Many locals had rented street vendor space, and I browsed a variety of handmade crafts, drifting farther and farther away from the bandstand and the crowd. Before I knew it, I'd wandered into the alley leading to Dottie's Burgers and Rings. Realizing there were no vendors back there, I turned to go back the way I'd come. An old-fashioned horse-drawn carriage waited at the end of the alley. Thinking Eddie Kennedy had stopped to check on me, I hurried.

My pulse quickened when I reached the carriage. This one didn't belong to Eddie. Instead of being open air, this carriage had windows. Up close, I saw it had real brass accents. The biggest hint this carriage didn't belong to Eddie, however, was the driver—a young man wearing black livery. I gave him an embarrassed wave and tried to pass around the carriage.

"A free ride miss?" The kid, who must have been a drama student from a nearby college or maybe even the high school, spoke in a silly, faux English accent.

"No, thanks," I said. Free was never free. I walked away.

The door to the carriage creaked open. Rather than turning to see who was inside, I walked faster. One of my high-heeled boots—*blasted feminine thing*—caught in the crack around a manhole and I engaged in the complicated dance of trying not to fall down. Hands clutched my waist and steadied me. I turned, expecting to see the carriage driver.

Benny Longstreet stood in front of me. Hysteria fluttering in my chest, I gasped and jerked away, but his grip tightened.

"I want to speak with you." His quick words brooked no argument. *Pompous bastard.*

I struggled, but he jerked me against him and dragged me toward the carriage. I shrieked and beat at him with my fists. Benny ignored me. We both knew I couldn't fight him off. The band playing several blocks away was perfectly audible. Between that and the roar of a couple thousand people, nobody would hear me.

"Help me, you little idiot," Benny said to the carriage driver. The young man hesitated, but something in Benny's expression got his butt off his seat.

Together, the men hauled me into the carriage. I bucked and scratched and swung my fists. Both men swatted me away. Benny sat on one bench and pulled me to sit next to him. The door to the carriage closed.

"Lock it from the outside," Benny called. The sound of the lock sliding home sounded so final. Fear rose and crested in me, and I screamed for help.

Benny cocked back one fist and stared at me. He'd already proved twice he would hit me. I shut up and sat still, my mind racing through escape plans. My mouth had dried to the texture of sandpaper, and my heart pounded against my chest. I sat back in the seat. The corners of Benny's eyes crinkled behind wire-rimmed glasses much like my own. He tapped the side of the carriage with his silver-topped cane. We began to move.

———

BENNY SAT BACK in his seat, smiling as though he hadn't just kidnapped me. I bet he'd treated my cousin just like this. My fists itched to pound his horsey face, but I knew I'd lose the fight.

"You gonna kill me now?" I scooted as far away from Benny as I could get.

Benny smirked. "If I wanted to kill you, I've already had two chances. Why would I do it now, in front of all these people?"

His words reminded me of what I'd said to Hannah. If Benny had murdered Rae, he would have taken her out of town, disposed of her so nobody ever found her.

"You hit me twice, you stinking piece of shit. Why should I believe you?" Even as I hissed mean words at him, I believed him. Benny had better sense than to kill me at the street dance.

"I'm sorry for hitting you. Damn it. I'm sorry." Benny's face darkened. His hands clenched in his lap, tightening until cords stood out in them. "That's why I want to talk to you. To explain what happened. And to warn you."

"Oh, hell." I made a show of rolling my eyes. "Now you

care what happens to me? In what alternate universe am I supposed to fall for that?"

"Do you think I'm proud of the way this has blown out of control?" He didn't wait for me to answer. "Haven't you ever gotten caught up in something you knew was wrong but couldn't stop?"

"I didn't kill my pregnant girlfriend because she blackmailed me." Rae's murder not matching Benny's personality slithered around my mind. But I imagined Rae's pregnancy and blackmail attempt scared him into some kind of action. Had he hired Veronica Spinelli and Billy Ryder to finish Rae? Rae owed Veronica money. If Benny offered to pay off Rae's debt in exchange for her murder, Veronica would have jumped on it. "Benny, just tell Dean what happened. If you give up Veronica Spinelli and Billy Ryder, you might get a lighter sentence."

Benny narrowed his eyes and cocked his head. "What in God's name are you talking about, child?"

His confusion threw me off. Either he missed his calling as an actor, or I had it all wrong. I slumped in the leather seat, wincing as the horrible corset bit into me. "Say what you have to say, but make it quick."

"No matter what you think, I didn't kill Rae," he said. "I got in over my head. I met her at The Chameleon while entertaining an investor. I meant to just do it one time, but I couldn't quit. She burned with life and passion. I'd never experienced anyone like her. Maybe I didn't love her, but I cared what happened to her."

I stifled the urge to kick him with my hard-soled, high-heeled boots. Benny had an aristocratic wife and two beautiful children. How could Rae, with all her schemes and nastiness, have made him feel alive? And how could he say he cared for her after everything he'd done? The way he'd twisted it all around sickened me.

"If you had nothing to do with Rae's death, what were you doing at her murder scene?"

"I need to tell you a little of what happened leading up to the murder." Benny shook off his embarrassment like a pro.

"You mean you need to rationalize whatever you did." No way I'd make this easy for him. Murderer or not, his behavior sucked.

"This is not a rationalization." Benny impressed me. His voice held no hint of whining or pleading. No wonder he did so well as a businessman. "You have to know what happened before to understand what happened that day."

"I bet I know more than you think." I held my eyes on his until he shifted and glanced at his feet. "Rae found out she was pregnant on Thursday before she died. She gave you the sex tape and tried to blackmail you. What then?"

"I refused to allow her to blackmail me. Instead, I offered to pay her expenses if she'd give the baby up for adoption. She became enraged. I called her bluff, told her to go on and tell my wife." Benny smoothed down his fancy suit, his trembling chin the only outward sign of his emotions. "She flipped out, told me this wild story about a fugitive who'd been on the run for thirty years and how she owed him money. I called her a liar, and she ran off mad.

"Sunday came around, and I hadn't heard from her. I

snuck through the woods between our properties. I went there to talk sense to her. Whoever...did what they did to your cousin had already come and gone, but she was still hanging on."

I went cold. All the food I'd eaten threatened to return in a spew of hot garbage. "Why didn't you call 911?"

"Just listen to me, okay? She was dying. You can—just tell. She said 'his neck...scar.'" Benny let out a long exhale. "At least, that's what I think she said."

"And you just sat there and watched her die?" Hot fury crept up my spine and throbbed in a vein on my forehead. No matter what excuses he gave, this cowardly douchetard watched my cousin die a miserable death and then beat me up so he could escape an out of control situation of his own making. I wanted to leap across the carriage and hit him and kick him until I ran out of energy. But I remembered how hard he hit. I drew in one deep breath. Then another. While I wrestled my temper under control, I remembered the gloves Benny wore that day. They'd sounded like balloons rubbing together.

"You're full of shit. You had on latex gloves, Benny. You either knew what you'd find in that trailer or you're the one who really killed her."

"I did not kill her. And I didn't know what I'd find. I went back to my truck and got some latex gloves so I could get her phone. It was one of those pay-as-you-go phones. I knew because I'd bought her minutes for it. If I took it, the police would never see the messages I sent her or my phone number on it." Benny stopped speaking and glanced around the carriage, even turning in his seat to peer out the window behind him. While he was turned, a light puff of wind moved his hair. He jerked back around and glared at me. I met his stare unblinking.

The undercurrent of tension in the carriage deepened. Rae. Her emotions crept into mine, her fear surprising me. Was Rae afraid for me? No. Her emotions centered on Benny. It slowly dawned on me that Rae had liked Benny. Now she feared for him. That meant Benny didn't kill her.

I had known, deep down, but still felt relieved. Benny, a vein pulsing at his temple and sweat coating his face, still searched the carriage for the intruder he could feel but not see. He shivered. I enjoyed his discomfort, perhaps too much.

"Please, Peri Jean. You have to believe me. Someone has to believe me." Benny's slick demeanor slipped, and a tear rolled down his face. He covered his face and gave in to a few convincing sobs. "I never wanted that to happen to her."

"All right," I said. "I believe you."

Benny raised his tear-streaked face and stared at me through brimming eyes. I wanted to puke. "Really? Can you forgive me?"

"Yeah. I believe you." I didn't answer the second part. I didn't think I could without screaming at him. "Let me out of here."

"Did I say we were done? I've not told you what you need to hear." Quick as a flash, Benny the ruthless businessman replaced the Benny who cried in front of me. He waited until I sat back on the bench. "Watch yourself.

Annoying as you were to me, I suspect you're an actual threat to the murderer."

He leaned forward and used his silver knobbed cane to knock on the carriage's wall. It rolled to a stop. The carriage shifted as the driver hopped down. A click sounded as he unlocked the door. I climbed over Benny, not caring if I jabbed him with my elbows, and grabbed the carriage door, opening it a little. With Rae here, I had the upper hand, but I'd take no chances.

"You listen to me, now, sleaze dick." I got right in his face. "This ain't settled. You best watch out."

"You best watch your mouth, honey." He reached for me, but stopped when he spotted something behind me. A blast of cold burned my back as Rae's ghostly arm reached over my shoulder and pushed Benny back on the seat. A dark patch appeared on his crotch as he pissed his pants. He looked down at the mess and back at me.

I wiggled my fingers and hopped out of the carriage and backed away. A solid wall of muscle stopped my retreat. I let out a little shriek and turned. Wade Hill leaned down to look at me, his frantic expression evident even in the shadowy half-light.

"You okay?" Wade gasped, as though he'd been running.

Benny shut the door to the carriage and moved away. Wade broke away from me and beat on the door, shouting at Benny that he ought to kick his ass. The carriage stopped, and Benny and Wade had a heated discussion. Benny slammed the door in his face, and Wade took off running toward the thickest part of the crowd.

A few minutes later, he and Dean Turgeau reappeared and chased down the carriage. Dean dragged Benny out and cuffed him. I stood at a distance watching the show. Dean motioned me over. He held Benny by his cuffed hands, waiting as a cruiser cut through the curious onlookers.

"Did he drag you into the carriage against your will?"

"He did."

"But I just wanted to help her. The real killer's still out there. He's after her. I just wanted to warn her." Benny looked more angry than scared as Dean stuffed him in the back of the cruiser.

Wade Hill approached me. "You okay?"

I nodded. "Thanks."

"Always happy to help a damsel in distress." He grinned and bowed. "Especially when she's as pretty as you."

I blushed.

Dean waved the cruiser off and walked over to us. He spoke to Wade. "I've got this." He didn't look real happy with Wade.

Wade shrugged and wandered into the crowd after winking at me. I lost sight of him in the writhing mass of people. When I turned back to Dean, a glare pinched his fine features.

———

HANNAH and I reconvened in the museum after the street dance. Dean had to work until the last reveler went home, and I opted to hang out with Hannah for a few hours. We invited Memaw to join us, but she claimed to crave the solitude and went home alone.

When Hannah untied my corset, I nearly fell down from the relief. In the night's last minutes, the pain had been nearly unbearable. Hannah poured herself a short glass of whiskey and told me to raid the refrigerator. I took a bottle of pomegranate juice.

"How'd you do? Several store owners have told me this is the biggest week of the year."

"I would've done better if Michael Gage hadn't written me a hot check. As is, I'll barely cover Memaw's Christmas present."

"Get out." Hannah clunked her heavy glass down on the vintage suitcase she used for a coffee table.

"Nope," I said.

"There's just something about that guy," she said. "I can't put my finger on it. What's his story?"

"He came here about four years ago, right after Pastor Reeves died. He said he'd done missionary work and talked his way into auditioning. They voted unanimously to hire him. The church was nearly dried up. Low membership. Gage turned it around."

"He's charismatic. I'll give him that," Hannah said. "But there's a dark side. The way he acted when he realized he wasn't going to hook up with you chilled me to the bone." She shook her head. "I met a guy like that in college. He— well, that's a story for another time."

We sat in silence for several minutes. Hannah seemed lost in the past. When she spoke, it was clear she wasn't yet done with the topic of Michael Gage. "That episode in the parking lot bothered me more than I'm probably conveying here. When I got home that night, I did some checking on Michael Gage. Before he came to town four years ago, he didn't exist online. Then, all of a sudden, he's all over the web."

"He was a missionary, remember? Maybe there was no internet where he lived." I went out with a lot of men. Michael Gage's antics had surprised me, but they didn't prove him guilty of anything more than being a tool.

"The missionary thing." Hannah pointed one freckled finger at me. "The night Veronica beat you up, you said you'd emailed that colleague of Michael Gage's. That Jerry guy from Guatemala. You ever hear back from him?"

I slapped my forehead. "I set up a fake email account. I've been so busy I forgot to log into it."

"Do it now." Hannah got her laptop off the mosaic-topped bar and handed it to me.

I logged into the phony email account and there it was —an email from Jerry Bower. He'd sent it almost a week ago. I barely skimmed through his polite answer and went straight into downloading the pictures. As the first one appeared on my screen, we sat speechless.

The man in the pictures had long legs, a red face, and a weak chin. Instead of black hair, his receding reddish-brown hair was curly. He wasn't the Michael Gage we knew. The woman, though, was definitely Sharon Zeeman Gage. I opened a browser window and showed Hannah the missing person's page.

After she looked at it, I sent Sharon Zeeman Gage's

sister an email with attachments of the picture and a summary of Jerry Bower's original letter, explaining that the Michael Gage it came to was the wrong man, but they might help her with her case.

"Things aren't adding up here." Hannah tapped at the corner of her mouth.

"I know a place we can check. He went to prep school. He had the picture on the wall of his office. Nightshade Preparatory Academy for Boys. Maybe they have an alumni page."

"Let's see about that." Hannah held out her hands for the laptop.

Hannah's fingers flew over the keys. Nightshade Preparatory Academy for Boys turned out to be in Vermont. Hannah clicked the link for alumni. The page seemed to take forever to load. Right there on the opening screen was the picture hanging in Michael Gage's office.

"There's the picture." I pointed at the screen.

Hannah scrolled down until the caption underneath the picture became visible. It read:

Nightshade's first graduating class: 1955

Each member of the class of 1955 was listed. Michael Gage's name was absent. He was too young to have been anywhere, much less high school, in 1955. Michael Gage lied about going to Nightshade Preparatory Academy for Boys and no telling what else.

Hannah suggested I get Dean to go with me to collect on the hot check. I argued, telling her I could handle myself. Michael Gage was a liar, maybe even a liar with a bad temper. But that was it. I'd handle things my way.

To change the subject, I told her about my carriage ride with Benny. "The louse came up on Rae still alive. Didn't even call 911. He knew she was dying and didn't want to get pulled into the stink. He told me Rae said 'his neck...scar' before she died. Benny left but decided to come back to steal her cellphone. That's when he ran into me."

"Whoever has the scar, that's Billy Ryder." Using the laptop, Hannah went into her favorites and pulled up Billy Ryder's mug shot. "See his tattoo? He must have had it removed sometime in the last thirty years. That's what the scar is from."

"I don't know anybody who has a scar on his neck." I took the photocopied sketch of Billy Ryder out of my bag, unfolded and set it on Hannah's lap. She enlarged Billy Ryder's mug shot and held up Rae's sketch of the biker dude next to it. "Look at the two pictures together. They look familiar, but I can't quite put my finger on it."

I peered at the two pictures. She was right. It was someone I knew.

"Now, about Billy Ryder." Hannah pulled up an email. "My college roommate works for the *Dallas Morning News*. I called her and asked about the Billy Ryder-Veronica Spinelli story. She has a contact who retired from the Dallas PD. The contact guarded Billy Ryder when they first picked him up. Apparently, Billy was a very entertaining guy. He kept them in stitches telling jokes and funny stories. Billy had a thick Texas accent he turned on and off at will. He could talk convincingly about any subject he chose.

"Larissa's contact worked the day Billy made his

escape. Billy's lawyer paid for a haircut and Billy shaved off the goatee you see in the mug shot. According to Larissa's contact, you never would have known him."

"It doesn't put us any closer to knowing who he is."

"I have a feeling—"

My cellphone's dying buzz cut her off. The stupid thing could barely ring anymore. I picked it up, checked the caller ID. Memaw.

"Yes, ma—"

"Come quick. She's here." An incredible ruckus rattled and pounded behind Memaw. Glass shattered, and Memaw screamed. Footsteps pounded, and the phone went dead.

———

MY CELLPHONE LOCKED UP AGAIN. I was already on my way out the door. Hannah trotted right behind me, trying to call 911, and got a message asking her to hold. It was a wild night for Gaslight City. Our small town dispatcher was probably swamped.

"You stay here and try to get the cops. I'm going out there."

"You're not going alone."

"You can't come. If you got hurt, your uncle and aunt would hang me on the old gallows behind the museum. Just keep trying to get someone out there." By this time, we were already at my car, two blocks down. "Go back and lock yourself in. Keep trying 911."

The Nova's tires squalled as I backed out of my parking

space, going ninety by the time I got to the end of Houston Street. I blew through a stop sign and headed toward Farm Road 4077. The shadowy pines sped by as the miles passed, but whatever was going to happen to Memaw had already happened. That didn't slow me down. I blew into the leaf-strewn yard, bailed out of the Nova, and ran toward the house. I bounded up the back steps and into the kitchen. There had been a hell of a fight in the room, but I saw no blood and no Memaw. I ran through the house, flinging doors open, and finally accepted that I was alone.

Dean. I needed to call Dean. Someone had Memaw. I got out my cellphone, but it was still locked up. In a fit of temper, I slung it against the wall. It smashed into several pieces. The house phone was dead. That's why Memaw's call had ended so abruptly.

I walked back outside in a daze. Headlights on the farm road sped toward the house and slowed down at the last moment. They turned into the driveway. Expecting Dean or Hannah, I ran toward the lights, realizing only at the last moment it wasn't either of them.

Michael Gage's window whirred down. "What's wrong, Peri Jean? Leticia called me all hysterical a little while go. I tried to call back, but I couldn't get through."

Thinking about the things Hannah and I had discussed not half an hour earlier, I stumbled backward. I took a good hard look at Michael Gage's face and saw Billy Ryder staring out of his eyes. I spun on my heels and ran for the house. A car door chunked open behind me, spurring me to run faster.

I slammed into the broken gate and tried to vault it, but still sore from Benny Longstreet's punch, I only made it halfway over. The man I knew as Michael Gage, but who was really a man with no name, dragged me off the fence.

"C'mere, you silly little bitch." The male version of Rae's spider ring glinted on Gage's finger. He curled his hand into a fist and slammed it into my face. Things got very dark.

23

I woke up on the floor of a tiny, cigarette-scented room. The light seemed impossibly bright, and I rolled onto my side to avoid it. A coat rack stood next to a knobless wooden door. On it hung a leather jacket with a lot of zippers and the Marlon Brando cap I'd seen in Rae's sketchbook. My mind flitted back to the shadowy face of the cap's owner. Gage was Ryder, and both names were likely stolen.

The real Michael Gage, the one who'd married Sharon Zeeman and befriended Jerry Bower, was probably rotting in an unmarked grave somewhere while this clown walked around using his identity. A nameless shadow that traveled the earth and created havoc wherever he went. Who killed Rae.

I rolled to my knees and used the wall as a brace while I got to my feet. My face throbbed and the room swam. The door opened. I backpedaled away from it.

"Well, hello, Peri Jean." The voice had a thick, flat Texas twang.

My breath caught as my chest tightened. Using every ounce of tough I'd cultivated over my thirty years, I faced the man who'd fooled all of Gaslight City, killed my cousin, and killed my best friend. He tipped me a wink and ran his tongue over his lips. My blood ran cold. Nobody knew where to find me. Whatever he had planned for me was going to happen.

———

MICHAEL GAGE, or the man who had played him so well, stood at the entrance to the room. For the first time, I saw him without a buttoned, collared shirt covering the sides of his neck. A muscle shirt hung on his wiry frame. On the left side of his neck was a circle about an inch in circumference where his tattoo had been.

One thought pulsed in my mind, bright as neon. *This shit killed Chase. Because of this killer—this liar—I'd never see my best friend again.* Fury, bright and pure, threatened to take over. I held it down and pretended to be whipped.

"Where's my grandmother?"

"She's in the next room. You'll see her once we have us a chat."

"How did you stay free all these years?" I asked, taking deep breaths to stay calm. When I hit him, I'd have to catch him by surprise to have a chance.

"Stealin' IDs. Got harder in the age of information, but

I managed." He stepped all the way into the room, blocking the way out. "Michael Gage was supposed to be my last identity...until your grandmother talked me into visiting your cousin in Hilltop Trusty Camp. Veronica spotted me, and I was fucked.

"Veronica insisted I help her get out when her parole came around. Your cousin wanted in on the deal because Veronica would no longer be around to protect her." Gage's dashing smile was downright evil. He'd hidden his true self from all of us. "I guess munching on one skanky bitch's pussy is a lot better than munching several skanky bitches' pussies."

I backed against the wall, behind the antique desk, trying to assess my injuries. My head buzzed too loud to concentrate. This time, I probably did have a concussion or worse. I couldn't fight my way out of here without a weapon. My eyes skittered over the glass-topped desk. Nothing. If I went for one of the drawers, Gage would be on me.

"I found this room right off, or at least the guys I hired to do the restoration did." Gage took slow steps toward me. "I read up on the Mace Treasure and thought it was in here. Still do, tell you the truth."

In a flash, Gage got in my face. He spun me around, grabbed me, and forced me to my knees. His fingers found a nerve in the back of my neck and pressed down on it. I stifled a cry. I wouldn't let him see weakness. Gage pushed my nose against the wall. Carefully hidden amid a carving of cavorting Victorian cupids was a keyhole.

"See that, you snotty bitch?" He shoved my face into

the wall. My nose pressed hard against the wall, and the nerve endings woke up screaming.

"That there is how your cousin talked her way into Veronica's plot to get out of jail. Know what your cousin told me?"

I shook my head no. Gage popped my head against the wall. I turned at the last second to protect my nose, but my cheekbone slammed against the wood, and I bit my tongue. I tasted blood.

"Answer me, snobby bitch."

"N-n-no." I barely said the word. It earned my head another pop on the wall.

"No, sir. I'm sir to you from here on out. Understand me?"

"N-n-no, s-s-ir." Fear pushed my anger down. I figured I'd die tonight. And that would be after some horrible stuff happened. A swell of emotion climbed up my throat. The first tear tracked down my face.

"Your cousin said you'd help her find the treasure. Then she wouldn't ask you." Gage leaned close, his breath hot and humid on my ear. I shuddered. He knocked my head into the wall again. "She ended up deciding to die instead of making you get your hands dirty. Thought it would protect you. Guess it didn't, though, did it? Answer!"

"No, sir." My words sounded slurred through my tears, but Gage nodded as though they were just what he wanted to hear.

"In case you ain't figured it out from that hot check I wrote you, I need that money."

"I can't help you."

"You'd better help me." Gage giggled, a sickening high-pitched whinny. "I've watched you bumble around trying to figure it out, but now it's time to get the job done."

I didn't answer. Instead, I listened for Memaw. Surely, I'd hear her yelling or arguing by now. She'd go down fighting.

"Ain't you got nothing to say, girl? Maybe it's time we go see your Memaw." He exaggerated the word, making a mockery of the way I said it. "Maybe she can talk you into helping me."

Gage yanked me toward the open door and into his study. We'd been behind his study the whole time. Memaw lay on a leather couch, her eyes closed. I jerked away from Gage and ran to her. When I touched Memaw's arm, her eyes opened. He had her gagged.

"Take off her gag."

"Suck my dick." Gage laughed at my expression. "I'm serious, Peri Jean, darlin'. If you want to talk to her, start bobbing."

I scooted away from him, shaking my head. Gage's face contorted in anger. He stalked toward me and yanked me upright.

"If you don't find the treasure for me—right now—I'm going to kill your bitchy old grandma right in front of you."

No. I struggled against Gage and bit back a cry as he tightened his grip. Footsteps rang on the hardwood floors in the hallway. Someone else was here. They'd help us. I screamed for help.

Veronica Spinelli strolled into the room. "Shut up, you dumb bitch." She dismissed me and turned her attention on Gage. "She about ready? We ain't got much time to get the money and get outta here. The po-lice is out at their house right now. Pretty soon, that pretty boy cop'll start looking for her."

They each grabbed an arm and dragged me back into the secret room.

Veronica whispered in my ear the whole way, her humid, stinking breath filling my senses. "Your cousin liked licking my clit. That's what you're gonna do for me. Anytime I say so."

Gage giggled. "And I'm gonna watch."

I glanced back over my shoulder and saw Memaw looking at me, the most fright I'd ever seen widening her eyes. Gage and Veronica yanked me into the secret room and shut the door.

———

"NOW WHO'S THE BOSS?" Veronica gazed upon me like a cat looking at mouse whose back she just broke. She bared her blocky yellow teeth at me.

I hung my head and didn't answer. Fear stung every part of my body and wormed its way into my brain. I had to think fast because soon the fear would paralyze me. After that, my ass was theirs—literally and figuratively.

"I've got the key." The words came out in a whisper, but neither Gage nor Veronica responded, so I repeated them.

"The key?" Veronica looked puzzled. She dismissed me and set a syringe filled with blue liquid on the desk.

"The key's around my neck," I told Gage. "See the

trinity symbol beside the keyhole? The top of the key matches the symbol."

"You better be right, little bit. I'll make you real damn sorry if you ain't." Gage untied the ribbon around my neck.

"Make her sorry anyway." Veronica shoved me at Gage. "I want to see her beg."

"You will before the night ends. She'll beg. I guarantee that."

Everything below my waist tightened. I tried not to think about what he meant but couldn't help myself.

Gage stuck the key in the keyhole and laughed in his horrible whinny when it fit. Instead of turning it, he spoke to me. "Isn't tonight exciting? Just think. We're going to do this again and again."

I stared at him. Terror had stolen my witty repartee from me.

"Think I ought to tell her our plan?" Gage spoke to Veronica. She shrugged. She didn't care about anything other than seeing me hurt.

"I'm going to use you in our best caper ever. There's all kinds of lost treasure around this country and in others. A fortune." Gage smiled his dangerous, scary smile. "We're going to use you to sniff it out. Rae told me all about how you see ghosts, you crazy bitch. Just think. You'll be a psychic bloodhound. And, of course, you and me are gonna fall in love."

He kissed me, ramming his tongue down my throat. I gagged and spat. Gage backpedaled.

"Kick her."

Veronica rushed forward and delivered a kick to my

ribs. I rolled into the fetal position, expecting more. Instead, Gage got back in my face, this time nearly crawling to do it.

"Every time you don't do what I say, she's going to do that. Understand? Say yes, sir, dear."

I nodded, unable to breathe, much less speak.

Gage nodded at Veronica, and she delivered a kick to my back.

"Yes, sir." My words came out in a hoarse sob. "Sir..." I rolled my eyes up to see if Gage was paying attention. He was. The look of pleasure on his face stole my breath.

"Please let my grandmother go...sir." I drew in a shuddering breath and bit back the urge to scream. Taking a breath caused a blast of pain in my right side. Veronica must have cracked a rib.

"Tell you what." Gage knelt down next to me and ran his fingers over my cheek. "I'll let her go as soon as we get out of state. When I see you're going to cooperate with us, that's when I'll let her go."

Icy tendrils of horror caressed my spine. No telling what these two would consider cooperation. And no doubt, they were lying about letting Memaw go. I had to do something to get out of this, or at least get Memaw out of it. I couldn't live with myself if she was hurt because of me.

Gage, still kneeling next to me, asked, "You understand?"

"Yes, sir." I squeezed my eyes shut as Gage continued caressing me. After a few moments of torturing me and getting no reaction, he stood.

"You know what?" Gage spoke to Veronica as though I

wasn't present in the room. "I thought it was gonna be hard to break her, but I think she's already halfway there. By the time we get to Virginia and that place you found online, we won't even have to fight her."

"She'll just bend right over and spread 'em." Veronica cackled and Gage joined her with his freaky whinny.

Gage went back to the keyhole where the trinity key still stuck out. He turned the key. Something clicked inside the wall, and a panel popped open. Gage peered inside.

Only I saw the dark shadow emerge from the open panel in the wall.

"Honey, it's stuck. I need some help." Gage's gaze rested on me, so I obeyed.

I staggered to Gage. Together, we tugged the box from the wall. White-hot pain bolted through my side every time I moved wrong. The black shadow coiled in the room's corner.

"Hate this damn house. It's always drafty in here." Veronica hugged herself.

"Fetch the letter opener out of the middle drawer, V." Gage struggled with the cedar chest.

Veronica produced a sharp letter opener. If I had just known about its presence, I could have threatened Gage with it. Maybe gotten out of here. As things stood, I was damned to some unimaginable degradation. Gage meant to break me like a work animal. My anger over Rae's and Chase's murders would keep me going for a while, but not forever.

Gage grunted as he worked to break the trunk's lock.

Veronica kept an eye on me, occasionally making suggestive tongue motions. I huddled into myself and tried to keep from visibly shaking. The trunk popped open, and Gage gave a triumphant whoop. Veronica grabbed me by the wrist and crowded behind Gage. They let out a collective groan.

Books, probably antiques, filled the trunk. Gage opened one and flipped through it, maybe looking for bills hidden in the pages. The book had Luther Palmore's name inside.

I doubted Gage and Veronica knew the burned out ruins behind Memaw's property had once belonged to Luther Palmore. Why would Reginald have hidden Palmore's books up here? I knew one thing. If he hid his fortune in the old Palmore house, it burned to ashes more than a century ago. My mind flashed back to the morning of Rae's murder and the ghost who came out of the Palmore ruins and stood next to me. *Luther?* The way everything tied together made my head hurt.

"Enough with the bullshit, little bit." Gage's eyes were hard with fury. He grabbed my wrist and squeezed until I screamed. Veronica's cackles and catcalls cut through my pain. "You show us what you're made of right now, or Veronica will go in the study, pick up that fire poker, and beat Leticia to death with it."

———

THE CLOUD of black smoke swirled in the corner of the

369

room. If I tried to enlist the dark spirit to help me, no telling what would happen. If I didn't, I would die.

"She can't talk to ghosts no more than Rae could." Veronica put her hands on her hips. "Just fuck her and let's go. We can find some family traveling, get a good ways on their credit cards."

Gage said nothing.

"I'll even kill her when you're done." Veronica took a step toward me. "Her and the old lady. You don't have to watch."

"I won't leave here with nothing." Gage's voice rose. "If it hadn't been for you—"

"If it hadn't been for me?" Veronica snorted. "You were in debt up to your tits anyway. You were more than ready to agree to Rae's little moneymaking scheme. You knew you couldn't stay here much longer."

Somewhere in the house, a door slammed open. Heavy footsteps ran through the house.

"Peri Jean Mace?" Wade Hill's voice boomed through the house. My muscles went loose with relief. I opened my mouth and screamed. Wade's footsteps pounded toward the study, echoing through the big old house.

Gage rummaged in the desk and came up with a snub-nosed revolver. Sweat broke out all over my body, my thoughts speeding to a hysterical jumble. He tipped his chin at me. "Keep her out of the way."

Veronica grabbed my ear and twisted it, smiling when I yelped. She followed Gage, dragging me behind her. Seeing the only chance I'd have to get the upper hand, I cooperated. Wade burst into the study as we got to the secret room's door. Things happened fast after that.

I twisted around, ignoring the pain from my ear, and bit Veronica's inner arm. She howled and shoved me away from her. I grabbed her arm and jerked her toward me, pistoning myself forward. Our foreheads cracked together. She staggered away from me. I followed, grabbing her hair and ramming her head into the wall. I did it until she crumpled to the floor.

Gage stared at us open-mouthed, and Wade charged across the room. Gage fired the gun. It sounded like the world crashing down around us. My ears rang painfully. Wade stopped in his tracks.

"Get Memaw," I told Wade. "Please. Just get her out of here."

"Don't move. I'll shoot." Gage trained the gun on Wade. "Put your fucking hands up."

I turned to the fireplace and grabbed a poker. I advanced on Gage, holding the poker. "Shoot him and I'll beat you to death."

Gage snorted. "I'll shoot you before you get in the first lick."

"Not unless you hit me in the head. What's that? Twenty-two caliber?" Wade moved closer to Gage. "Unless you kill me with the first shot, I'll take that gun away from you and shoot *you* with it."

Gage slumped, his eyes darting between Wade and me. Wade took another step forward. Gage straightened again and pulled the hammer back on the revolver. "Stop."

"Let him take Memaw," I said. "There's no way you can win this. Let him take her, and you'll still have me."

Gage turned to me, his scary eyes wild. "Put down the poker. And come here."

"Peri Jean, don't," Wade said.

The poker hit the floor with a clang. I walked toward Gage. He grabbed me and dragged me the last couple of feet, sliding his arm over my chest and holding me in front of him. The gun's barrel dug painfully into my temple. I flinched, sucking in my breath and holding it. The ringing in my ears and the pounding of my heart took over my world.

"Get the fuck out," Gage yelled at Wade.

"I can't leave you." Wade held his hands out in a pleading gesture.

"Please. Just take my grandmother and go." I locked my eyes onto Wade's and tried to telegraph how much I wanted him to get my grandmother out of there. After a long moment, he jerked a nod and walked to the couch.

He got his arms around Memaw and picked her up as though she weighed nothing. After giving me another long look, he left. His footfalls sounded heavy and final. Veronica staggered to her feet and lurched after him.

"Forget it," Gage yelled at her. "We can still get out of here. Every cop in town is probably out at that farm. Take 'em fifteen minutes to get over here."

Veronica swayed, holding one hand to her head. She looked at me with murder in her eyes. If she got a chance, she'd kill me. I raised one hand and gave her the finger. *It's on, babe.* She stalked toward me, her face contorting into a hateful expression.

"Stop it or I'll kill you." Gage pointed the gun at her. "Just help me get us out of here."

"And you..." He turned the gun on me. "Call Reginald Mace. Find the treasure. I'll kill you if you don't." He had no idea what he asked, and really, neither did I. But if an encounter with a ghost was what he wanted, then that's what Gage was going to get.

———

I GATHERED my nerve and concentrated on the black spirit, willing it to come forward. With no idea how to survive the night, I'd concentrate on surviving the next minute. The swirl of black in the corner room rose up and rolled toward me. Chaos filled my mind, convincing me I could whup the world.

I could tell Gage saw the black smoke swirl around me and caress me. His eyes met mine, and whatever he saw there made him take a step back. I closed my eyes and drank in the dark spirit's power. *Help me*, I thought.

Another otherworldly presence registered. I opened my eyes to see Rae, blood tinting her skin, float into the room. I thought I was the only one who saw her until Veronica put her hands to her face and screamed. Behind Rae followed our wild-haired, wild-eyed ancestor, Reginald Mace. As crazy as he appeared in old photographs, it didn't compare to the way his ghost looked. His eyes held a madness I'd never seen in a person living or dead.

Together, Rae and our many-greats grandfather advanced toward Veronica.

Veronica's fear was so intense she could never have worked with someone like me. She clenched both fists and screamed over and over again, taking a breath between each scream. Rae kept moving toward her until Veronica stumbled from the room. A crash sounded. Veronica's scream ended with a gurgle. A rush of emotion came from the study. Rae was happy she'd hurt Veronica.

I concentrated again and said the words out loud. "Help me."

The dark spirit's power swelled, and the rush strained my pounding heart. Arctic wind came from nowhere and blew the small room's contents into a tornado of flying objects. Instinctively, I flicked my fingers at the black mass swirling around me.

It surrounded and closed in on Gage. He swung his fists, his punches whistling through the air. The black swirl pushed Gage, and he bounced off the wall. Rage twisted his features. He pointed the gun into the black mass and fired. I hit the ground and lay there listening as Gage emptied his gun. The dark spirit never stopped swirling. Gage screamed, a sound as full of fear as it was violence.

Rae leaned over me and motioned me to stand. She directed me toward the desk. I opened a deep bottom drawer and spotted the heavy glass of an ashtray full of cigarette butts. I grabbed the ashtray and snuck up behind Gage. Occupied fighting off Reginald and the dark spirit, he never saw me.

I reared back and swung the ashtray with all my might. Cigarette butts and ashes flew everywhere. The heavy glass connected with the back of Gage's head and thumped hollowly. Gage put his hand to the back of his head, where blood immediately seeped through his fingers. He dropped to the floor. I hit him again. He collapsed with a dazed expression on his face.

I stood over him and raised the ashtray again. "This is for Rae and Chase, you useless turd."

"You bitch." The voice came from behind me.

I turned to see Veronica charging with a big handgun pointed right at me. Rae shoved me out of the way. A deafening roar crashed through the room, and something seared across my left bicep. I screamed and clapped my hand to my arm. The muscle thrummed with a low, deep ache. Veronica stopped and pointed the gun at my head. She smiled.

"Stop or I'll shoot."

Veronica's grin faded, and she turned. Dean stood in the doorway with his pistol trained on her. He moved his thumb, and a red dot appeared on Veronica's forehead.

"Drop the gun," he screamed. "Do it, now."

Veronica pointed the gun at Dean. Without a second's hesitation, he shot three times. She crumpled, and a pool of blood spread around her. A transparent Veronica rose from the still body. When she realized I could see her, she bared her teeth at me. Her fury rolled into me like molten lava. The dark sprit flew at her and swirled around her as it had me. Veronica's ghost screamed silently as she faded into nothingness.

HANNAH and I sat on Mace House's lawn, my arm around her as she sobbed into her hands. She had arrived right after Dean. Along with Wade and Memaw, she heard the shots coming from the house. Of the three, Hannah was the most upset. Memaw knew Dean would take care of me. Wade probably figured I'd take care of myself. Hannah hadn't known what to think.

She finally slowed down to the type of crying where her chest only hitched every few minutes. She used the hem of her shirt to wipe off her face.

"So your arm is going to be all right?" she asked.

"Sure." I nodded. "I think my ribs are worse. It hurts to breathe."

"I guess I just freaked out when I first saw you." She shivered. "All that blood."

The results of yet another nosebleed decorated my t-shirt. I probably looked like I'd been in a war. And I had, sort of. The nosebleeds, which started the night Rae came back in spirit form, worried me. But I had a feeling no medicine existed to fix them. I told the paramedics I got this one when Veronica punched me in the nose. Maybe it wouldn't happen again.

Wade walked over to us holding two bottles of water so cold condensation beaded on them. He handed one to me and one to Hannah.

"Thank you," I said as I took my water.

"It's the least I could do." He gave me a long, reproachful look.

"Thank you for taking Memaw out of there." I needed to explain. "Gage threatened to let Veronica beat her to death."

Hannah gasped. Wade gave me a quick nod.

"So," Wade said, "did you find the treasure?"

I told Wade and Hannah about the books.

"What does it mean?" Hannah asked.

"It means exactly what I thought all along. That treasure is bullshit and always was. Reginald Mace was a crazy man." But that crazy man came to help me when I needed it. Had I called him or had the dark spirit? No matter. I didn't want to get up close and personal with that thing ever again.

Two paramedics loaded Gage's still form into Gaslight City's one ambulance. I must have hit him harder than I thought. He hadn't regained consciousness. It might have been wicked of me, but I hoped he never did. Hooty Bruce and another man loaded a black body bag containing Veronica's remains into the funeral home's hearse.

The ambulance pulled away from the curb and revealed a teenage girl standing in the street. Without the bleached blonde hair, the boob job, and the hard look on her face, it took me several seconds to recognize Rae.

She wiggled her fingers at me. I inclined my head toward her. She'd saved me, not once but twice, and I owed her a break. Her emotions rushed to me. I leaned back and let them envelop me. Love, joy, and appreciation tinged with just a little bit of jealousy flowed over me. I didn't blame her. Figuring out how to live this life took more than thirty measly years. She got robbed.

We stared at each other, and I let go of whatever resentment I had left. A glow rose from the ground and pulsed around Rae. Though I doubted I'd miss her, a lump formed in my throat. The light made Rae brighter and brighter until she just winked out.

"You cold?" Hannah asked.

"Huh?"

"You're shivering." She spoke slowly, maybe thinking I couldn't understand. "I asked if you were cold."

"I'm okay." I pulled my jacket around me and stuck my hands in the pockets. Something brushed my hand. I pulled the scrap of paper out of my pocket, unfolded it and used the streetlight to read it.

Scribbled in Rae's handwriting, it read:

Life ain't no dress rehearsal. Do it right. You are worth it.

Can I borrow fifty bucks?

I couldn't help smiling. She must have put the note in my jacket last spring, and I put it away for the summer without finding it. My cousin had been one of a kind, her silly advice spot on. From now on, I would remember I only had one shot to do it right.

Dean joined us, looking much the way he had the first day I met him—upset and tired. He sat down next to me and put his arm over my shoulders. I leaned into him.

Dean glanced at Wade and scowled. "You still here? This is an official crime scene."

"Settle down, little buddy. I'm *officially* about to leave," Wade said, as though they'd already had this discussion. "I wanted to bring the ladies some water."

"Your help, while greatly appreciated, is no longer needed," Dean said with more force than necessary.

Wade turned to me. "You sure about this? He has a Napoleon complex."

Hannah laughed. Dean scowled. The world was right again.

EPILOGUE

A Few Days Later

A LIGHT NOVEMBER wind blew over Piney Hill Cemetery, the areas in shadow about ten degrees cooler than where the full sun beamed down. Summer was gone for one more year.

Despite the robin's egg blue sky and the brilliant sun, a deep sadness filled me, weighting my steps with a fatigue I couldn't shake. Dean's firm grip on my arm grounded me, kept me from wandering into shadow. He guided me to the front row of metal folding chairs. I turned to him.

"I can't believe this is happening." My voice sounded disembodied, like maybe it belonged to someone else.

"Go on and sit down." Dean put one hand on each of my shoulders and gave me a gentle push. I sat because I didn't have the energy to do anything else. "They'll expect you to say something. Have you thought about what you want to say?"

The sun illuminated the highlights in Dean's hair. He squinted his eyes against the sun, but I saw caring in their depths. Not a day went by that Dean didn't surprise me.

I glanced toward the ladies from Gaslight City First Baptist who wove mums into an archway near where the casket would be placed. Eddie Kennedy worked to stabilize the archway so the wind couldn't blow it over. I spotted Memaw working next to Hannah. Memaw's head rose as though she sensed me looking for her. She tipped her chin and gave me a wave. I returned the gesture.

From this distance, she looked normal. She didn't look like a woman dying of cancer. But if Dr. Longstreet knew his stuff, her health would fade fast. Sooner rather than later, I'd be sitting in a metal folding chair at her funeral. A dark hand on my arm drew me out of my reverie. Hooty Bruce—father of the formidable Rainey—knelt in front of me, next to Dean.

"Now, I'll be giving the sermon just like Jolene and Darren Fischer asked. We'll have a song, I'll talk, we'll have another song, and then I'll call on you." Hooty stopped speaking and turned his attention to Dean. "Is she going to be able to speak? No shame if she can't."

"I can speak," I said, my voice still sounding as though it came from afar. I had no idea what to say, but I wanted to send the best friend I'd ever had off in style. Not many people—other than Chase's parents and me—understood what had been good about him. They only remembered him as a drunk and a druggie.

Hooty and Dean exchanged a long look, one I couldn't interpret. Hooty finally nodded and stood. He gave me a rough pat on the shoulder and wandered over to Memaw. The two talked, their gazes wandering to me every few seconds. I had to pull myself together but the lethargy in my bones weighed a ton. Going back to bed sounded like a great idea.

"I need to make sure I parked the car in the right place." Dean, still kneeling in front of me, took my hand. "I'll be back."

"I'm okay." I leaned forward, ignoring the stab in my back from a cracked rib. Putting my arms around Dean caused more screams of pain from my bruised body, but I did it. I gave him a squeeze and wondered for the millionth time how things would end up between us. For once in my life, I decided to enjoy the ride and not worry about controlling things. I brushed a kiss on Dean's cheek, enjoying the thrill of pleasure. "I appreciate everything you're doing right now."

Dean's lips curved into a smile, one that touched his eyes. "That's all I need to hear." He got up, brushed off his pants, and wandered toward his ratty old Trans Am.

I sat back on the hard metal folding chair with a grunt. My body still ached from the beating Michael Gage and Veronica Spinelli gave me. Gage had fared much worse. He languished in a coma at Mother Francis Hospital in Tyler. The doctor said he couldn't understand what caused the coma since the skull was not fractured. Armed law enforcement guarded Gage twenty-four hours a day.

According to Dean, Veronica Spinelli lay unclaimed at the Smith County Coroner's office. Dean offered to pay for a pauper's burial. His guilt over the shooting surprised me.

His killing her saved me, and Veronica was a horror of human being. I didn't feel bad about her demise.

Benny Longstreet used his millions to make bail. He faced a long list of charges for offenses ranging from failure to notify authorities after he found Rae dying to assault and kidnapping. Dean speculated Benny would escape a little poorer but relatively unscathed. I withheld comment. Benny and I had unfinished business. I'd make sure he knew he picked a fight with the wrong Mace.

"Hey." A hand closed on my shoulder. I tipped my chin and found myself looking right into the bright sun. The person touching my shoulder was lost in silhouette. Then Wade Hill moved and sat down next to me. He pulled me into a one-armed hug and squeezed until I uttered a pained squeak. He let go.

"I'm surprised you came." And I was. After the smoke cleared, Dean and Wade had some scathing exchanges. Dean suspected Wade had known exactly who killed Rae and where to find them and had followed me around town, trying to keep me out of danger instead of calling the police. Wade told Dean he suffered from short man syndrome.

"I've been feeling a million kinds of guilty since that night at Mace House." I noticed he omitted any mention of the horrid events. Maybe for the best. The nightmares from that night would haunt me for the foreseeable future.

"Don't. You saved my bacon." I squeezed his arm to let him know I meant it.

"At least let me explain." Wade kept his eyes focused on a distant point. "I worked at Long Time Gone because I needed money, but also as a favor to a friend who has a vested interest in what goes on there. I knew exactly who Billy Ryder was the whole time."

I went still, and then turned my body so Wade got the full force of my glare. His eyes widened, and he developed a case of verbal diarrhea.

"At first, see, my job was to figure out the scam he had going with Olivia. Then I was to either make him pay tribute to the right people or figure out where to find him away from Long Time Gone so he could be...dispatched." Wade stopped, closed his eyes, and slumped.

I twitched, remembering the rumors of the outlaw biker gang associated with Long Time Gone. I didn't want to think about how Wade knew them or why he helped them. Some other time.

"Then Rae got killed. Once we figured Billy Ryder did it, my employer changed my job description to leading the cops to Ryder. But I never figured out Billy Ryder and Michael Gage were one and the same. Then you showed up with that drawing, looking for Billy Ryder. I didn't want to see you end up like Rae. So I quit focusing on leading the cops to Billy Ryder and tried to watch over you."

"I don't need anybody to watch over me." If it wouldn't have hurt, I'd have put my hands on my hips.

"Peri Jean, please. If anybody ever needed a keeper, it's you. Believe me on this." He snorted and shook his head. "And I did a good job. But the night of the street dance, I lost you when you went to Hannah's apartment. One minute you two were chatting with your grandmother, and the next you disappeared. I went out to your grandmother's house, figured out you weren't there, and went back to town. Couldn't find you anywhere. Finally, I went to talk to Hannah—scared the hell out of her—and we figured out who Billy Ryder was and where to find you. You know the rest."

I wanted to be irritated with Wade Hill, but he'd risked annoying a dangerous someone to help me. I didn't even have the energy to think about the rest of what he'd told me. His honorable intent overrode his lack of success. I touched his arm. "Thank you."

He shrugged. "Just another day in the life of a modern day knight in shining armor. Plus"—he dropped his voice to a whisper and leaned close—"I have an ulterior motive."

"Oh?" I thought I knew, but his delivery amused me.

"Let's say it like this: if it doesn't work out with Mr. Short and Surly over there"—he gestured at Dean—"give me a chance. I'll show you my tattoos. All of them."

Wade and I locked eyes for a moment. Again, I wondered what it would have been like to be more than friends. A mischievous smile spread over his face as though he knew my thoughts.

"And I knew it would piss him off if I came." Wade's smile widened even more, and his dark eyes twinkled. A shadow fell over us. We both raised our eyes to find Dean standing over us, scowling. His good mood from a few minutes ago had vanished.

———

"Get up." Dean narrowed his eyes and turned down his lips when he spoke to Wade.

"No. You might be a cop, but you're not king of the world." Wade crossed his arms over his chest.

"I didn't arrest you for obstruction of justice because Peri Jean begged me not to." Dean's voice rose and people turned to watch the three of us.

"Y'all, please stop this..." I trailed off when I realized they were ignoring me.

"And because you knew you couldn't make anything stick. If I hadn't walked into that house a few nights ago—"

"We'd have done just fine, you big baboon." Dean had his hands near his hips like an old west gunslinger.

"What's going on here?" Darren Fischer leaned into our conversation. His red-rimmed eyes and tear-stained cheeks gave both Wade and Dean pause.

"There's not enough room for him to sit here." Dean gestured at Wade. "He's taking up space reserved for the family."

"You're right." Darren nodded. "Why don't you two men sit over there?"

Dean, Wade, and I looked in the direction Darren pointed. The back row. Dean flushed and cracked his knuckles. I bit my lip to keep from smiling. For the first time since Chase died, I wanted to laugh. One glance at Dean's shocked scowl and I dropped my head so he wouldn't see my amusement. Wade took the rebuke with a smile.

Hannah rose from where she'd been sitting next to Memaw in the row behind us. "Come on, gentlemen. I'll join you. Make more room for family and people who knew Chase well."

"After you, Officer Turgeau." Wade stood and swept his arm out for Dean to pass.

"It's not Officer," Dean groused. "It's Deputy."

As the two men walked away, Wade said, "I don't give a shit."

To my utter shock, Wade and Dean sat next to each other in the back row. Their stiff postures suggested they were not finished sparring. Cords stood out in Dean's neck, and Wade's smile was predatory. Hannah sat down beside Dean. She rolled her eyes at me. I smiled at her in thanks, and she winked.

As my eyes swept over the crowd, I noticed Felicia Holze and Chase's son, Kansas. The boy looked uncomfortable and confused. He'd barely known Chase, I realized. And now he never really would. That brought the grief crashing back, its tide rising until I could have howled. Tears dripped off my chin as I lamented the way life can suck.

That's when Darren and Jolene sat down on both sides of me. Jolene reached over and grabbed my hand in a death grip. The buzz of conversation trickled into silence as Hooty took his place at the pulpit and fussed with his Bible. When the morning air was still except for the squawk of a few birds, Hooty looked out over the crowd with a solemn expression on his face.

"I knew Chase Lawrence Fischer from the time he was about a week old. He grew to be a sensitive boy with a tender heart who couldn't quite stand the sadness in the world around him. His sensitivity helped him become an accomplished musician..."

Something moved at the corner of my vision. I took my eyes off Hooty and squinted into the outcropping of tombstones. The air wavered like a heat mirage, and a figure came into view. The lanky body moved with fluid grace. The sun blazed down on blonde hair, creating an impossibly white sparkle. My heart caught in my throat, and the sting of tears burned my eyes. Chase Fisher, younger and healthier than I'd seen him in a long while, stepped to the periphery of his own funeral. Hot tears tracked down my face as we watched one another. The sun damage was gone from Chase's skin, and he looked the way he had the year he broke my heart—back when he still thought he'd be a rock star. He smiled at me, and a sob jerked out of me. Jolene squeezed my hand even tighter.

"They're ready for you," Darren whispered in my ear. I struggled to my feet, my abused muscles protesting. Darren stood to help me to my feet. Hooty shot out from behind the pulpit and escorted me to it. He adjusted the microphone, gave me a pat on the back and stepped away.

Everyone watched me expectantly. Everyone, that is, except for Wade and Dean who glared at each other in the back row. I turned around to see if Chase's ghost had left, and the crowd followed my gaze. Chase still stood near a tombstone, watching me. A rustle went through the crowd, and I turned back to them. I opened my mouth to speak, not knowing what I needed to say. The words seemed to come on their own.

"Chase Fischer was the best friend I ever had. I loved

him more than I've loved anybody...except my Memaw. He wasn't perfect, but none of us are..." I turned to look at Chase's ghost again. The glow I saw before Rae winked out blanketed Chase. He raised one hand to wave at me and faded from sight, traveling down his forever road. I choked back a sob and waved goodbye to the best friend I ever had. Confused whispers rippled through the audience. For once, I just didn't care.

THE END

Visit Catie's website:
www.catierhodes.com

Find Catie on Facebook:
http://www.facebook.com/catierhodesauthor

Sign up for Catie's mailing list:
Read Black Opal (Book #2) FREE. Hear about new releases
and discounts first. Enjoy opportunities to read free stuff.
Visit: http://smarturl.it/lrdemailchimp

ABOUT THE AUTHOR

Catie Rhodes is the author of the Peri Jean Mace Ghost Thrillers. Her short stories have appeared in *Tales from the Mist*, *Allegories of the Tarot*, and *Let's Scare Cancer to Death*.

Catie was born and raised behind the pine curtain in East Texas. Her favorite memories of childhood are sitting around listening to her family spin yarns. The stories all had one thing in common: each had an element of the mysterious or the unexplained.

Those weird stories molded Catie into a purveyor of her own brand of lies and legends. One day, she found the courage to start writing down her stories. It changed her life forever.

Catie Rhodes lives steps from the Sam Houston National Forest with her long-suffering husband and her armpit terrorist of a little dog.

When she's not writing, Catie likes to cook horribly fattening foods and crochet or knit stuff nobody wants as a gift. She also reads a whole helluva lot.

Find me online:

www.catierhodes.com